For the artists. Keep creating.

ACKNOWLEDGEMENTS

First and foremost, I'd like to thank my family for their unending support. Additionally, my sister, Mallary. You are the first person to tell me if something is bad, as well as the first person to encourage me if something is good. I could not have completed this without your support.

FOR IT WILL BE YOURS

Trey Everett

Black Rose Writing | Texas

ISBN: 978-1-68513-277-4
PUBLISHED BY BLACK ROSE WRITING
www.blackrosewriting.com

Printed in the United States of America
Suggested Retail Price (SRP) $21.95

For It Will Be Yours is printed in Baskerville

*As a planet-friendly publisher, Black Rose Writing does its best to eliminate unnecessary waste to reduce paper usage and energy costs, while never compromising the reading experience. As a result, the final word count vs. page count may not meet common expectations.

FOR IT WILL
BE YOURS

"I have put my heart and my soul into my work, and I have lost my mind in the process."

–VINCENT WILLEM VAN GOGH

CHAPTER 1

"He'll never be his uncle."

An elegantly dressed patron spoke under her breath as she delicately held the thin stem of a plastic champagne flute between her index and middle fingers. The dim candlelight in the main room of the exhibition space, combined with the hushed murmur of the patrons privately criticizing each piece of art, made each attendee in the gallery feel singularly more important than they probably should. They were all the main characters of their own stories.

"Oh, come on, be nice," a second woman responded back to the first, as they both stared at the exhibit's main piece of art. The gallery's centerpiece was a large canvas splattered with black and dark green paint in no apparent rhyme or reason. The painting's size made it the gallery's primary focal point.

"Be nice? It looks like a Jackson Pollack fever dream." The first woman said with a tinge of disgust and offense.

"Well," the second woman shrugged, taking another sip of her champagne, "I think it's quite... bold, daring even." At the word "bold," the first woman could not help but laugh, and almost choked on her drink. She put her hand to her mouth, and tried to not make a scene.

"Daring?" she said.

"He's trying," the second woman countered.

"I know he's trying. 'Try' being the operative word. There's just... there's no life in this piece. In any of these pieces, for that matter." The sharpness of the woman's words conveyed how truly genuine she felt them.

"I'm sure he'll keep trying, and keep improving," the second woman responded again.

"He'd better keep trying, because this ain't it." If the first woman's eyes rolled any farther back in her head, she would be looking in the opposite direction.

"He's still young." This caused the first woman to guffaw loudly, which drew some attention from a few of the patrons standing closer to the two women.

"Young, right. As if that's an adequate excuse in the first place. Also, he isn't that young. Akiane Karamarik painted 'Prince of Peace' when she was eight years old. Eight years old... *that's* young. That was also significantly better, for the record."

"Maybe he just needs to die and meet Jesus first, then his —" The second woman tried to joke, but the first woman plowed through the attempted humor, and continued her verbal assault.

"Van Gogh painted 'The Starry Night' when he was thirty-six. Thirty-six years old! You think he's close to creating the next 'The Starry Night'?" The first woman refused to let the matter go.

"Maybe he is, who am I to say?" The second woman continued to try to reason with her, playing an *angel's advocate* of sorts.

"You know 'The Girl with the Pearl Earring?' Vermeer painted 'The Girl with the Pearl Earring' when he was thirty-three. Thirty... three..." The first woman tilted her head, and looked at her friend with disdain. The second woman's eyes pleaded with a thinly veiled *"people can hear you"* message, and she responded with an intentionally lower tone of voice.

"Okay, okay. Jesus, Carol, point taken. He's no Van Gogh, he's no Vermeer." The second woman quietly conceded.

"And he *isn't* his *uncle*. By this point in his career, his uncle was already changing the art world. Just look at this. Look at this canvas," the first woman sneered, and pointed at the piece again. "He's just… he's *trying* to be his uncle, but he will *never* be his uncle." The first woman snapped back, as she slurped her complementary champagne. Then, after recognizing that she had drawn a little more attention to them both than she had meant to, the first woman finally decided to lower her tone, before she added, "At least there's booze."

"Oh, stop," the second woman responded, snickered, and playfully hit her friend in the arm.

"I won't stop. It's insulting. His uncle's work is so… it's so full of … joy? Life? Soul? *Wonder?* Whatever it is, you get it. This work… it's just not that. It's trying to be that, and it is not that."

With that, the two women stood silent and continued staring at the piece. The soft, orange glow of the LED Edison bulbs strewn about the space reflected off the canvas, and perfectly complimented its unpredictable color scheme.

The unfortunate subject of their ill-deserved, and subjective derision was not this specific painting, but the host of this particular gallery opening. Wyatt Brone stood just within earshot of the two women, as he stared, defeated, at their silhouetted profiles. Every inch of his six-foot, broad frame debated whether to confront the women and ask them to restate their dismissive opinions to his face. A level of courage and brazenness he knew full well they would not possess. Most people, as Wyatt knew it, were only courageous in their opinions when they assumed they were not being heard. Wyatt had unfortunately heard every word of their brief but incredibly harsh critique.

Though he was only three months shy of his thirty-third birthday, Wyatt had already spent most of his life unsuccessfully working towards his only true passion… painting; being an artist. He always felt drawn to putting paint on canvas. By his late teenage years, it had become the only way he truly knew how to express himself. Though as an artist he was largely unknown, he found comfort on the canvas. He found hope and inspiration in his brush strokes. He found himself in his work. The one thing he could not seem to find in his art was success. A nuanced thorn in the side of his painstaking professional journey, Wyatt also happened to be the nephew of arguably the most popular artist in the world; abstract phenom, Jackson Brone.

Wyatt's uncle had erupted to international fame with a few of his works in the early 1970s. Critics unanimously decided that Jackson was undeniably "changing the game," and the art world ate it up. Newspapers and magazines from all around the world aided in skyrocketing Wyatt's uncle to a level of fame never before achieved by an artist in their time. Specifically, it was a *New York Times* article in 1972 that catapulted Jackson to becoming a recognizable, household name. Renowned art critic Joseph Benson wrote Jackson had "made art truly accessible to the public, writ-large, for maybe the first time ever." Galleries showcasing Jackson's works immediately sold out and demanded more stock. Celebrities went out of their way to add an original Brone to their exclusive, at-home collections. Not even the harshest art critics in the world could deny Jackson's brilliance, nor did they have any interest to. Everyone from the most casual art observer, to the most fervent collectors agreed: Jackson Brone was the greatest artist ever to put paintbrush to canvas.

"I'm just saying, he'll never be his uncle," the woman said one last time before she exhaled, and rolled her eyes again. Jackson watched from a dark corner of the gallery as the two women finally walked away from the main piece, set down their cheap, plastic flutes of half-consumed, expensive champagne, and promptly left the gallery.

The fact of the matter is that Wyatt never felt like he was truly trying to be his uncle. Not only did he understand, practically, that he would never be able to achieve the unrealistic level of notoriety his uncle had achieved, but he honestly never had any interest in it either. He did not care to. Wyatt was an artist's artist, and he prided himself on being as such. Wyatt painted not because he wanted to, but because he had to. Realistically, there was nothing else for Wyatt to do. There was nothing else Wyatt could ever see himself doing with any semblance of happiness or fulfillment. Nevertheless, he had always hoped that his work could be appreciated for what it was. Just that: his work. His passion, his expression, his art; his work was himself. He just wanted these pieces of heart and soul to be appreciated for what they were: pieces of himself.

As he watched the door glide shut behind the women as they left the gallery, he walked over towards their not quite empty glasses, and picked them up. With both flutes in his hands, Wyatt turned to find a trash bin to drop them in. After searching for just a moment, one of the serving staff quickly passed by, and tapped Wyatt on his right shoulder. He turned, fully ready to be introduced to a patron hoping to buy one of his pieces.

"Bins over there, hun. Then get back to the bar, they're getting a little backed up," the server said as she quickly passed him without even really looking at him.

"Oh, I —" Wyatt started to respond that he is not on staff, but is actually the artist being showcased, but stopped himself. He realized it did not ultimately matter. *What difference does it make?* He thought to himself. He walked over to the nearest trash bin, and dropped the plastic flutes in.

"Man, I've heard of artists not having great openings, but I've never seen one so bad they put the talent to work." The voice was familiar, and made Wyatt roll his eyes before he even turned around to see from whom it came.

"You gonna kick me while I'm down, eh?" Wyatt responded with a smirk.

Melody Brone stood just behind him. Wyatt's sister smirked right back with the air of condescension that only a sibling could understand. Melody was dressed for the event, a lovely dark emerald green dress, with a pair of shoes worth more than one or two of Wyatt's paintings.

"Kick you? This is costing me money too, ya know. You don't make money, I don't make money." The smirk left her face, and she looked more disappointed than anything. She casually sipped another taste of champagne. "At least I have good taste in bubbly."

"It isn't that bad, Mel." Wyatt tried to find the bright side in the dark room. "There's actually a great turn out. Better than last time, for sure." Another member of the serving team slowly walked past, and Melody grabbed two more flutes. She handed one to Wyatt, and took another sip of her own.

"Find the dealer," Melody said. "See what the damage is so far." Melody started to walk away, before turning back to Wyatt. "And go talk to some fucking people. At least try and sell something tonight. For both our sakes, please?" And just like that, Melody disappeared back into the sparse crowd of patrons.

"Thanks for the confidence, sis." Wyatt responded dryly.

Ultimately, Wyatt knew she was right. Since Melody started her artist management firm with Wyatt as her initial, and only client, Wyatt had become the pariah on her ever blossoming roster. She made the least commission from him, and constantly found herself having to make up excuses as to why Wyatt reneged on various artist commissions and commitments. Wyatt had hoped that this gallery opening would be the moment their luck changed — his luck, anyway. "Come on, Melody, tonight could change everything," he had told her just a few hours before.

Unfortunately for him, the night had not changed anything yet. Wyatt knew if he had any chance of altering that course, he needed to take the advice of his sister, and "go talk to some fucking people."

Admittedly, confidence was never something Wyatt lacked when it came to his art. Every stroke, every color choice, every decision came like a blur of inspiration and ended up meticulously placed on each of his canvases. His passion, his technique, and his precision were all things he accomplished without any doubt or insecurity. *Talking* about these things, however, was never one of Wyatt's strong suits, especially not in a setting such as this. Yes, this evening was singularly focused on showcasing his blood, sweat and tears. Yes, every single one of the patrons in attendance were only there to look at his newest batch of paintings. Yes, he would likely sell *some* pieces from the gallery tonight. No, none of those facts would help subvert the incessant nagging of his own destructive anxiety.

In his defense, Wyatt never felt confident walking up to a stranger, and starting a dialogue in any situation. He had always been one to feel more comfortable ordering another round alone at the bar, rather than approaching and talking to the person who had been making eye contact with him all night. Then there is the idea that even if he decided to interject himself into someone else's conversation, what would he say? *"Oh, hi, yes, it really is me,"* wink. Just the thought was entirely cringeworthy, and he knew it. Melody's pseudo-supportive words came back into his mind, and Wyatt knew if he had any chance of making the evening at all successful, he needed to bite the proverbial bullet, and talk to some fucking people.

Across the room, Wyatt noticed a younger couple dressed in trendy outfits admiring one of the pieces he, personally, felt more fondly of. The twenty-four by thirty-six inch, horizontal canvas featured a work he had spent the better part of six months on. One of his more abstract pieces, featuring the depiction of how Wyatt felt when he found out his mother had passed away. The deep blues, and contrasting grays represented a conceptual, and impressionistic skyscape. With not much real structure, Wyatt allowed for the viewer to add in their own interpretation to the clouds, and the storms. Entitled, "A Place to Rest," this piece was one Wyatt had marked down from his initial pricing ask, in hopes it would find someone that truly needed to have it.

Wyatt watched as the trendy husband pointed at one portion of the painting, and gestured with his hand to his wife, speaking something Wyatt could not hear. As he finished his words, Wyatt saw the wife put her arm around her husband's, and pull herself slightly closer in. As he watched her rest her head on the husband's chest, Wyatt smiled. The husband took a sip of his champagne, and slowly shook his head. Their body language spoke to Wyatt. They were at peace; they were at rest.

This is the couple, Wyatt thought, and a smile crept across his lips.

With a new sense of energy, and hope, Wyatt started making his way over to the admirers of his work. He could not help but feel excitement at the prospect that this particular work would go to the right people. A couple who would proudly display this piece as a focal point in their home, and be able to tell the story of when they met the artist at his gallery opening.

"We saw it, and we just knew we had to have it," the husband would say to their guests.

"He convinced me straight away," his wife would add. "I knew I loved it, obviously, but hearing the actual artist speak about it with such passion and conviction, we knew we needed to have it."

The fantasy was quick, but profound for Wyatt, as he picked up his pace towards the couple. He took a breath as he got closer to the two, and planned how he would introduce himself. Once he was within earshot, he was finally able to hear the husband's words as he spoke to his wife. Wyatt's entire fantasy crumbled under the frill twang of the man's surfer accent.

"It just, like, looks like a kindergartener could have done this, ya know? Like, is this art? Look at it," the husband said as he pointed to another area of the canvas. "It's just, like. It's… it's just bad. What a disaster…"

The man's words stopped Wyatt in his tracks. The smile left his lips, and the excitement was evicted from his mind. Wyatt had no delusions of grandeur, but even this felt a little excessive.

The couple must have noticed the sudden stop in momentum and both turned to find themselves face to face with the creator himself. Wyatt must have looked like a deer caught in the headlights of an on-coming semi-truck. Unsure of what to do, he simply did the first thing his brain transmitted to the rest of his body.

"Hi, I'm Wyatt Brone. This is my gallery." *Well-done, Wyatt.*

If Wyatt looked like the deer that had been caught in the headlights, the couple looked like the deer that got smashed to dust by the truck behind the same headlights. Several awkward, and silent moments passed. The couple, not knowing what to say to the man whose work they had just utterly denigrated, and Wyatt, unsure if they realized he had heard every word. Again.

"Wow," the husband finally said. "Amazing work, Wyatt. You must be, like… super duper proud." The expression on Wyatt's face was not subtle, and the couple immediately became aware of their blunder. The wife tried to break up another beat of awkward silence by echoing her husband's sentiment.

"Great turn out, too. Thanks for such a wonderful evening." She replied, and forced a smile.

Avoiding any further compulsory niceties, the couple meandered over to another piece, and Wyatt ironically was left standing in front of "A Place to Rest." He studied the piece again, and the last glint of joy from just a moment before faded into nothing. He knew somewhere deep down he still felt great pride in this work, but the feeling was lost on him now. Before this embarrassing encounter, when Wyatt looked at this piece, he saw the phone call from Melody. He saw the hospital hallway, the doctor's face. Now, in this moment, he simply saw splatters of blue and gray paint thrown against cotton and hemp stretched over a rectangular, wooden frame.

A few minutes later, Wyatt found himself in the alley outside of the gallery. Sparks flew from his lighter, as he lit the end of his final cigarette. Instead of tossing his empty pack into the trash-cluttered street corner, he shoved it back into his coat pocket. The city sounds of car horns, police sirens, and the Los Angeles Police Department helicopters overhead were drowned out as the nicotine and tar filled his lungs. His throat burned slightly, and he exhaled his frustration into the surrounding air.

Wyatt wondered how it had come to this. He had given more than a decade and a half of his life to this craft that to this point had offered nothing in return other than the emotional burden of needing to be fulfilled. Had he wasted all of this time?

The sudden burst of a car horn jerked Wyatt out of his self-deprecating, internal thought spiral. The silver sedan's tires screeched to a halt, and the driver threw his hands in the air. The driver threw a fit, and screamed at the car in front of him.

"Pull up! Pull the fuck up! Come on," the silver sedan's driver yelled. Wyatt looked at the woman driving the car in front of the man. He noticed the woman looked nervous, and she gripped her steering wheel tightly. She slowly crept just somewhat farther into the intersection. "Pull the fuck up!" The man screamed again, and honked his horn to match his anger. Wyatt looked at the intersection closer, and realized that they were in an unprotected left turn lane, and the light was likely going to turn yellow at any moment. The man apparently was trying to avoid getting stuck at the intersection. "Pull up, goddamnit!" The driver slammed on his gas pedal only to again immediately slam on his brakes, and avoid crashing into the car in front of him. The angry seesaw caused his entire silver sedan to rock aggressively back and forth. Eventually, Wyatt had had enough of the sedan driver's irrational anger, and finally spoke up himself. Since the driver's window was down, Wyatt knew he would hear him.

"Hey man, chill out, yeah?" Wyatt took another drag of his cigarette. The silver sedan's driver looked over to Wyatt and kept his anger at the same level.

"Oh, fuck you," the man shouted back at Wyatt.

"You look dumb." Wyatt retorted, and let out a small sliver of laughter. "Just relax, there's nowhere for her to go."

"Mind your own fucking business." Wyatt chuckled to himself again, and snapped back at the angry man.

"You look so pathetic." Wyatt laughed through his words, which only made the driver more angry. Wyatt then found himself yelling at full volume to the stranger behind the wheel of the silver sedan. "You look so fucking stupid! You look so dumb!" Wyatt shouted through maniacal laughter.

The light turned yellow, and the woman carefully took her left turn, like a normal driver. The silver sedan peeled out behind her, and sped through the red light. Wyatt held up his middle finger as the man looked back towards him.

Wyatt wondered if the slight catharsis he felt from lashing out at this stranger scratched the itch of scolding himself. After yet another unsuccessful gallery opening, was he the one he thought looked stupid?

The gallery's back door swung open, and a woman walked into the alleyway. She also lit a cigarette, and leaned against the building. She saw Wyatt, and nodded his direction. Wyatt, still held his middle finger in the air, smiled back at her. The gallery dealer took a long drag, and then noticed Wyatt's gesture.

"Rough night, eh?" She said and blew out a cloud of smoke.

"You can say that." Wyatt took another drag, himself. "What's the word?" Wyatt hesitated even asking, as he knew he did not want the answer.

"You really want to know? Right now?" She looked down to her heels. Wyatt looked in the opposite direction, just in time to see one of those helicopters loudly fly over.

"Not really," he responded, "but I don't know that I really get a choice."

"I mean… If tonight is any indication, I probably won't take up the second-week option on our showing agreement." Wyatt exhaled, and watched the helicopter disappear behind nearby buildings.

"Ouch," was the only word Wyatt could think to respond with.

"Don't sweat it. I'm sure we'll sell something. Just probably not tonight, ya know? People will come back, next couple of days. Word of mouth and all that. But yeah, I probably won't extend the showing beyond this week unless we start going through them." The dealer dropped her cigarette down to the street, and stamped out the flame with the front sole of her heels. "Listen, if you talk to your uncle, will you let him know that I took care of you tonight? Like… made things easy, and what not. I'd love to get a chance to show his work here. Would be a real opportunity to bring some notoriety to the space." Wyatt did not look towards her, and instead kept his gaze to the sky. It took every ounce of focus to not drift away into the stars he stared at. He wanted to be anywhere but where he was.

"Sure thing," he said back. He finally worked up the courage to look the woman in the face. "I appreciate your honesty." Wyatt said as he took another drag.

"It'd probably help if you got back inside and talked to people. Not many people still here, but it wouldn't hurt." Melody's words echoed again in Wyatt's mind.

"Yeah, I think I'm probably going to head home. I'll reach out later this week and see how it's going." Wyatt too put out his cigarette. "My sister, Melody, she's my agent. She helped coordinate all of this. She'll be the one to settle with you before you close up for the night. Would you mind letting her know I took off?"

The dealer nodded, and replied. "Yeah, sure," before she went back inside. Wyatt, now alone in the alley, put his hands in his pockets, turned towards the street, and started walking away.

Even on the most beautiful of nights, there is already something depressing about Downtown Los Angeles, and for Wyatt, tonight would be no exception. The streets are lined with unhoused residents that are regularly demonized by tourists, and locals with a sense of entitlement. Law enforcement stands idly by, not engaging with anyone until they demonstrate peacefully over some unjust action likely perpetrated by those same officers. Downtown Los Angeles was not a friendly place, and oftentimes, not a safe place either. Tonight, Wyatt did not seem to care about any of it. He walked slowly, and spent most of the time within the confines of his own mind.

He pulled out his cigarettes and remembered that his pack was empty. He tossed the package in a trash bin on the sidewalk, and then saw a small magazine stand a few feet ahead of him. He walked up to the stand, and saw a copy of *GQ Magazine* sitting in front of the display.

After signaling to the employee he wanted a new pack of *Marlboro Lights 100s*, Wyatt picked up a copy of the magazine. The cover displayed an animated image of a man with a grey beard, in a perfectly pressed suit. The caption simply read, "What's left to accomplish?" Just above the caption, Wyatt saw the name of the magazine's subject… his uncle, "Jackson Brone."

The employee snapped Wyatt out of his trance with a simple, "Did you want that too?"

Wyatt nodded, and paid for both. As he walked away, he did not break his stare into his uncle's judging, illustrated eyes on the cover of *GQ.* Wyatt slung the magazine under his arm as he pulled out a cigarette from his brand new pack, and lit it up. He took a long drag of the fresh cigarette before he grabbed the magazine from under his arm, and tossed it into another sidewalk trash bin.

Wyatt made it back to his workspace loft after about a twenty-five-minute walk through downtown. He pulled his front door open slowly, picked up some mail from the ground just inside, and flipped on the lights. The loft itself was beautiful. Huge, with twenty-foot ceilings and tall windows that overlooked the vastness of the fatigued city streets he had just walked through. Lights twinkled in the distant Hollywood Hills, and the faint sounds of the chaotic city below barely made its way through the windows. A small kitchen rested in the corner of a main living space, with multiple work-space rooms connected to it. The living space doubled as Wyatt's bedroom, with his bed chaotically placed in the middle of the area. It's rent controlled, micro-rate seemed to be the only reason Wyatt could still afford this place; a fact he never let himself forget.

Wyatt walked into his kitchen, and pulled his cell phone out to make a call. Wyatt fingered through his mail, and held his cell phone up to his ear. After a few moments of silence, he heard a gentle voice speaking through his phone's speaker.

"Hi, you've reached Samantha, I'm sorry I missed you. Leave a message, and I'll get back to you as soon as I can! Or just text me, that's probably better. Bye!" *Beep.* Wyatt ran his hand through his hair, and spoke into his phone.

"Hey, babe, it's me. I didn't see you tonight, so I was calling to see if everything was okay. I assumed you'd be late, but I thought you'd at least be there. Okay. Well, give me a call back, I guess. Love you." Wyatt gently tapped the red "End Call" button on his cell phone's screen, and stared at the photo of he and Samantha that served as the wallpaper of his phone before he slid it back in his pants pocket.

He shook his head, and noticed his answering machine blinking with an unread message. Much to the chagrin of his sister, Wyatt always insisted on keeping a landline as his "business line," versus just using his cell phone for both work and pleasure.

Wyatt continued looking through his mail, walked over to the machine, and pressed the "play" button to listen to his unheard message.

"Hi, Wyatt, this is Maurice Pallen. I — uh, my apologies, I'm your uncle's attorney." The words caught Wyatt's attention and he turned towards the answering machine. "Listen, I am very sorry to say this to you in this way, but your uncle is dead." Wyatt lightly tossed his mail onto the countertop. "Again, I'm very sorry to leave this in a voicemail, but I need the chance to connect with you regarding your uncle's estate. There's a particular item I need to discuss with you. If you could please give me a call back tomorrow, so we can go over some logistics, I would greatly appreciate it. Thank you, and again, my condolences."

Wyatt stood silently in his kitchen, and stared at the answering machine. After a few moments, Wyatt hit the button, and listened to the message again.

"Hi, Wyatt, this is Maurice Pallen. I — uh, my apologies, I'm your uncle's attorney. Listen, I am very sorry to say this to you in this way, but your uncle is dead. Again, I'm very sorry to leave this in a voicemail, but I need the chance to connect with you regarding your uncle's estate. There's a particular item I need to discuss with you. If you could please give me a call back tomorrow, so we can go over some logistics, I would greatly appreciate it. Thank you, and again, my condolences."

Wyatt stood in silence and disbelief, as the truth of this message sank in.

The world had lost one of its greatest artists. The art world had lost one of its most influential talents. The revered, unconventional, disruptive, and once-in-a-generation talent Jackson Brone had died.

Wyatt's uncle was dead.

CHAPTER 2

"Yes, I'm terribly sorry, but yes. Your uncle is dead."

Wyatt stared at the short man in a wool, three-piece suit. The suit itself probably cost more than Wyatt's entire workspace loft mortgage, but Wyatt could not seem to get it out of his head how uncomfortable and itchy it must feel to wear in this summer heat. His intuition proved to be accurate by the man's incessant fidgeting. He tugged gently on his collar, straightened his lapels, and pulled a small, folded handkerchief out of his breast pocket to dab at the beads of sweat on his forehead.

Maurice Pallen stood just inside the entryway of Wyatt's workspace loft. He was shorter than Wyatt remembered, but his face just as round, and his head just as bald. His shoulders slightly slumped forward towards the ground, and his head hung just low enough for the light above the two men to reflect off of his transparent, plastic frames, and into Wyatt's eyes. Wyatt observed how this normally dominant, alpha-business-male's knuckles were white from the intense grip he had on his briefcase. Maurice was nervous. He was feeling *something,* at least, Wyatt thought.

"I am truly, very sorry," Maurice continued. Despite his meek posture, and the physics of his blood flow betraying his normally non-emotional tendencies, Maurice said the words with such a calculated, and disinterested cold tone. Wyatt was confident that he meant no disrespect whatsoever, but rather intended that this conversation would simply be another aspect of the business relationship Maurice had had with Jackson for decades.

Maurice Pallen was one of Los Angeles' most well-known, and most rightfully feared, entertainment lawyers. His firm, Pallen & Wall represented some of the world's most recognized names in "Hollywood." While the firm primarily represented actors, directors, and writers, Maurice found that Jackson Brone was an incredibly rare talent who garnered such universal, and global success that he simply would not miss the opportunity to negotiate, and secure, his deals for him. Maurice was a brilliant and shrewd attorney, and Jackson's career was always better off for it. For Jackson, the feeling was mutual.

When Wyatt had decided to take the leap of faith, and pursue art full-time, Jackson had recommended Wyatt get an attorney to protect his pursuits, and assets. When Wyatt had mentioned possibly meeting with Maurice to discuss what the process of finding an entertainment lawyer could potentially look like, he remembered his uncle saying, "No, not that lawyer. That lawyer is mine." Jackson was incredibly protective of his relationship with Maurice, and Maurice was equally protective of Jackson's estate.

"All right, then." Wyatt said to Maurice. They were the only words he could think of to respond to the blanket statement that his uncle was dead. "Good to see you too, Mo."

Wyatt extended his arm out towards his loft, and welcomed Maurice into his space, and offered him the only seat that wasn't covered in paint supplies, and half-completed canvases. A small, green, one-seater positioned directly opposite of Wyatt's unkempt California King bed. Maurice walked over to the chair, and he gently dabbed the tip of his index finger into a splotch of paint on the worn upholstery, ensuring it was old and dry before he sat. He tried to take up as little real estate on the broken in chair, and set his laptop onto his lap. Wyatt stood in the kitchen and poured himself a cup of coffee.

He glanced over towards the visibly uncomfortable Maurice, and watched as he shuffled his briefcase in his lap, and ran his multi-ring cladded hand over his meticulously groomed beard. Wyatt watched the small man fidget in the maybe too comfortable chair cushion.

"It's old," Wyatt said, gesticulating his coffee cup towards the green seat. Maurice didn't respond. He artlessly sat, humdrum, and nodded. "Jumping right in, I guess." Wyatt said. The thick residue of sarcastic, dark humor slowly melted over each word. "Would you like some?" Wyatt asked, offering a cup of coffee to Maurice, who politely declined.

"No, no… Thank you, though," Maurice again awkwardly shuffled in the deep cushioned chair, and maneuvered to click open the worn, leather briefcase that also sat in his lap. He shuffled around a few papers, pulled a small stack out, and then struggled to click the briefcase closed again.

Wyatt added a small amount of oat milk to his black, single-origin drip, and stirred it in as he walked back out from behind his counter into the main living space.

"My apologies if I seem unsympathetic. It's just business for me, you understand." Maurice was sincere, but still very calculated.

"No need to apologize, I totally get it." Wyatt sat down on the edge of his bed, faced Maurice, took a sip of his coffee, and gestured for Maurice to continue. "So, how can I help?"

"Well, first, thank you for making time today on such short notice," Maurice started again, and got straight back to business. Another aspect of being one of, if not, the most successful entertainment lawyers in the business was the seemingly simple ability to skip the small talk. Time was money for Maurice, and Wyatt appreciated the lack of unnecessary pleasantries. "And again, I am truly sorry for your loss. It is my understanding that Mr. Brone was some of your only remaining family."

"Uh, yeah —" Wyatt responded, somewhat surprised by Maurice's depth of family knowledge. Then again, he knew that

Maurice was intimately close with his uncle's business dealings, and had been his uncle's most consistent professional alliance for nearly four decades. Naturally, personal details were shared throughout their time working together. "He and my sis, Mel, yeah. Not really anyone else."

"Mr. Brone was —" Maurice began again, before Wyatt interrupted him.

"You can just say Jackson. It's okay. He's dead, and I won't tell anyone, I promise." Wyatt's sarcasm was lost on Maurice.

"… Jackson… was extremely particular about his final Will and Testament. Every detail of his estate was meticulously planned. Everything is being left precisely how Mr. — how Jackson wanted it to be." Maurice handed Wyatt the small stack of papers held together with a paperclip. Wyatt looked at the title page, and just saw the words *Will and Testament*, and again, the realization of this conversation came full force into Wyatt's mind.

"I don't need anything from him," Wyatt responded, as he started to hand the papers back to Maurice.

"Jackson was aware that you would likely disclaim any inheritance he left to you, so to be fully transparent, most of his estate is being left to your sister, Melody Brone." Wyatt smirked at how Maurice mentioned Melody, as if Wyatt needed reminding of his own sister's full name. Part of him wanted to make a joke by asking, "Who?" But he thought better of it. Maurice did not strike him as the funny type. *Some "entertainment" lawyer,* Wyatt laughed to himself, in his mind.

"Beyond what is being left for Melody, the rest of Jackson's estate is accounted for, excluding this one final asset." Wyatt looked to the papers again, then back to Maurice, who was making focused eye contact.

"What?" Wyatt asked, hesitating and nervous for the response. Maurice's focus confused Wyatt momentarily. "What is it?"

"Your uncle is leaving you a piece of art." Maurice said.

Are you fucking kidding me? Wyatt thought, instantly annoyed at the revelation. Over a decade of unsuccessfully pursuing a career as a painter, living in the shadow of his ultra-famous uncle, only for his uncle to pass away, and leave a constant reminder of his lack of notoriety. A piece of his uncle's work.

"Oh," Wyatt said instead.

"Admittedly, I have very few details of this piece. It's… strange, if I may speak plainly. Every other aspect of your uncle's will was, as I previously stated, meticulously designed, and yet, with this one asset… I essentially just know it's being left to you."

"Why such secrecy?" Wyatt asked, still piqued at the prospect of taking in a piece of art he had no interest in keeping.

"I have no idea. There are no other actual instructions, simply 'This piece goes to Wyatt.' Given the backdrop of your uncle's methodical nature, it's… peculiar, if I'm being honest." Wyatt thought it strange, as well. Wyatt had always known his uncle as being the type to plan out every minute detail of everything; from his life, to his estate, and especially his paintings.

"Any guesses?" Wyatt asked candidly, as he burned his tongue just slightly, slurping down another sip of coffee.

"None," Maurice responded, giving Wyatt nothing to work with. "Other than, maybe, it was of… particular importance to him."

Aw, it was important to him, Wyatt thought as he rolled his mind's eyes. *Thanks, Uncle Jack.*

"You may have been aware, but your uncle hadn't been starting new pieces recently. Over the last few months, I'd say. This painting, the one being left to you, is to my knowledge, his final unfinished work."

There was something about this conversation that did not make any sense to Wyatt. For as pragmatic as Wyatt knew his uncle to be, he was even more shrewd. Wyatt knew his uncle would have never left Wyatt something of particular value or importance. If a piece of his uncle's work was important enough to be kept shrouded in such secrecy, Wyatt was confident his uncle would have left it to somewhere of significance and prestige, like the Smithsonian American Art Museum to be displayed next to Frederic Edwin Church's *Aurora Borealis.* Wyatt was confident a renowned art museum would have been salivating at the mouth to showcase the famed Jackson Brone's final, unfinished painting.

"It comes with a letter, as well." Maurice continued.

"I'm sorry?" Wyatt was not sure he had heard Maurice correctly.

"The painting. It comes with a letter as well." Maurice clarified.

"What's it say?" Wyatt pushed his eyebrows together, more confused than before.

"I — uh — I have no idea. I haven't read it. No one has, except your uncle. It was sealed before his passing, and has remained so. It will remain so, until you open it, presumably."

Wyatt listened to Maurice, carefully took another drink of his coffee, and still tried to put the pieces of this strange puzzle together in his mind.

"So my uncle, the man who trusted you with possibly every aspect of his professional life, is leaving me a single piece of art from his personal collection, and a letter. And you, his longtime lawyer, arguably his closest confidant, have no idea why you don't have more details around it? Am I understanding all this right?" Wyatt was trying to not sound sarcastic, but he understood he was likely not succeeding in that feat.

"That is correct," Maurice responded laconically.

"It's a little weird, right?" Wyatt asked, smirking somewhat at the uncomfortable lawyer.

"I think so, yes." Wyatt looked at Maurice for a moment, before he hopped up, and walked back into his kitchen.

"Seems a little shocking to me, I guess. Unexpected," Wyatt said as he stood in his kitchen and refilled his chipped, stained, porcelain mug.

"Yes, I agree. But so does killing yourself." Maurice again spoke with that same calculated cold. Wyatt stopped in his tracks, and stood still in his kitchen for just a moment. With those words, Wyatt realized he had not yet known how his uncle's life ended. His uncle had seemed to be in good health, so Wyatt had likely assumed it was a freak anomaly. The idea of his uncle taking his own life had not even crossed Wyatt's mind.

Maurice saw Wyatt stop, and stand still, and he was immediately flushed with a hot flash, and his entire person began perspiring almost immediately.

"I'm sorry?" Wyatt asked the only words that came to his mind. Maurice struggled to find a response, mortified with his blatant disregard for Wyatt's feelings.

"Wyatt... please forgive me. That was a wildly inappropriate thing for me to have said."

"No, no, it's... fine. I think." Wyatt was quick to absolve Maurice.

"You didn't know," Maurice said with almost a question-like inflection.

Wyatt shook his head "no," and set his mug down on his counter. There was a palpable silence as Wyatt leaned his back against the granite countertop.

"I did not. I only know what you told me on the phone," Wyatt finally said. "That my uncle had..."

"Passed... Wyatt, I am so deeply sorry."

"Mo, it's fine, really. Don't beat yourself up about it, it is what it is."

Another short silence fell over the two. Neither sure what to do or say next. After a few moments, and a couple guarded sips of his coffee, Wyatt finally spoke up again.

"How... how did he do it?" Wyatt asked, careful to not go down a rabbit hole from which he would not return. Maurice looked down at his hands, and twirled one of his many rings.

"Do you want to know?" Maurice asked, equally carefully, before he looked back up to Wyatt who unaffectedly nodded his head. Maurice cleared his throat, and tugged slightly at his tight collar. "He — uh — he cut his throat."

Wyatt was not sure how to respond to the news, so he instead stood in silence. The silence only disrupted by Wyatt's occasional slurp of black drip.

"Wow," Wyatt finally said. "That's... kind of intense." Wyatt smirked when he said it, which caught Maurice off-guard. "I guess it's only fitting that he go out on his own terms. Who found him? Do you know who found him?" Wyatt could not tell if the turning he felt in his stomach was from the gruesome development about his uncle's death, or the fact that he was now on his fourth cup of coffee, and still had not eaten any breakfast.

"A member of his staff."

Wyatt shook his head, and exhaled, "Fuck, man. Are they okay?" Maurice nodded again, still fidgeting with his hands.

"Yes. Yes, it was overwhelming, understandably. But your uncle had known that they would likely be the one to find him, so he made every possible accommodation ahead of time. To try and... make it... less... traumatizing, I suppose."

"Kind of fucked up. Seems like he could have done something less... dramatic."

"Well. You know Mr. Brone." Wyatt laughed, but was not sure whether he was meant to. It seemed like a quip, but again, Wyatt knew "quips" were not Maurice's specialty. He looked at Maurice, and when Maurice caught Wyatt's eye, he smirked a slight smile. Wyatt smiled back, and chuckled a little.

Good for you, Mo, Wyatt thought.

"Fair," Wyatt said through his smile. "So what now?" Wyatt sat back down on his bed, facing a seemingly more relaxed Maurice.

Wyatt had begun to realize that his question held more weight than it probably should have. *What now?*

If Wyatt was being honest with himself, he was not simply asking about the logistics of getting his newly inherited piece of art from his deceased uncle. Wyatt was also asking about what he could do next, after learning all of this new information. After all of the conversations he had been having, quite recently, with his sister regarding his own future in this craft. Now that the most famous artist walking the earth, his uncle, was no longer doing so, who would fill that void? Would that void need someone to fill it? Could Wyatt possibly be that person?

Truthfully, the thought was initially exciting, and Wyatt felt his racing heart pound hard within the confines of his chest. The second wave of emotion, however, was more somber in tone. The reason he was having these thoughts is that his uncle slit his throat until he bled to death on the floor of his home.

You're sick, Wyatt thought to, and of, himself.

"You do not need to do anything," Maurice continued. "I have already made all of the arrangements for the piece to be delivered. I tentatively scheduled it for tomorrow, late morning, around 11:30 A.M. Will that work okay with your day?" Wyatt nodded, and took another sip.

"Sure, that works fine."

"Great. In that case…" Maurice popped open his briefcase, and again, shuffled through the chaotic stack of papers until he found what he was looking for.

From out of the depths of his briefcase, Maurice pulled out a single, off-white envelope with just the word, "Wyatt," written on the outside. It was sealed, and wax-stamped, with his uncle's personal insignia.

Wyatt took the item from Maurice, and looked at it a little closer. The blood-red wax was smeared just slightly, like his uncle struggled to press it down onto the envelope.

"I'm guessing this is the letter?" Wyatt asked, looking back to the lawyer.

Maurice nodded.

"That is the letter."

"And you didn't read it?"

"No one has. Except your uncle."

Wyatt again looked over the envelope. The color was an off-shade of white, almost tea stained. The paper's rough texture made it feel old. The wax stamped with an olde English letter "B" held the paper together in neat folds. Wyatt thought, again, that it seemed dramatic.

"Probably could just have emailed me, or something," Wyatt said, as he set the letter down on the kitchen counter on his way to what would likely be his last refill. Not because he was emotionally finished with coffee for the day, but simply because he had run out, and did not feel like going through the trouble of making another pot.

"It seems that would have been more convenient." Maurice responded, not really needing to. "The movers will be by tomorrow morning, they just requested that you create a space for the piece to be set in. They will take care of everything else. From what little information I have regarding this particular asset, it does seem important that the piece have… a space. Somewhere it can be."

"All right, then." Wyatt smiled gently at Maurice, and the two made their way back to Wyatt's front door.

"Thank you again for making the time to connect today, and it cannot be overstated… I am truly sorry for your loss. Jackson was a rare person." Maurice said, as he extended his hand. Wyatt smiled back, and took Maurice's hand in his, shaking it.

"Appreciate it, Mo. Thanks for helping out with everything." Maurice nodded, and turned to open the door and leave. As he stepped through the doorway, Maurice stopped himself, and turned back to Wyatt. Wyatt noticed Maurice's abrupt stop, and looked up.

"Oh — I wanted to tell you." Maurice looked to the ground, again seeming nervous.

"Yeah?" Wyatt asked, curiously raising his eyebrows. Maurice smiled cordially, and looked back at Wyatt.

"I'm a big fan of your work, Wyatt. I am excited to see what you do next."

Maurice turned, and left. Wyatt stood in the doorway for a moment, a little taken aback at Maurice's candid compliment.

It is both sad, and remarkable; the fragility of the mind of an artist. Words, from insignificant people, can either create a whirlwind of momentum, or completely reduce to rubble the confidence of the creator.

Those seven words, spoken from someone of no real consequence to Wyatt's attitude, decision-making, or intellectual care, shot through Wyatt's psyche like a small bolt of lightning.

Maurice is a fan of Wyatt's painting.

The man who represented Jackson Brone has not only seen Wyatt's work, but it brought him joy. Wyatt stared into the empty hallway. He cracked a smile, let out a small "huh" grunt, and turned to walk back inside as the door slowly clanked shut behind him.

Back inside his workspace, Wyatt's mind immediately resumed the war it was beginning to wage previously. To make more coffee, or to not make more coffee. He walked back into his kitchen, to further tempt fate, and picked up an apple from a small basket on his countertop.

As he sunk his still not brushed teeth into a crispy, sweet Gala, his eye caught the letter from his uncle, sitting on the counter next to the fruit. Again, his mind was fixated on the conspicuous design of the envelope.

The crunch of his chewing was loud in his head, but it was still not enough to overpower the intrigue he felt towards this piece of Couché-style paper held together by only the wax seal.

Wyatt again sunk his teeth into the apple, holding it in his mouth, as he grabbed a butter knife from inside the drawer, and picked the letter up. As the apple juice started to dribble out of his lips, Wyatt slid the knife through the crease of the paper, and pealed the wax seal away. The letter fell open, and Wyatt noticed a slight discoloration underneath the wax seal.

The seal his uncle had used was a deep, blood red color, but there were hints of dark blue, and maybe green too. Wyatt thought it was strange that his uncle would have used two different wax drips before settling on the blood red color used.

Then again, Wyatt thought, his uncle was not the most rational or normal. Wyatt slurped up the apple juice trying to escape through his teeth, and grabbed the apple with his hand, taking a big bite out of it in the process.

The crunch again was loud, but Wyatt was transfixed on the letter. With his free hand, Wyatt flattened out the paper, sprawling it out flat on his countertop. Wyatt legitimately could not explain anything about this letter.

The first thing Wyatt noticed about the letter is that the paper felt impossibly old. Coated, and with a faded glossy finish, it was heavy and thick. He kept gently sliding his thumb and index finger back and forth on either side of the page. The texture was soothing, but odd.

Next, Wyatt noticed the writing on the letter itself. There was one primary block of text, but he noticed there was scribbling all over the rest of the page. The script looked to be in different handwritings, and with no apparent rhyme or reason.

On top of the main text, on all sides, below, in the margins, there were scribbles of writing everywhere. Wyatt's heart sank, slightly. He felt sad for his uncle, who was obviously suffering from intense mental decline in his final weeks. Nothing else could account for how chaotic, and seemingly indecipherable this letter truly was.

Wyatt tried his best to read the main block of text. It was written in such elegant, cursive penmanship, that it was almost difficult to make out. He slowly spoke it aloud to himself as he read it.

"To nev'r showeth and nev'r bid, f'r 'twill beest yours.
To nev'r stand ho and nev'r selleth, f'r 'twill beest yours,
Followeth these to wildest dreams, f'r 'twill beest yours."
Huh, Wyatt thought again, *thanks, Jack. What a beautiful letter.*

Wyatt rolled his eyes, and tossed the letter aside. *What the hell was that supposed to mean?* He thought. Wyatt was not even sure it was in English. He took another large bite of his apple, and walked from the kitchen into his secondary work room.

Wyatt's workspace loft was segmented into three main areas. First, his main living space, where his bed and awkward meeting with Maurice was held. Second, his primary work space, where his most current painting awaited completion. And lastly, a smaller, secondary workspace room, where he cast away pieces he was not ready to destroy quite yet. It was a room Wyatt affectionately referred to as his "Island of Misfit Paintings."

This room, Wyatt decided, would be the easiest, and unfortunately, most appropriate place to make space for the painting Wyatt did not have any interest in keeping.

Wyatt never dreamed.

From the time he was a boy, he prided himself on his ability to drift in and out of his own reality whenever he chose. Most of his painting ideas typically came to him during his many visceral daydream states. Wyatt always felt most creative when he knew he was awake.

That night was different.

Maybe it was learning of how his uncle had passed away, maybe it was residual stress of another failed gallery opening, or maybe it was the fact that both of these things happened on the same ill-fated evening.

Most of his night was spent completely restless. Wyatt knew of an abnormally long heat wave raging in his region, and tonight seemed like an apex. Since his downtown Los Angeles, workspace loft had no centralized air conditioning system, the heat was felt even more oppressive. He had already shed his normal "sleep shirt," and still could not get over the sticky, night sweat feeling.

Whether or not there was any truth to it, Wyatt had heard that it is better to get up if you cannot sleep, instead of restlessly laying in bed. Supposedly, the stress of laying restless for hours on end was worse for trying to turn your brain off than just getting up until you feel tired again.

After failing to win the battle of discomposure, Wyatt gave in, and stood up from out of his bed. He walked into the kitchen, and grabbed a glass from his cupboard. His 10-cup Brita pitcher was almost empty, but he managed to pour a full glass. He set the pitcher in his kitchen sink, and turned the faucet spout on to fill it up again before he took a drink. Wyatt could feel the ice cold water as it traveled down his throat before settling into his stomach. A strange sensation that no one ever really discusses.

Wyatt turned the water off, and slide the heavier pitcher back into his refrigerator. He took another drink of the ice cold water, and walked over to the floor-to-ceiling windows overlooking the thick of downtown. He was not sure what time it was, but he knew it was early. Or late, depending on how you think of it. He looked down at the bustling street below him. Crowded, even still, with cars, vagrants, and the occasional tourist likely coming back to their hotel from an underwhelming night out in the city of angels.

Wyatt always felt bad for people visiting the city for the first time. Growing up outside of California, he knew people thought of Los Angeles as a city of glitz, glamor, and celebrities. The city where just by going to a nearby Starbucks for a six dollar, artificially flavored latte could provide the chance to bump shoulders with that year's "Sexiest Man Alive." Urban legends of celebrities getting their big break in such a scenario filled the shallow dreams of everyone hoping for the same outcome. Wyatt remembered hearing a story of Cameron Diaz being discovered at a local, Hollywood coffee shop and being offered her role in "The Mask" right there on the spot. He knew it was most likely bullshit, but he also assumed if he had heard that story, he surely was not the only one. And at the same time… what if?

The lie that perpetuated the problem.

He looked down to the sidewalk below him, and he saw a homeless man talking to himself on the street corner. Two girls, who were clearly not from here, noticed the man from down the block, and intentionally crossed the street in an effort to avoid an unwanted confrontation. Wyatt watched the women as they continued their conversation, but kept an obvious eye on the man yelling at the air across the street. His heart sank a little, understanding that there was nothing unique about this experience. Whether it was Los Angeles, or New York, or any city really, and also regardless of the time, this was something women have to deal with, constantly. He took another drink of water, and shook his head, watching the women pass the man safely.

Wyatt had not traveled the world very extensively, but he had visited other American metropolitans, and he always noticed one key difference. The unhoused population in Los Angeles seems to always be performing. An invisible and unknown audience, driven by that lie that if the right person were to come along, their entire circumstance would change in an instant. Fame, fortune, and notoriety at the drop of a dime… just like that. Wyatt chuckled to himself, and wondered which was worse. Who was better off? The man on the street corner, unafraid to be a nuisance to everyone around him, yelling into nothing. Or him… a failed artist unwilling to give up on his own dream, pouring his madness deeper onto canvas.

Perhaps they were not so different after all.

Without realizing it, Wyatt was knee deep in a very welcomed yawn. A yawn so intense it made his eyes water. It was time.

Using as little energy as possible as to not lose the sleepy feeling, Wyatt set the half-empty glass on his counter, and crawled back into bed. The sheets and pillow felt cooler with the absence of his body on them. A welcomed cool.

Finally, after what felt like forever and somehow also like no time had passed at all, Wyatt drifted into profound, dreamless rest.

CHAPTER 3

The sun was hot.

A searing hot Wyatt had only felt in the dead of summer growing up in Houston, Texas.

It was a sweltering that flushed Wyatt's cheeks, painting them with a healthy shade of red, as it fully crept past the edge of his curtains, and tinted everything orange from behind his still closed eyes. In just an instant, Wyatt opened his eyes to an entirely new world.

The city still buzzed below him, car horns, and strangers screaming at the air. The sun, however, shone brightly through his tall, thin loft windows. Wyatt reluctantly got out of bed, still hoping the gallery and his conversation with Maurice just the morning before were both somehow part of a terrible dream.

Wyatt walked over to his tall, curtained windows, rotated the small handle, and cracked them open slightly. Even with the almost unbearable heat from the sun, the breeze immediately rushed into Wyatt's space from the window, and the cool air brushed brilliantly against his face. He exhaled in quick relief.

"Oh, man," he said out loud to himself, laughed, and then yelled into the city noise, "LA, it's fucking hot!"

He stood silently for a moment, and focused on how nice the wind felt against his cheeks. The new, cooled life of air breathed into his stagnant, warm home. His hair tousled in the force of the wind. Wyatt welcomed the moment of quiet, peace.

Still unsure of the what time it actually was, Wyatt knew it was at least time for his habitual morning coffee routine. He eagerly made his way into his kitchen.

"Alexa," Wyatt said in the nothingness of his empty loft, "what's the weather today?"

As his robot assistant answered his question, Wyatt filled a brushed steel tea kettle with tap water from his deep sink.

"Right now in Los Angeles, it's eighty-seven degrees Fahrenheit, with clear skies. Tonights forecast has mostly clear skies, with a low of sixty-eight degrees. By the way, looking to get outside? Ask for nearby parks you can —" Wyatt interrupted her.

"Alexa, stop, Jesus." He set his full kettle onto the smallest circle of his electric stovetop.

The phrase "a watched pot never boils" came to Wyatt's mind as he watched the temperature gauge on his metal, pour over kettle slowly rise as it sat on his stove. Wyatt always hated that phrase. He knew if he continued watching the temperature gauge, it would obviously continue to rise. *For an artist,* Wyatt thought of himself, *you sure don't have much imagination.* Wyatt took a deep breath, lifted his arms over his head, and stretched the last remnants of a terrible night's sleep out of his body. He exhaled slowly, and thoroughly, and shook his head like a rag doll, side to side, hoping to release any left over tension.

Wyatt heard the building buzzer sound off, and he remembered that the painting he was inheriting was to be delivered today. He walked over to the door, and pressed the "talk" button with his thumb.

"Come on up, door's open," Wyatt said, before walking back into his kitchen.

He walked into his loft's secondary workspace, where he had decided to keep his inheritance... the extremely unwanted "Jackson Brone original." He had moved some of his other works out of the way, placing them against the wall to clear a space in the middle of the room. He was not sure how large the piece was, but knowing his uncle, it was not going to be as small as he hoped it would be. He took another deep, calming breath and exhaled a disappointing sigh. Wyatt looked around the small room. He never thought he would own so many paintings that he would preferably have destroyed. He never thought he would willingly add to the collection. He definitely never thought he would willingly accept one of his uncle's pieces for said collection. *Here we go,* Wyatt thought. *Thanks again, Jack.*

"Hello?" A gentle voice called out from the entryway. "Mr. Brone?" Wyatt heard the voice calling out, and he started making his way to his front door.

"Yeah, I'm coming. Come on in," he called back. He walked lazily towards the voice in his entryway, and started in again just as he turned the hallway corner to see the movers. "You can come straight back here, I have an area I've set aside —" Wyatt stopped at the sight of two men in suits standing in his entryway. One held a badge in his hands, and lifted it up for Wyatt to see clearly.

"Mr. Brone?" Wyatt stared back at the two men, without responding. Expecting to see a couple of rough around the edges movers in jumpsuits, seeing the business suits and badges threw Wyatt off momentarily. "Wyatt... Brone?"

"Uh — yes, sorry." Wyatt laughed for a moment, and tried to figure out if he knew who was speaking to him. "Yes." The two men stared back without responding immediately, returning the favor. "Who are you?" His earnest question was met with an equal chuckle from the man holding the detective's badge.

"Sorry for stopping by with no notice, we were just at HQ down the street, and thought we would swing by to see if you were in. I'm Detective Thomas Johns. This is my partner, Detective Gerry Foss. We're with the Homicide Division at L.A.P.D." Wyatt instinctively held out his hand to both men, shaking their hands in greeting, still completely unsure as to why they were at his home.

"Oh, got it. It's — uh — nice to meet you both," Wyatt said almost robotically.

"We were hoping to ask you some questions about your uncle? Did we catch you at a bad time?" Det. Johns again showed Wyatt his badge and a department issued photo identification card, as if to confirm that he was, in fact, who he said he was. As if Wyatt would have any real reason to be suspicious. Or any idea what these things were supposed to look like for that matter. Wyatt was anything but a habitual rule follower, and had a healthy distrust of organized authority, but even he knew he would have no idea if he was being swindled by an imposter. Wyatt looked at it anyway, and saw his name, badge number, and the words that he had just heard, "Homicide Division."

"I — uh, not really, no. I'm expecting someone shortly, but it's fine." Wyatt struggled through his response. His brain finally catching up.

"Can we come in? Chat for a minute or two?" Det. Johns again asked. Wyatt nodded.

"Please, yeah, uh, come — come on in." Wyatt gestured to the inside of his home as he turned and walked towards the kitchen. The two detectives slowly followed him into his loft, both men looking around as they entered.

The kettle whizzed and screamed steam across the kitchen air. The piercing noise echoed through the hallow space until Wyatt was able to make it over to the stove, and move the pot over to an unused burner. He clicked the electric stove top off, and turned back towards the detectives. "I was just about to make a pot of coffee, can I get either of you some? Light roast."

"No, thanks," Det. Foss responded.

"No, thank you, though," Det. Johns also said. Wyatt watched as Det. Foss slowly walked through the space, and looked around at the scattered nature of the loft. Det. Johns kept his eyes on Wyatt's movements. They were quick, and a little chaotic as he prepared his coffee. Wyatt grabbed his Chemex, and poured the boiling water over the coffee grounds with a slight hint of cinnamon he had already prepared in the triangle, paper filter.

"You do your work here too?" Det. Johns asked.

"Yeah, it's a workspace apartment lease. I live and work here, as you can tell by everything being just slightly covered in paint. I should probably clean it all up, but who am I kidding? It'd be back in a day or so." Wyatt chuckles to himself, but the humor was lost on the two men. "Because I'm a … a painter. And… I work here." Wyatt quickly lifted his eyebrows, and thought to himself, *moving on.* "I'm sorry. Did you say *homicide division?"* Wyatt asked as he let the water percolate into the glass, pour over carafe.

"Yes. We're overseeing the investigation into the death of your uncle, Jackson Brone." Det. Johns spoke slowly, and clearly. Wyatt could tell he was a veteran on the force. Wyatt saw Det. Foss looking at some of his painting scattered throughout his space. The detective reached to pull out of the canvas' away from the wall to look at the art, and Wyatt called out to him.

"Careful, please. Some of those pieces are still wet," Wyatt said to Det. Foss with a gentle smile. Wyatt felt nervous, and he was not entirely sure why. Det. Foss lifted both his hands into the air in an exaggerated "I am not touching" gesture, and he half-heartedly smiled back. Wyatt turned again to Det. Johns. "I was under the impression that my uncle killed himself..? Is that not the —"

"Sorry, yes. We are responsible for investigating your uncle's … unfortunate suicide. We don't even really like using the word 'investigation,' to be honest. This is sort of, just a formality, like I said. California State law requires that we still conduct a thorough investigation, as our team confirms the appropriate cause of death. Just so we can officially rule out foul play, things of that nature. Just for your own peace of mind, however, the primary investigation into Jackson Brone's passing *is* as a suicide. Detective Foss and I have no reason to suspect anything else, but we still get the, uh… pleasure of doing the paperwork part. All part of the gig," he said, and tapped his badge, "and all just part of the process. Bureaucratic stuff, nothing more. Nothing to worry about." Det. Johns and Det. Foss both smiled at Wyatt, in an almost choreographed moment.

"Why would I be worried?" Wyatt asked. Det. Foss turned to Wyatt, and both detectives stared at him.

"No reason to, really. Just doing our due diligence, is all," Det. Johns replied. "Everyone responds to our kind differently, so we just like to be… delicate with our wording. Helps put people at ease, I supposed."

"Got it, I — uh, didn't know you had to do that." Wyatt smiled back at the men.

"Not many folks do. And we really are sorry for your loss. Jackson seemed like a really… interesting person. And a real talent. Anyway, part of the 'investigation' is interviewing next of kin of the deceased. As of now, you and your sister are the closest people we were able to track down. The only people, really. But if now isn't a great time —" Det. Johns canned speech was interrupted by Wyatt being overly accommodating.

"No, no, please. Ask away. How can I help?" Wyatt started pouring himself a cup of coffee.

"Well, just wanted to touch base and introduce ourselves, really. We were hoping you would be willing to — well, it might be easier if you were to come down to the station and submit a statement for our team?" Det. Foss took a couple of steps towards them, as Det. Johns continued speaking. "Would that be all right, Wyatt?" Wyatt crinkled his forehead and looked back at the men.

"Is that … totally necessary?" Wyatt asked before grabbing his small container of oat milk out of his refrigerator. The detectives looked at each other, before turning back to Wyatt.

"It would be really helpful. It's a pretty standard process." Det. Johns said.

"I just don't know that I really have a lot to say. I didn't even know about any of this until yesterday, anyway. I don't know how a statement from me would be of help."

"Merely a formality," Det. Johns responded.

"I guess I just don't understand why I would need to go all the way to the police station to make a statement." Wyatt tried not to sound too confrontational, but he already felt the annoyance as it boiled up within him. He had successfully avoided connecting with his uncle while he was alive for as long as he could remember. Ironically, now that his uncle had died, he found himself having to talk exclusively about him; Wyatt's actual nightmare.

"If that is not acceptable, we could do something a little more informal?" Det. Johns asked. "If you have some time now, Det. Foss and I could just ask you a couple of questions here, now."

"Yeah, that's fine," Wyatt stirred his coffee before bringing it to his mouth and taking a small sip. He watched Det. Foss pull out a small notebook, while Det. Johns continued to look straight at him.

"When did you last speak with your uncle?" Det. Foss finally spoke. His voice low, and choppy like wheels rolling over an old, gravel parking lot.

"Maybe… a week ago? Maybe two."

"Can I ask what you discussed?" If Det. Johns was the good cop, Det. Foss was desperately trying to be the bad one.

"I had a gallery opening a couple of nights ago, and my uncle is friendly… *was* friendly with the curator. We discussed some logistical details about the space, and the event." Wyatt responded, slowly. His conversation with the curator in the alley during his failed opening popped into his mind. How she asked Wyatt if he would help her get his uncle to show some work in her gallery space. Det. Foss noticed the hesitation in Wyatt's tone.

"And when was the last time you *saw* your uncle?" Det. Johns continued to jot down notes as he asked the next question without looking up. Det. Johns asked and wrote, Det. Foss stared at Wyatt.

"I — uh," Wyatt thought. He was not sure he knew. "Jesus, um, I guess it's been… a month maybe? I don't actually know. A month, maybe, yeah." Wyatt took another sip of his coffee. Both detectives stared at him.

"So a month? Or maybe a month?" Det. Foss clarified. Wyatt could not tell if Det. Foss was being intentionally dismissive, or if he was just agitated about something unrelated.

"Yes," Wyatt responded a little more cold, "it's been about a month."

"And do you remember the nature of *that* interaction?" Det. Foss continued on, unphased, and still unpleasant.

"I — I don't remember. I'm sure it was nothing important."

"Wasn't about your gallery opening?" Det. Foss asked with a hint of sarcasm in his tone.

Wyatt stared directly at him, "maybe. I don't really remember."

"It would be helpful for us if you could try and remember, anything at all, really." Det. Johns said in his much more pleasant tone. "Anything helps."

"I — uh — to be honest, my uncle and I didn't have the best relationship, so we didn't talk a whole lot. When we did, it was usually about business, or something awesome he was doing, or planning. So it was probably something like that."

"You sound a little frustrated by that," Det. Foss dug a little deeper. "Was that conversation an argument?"

"No, we never argued." Wyatt responded quickly.

"Never?" Det. Foss pushed back.

"We were always more passive aggressive towards each other than anything." Wyatt said plainly.

"Do you think that conversation was upsetting to your uncle?" Det. Foss continued.

"I don't think he cared what I thought about most things," Wyatt snapped.

"Was committing suicide something you thought your uncle was capable of?" Det. Foss dug deeper.

"Excuse me?" Wyatt asked, surprised.

"Do you think your uncle killed himself?" Det. Foss took a step towards Wyatt.

"If he did, then he did. I don't see how my opinion on the matter is relevant." Wyatt said pointed, and dry.

"It just… it seems odd, don't it?" Det. Foss continued. "Someone as well-liked and revered as Jackson Brone was. Someone that successful, just up and ends it. It's weird, right?"

"Well, I'm sure my uncle wasn't without his demons." Wyatt responded.

"Aren't we all," Det. Johns jumped in, again in his soft tone, breaking the building tension.

"I'm sorry, can we not do this now? I'm expecting someone any minute, and I still need to wrap a few things up here first."

"Of course," Det. Johns said with a smile. "If you change your mind about coming down to the station to make a statement, it really would be a great help for us. Might get us out of some unnecessary paperwork in the long run."

"Sure, yeah, sure. I can come in some time this week maybe." Wyatt smiled, as he started walking towards his front door. The two detectives followed him.

"Listen," Det. Johns said carefully, "one last thing. Is there any reason your uncle would have to … how do I say this … is there anything your uncle would have been holding against you recently? Any grudges or… anything like that?" Det. Johns asked delicately, and Wyatt picked up on his curious concern.

"No." Wyatt responded plainly.

"And you two never had any issues over things like… money? Or anything like that?" Det. Johns asked, again in as pleasant a tone as he was capable of.

"No, not at all. Why?"

"No reason," Det. Johns again smiled. "We just had the impression that there was maybe a falling out between the two of you. We were hoping to get to the bottom of what had maybe happened, that's all."

"My uncle and I had a very strained relationship. He was a difficult person to be around. But we were still family. He was still some of the only family I had left."

The two detectives walked past Wyatt, back into the hallway outside of his loft.

"I understand," Det. Johns said. "Thank you for the time today, Wyatt. Really, it helps. And sorry, again, for showing up unannounced."

"Of course, no worries. Happy to help. Let me know if there is anything else I can do." Wyatt responded, trying to wrap up the conversation as quickly as he could.

"The station, this week? If you can make that happen, it would be really great."

"Sure. I'll make it work."

"Due diligence," Det. Johns said. "You understand."

"Yep," Wyatt tilted his head, and smiled.

Just as the silence transitioned into an untempered awkward moment, the three men were interrupted by the sound of the building's freight elevator pinging Wyatt's floor. The chime and squeal of the door opening echoed through the hallway, and all three men shot their glances over towards the noise.

They all watched as two movers, wearing the very jumpsuits Wyatt had been expecting, stepped out of the elevator. They carefully removed a large, covered object from the elevator, and rolled it on a dolly cart into the hallway.

Once the object was safely out of the metal lift, and into the hallway, one of the men lifted a clipboard, looked at the paper, and then towards a nearby apartment number. He looked down again at his paperwork, and then up again. He made eye contact with Wyatt, and Wyatt nodded.

The object on their dolly cart was gigantic. Covered in a neutral toned, beige drop cloth, it nearly touched the ceiling of the hallway, and Wyatt wondered how they even fit it inside of the elevator. *Great,* he thought.

"Wyatt Brone?" The mover with the clipboard called out.

"Yeah, right down here." Wyatt responded. The movers started walking their way down the hallway, and Wyatt turned back to the detectives. Det. Foss stared, and Det. Johns smiled.

"Thank you again, Wyatt. And again, we're sorry for the loss." Det. Johns said.

"Thank you," Wyatt responded.

The movers approached the doorway, and the mover with the clipboard got Wyatt's attention.

"You Wyatt?" The mover asked.

"Yeah, that's me." Wyatt said in response.

"I.D., and just sign here, please." The mover handed Wyatt the clipboard, after Wyatt showed him his driver's license, verifying his identity. Wyatt signed the paper, and handed the clipboard back to the mover.

"Here you go," Wyatt said.

"Where do you want it?" The mover with the clipboard said. He either did not know what the object was, or he simply did not care. Wyatt assumed the latter.

"Uh — around the corner to the right. There's a room. I made space for it. Just in there is fine," Wyatt said motioning around the entryway's corner, towards his "Island of Misfit Paintings."

The movers made their way past the men, and into Wyatt's loft. Wyatt and both detectives could not take their eyes off of the drop cloth covered painting as it slowly rolled into Wyatt's loft. There was an energy to it, and even though none of them could actually see the artwork, they were all captivated by it.

Once they all watched the shipment and movers turn the corner, disappearing into Wyatt's space, they seemed to snap out of their trance. They looked back at each other, and all three of them seemed somewhat at a loss for where they were.

"What is it?" Det. Foss asked, not expecting Wyatt to answer.

"That would be my inheritance. It's a painting from my uncle, actually." Wyatt responded, and shrugged. Det. Johns looked at Wyatt, then quickly back to where the covered canvas had just rolled past, then back to Wyatt.

"You mean there's an original Brone in there?" He asked. Wyatt's expression was less impressed than Det. Johns tone. He shrugged and nodded.

"All your uncle left you was a painting?" Det. Foss interrupted, his tone suggesting disbelief.

"Like I said, we weren't super close."

"Got it. Always was a fan of his. Your uncle's. Mind if we sneak a peak?" Det. Foss continued.

"No," Wyatt snapped quickly. The speed of his response caught them all off-guard, Wyatt included. Wyatt could not figure out why he responded so fast, or so stern. Something inside of him compelled it. "No, sorry, I don't have much free time right now, I have to be somewhere."

"This week... We'll be in contact." Det. Johns smiled, again breaking another moment of uneasy silence.

"Yeah, uh — sure." Wyatt smiled back "Thanks."

The two detectives turned to walk away, and catch the elevator while it was still on Wyatt's floor. Wyatt watched then men as they walked into the elevator, and the door slid slowly shut. Once they were officially out of sight, Wyatt let out another sigh. *What was that?* He thought.

Wyatt walked into the kitchen to grab his coffee before moving towards the secondary room just as the movers were placing the painting on its easel in the center of the room. The work took up most of the space, demanding the attention of anyone remotely nearby. They placed it facing away from the doorway, so Wyatt stood staring at the back of the beige drop cloth.

"Do you want us to take the cover away for you?" The mover with the clipboard asked.

"Is it yours?" Wyatt asked. His tone curious and genuine.

"No, sir. Just cloth, we can toss it for you on our way out, if you'd like." The mover replied as he checked the last couple of boxes on his paperwork.

"No, that's okay. I can take care of it." Wyatt exhaled, and took a sip of his coffee.

"Okay, great." The mover with the clipboard handed it back to Wyatt. "Just one more signature here," he pointed to a spot on the page, "one more initial here," he pointed to another spot, "and that's it. She's all yours."

"Great. Thank you, guys."

"Are you sure we can't take the cloth for you? Would be nice to see what we lugged all the way up here." The mover asked.

"No, sorry," Wyatt smiled at the men, even though he felt this was a slight overstep. Wyatt took another sip of his coffee. "That's great. Thank you."

"All right, well, have a great rest of your afternoon. We'll show ourselves out."

The movers left the room, and Wyatt stood, staring at the gigantic, covered canvas in his self-proclaimed "reject room." He heard his front door click open, and then slam shut again behind the men. He was alone again.

He took another sip of his coffee, and just stared at the back of the painting's drop cloth draped loosely over the canvas. He thought the easel seemed too small for the size of the canvas.

Unsure of what to do now, Wyatt just stared at the piece of covered art from the room's opened doorway. This was it. The culmination of his uncle's career, and the end of the tunnel on the whirlwind forty-eight hours he had just experienced. He had woken up just two mornings before with an exciting gallery opening planned, and his uncle was the world's most famous talent. Less than two days later, he was on the brink of throwing away his brushes, and his uncle's final, unfinished work of art sat in his reject room, a mere seven feet away from him. *Life's fucking wild,* Wyatt thought. He took another sip of coffee. After he stared at it for a few more moments, Wyatt left the room, and walked back into his kitchen.

Wyatt checked his watch. It was fifteen passed eleven in the morning. *Oh shit,* he thought. Wyatt remembered he had scheduled a "recap" breakfast with Melody that morning. Scheduled in hopes of celebrating his gallery opening's success, Wyatt now feared this meal would become a "come to Jesus moment" of sorts from his sister.

Wyatt poured out the remaining coffee in the glass, pour over carafe, and immediately washed it out with water. He did the same to his blue, homemade, porcelain mug before quickly washing his hands. He walked towards his front door to grab his keys and leave when his eyes again caught the massive, drop cloth covered painting standing solitarily in his secondary workspace room.

Once again, the giant piece grabbed onto his attention, and would not let go. Wyatt felt stuck again, like he had in the hallway, and he was overcome with the urge to uncover the piece. A primal urge. It was taking over his whole ability to think.

Before Wyatt knew it, he found himself walking into the room to stand directly in front of the covered canvas.

He stood for just a moment, solemnly, before grabbing his palette and a single brush.

Wyatt looked down at the tools in his hands, and wondered why he felt so compelled to work. *What the hell is going on?* He thought. It was an impossible sense of urgency. Wyatt felt his hands tremble, and he slightly lifted them towards the covered canvas almost upon their own accord.

Wyatt felt the hairs on the back of his neck stand up, and he quickly set down the palette and brush. He slowly backed away out of the room, and decided to leave before he let his brain spiral out of control on what he just experienced. Nothing, he knew, he would ever be able to describe or explain in any adequate way.

Before he walked to his front door, he again looked at the painting in the room.

Again, he felt compelled to it.

CHAPTER 4

The downtown city streets were busy.

The streets in Downtown Los Angeles were always busy, morbidly busy even, and today was no exception. Rarely did it matter the day or time, the season, or the occasion. Los Angeles is simply always busy, congested, and rarely convenient. The traffic of Los Angeles is a legendary facet of the city's lore. People have, and will continue to write about it, pontificating the reasons. Experiencing it firsthand, however, was a different thing entirely. The truth of the matter is that the city of Los Angeles stretches roughly just over five-hundred square miles, but houses more than four millions residents. If you were to do some quick math, you would find that you would be left with just about eight-thousand residents per square mile. Combine that already uneatable statistic with the inevitable tourism destination of "Hollywood," and naturally, you will have lots, and lots, and lots of traffic.

Of course, the traffic is always worse when you were supposed to be somewhere twenty minutes earlier. A particularly unique type of frustration that Wyatt was maybe a little too familiar with.

Wyatt again found himself in the backseat of a Lyft. From inside his pocket, he felt his cell phone buzz. A notification pinged him physically. He pulled his phone out of his pocket, looking down at the screen as it illuminated, and he saw his sister's name just above the simple, but poignant question, *Where the fuck are you?* Wyatt tapped the message, and unlocked his phone to reply. *So sorry, Mel. Ten minutes away.* As with most other aspects of Los Angeles, this was also a lie. He was twenty-five minutes away, at best.

Wyatt was not fooling anyone, least of all, his sister Melody. His phone buzzed with a response.

So you haven't left your loft yet. Great.

Wyatt smiled, amused with his sister's annoyance.

Parking, I swear. Wyatt replied with a smile.

Fuck you. Wyatt could almost hear Melody's voice speak the words aloud.

I love you too. Wyatt replied, beaming ear to ear. He really enjoyed pushing her buttons.

Whatever. Just get here, fast. Wyatt laughed a little to himself in the backseat of the car.

Melody Brone had graduated at the top of her class, getting her Juris Doctor degree from Stanford Law School just about a decade prior. Even though she had always known she wanted to be in talent management and never for one-second had a desire to actually practice law in any capacity, she still took the California Bar exam. Melody Brone passed on her first try.

That is just who Melody Brone was.

She spent her first several years, post Summa Cum Laude, fastened directly, and securely, to her uncle Jackson's hip pocket. Anywhere and everywhere Jackson went, Melody surely followed. Jackson loved having the companionship she offered him, and the two had a much stronger relationship than Jackson and Wyatt had. She soaked up not only understanding the life of an artist from her uncle, but also focused intensely on building strong relationships with her uncle's professional team.

She learned the role of a talent's manager, the power of a good entertainment lawyer, and she engrossed herself in the sometimes necessary placating of a talent's ego. Jackson understood what she was hoping to gain from this time, and fully embraced her. He did everything in his power to ensure that Melody could tag along to any and every meeting and experience he had. Jackson encouraged Melody to connect with his team whether he was present or not. He wanted her to learn from them, and ultimately use them as resources. A courtesy Jackson had never extended to Wyatt, and something that Wyatt instantly, and resentfully, took notice of. This was one of the primary arguments Wyatt made when petitioning his sister to take him on as her first, official client.

"If Jack had provided me with half of the resources he's provided you, I would already have a team working for me, and you fucking know it, Mel. Come on, sis," Wyatt had pleaded.

Melody reluctantly agreed, but also made it clear from day one, that when she was his representation, she was not his sister, and vice versa. She left no grey area in terms to their familial relationship and their professional relationship ever crossing paths. She was very clear that she would not be allowing that to happen, ever. And she made sure of it.

"When I'm your rep, I'm your rep. I'm not Mel, your sis. You get it?" She said pointedly. Wyatt nodded in response, and in true Melody fashion, she dug in. "I need you to use your words, Wyatt. Do you understand me?"

"Yes, Mel, I understand, Jesus," Wyatt chuckled back.

"It's not funny, Wyatt. This is how things like this get ruined." She responded.

"Name three examples," Wyatt smirked, poking the bear.

Without missing a beat, the bear snarled back, "Oasis, Creedance Clearwater, The Jonas Brothers, Fleetwood Mac. And these are just in music, should I continue?"

"First of all, no one in Fleetwood Mac was related, were they?" Wyatt asked, genuinely curious. "Weren't they all just fucking each other and doing LSD?"

"I don't think so, but they, you know, let their relationships get in the way." Wyatt could tell that Melody was starting to get flustered with this particular response, and she started to let it get to her, "It's besides the point, you know what I mean. I'm not letting our relationship get in the way of our business. Okay?"

Wyatt laughed, "Okay, deal."

The truth is that Melody was a shark in the best of ways. A true apex predator in a world dominated by ill-intentioned men; the entertainment industry. She assumed the role of a remora, effortlessly gliding between men who assumed they were in control, when she knew all along that she was the Tiger Shark in the water. Her first year in business for herself was somewhat rocky, to say the least. Wyatt being her only client did not bring in a ton of business, but leveraging her persuasive skills, and her acumen for shrewd business dealings, she was able to fill out her roster with two, highly sought after television actors. They both happened to book leading roles in the same CBS comedy pilot, and when it was announced that the series was getting a a full twenty-six episode order, something unheard of in today's television market, Melody signed the lease on a brand new office space in Beverly Hills. From there, Melody was slowly taking over the industry, becoming one of the hottest talent managers in Hollywood.

She was featured in all of the major, industry publications such as *Variety* and *The Hollywood Reporter*, as a "top rep to watch," or, "the hottest non-actor there is."

And then there was Wyatt.

A classic dim Yin, to her brilliant, and shining Yang.

Yes, Wyatt was her first client. Yes, Wyatt was her longest running client. Yes, Wyatt was her brother. But no, Wyatt had not been blossoming her success like her now-full, award-winning roster had, in fact.

Wyatt felt his phone buzz in his hand again, as his Lyft creeped to a stop outside of a restaurant in West Hollywood. He looked down at the screen, and after reading the words, Wyatt rolled his eyes. *Wow, if you were as good of a painter as you are a liar, we might have sold something last night.*

Melody was not known for pulling punches, she was known for throwing most of them. It is, admittedly, what made her such a great representative.

Wyatt walked through the open front doors of the restaurant, and started looking around at the crowd inside, at their tables and at the bar. A small hostess in a black button up and black pants, clearly the restaurant's uniform, approached Wyatt.

"Hi, sir, can I help you with anything?" She asked with a smile.

"Hi, uh, yeah, I'm supposed to be meeting my sister, she is already —"

"Wyatt, right?" Flattered that the hostess recognized him, Wyatt smiled and nodded in response. He started to speak to his appreciation for her fandom, when the hostess, unfazed continued. "Your sister told us you would be late. Right this way," the hostess said as she immediately turned and led Wyatt through the restaurant's cluttered dining room, chaotic with the lunchtime rush. She did not know who Wyatt was at all, and from the tone in her voice, she did not care. She most likely just wanted the table back as soon as possible. Wyatt swallowed his pride, and quickly followed behind her.

When they arrived at the table, Melody did not even look up from the menu covering her face. She wore Tom Ford sunglasses, a nice blue dress she got on sale at Nordstrom Rack, and a beautiful Brandon Blackwood handbag gifted to her from the creator himself. Wyatt did not need to see her eyes, he could already tell she was angry with him.

"Sorry, sis," Wyatt started, as he pulled the chair out to sit.

"Sorry, Melody," she responded, still not looking up. "This is a business lunch."

"Sorry, *Mel.*" Wyatt said sarcastically. A compromise between professionalism that he knew would annoy her. He was right, Melody plopped her menu down onto the table, and the silverware clinked together. "Jesus, I was joking. I know, this is a business lunch. I'm sorry I'm late."

"You're always late, what's new." There was a faint sibling annoyance behind each of her words. The kind of annoyance that only a sibling can feel towards another sibling. Not quite rage, not quite disinterest, and it is so subtle that if you were not paying attention you would likely miss it entirely. But it is there.

"Have you ordered anything?" Wyatt ignored her insult, and picked up the menu on his side of the table.

"Just a cocktail," Melody's voice remained monotone. Wyatt smirked at his sister, assuming she was not looking at his face.

"A cocktail, eh? It's only noon." Wyatt's dangled his sarcasm just over her head, and Melody left it alone. She had no interest in sparring with her big brother today.

"Well, consider it a way of getting through this conversation." Melody finally looked over at Wyatt, and smiled sardonically.

"It's nice to see you too," Wyatt said back, shaking his head slightly. The honest truth is that Wyatt and Melody were siblings, yes, but they were also the absolute best of friends. They trusted each other intimately, personally and professionally. They had an ability to be so abrasively honest with each other, and they were simultaneous fiercely protective of each other. Wyatt's pain was Melody's pain as well. Melody's successes were Wyatt's successes. Since they had no other real family other than their now-late Uncle Jackson, they truly were all each other had. They would not ever let that diminish or be broken apart for any reason whatsoever.

Their server walked up to the table, and addressed them, setting down Melody's cocktail.

"Hi, happy to see your guest has arrived." Then looking to Wyatt, he continued, "Can I get you anything to drink?" Wyatt looked over at Melody's cocktail, then back to the waiter.

"I'll just have one of those, thanks." The server looked at Wyatt for a moment, almost not believing him. Wyatt stared intensely back at the server and crinkled his forehead, when the server snapped out of it, smiled, and walked away again.

"Craving a Cosmopolitan?" Melody smirked as she asked, almost laughing at her brother ordering the stereotypically feminine cocktail.

"Hey," Wyatt jumped all over it. "It's the twenty-first century. Men are allowed to order whatever cocktails they want. And also, I didn't know that's what it was, it just looked delicious." Wyatt shrugged, unaffected.

"It is delicious," Melody retorted, taking a sip and humming an, "Mmm."

"Besides, what can I say," Wyatt said laughing, "I've been watching a lot of 'Sex in the City.'"

"And." Melody looked back at her menu. She cleared her throat, and stared dead ahead at the food options. Wyatt blankly stared back at his sister, and thought for a moment without saying anything in response. Finally, he decided to speak up.

"Huh?" Wyatt asked, confused.

"It's 'Sex *and* the City,' not 'Sex in the City.'" Melody responded without looking up, as she still stared into her menu.

"I … I don't care." Wyatt said honestly, and laughed, before the two siblings began bickering like a stereotypical brother and sister.

"Obviously you don't care, because 'Sex in the City' isn't actually the name of the show, and 'Sex and the City' is."

"I was obviously joking, I don't —"

"And I'm just saying that your joke wasn't even any good. 'Sex and the City' is the name of the blog that Carrie writes for *The New York Star* —"

"That's not even an actual publication, because it's a fake, mediocre television show. Why are you being such an asshole, I just —"

"Mediocre? You want to talk about mediocre art, Wyatt? Do you? You pride yourself as an artist, just get the fucking name right —"

"It's a show I don't even watch, I was just making a —"

"Well, clearly you don't, you can't even get the name right."

Finally, there was a beat of silence. Wyatt cracked a little smile, and stared at Melody until she looked back at him. Seeing his smirk, she laughed, and looked down.

"You're a brat," Wyatt chuckled back, unable to remove his mischievous grin.

"And you're an asshole sometimes." Melody replied.

"It's nice to see you, sis," Wyatt said through his smile.

"It's nice to see you too, big brother." Melody shook her head, smiling, but still annoyed.

Wyatt's Cosmopolitan was dropped off at their table, and they both ordered a light meal each. Melody ordered an arugula and quinoa salad with roasted cauliflower, crispy Brussel sprouts, toasted pine nuts and a lemon zest vinaigrette, and Wyatt ordered the salmon bowl with a mango habanero glaze. This particular rooftop cafe had become a consistent favorite of the two siblings, and the place they typically met at if they were meeting on "official business."

"I'm not going to lie," Wyatt started, "I was hoping the circumstance of today would have been different." Melody could tell there was a hint of embarrassment in Wyatt's tone.

"You and me both," she delicately said back.

"So what is the damage?" Wyatt finally asked after a few moments of silence.

"Wyatt, it isn't good," Melody lamented, showing her first glimpse of genuine, non-contemptuous care.

"I mean, I assumed that. The gallery mentioned not selling many —" Wyatt started to justify his galleries' opening night's shortcomings, but Melody was quick to interrupt him.

"It isn't just last night, Wyatt. This is our fourth opening in the last three years with nothing real to show for it." Melody said.

"That isn't entirely fair, Mel," Wyatt began his defense strategy.

"It might not seem fair, but it's the truth."

"It was just a bad night," Wyatt said again.

"No, Wyatt. It was a bad night, after a bad month, after a bad year, after, yadda yadda yadda. You need to start thinking about what your plans are." Melody hesitated, before she took another sip of her drink.

"My plans? What do you mean 'my plans?'" Wyatt pushed back.

"I mean, we can't keep doing this over and over again. I can't keep doing this over and over again. You haven't sold a piece in months. You're barely fulfilling commission agreements, your openings' bust... maybe it's time to hang it up."

"Wow. Hang it up? Are you kidding me?" Wyatt caught himself before he let his voice raise too loudly to draw attention from other restaurant patrons. "Are you kidding me?"

"I'm not trying to be mean, Wyatt. I'm just saying. You've had such a specific idea of what your life would be since you were a kid. Your life has never once resembled that idea. Maybe it's time to *evolve* that idea into something more..."

"Realistic?" Wyatt may have controlled his volume, but he could not control his frustration. He did not even try to.

"Attainable," Melody said gently, "something more attainable. A future within reach that you actually have control over."

"So much for a relaxing lunch with my sister," Wyatt responded in an irreverent tone.

"Fuck off, Wyatt. I have given you everything, what else do you want? This was also planned as a business lunch, and you fucking know it. So don't play that bullshit game with me." Melody was not having any of Wyatt's "woe is me" plight. "You are the first person I ever represented, and you've achieved the least amount of success. We were children back then. I have a company that I have to provide for now, things are different now. People's lives. I have to be smart about where I allocate resources."

The two sat in a brief, heavy moment of silence. They did not look at each other. For as close as they were, sometimes their fearless honesty could cross the line. Wyatt and Melody, both being fairly sensitive individuals, were careful to keep arguments and disagreements as polite as possible, especially when they were the subject matter. Wyatt knew she was right. Wyatt had not seen any semblance of success in years. He often contemplated on his own what his future looked like as an artist, but he was too insecure to admit it. Melody finally broke the silence, by adding, "also, 'realistic' isn't a bad thing, ya know."

There they sat. Wyatt sipped his Cosmopolitan, finished it then ordered a Hudson Manhattan Rye Whiskey neat. The drink he really wanted, and unfortunately needed. After another few moments of silence, the server brought their two meals, and the siblings dug in. Wyatt took a large mouthful of rice and salmon, thankful for the interruption.

"I heard Maurice came by and saw you?" Melody asked, hoping to briefly change the subject.

"Yeah, he just wanted to talk inheritance stuff."

"Did he —"

"Tell me that Jack left you everything?" Wyatt interrupted, then chuckled to himself. "Yes, yes he did."

"That's not what I was going to ask," Melody rolled her eyes.

"I know," Wyatt said and took another bite. "I prefer it that way, anyway. You were always closer."

"What did Jackson leave you?" Melody asked, and was legitimately curious.

"Oh, I'm so happy you asked. Good 'ole Uncle Jack left me one of his paintings." Wyatt stared at his sister, and she immediately read the disdain in his eyes.

"You're joking," Melody responded.

"I wish." Wyatt said. He knew Melody could see the smirk on his face.

"Uncle Jackson left you one of his paintings?" Melody made a face that suggested she was cringing.

"His 'final piece,' as Mo said to try to soften the gut punch."

"Yikes… That seems… bold." Melody tried to muffle her laughter.

"Yeah, you think? It's so strange too, Mo didn't know anything else about it, really." Wyatt continued. "With how close he was with Uncle Jack, and how tight he was on finances and such, I thought he would have known every detail."

"That is odd," Melody added. "It always felt like Maurice knew everything about everything."

"Because he did," Wyatt laughed. "I asked Mo why he thought Jack would leave me a painting, and Mo said because he thought maybe it was important, and I —" Melody burst into laughter before Wyatt could finish his thought.

"Yeah right, Jackson would rather die than give you something he deemed important." Melody laughed again, hard.

"That's literally, exactly what I said, I don't think Mo believed me," Wyatt joined his sister as they essentially laughed at Wyatt's misfortune. "Have you moved your team into the office space yet?"

A bright smile swept across Melody's face. She beamed at the question. "Mo told me you got basically everything, so I assumed the building was one of those things," Wyatt continued.

"Yes, we made the move official yesterday. This coming week will be our first full week in it. Wyatt, it's perfect. It has the perfect amount of space for my team as is, and I even have a little room to grow, and a few floors to have rented out to other businesses."

"That's amazing, Mel. I'm really glad to hear that."

Wyatt knew Jackson had left his recently shuttered business' office space to Melody so she could run her management company out of it. It was a big, eleventh floor office space in the heart of Beverly Hills. The ability to be in an office space in Los Angeles without the burden of having a mortgage to pay made Melody more comfortable than she ever thought she would be. A privilege she did not plan on taking for granted.

"I just feel so much more comfortable taking more risks with my clients. I know a misstep won't sink the company, it's a gigantic monkey off my back."

"I bet, that's so great."

"Yes, it's just been a huge burden relief."

"What sorts of risks are you taking for your clients?" Wyatt asked expecting Melody to talk about independent films, and non-financed television series. He was not expecting the response he received.

"Keeping you as a client, for one," Melody said, unironically.

"Jesus, Mel, tell me how you really feel." Wyatt awkwardly laughed.

"I'm serious, Wyatt. You're the only client on my entire roster that isn't bringing in more than I am sending out. That isn't bringing in anything, really."

"I know, I know," Wyatt instantly was back into his defensive mode.

"If Jackson hadn't left me his office, I don't think I would have the option," Melody said. "That's a big problem, Wyatt."

"I'm just in a funk," Wyatt said.

"A funk? It's been sixteen years, Wyatt. This isn't a funk, it's a reality."

"I just — I'm struggling so hard with insecurity. My work, my relationship, just everything." Wyatt finally admitted.

"Your relationship? What's up with Sam?" Melody asked.

"I mean, nothing. She's great. I just think she's over it too."

"Can you blame her?"

Wyatt let the question sit unanswered. He knew the answer, even though he did not want to.

"You don't have any bites, Wyatt. There's literally no heat. There's nothing but disinterest in you as an artist. I can't do a whole lot with that."

"I know, I know," Wyatt still defended himself. "I just haven't been myself lately."

"Well, I have a roster of people very much being themselves, and booking gigs, and bringing in income, and that list is growing, rapidly. Wyatt, I can't keep devoting all of this time to my least productive client. Even if it is my brother. It isn't fair to my team, or my clients."

"I know," is all Wyatt could respond with.

"I'm thinking of keeping my old office space, and using it as a second location. Grow my team, build out our roster. I have big ideas and plans, Wyatt. I need to feel confident in the clients I continue to represent that they can help me reach those things. And if they aren't, then I need to be economical about my decisions on who to continue to represent."

"Melody," Wyatt felt very close to pleading.

"What? What Wyatt? Say what you need to say." Her words were quick, and harsh. Still in a loving way, but Melody was not sugar-coating anything. Deep down, Wyatt knew he appreciated it.

"I just —" Wyatt was not sure what to say.

"Wyatt —" There was a hesitation in Melody's voice that broke Wyatt's heart. For this first time in a long time, he truly felt pathetic. Melody looked at him, and in his eyes, she could tell just how pathetic he felt. "I planned this lunch fully prepared to take you off my roster. There's just… Since Uncle Jack died, I feel like you could be on the verge of something. But I have to think of my business."

"I can turn it around, Mel, I swear I can." Wyatt stared at his sister, his eyes pleading in a way his words never would. Then Wyatt said the word he had been trying to avoid using with Melody. "Please." Melody exhaled, as that one, single word cracked her tough exterior. Yes, Wyatt was her least successful client. Yes, Wyatt was becoming a financial drain on her wildly successful business. But yes, Wyatt was still her brother. She knew how much this meant to him.

"You have one month, Wyatt." Melody just stared back, blankly.

"That's all I need," Wyatt said.

"I'm serious. One month," Melody echoed his words.

"One month," Wyatt said as he smiled, and beamed from ear to ear. Melody could see the excitement on his face, and quickly shut it down, bringing back the severity of the situation.

"I'm serious —" she said. Quick, calculated, and without compassion. "I'm serious, Wyatt. One month. Four weeks. That's it."

"I know. One month. Thank you, Mel." Melody exhaled, and shook her head. The server walked by again, and dropped off the check. Wyatt looked at the black, leather book and then back to his sister. "This is a business thing, right? I mean, you're covering —" Melody and Wyatt both stated laughing.

"You're an asshole." She said through her laughter.

"I'm just kinda hard up lately, on account of —"

"Being poor, yes, I know, trust me." They both laugh again.

"Oh, shut up," Wyatt said.

"Yes, unfortunately for me, this is a business thing." Melody said as she picked up the check, opened it to look at the small piece of thermal paper, and slid her black American Express card into the clear, plastic slot.

"Thank you," Wyatt said.

"It's a tax write off. Don't thank me, thank Brone Talent." Melody shrugged, and sat back in her chair. She sipped the last bit of her cocktail from the glass.

"I don't mean just for the lunch, Mel, I mean for everything. You've always been the only person who sees in my art what I want people to see. You see me. And you've put up with my bullshit for years. You are the first person who ever believed in me, and you'll most likely be the last one too. I owe you a lot. Everything, probably." Wyatt looked down, and Melody smiled just slightly. She appreciated the words he was saying regardless of whether she needed to hear them. She often put Wyatt ahead of her own needs, and they both knew it.

"You're so talented, Wyatt. You know I think that." Melody said lovingly.

"I know, I know, it's just tough to get past the imposter syndrome, ya know?" Wyatt added. "Especially with the last few years that I've had," he laughed a little.

" I get it. I genuinely believe that we just haven't gotten the right eyes on your work yet. I guess, ultimately, I just want to know that if we never do, you'll still be okay."

"I know." Wyatt said, as he smiled and looked back to his sister. "I hear you."

"One month," Melody reiterated.

"One month," Wyatt repeated.

CHAPTER 5

Wyatt was silent in the car.

He sat in the backseat of another Lyft on his way back to his loft downtown, and did not say anything. The driver was friendly, offering Wyatt some water and gum, but was quick to pick up on the hint that what Wyatt actually wanted was silence. That, and for once, Wyatt had actually remembered to turn on the feature for this ride where the driver is notified before picking you up that you are not interested in small talk. For someone that hated small talk as much as Wyatt, he constantly forgot that this feature even existed. Other than the occasional check in on the car's temperature, and making sure the music was not too loud, or too obnoxious, the driver provided Wyatt the quiet he craved. And the quiet he digitally requested.

For most of the entire drive, Wyatt's mind was consumed with the deal he had just agreed to with Melody. One more month of pursuing this craft as a career before he moved on to something more attainable. One more month of putting paint on canvas, and pouring his soul out. One more month of his art resonating with someone enough to make him a financially viable artist. One more month to try to make a living out of what is a hobby for most other people. Wyatt never considered himself as "most other people," but maybe he was. Maybe these ideas and dreams he had held onto since he was a child were nothing more than delusions of grandeur.

The delusional ideas that had been force fed to him by well-intentioned parents, and generations of Americans buying into the dream of, "if you work hard enough, you can do anything." The delusional idea that he was somehow entitled to success in his art. Wyatt knew the "American Dream" was bullshit, but he had always hoped it would still be achievable… for him, at least.

How could Wyatt truly stop pursuing art? He knew it was the only thing in his life where he was ever provided quiet. The only thing he could do that truly quieted his mind from the chaos it normally screamed. The world around him was always so loud, and yet, when he put paint brush to canvas, the world calmed down like a teething baby finally finding rest. *What would I even do?* Wyatt thought, staring at the city streets passing by through the backseat window.

Wyatt graduated from his high school a year early, and moved to Los Angeles to pursue this dream. This dream of creating art, and being able to share that art with the world. Even in the worst of times, he knew he could always rest back on the idea that he was supporting himself with his art — something he knew was such a privilege, and something that not many people could adequately claim.

Even other people in Wyatt's life that he considered genuine friends would stake that claim, when Wyatt knew that their parents were paying half of their monthly expenses. Wyatt, unfortunately for him, did not even have that as an option.

Wyatt and Melody's parents had both passed away when they were just children. In lieu of being put into their state's child welfare system, their uncle, Jackson, stepped up. He did not take them in directly, but he provided a stable housing situation for them. He covered their financial needs, he paid for Melody's college schooling, and in his credit, he did offer Wyatt the same. Wyatt already knew that what he wanted to do would never require the degree that Melody sought.

Wyatt wanted to paint. He wanted to create. He needed to.

And so he did.

Well, he tried to, at least.

It had been sixteen years since he decided that he was finished with his schooling, and began "officially" pursuing art. Wyatt thought of his younger self; so hopeful, and energetic. He was convinced that he would arrive in the art scene, immediately make a splash, and become a household name. His earlier works focused mainly on landscapes, and scenic depictions, that at one point his Uncle Jackson had mockingly referred to him as "Rockwell of the Woods."

Wyatt chose to take it to heart, and stopped painting landscapes altogether.

He played around with different techniques, and different styles, before he truly found himself in the abstract impressionistic work he had been focusing on for the last decade or so. Wyatt knew that if he were to make a name for himself, it would be for what he is creating now. Wyatt also knew that he was not anywhere near where he would prefer to be, in terms of making a name for himself.

He meant what he said to Melody. He knew he owed her for any success he had found to date, albeit, it was not much. She had been the first, and so far, only person to champion Wyatt's art, including his uncle. Melody had negotiated his first commercial deal, creating wall art for Target's North American market locations.

No, it was not a glamorous gig, but it provided Wyatt the chance to create art, and be compensated handsomely for it. Of course, his name was never featured on the art, and no one in the universe would ever know it was his. But Wyatt knew. And Wyatt knew that Melody was to thank. Melody also promised to never let Jackson find out about it, for fear he would completely disown Wyatt.

Wyatt often failed to see the forest for the trees. When he was being less aggressively diminishing to himself, Wyatt understood that he had moved out on his own at around seventeen years old, and had financially supported himself since. For most other people, this in itself would be a massive accomplishment. Wyatt just understood that he wanted more. In moments when he was being very honest with himself, he knew he *needed* more.

With every passing birthday, Wyatt became more and more obsessed with the idea of what his legacy would be. What legacy would Wyatt leave the earth with? The dread of the realization that the answer could in fact be "none" constantly kept him up at night.

Wyatt stayed staring out of the backseat, passenger window, when he felt his phone buzz. He looked down at the illuminated screen, and saw a text message pop up.

Hey babe, I'm here. Are you close?

A soft smile crept across Wyatt's face, before an entirely new set of anxieties swept in. He swiped open his phone to respond. *Be there in five.*

Wyatt had been dating Samantha for the better part of five years. They met at one of his gallery openings. It also just happened to be one of his most successful gallery openings. A rare anomaly of success throughout his lackluster career. That night, Wyatt sold seven separate pieces, all above what he had declared to the curator as their "initial value."

At the end of the night, Melody brought over a bottle of champagne to share with Wyatt, when Samantha sheepishly approached him to tell him how much she loved his work. Melody finished the bottle herself, while Wyatt and Samantha stayed up all night, talking.

Samantha was in her final year studying art history at the University of California, Los Angeles. Wyatt was immediately consumed by her knowledge and excitement over their shared interest in abstract expressionism, and the works of legends such as Pollack and Rothko.

Wyatt remembered gushing over Samantha to Melody the next day at their "recap" lunch meeting. Wyatt with his salmon bowl, and Melody with her quinoa salad. Melody rolled her eyes when Wyatt mentioned that part.

"Everyone loves Pollack and Rothko. And if they don't, they say they do. Ask her to name two others. Any two." Wyatt laughed at Melody's cynicism. He did not care. He already knew he was in love.

For months, Wyatt and Samantha spent every moment together. They visited different art museums all over the country together. She attended every one of Wyatt's gallery openings, and played an instrumental role in the few night-of sales he saw. Regardless, she was the constant source of encouragement he had wanted in a partner. Whether his night was a commercial success or not, she was there, at his side, her hand in his, saying the words, "I'm proud of you." All Wyatt ever truly needed to hear.

Samantha graduated from U.C.L.A. and was almost immediately offered a job as an educator in the program she had just graduated from. Though art was a giant passion of Samantha's, all she ever wanted to do, professionally, was teach. Being able to teach a subject with which she was so in love was a dream come true for Samantha.

Dating the nephew of Jackson Brone also was not without its perks.

Jackson adored Samantha, and always found his way into conversation with her the few times they would all get together. For some of the more major holidays, Melody would try to get together what little family they had for a meal. These dinner's usually just consisted of Melody, Wyatt, Jackson and Samantha.

Melody would be a basket case of stress, preparing the meal and all of everything else involved, Wyatt would dread sitting in the same room as his uncle for more than twenty-five minutes, and Jackson and Samantha would sit at the table, gabbing away for hours.

Once Samantha started teaching at the university, Jackson immediately offered to come lecture her classes. And he did so, regularly. She became the shining star on campus. Professor

Garcia, the one who brought in Jackson Brone. Her classes became the hottest commodity in U.C.L.A.'s art history department, sometimes boasting a two year waitlist.

It was not lost on Wyatt that Jackson willingly included himself into almost every aspect of Wyatt's life other than his pursuit of art. His sister and his girlfriend had both benefited from Jackson's acclaim. Wyatt never saw the same favor from his uncle. While Wyatt did not resent Jackson for that, it was something he thought of often. It was another reason why his inheritance felt like such a humiliating affront.

In more recent months, Wyatt's relationship with Samantha had begun to feel strained. Whether it was Wyatt's own lack of self-appreciation, or the fact that his lack of success was coming to a boiling point even for himself, Samantha had seemingly started pulling away emotionally. The thing about anxiety, however, is that you can never really tell if your reality is being truthful.

Wyatt understood that his brain was broken.

He was an artist, it was to be somewhat expected. More likely, anytime Wyatt began feeling the pressures of anxiety, most other people close to him were not far away from experiencing the same feelings.

For the last several weeks, as Wyatt began picking up on the distance he felt Samantha was building into their relationship, he would delicately broach the topic only for Samantha to shut it down completely. This game of cat and mouse repeated itself a few times in the more recent weeks, but Wyatt had a knot in his stomach that today was the day it would come to a head.

When he saw the words pop up on his phone, he almost knew it for certain. Today would be the day Samantha left him.

Of course, he had no evidence for this outcome to take place, it was all just an internalized, and likely irrational fear he carried unnecessarily. The other tricky aspect of anxiety is how much more harsh your brain is when you have been correct in the past.

You know this is it, Wyatt's brain would taunt him. *I hope you're ready to die alone.*

Wyatt took a deep breath. He exhaled all of the air out of his lungs, and then slid his phone back into his pocket. He kept his gaze out the backseat window, as he felt his Lyft come to a stop outside his building at the corner of Sixth Street and Spring Street, downtown.

"Thanks," Wyatt said to the driver, as he opened the door and stepped out onto the street. Wyatt stood on the sidewalk for a moment, adding in his rote five-star rating into the app on his phone. The driver was so quiet on his drive back home that Wyatt would have even given him a sixth star if it were possible.

The driver drove away, and Wyatt looked up towards his floor, and exhaled. *It's now or never,* Wyatt thought to himself.

He walked into his building, and nodded to the doorman at the front desk.

"Afternoon, Mr. Brone," the doorman called out, as he remotely called the elevator to pick Wyatt up. He only had to wait for a moment before the elevator chimed and screeched open. Wyatt stepped in. He clicked his floor's button, and the doors squeaked as they closed.

Every time Wyatt stepped into an elevator, his mind would race with the idea of the elevator breaking down. Admittedly, a morbid thought, but Wyatt could not help it. Then there were stories that added fuel to Wyatt's brain's fire. Stories like Nicholas White, a 34 year old New York production manager who was stuck on an elevator with no water for over forty hours back in 2008. The worst part was that the elevator's security camera caught the entire ordeal, but no one noticed. Or more recently, the grim security camera footage of Elisa Lam before she ultimately went missing.

Whether it was being stuck, or being in an alternate universe's game of psychotic chicken, Wyatt did not want to be involved.

Just then, his elevator chimed, and the door slid open on his floor. Wyatt could feel his heart rate tick up a notch. Regardless of how emotionally prepared he felt for the conversation he believed was inevitably about to take place, Wyatt still was not looking forward to it. He pulled his keys out of his pocket, as he stepped out of the elevator, and walked towards his door. He opened it, and walked inside of what seemed like an empty loft.

"Sam?" Wyatt called out. "Samantha?"

"Yeah, in here," Samantha responded. Her voice rang out from around the corner, to the right. Wyatt tossed his keys down on an end table just inside the door, and walked around the corner towards his reject room. He stopped just at the room's doorway, and leaned gently against the door frame. There, he saw Samantha standing in front of the painting, still covered by its drop cloth. He could not tell if she felt the same, frenetic draw to the piece. Then again, she was standing in a room, silently staring at a covered painting.

"Hey you," Wyatt finally said. She did not look at him, but she barely smiled.

"Hey," Samantha responded. She finally broke her stare at the work, and turned it to Wyatt. "Is this something new?" She asked.

"It's from Uncle Jack... it's my inheritance." Wyatt said with a sarcastic smirk, and Samantha tilted her head slightly. She could hear the tension in Wyatt's voice.

"You sound mad," she observed out loud.

"Annoyed, maybe. He left me a painting. How else am I supposed to feel?" Wyatt complained, as he turned away and walked towards his kitchen.

"Wyatt, that isn't fair. You know how important your uncle's work was to him. If he left it to you, then he must have —"

"Please, don't. Please, don't, Sam." Wyatt snapped back, as Samantha followed him out of the secondary room, and into the kitchen. He could feel her eyes roll as she followed him into his kitchen.

"Why do you have it covered? Can I see it?" Samantha asked gently.

"It came like that, I just haven't taken it off yet. I don't know if I want to, to be honest."

"Wyatt, you have to…" Samantha made a face, and Wyatt looked away. He could feel his chest tighten a little.

"I don't feel like talking about it right now, to be completely honest. Sorry, I just," Wyatt's voice trailed off as he leaned against his kitchen counter.

"Can I see it?" Samantha asked again.

"See what?" Wyatt asked, still preoccupied with the impending doom building in his mind.

"The painting… what else," Samantha raised an eyebrow, and sort of snickered.

"Goddamnit, Sam, I just said no. Just drop it, please." Wyatt snapped, and immediately regretted his outburst.

"What's wrong with you?" Samantha asked rightfully. "You're being an asshole."

"I'm sorry, I just think it's a little insulting that my uncle left me a constant reminder of how fucking pathetic I am, and I don't want to spend the rest of my night with my girlfriend gawking over a painting that I don't even fucking want."

Despite regretting his outburst, there was a slight cathartic release he felt when doubling down.

"You're being a dick right now. Your uncle, whether you like it or not, is one of the most influential artists in history. And he left *you* a piece of his legacy? That's amazing, and should be celebrated. So like… get over it."

"Oh, wow, Samantha is taking Jackson's side, even from beyond the grave. Color me shocked." Wyatt turned his back to her, but it did not deter either of them. This argument was on its way one way or another.

"What is that supposed to mean?" Samantha pushed back.

"You always sided with him. He fucking dies, and I still can't get you to be on my side for once. It's unbelievable."

"Can't get me to be on your side? Wyatt, I've been a champion for you and your dreams since the moment we met. I am one of the *only* reasons you even sell pieces at openings, all of which I have been to over the last four years." Wyatt could hear the anger building in Samantha's voice as she spoke to him.

"That's funny, I don't remember seeing you last night." Wyatt finally turned to look at her, and he could see tears pooling in his eyes. For a moment, Wyatt wished the same for himself, but he was not getting there.

"Wyatt, I cannot continue to make excuses for your shortcomings, and your lack of confidence. And honestly, it's … it is so exhausting trying. So I am sorry if you have some weird, ego, God complex, and compare yourself to your uncle who just so happened to be a once-in-a-generation talent, but you need to grow up and be your own man." Samantha was as kind as she could be with the words and sentiment she chose. She was also absolutely correct, and Wyatt knew it.

He did not respond for a moment while he took in her brutal honesty.

Wyatt knew she was right, and it was just another moment of a powerful woman telling him to grow up that he had experienced in the last two hours. A part of Wyatt felt extremely annoyed, and another part of him was thankful to have these voices in his life.

"I'm sorry," he finally said. "You're right, I'm sorry. It's just… it's been a shit couple of days." Wyatt looked down, and then back to Samantha.

"It's okay, but you have to do better." Samantha said. Wyatt nodded.

"Have you thought at all about what you want for dinner?" He asked.

"Listen, I don't think I should stay tonight," Samantha said. Wyatt noticed she still had her purse around her shoulder.

"What are you talking about?" Wyatt could feel his breath thinning.

"I had a thing come up at work, and I have to go in to help figure it out, I'm sorry. I just wanted to see you first, so we could talk about things." *Here it comes,* Wyatt thought. "Wyatt, I just think — "

"Sam, don't. I get it. You aren't happy. I'm a loser, I'm pathetic. I get it. You don't have to say anything else, I understand." There it was. Everything Wyatt feared she would say, he simply said for her.

"Just for the record, I wasn't going to say any of that. But you can't help yourself." Wyatt wasn't sure how to respond, so he just stared back at her. "Wyatt, I can't continue to be the only one that believes in you. At some point, you need to take that responsibility onto yourself. But until you do, it isn't fair for me to stay."

The tears found Wyatt's eyes, and he turned away from her again. He nodded, exaggerating the movement to ensure that Samantha saw he was agreeing with her. She saw.

"When you find the ability to do that," Samantha added, "Jesus, please let me know."

And almost in an instance, she was gone. Wyatt broke down for a moment alone in his kitchen, and he heard his loft door click shut behind her. The faint chime of his elevator rang out through the closed door. Wyatt tried to breathe and calm himself down.

Wyatt grabbed a bottle of whiskey from on top of his refrigerator, and poured himself a heavy two finger glass of neat rye. He quickly threw it back, and poured another.

Wyatt was not sure if that conversation was inevitable, or if his nagging subconscious made it so. Either way, it happened, and it was over. Wyatt, with his drink in hand, slowly walked back into the second room from his kitchen, and stared at the beige drop cloth. Again, he felt that energy pulling him closer to it.

Finally, he pulled the cloth away.

For the first time, Wyatt looked at the painting his uncle left to him.

His initial thought was confusion.

The painting was not anything like he had seen from his uncle before. Jackson Brone was known as an abstract expressionist, not unlike the aforementioned Pollack or Rothko, but this was something different altogether. There was no connection in the colors. There was no reason in its structure. There was no depth. Even so, Wyatt could not look away. If he had felt drawn to the canvas previously, he was fully inside the canvas now. Wyatt looked closer, and noticed that there had to be multiple layers of paint on this particular canvas. Red's on top of blue's, green's on top of white's, all bleeding through. Wyatt thought by looking at the canvas that Jackson must have painted over this piece a dozen times. It was a mess, but it was still calling to him. It frustrated Wyatt that he could not figure out why he felt so immediately connected to the piece.

He remembered the letter that had been given to him by Maurice, and walked back into his kitchen to pick it up. He came back into the room, and stood in front of the work when he looked back down at the letter itself.

Again, Wyatt slowly spoke it aloud to himself as he read it.

"To nev'r showeth and nev'r bid, f'r 'twill beest yours,

To nev'r stand ho and nev'r selleth, f'r 'twill beest yours,

Followeth these to wildest dreams, f'r 'twill beest yours."

This time, however, Wyatt paid more attention to the scribbles around the letter's blank space. Above each line of original text, Wyatt noticed the same instructions in layman's terms. He, again, took it line by line.

"To nev'r showeth and nev'r bid, f'r 'twill beest yours... to never show and never tell, for it will be yours.

To nev'r stand ho and nev'r selleth, f'r 'twill beest yours... to never stop and never sell, for it will be yours.

Followeth these to wildest dreams, f'r 'twill beest yours... follow these, to wildest dreams, for it will be yours."

He still did not understand it fully, but he continued reading some of the other descriptions jotted down on the paper.

"Add new paint every day," Wyatt read aloud to himself. "Any amount will do … Don't let anyone else look at it." Farther down the page, "Do not remove or destroy the paint, just add in new layers." On the far right, "Do not let anyone see, ever." On top, "Everything will come true, everything will happen... everything."

Wyatt took a step back, and looked at the painting again. He thought about what these words could mean. He thought about all of them placed together on this page, and what they could mean as instructions.

"To never show, and never tell," Wyatt thought. "Okay, don't show it to anyone, and don't talk about it... easy enough." Wyatt knew neither of those would be a problem. "To never stop, and never sell." Adding new paint to the canvas every day seemed a little extreme, but also a simple idea. "Follow these to wildest dreams," Wyatt stopped for a moment. He thought if this meant that his wildest dreams would become reality if he followed these instructions. *How is that even possible,* he thought again. Wyatt laughed to himself, and shook his head. *What the hell is wrong with me,* his mind asked. He laughed at how insane he sounded. He looked back down towards the bottom of the letter and read again, "Everything will come true, everything will happen... everything."

Wyatt wondered what would the odds be that his uncle left him a blessed painting? Slim to none, was his answer. He knew, realistically, that if his uncle would leave him anything enchanted, it would be a curse. Hence, the reason his uncle left it to him, and not his sister. *Do not be a fucking child,* he chastised his psyche.

Still, he felt the painting pulling his hands towards it. He felt the painting pulling his mind to it. He felt physically drawn to work on the canvas. If it was not a curse, he truly could not explain what it was. He remembered Samantha had just seemed sort of entranced by it. Even the detectives also seemingly captivated by it.

Before he could realize it, Wyatt looked down at his hands. The letter had fallen to the ground. His glass of whiskey had also fallen, and laid shattered on the floor at his feet. Again, Wyatt held his paint palette in one hand, and a brush in the other. Both again featured fresh paint.

Wyatt thought his heart was going to burst out of his chest. It was raced like a horse on the final lap of a Kentucky Derby winning run. *How was this possible?*

There was little about this experience that Wyatt could confidently explain, but he knew he had a decision to make and there were two clear options.

Option one, he ignores everything that is happening, and leaves the room. Option two, he acknowledges the idea that there is something special, and unexplainable, at play, and he leans in. After all, if all of your "wildest dreams" are at stake, what's a single stroke of paint?

"All my dreams," Wyatt quietly said aloud, as he stared at the painting in front of him. He cleaned up the broken glass off the floor, fixed himself another whiskey, and after deciding he would be drinking more that evening…

Wyatt added a stroke of paint.

CHAPTER 6

The heat was unbearable.

Again, Wyatt found himself woken by the blaring sunlight streaking through the swaying plates of his window shades; an archaic feature of his otherwise modern housing that he had sworn to himself when he moved in that he would immediately have replaced. This morning, however, he could instantly feel the beads of sweat building on his forehead. The thin beams of light, illuminating the specs of dust floating in the air between his window and his bed, sizzled against his skin. He had suddenly become aware of his own internal temperature when he slowly moved to his side, and felt the warm, sticky sweat on his legs under his covers.

There was a heat wave crushing the city, and the several fingers of whiskey Wyatt remembered from the night before, along with several he was sure he did not remember, made the sunlight feel even more intense. He groaned, as he slowly pulled his duvet cover away from on top of his legs, hoping to find a small burst of cool air against his skin. The hot air showed no relief. Wyatt took a deep breath and laughed through another groan. His body made sure he was well aware that he was not a kid anymore. He could not help but smile at the cruel reminder.

Even without the crushing heat from the sun, Wyatt felt pressure in his head not unlike that of a deep-sea diver. Every moment itself felt somewhat underwater, sluggish with the stink of triple Rye, neat, after triple Rye, neat. *Kill me now,* Wyatt thought as his feet settled on the ground to the right of his messy bed. He even remembered to take two Tylenol and drink his entire sixty-four ounce water bottle before he fell asleep. He really was not a kid anymore.

Through the pounding of his head, and the underwater, sluggish, marginally controlled movement of his limbs, Wyatt could still manage to laugh at himself. After all, this was legitimately no one's fault but his own.

He managed to sloth his way through his cluttered living room area into his kitchen to grab his pour over kettle, fill it with water, and plop it onto the closest stove top burner. Not one bit of Wyatt's fragile physical state cared that it was over ninety-five degrees outside… he would have his morning coffee. As the water slowly came to a boil, Wyatt thought of the idea that hot beverages are better for hot temperatures. He remembered hearing something about how drinking a hot beverage in hot weather can actually help cool your body temperature down, because your body leverages the temperature of the beverage to help lower your core temperature. He did not know if it was true, but it was now his story, and he was sticking to it.

The faint whistle of his kettle had begun singing out, and Wyatt realized he had not prepared any coffee. He quickly tossed two scoops of his already ground blonde roast, mixed the scoops with a dash of cinnamon, and began to pour the boiling water over the awaiting mixture. The steam, immediately masked with the smell of the grinds, wafted towards his face, and for just a moment, he felt normal.

Wyatt listened to the bubbling of the steaming water percolating through the grinds, and dribbling through the paper filter, into the glass carafe awaiting below. It would only be moments now.

As soon as he poured the last of the water, he quickly lifted the filter, still dripping water through, and filled his hand-made, blue ceramic mug. Wyatt carefully placed the filter back into the glass carafe, and desperately pulled his mug to his lips. It burned his tongue, a welcomed pain; a well-worth it pain. He could feel the hot, black drip slide into his belly. He exhaled, finally at peace. Even with a still pounding head.

Wyatt walked his coffee back over to his towering windows, and pulled the plastic shades back. He had left his windows open in hopes it would create a slight escape from the brutal heat expected for today, but all it accomplished was keeping him awake with the sounds of the second city that mostly never sleeps.

Ride sharing cars sped through the busy downtown streets, the same houseless man shouted at tourists walking by, and the heat… *My god,* Wyatt thought. He closed the shades, and walked back into his kitchen to refill his mug. He poured himself a glass of water in the process, and drank it down quickly. It was a stark, room temperature contrast to the still steaming cup of coffee.

After a few more gulps, and a quick splash of water to his face, Wyatt decided it was probably time to start his day. He slowly walked into his main painting space, one of the side rooms connected to his main living space. His most recent work was prominently displayed in the middle of the room on a large easel, paint splattered everywhere.

He stood in front of this work, and looked at it. In total, he had probably spent around four months on this piece, and he still was not sure what he thought of it. If all of his works had existing "this looks like" artists, he felt this most recent work would be compared to Kirchner, the German expressionist who started a group that was fundamental to the foundation of Expressionism in twentieth-century art. Wyatt's work was still a little more abstract, but he knew he would be happy to be compared with someone the Nazi's referred to as "a degenerate." *At least it's good company,* Wyatt thought to himself.

He stood in the room, and stared at the work, still neither pleased or displeased. Truthfully, Wyatt felt nothing from this piece. The lack of feeling is what Wyatt felt was disappointing. He would always rather hate something, or love something, but he dreaded when he would dedicate so much time to something he felt nothing towards. He could still at least sell something he hated.

Perhaps it was his chosen color scheme. Perhaps it was the vague, tower-like structure he had constructed on the feminine side of the canvas. Perhaps it was simply that it was his. Wyatt's confidence had admittedly been waning, flailing, really, in recent months. As he stared at his canvas, Melody's words came to his mind. Her idea that maybe it was time for Wyatt to pack up this dream, and exchange it for something more "attainable." *Attainable, ha. Right,* Wyatt thought.

Then again, he thought, *maybe she is right.*

Wyatt had been *at* this insane dream for longer than he could remember. Longer than he cared to remember. Yes, Wyatt had seen glimpses of success, and yes, Wyatt had sold pieces at galleries across the country, but it was never enough… not for Wyatt, at least.

Wyatt never had delusions of grandeur, he never had any idea of becoming the household name his uncle had, but he still wanted more than he had ever achieved. After all of these years, grinding, sacrificing, and never bearing fruit from the seeds he relentlessly planted, maybe it was time to do something more attainable. Surely it was possible to find joy, and stability in the same professional endeavor… *Right?* Wyatt hoped.

The truth of it, as Wyatt understood, is that he would never find happiness outside of his art. Realistically, however, he knew he would never find happiness inside of his art, either. Impossible, yet simultaneous, truths that were both dangerous and destructive.

Wyatt tried imagining what he would be outside of this space. Outside of painting his heart onto canvas with paint that called out to him from his color palette. These works were not just his emotion, and his desires, they were his truth. He knew in both his best and worst moments, he ran to his paintings, but was he hiding in his paintings? He always felt that he was living in his paintings, but maybe he ran to his work to escape the reality of what he never wanted to understand.

"Maybe it's time to evolve this dream into something more attainable," Melody's words again rung out in his mind as he stared at his most recent work.

"Maybe you're right," Wyatt spoke aloud to himself.

In the back of Wyatt's mind, a slight, white noise crept in. At first Wyatt assumed it was slight tinnitus from his years of banging on drums as a teenager. Then Wyatt realized it was coming from his second workspace; the room with his uncle's painting. Confused, but intrigued, Wyatt walked out of the room he stood in, and towards the secondary room. The white noise had started to build as he got closer to the room's entrance. Louder, and louder, more and more static, it was almost becoming unbearable. It got so loud, and chaotic, that Wyatt found himself pressing his hand into his temples, in hopes to tame both the ringing, and his established headache. His pace quickened as he turned the corner.

As soon as he passed the second room's door frame, and his uncle's painting came into sight, the ringing ceased. The static disappeared, the white noise was gone. Wyatt stood in the doorway, staring at the painting, and suddenly realized that even his headache had seemingly faded into obscurity. *This is impossible,* Wyatt thought.

He entered the room, and set his coffee down. He walked in front of the work, and stood, staring at it. Again, he thought about how *nothing* about this painting made any sense. The painting's size, color scheme, style, structure... nothing made any sense. There was no connectivity. There was no rhyme or reason that

Wyatt could decipher. Jackson was a chaotic artist, but he was structured and disciplined. This painting was anything but.

Wyatt again noted the colors on top of colors.

Every artist, at some point, starts over. Artists usually, however, either sand the canvas down to smooth nothing, or more commonly, use an oil solvent to strip the canvas of its prior paint. No artists will simply paint over a painting without removing as much of the previous coat as possible.

Wyatt thought about the painting's size.

Most of his uncle's pieces were a standard twenty-four inches by thirty-six inches, his uncle's preferred canvas size. All of his works were always twenty-four by thirty-six inches. "You never need anything bigger, and nothing should ever be smaller," Jackson would always say, like a slogan or a company jingle. This piece, however, was massive. Just at a glance, Wyatt believed this particular canvas to be at least four feet wide, and six feet tall. The easel held it just above the ground, and it was almost as tall as Wyatt was. Wyatt had never known his uncle to work on a canvas that was anything close to forty-eight inches by seventy-two inches. It seemed wildly uncharacteristic.

Finally, Wyatt thought again about the note.

Wyatt knew his uncle's health had been in a slight decline over the last few years, but Wyatt still could not explain the rambling scribblings on the letter, or even the letter itself. What did it mean? Why was it even included? *Were these rules actually real?* Wyatt shook his head, and chuckled to himself. *You sound insane right now,* Wyatt thought.

Then, as if he should have expected it to be, Wyatt looked down to see his brush and color palette in both of his hands. Again, unsure of how they came to be there, and again, terrified at the idea that this painting was somehow cursed. He looked at the fresh paint on both his palette and his brush, and thought, again, of the letter.

"Never stop," Wyatt quietly said aloud to himself. He looked back at the piece, and again, felt inexplicably drawn to its surface.

Wyatt added a stroke of paint to the canvas.

As soon as the brush left the surface of his canvas, Wyatt heard his phone ring. It was not his cell phone, however, it was his outdated landline. Something he had dedicated as his "business line," mainly so he could write off his living expenses. He felt confused at first, however, because even though he had this landline dedicated for business purposes, most people, including Melody, simply called his cell phone.

Being a late-stage millennial, with a fair and expected amount of anxiety fueled by a lifetime of crippling world-crisis, Wyatt screened the call. After several loud rings, the call went to his voicemail machine, but Wyatt heard no message. Instead, after a moment or two of welcomed silence, Wyatt's landline rang yet again. He decided to follow his self-established telephone rule of, "If it rings once, ignore it. If it rings twice, maybe answer it," and he walked into his kitchen, over to the early twenty-first century device… a telephone with a cord. He picked up the phone, and held it to his ear.

"Wyatt Brone's studio," Wyatt's voice cracked and held the deep tone of someone who had not spoken in a decade.

"Wyatt, where the fuck have you been?" Melody's voice barked out on the other end of the line.

"What? Mel?" Wyatt asked, confused.

"Answer your fucking cellphone, you idiot!" Wyatt could not tell if she was angry, as he felt there was a slight sense of joy behind her shout.

"What are you talking about?" Wyatt said defensively, when he heard Melody laugh. He looked for his cell phone around him, but could not see it anywhere.

"Do you have your cell with you?" Melody shouted again, but Wyatt could tell she was smiling.

"Hang on," Wyatt said as he set the receiver down on his kitchen counter. Still unsure if he should be celebrating or panicking, Wyatt searched his bed and nightstand for his cell phone. It was nowhere to be seen. Wyatt then heard the faint vibration coming from underneath his pillow. He reached under it, and pulled out his cell. The screen illuminated with the most missed activity Wyatt had maybe ever seen.

Thirty-six missed calls, and eighty-seven missed text messages.

What the fuck... Wyatt thought. His mind immediately went to the dark idea that someone else had passed away. Morbid yes, but most realistic... also yes.

Wyatt quickly walked back to his landline, cell phone in hand. He picked up the receiver and held it back to his ear. He stood for a moment in silence, unsure of quite what to say to his sister.

"Mel, what is going on?" He asked with a careful trepidation.

"Do you have your phone?" Melody asked, and Wyatt heard her laugh in the background. Wyatt looked down at his screen as more text messages came in, and another voicemail notification popped up.

"Yes, it's in my hand... Melody, what is going on?" Wyatt asked again, his tone more forceful, rather than concerned.

"I don't know, Wyatt, but people want you." Wyatt unlocked his phone, and skimmed through some of the text messages. Almost all of them were from numbers he did not have saved, and he was only able to recognize certain words.

Words like "interview," and "gallery," immediately stood out. He almost noticed several messages from Melody, and after opening his entire text message conversation with his sister, saw several, "wake the fuck up, you big, dumb, idiot," loving notes.

"Melody, what is going on?" Wyatt asked a third time, putting his proverbial foot down. He wanted answers, and he hoped to God that Melody had them.

"Honestly, I have no idea, but right now it doesn't matter. You need to call Sylvia Peregrine back immediately. Wyatt, Sylvia is the curator at Porter & Herth. Porter and fucking Herth! They want to showcase your work! Are you hearing me? Porter & Herth wants to showcase your paintings, Wyatt!"

Wyatt stared down at his cell phone screen, and found the correlating text message. He read the message he had missed from a couple of hours before.

"Hi Wyatt, my name is Sylvia Peregrine. I tried reaching you, but I got your voicemail. I'm with Porter & Herth, we are very interested in showing some of your pieces at our gallery here in Los Angeles. Please give me a call when you can."

"Porter & Herth?" Wyatt said to Melody. "What the hell does Porter & Herth want to show my paintings for?"

"Who fucking cares, Wyatt! They are one of — if not *the* most prestigious art gallery in the city. They don't showcase paintings they don't sell, Wyatt. This is huge. You need to call her back right now!" Melody shouted through her joy and laughter on the other end.

"Okay, okay, yeah, I'll give her a call back right now," Wyatt stumbled through his own words.

"Wait!" Melody shouted again. "After you call her back, you need to call Caroline Haynes back as well."

"Who is Caroline Haynes?" Wyatt asked.

"She's with *The Times*, Wyatt. The fucking Times!" Melody yelled again, laughing and smiling still.

"*The Times*?" Wyatt asked, more confused than before. "As in…"

"Yes, Wyatt! The New York fucking Times! They apparently want to do a write-up on you, or something. Can you believe it?! *The New York Times*, Wyatt!" Wyatt could hear Melody beaming, and he realized this was the most proud she had ever sounded in a conversation with him; especially, regarding his art.

"Wait, wait, wait… *The New York Times*?" Wyatt was in shock.

"Yes, now go! Call them both right now!" Melody shouted again.

"Okay, okay! I'll call them both now."

Wyatt heard his call disconnect, and he stood silently in his kitchen, still staring down at his cell phone screen. He sifted through more messages, and then he saw a text message from Caroline.

"Hi Wyatt, Caroline Haynes with the NYT here. Please give me a call when you can! Would love to chat about an article."

What the fuck is going on? Wyatt thought, in disbelief.

Instinctively, he called Sylvia back first. Nervous, he felt his hand quiver as he held his phone to his ear. With every ring that passed, Wyatt felt his heart pound a little heavier. Finally, after almost giving up hope that she would not answer, Wyatt heard a faint voice pick up on the other end.

"This is Sylvia," she said in a soft, but focused tone.

"Uh — hi, is this — uh, is this Sylvia Peregine?" Wyatts voice shook almost as much as his hands.

"Yes, may I ask who is calling?"

"Hi — uh, this is Wyatt Brone," Wyatt said. Somehow, the sound of his own name made him feel even more nervous.

"Wyatt! Yes, hello!" Sylvia's tone was immediately brightened, and she seemed to sound authentically excited to have him on the line. Wyatt unintentionally laughed out loud. "Thank you so much for getting back to me!"

"Of course, are you kidding?" Wyatt nervously put his free hand through his hair, unsure of what to do with it.

"Listen, I'm sort of in-between meetings, so I'll cut right to the chase," Sylvia spoke with hurried words. "We would love to host a month-long showcase of your catalogue of works. Fifteen to, maybe, twenty of your pieces. An exclusive artist showcase, our whole gallery, just your paintings. We would start with a month, and depending on the reception, maybe extend. But of course, we would defer to you. You can choose the works, we'll give you full creative control. Anything you want to do. New, old, staples, abstract, we don't care. We just want Wyatt Brone's unfiltered paintings in our gallery. We can negotiate this with your representation, but we would really love to purchase the works from you upfront, since we are pretty confident that we will sell them all. We are also willing to offer a 35% commission on the pieces we sell, in addition to our upfront payment. It's a little unorthodox, but like I said, we are really excited to have your works showcased. What do you think?"

Sylvia said all of this in such a matter-of-fact way that Wyatt was not sure exactly how to respond. The truth was that he had never been given this type of offer before. Never this much commission, never any payment upfront, and never with the confidence that the gallery would sell *all* of his pieces.

"I — uhh — I don't know what to say…" Wyatt responded, a smile in his voice, and his heart still racing.

"Please, think it over! I don't need an answer right now. But listen, I'm actually walking into another meeting. Connect with your reps, and let me know! We are so excited to finally possibly host Wyatt Brone. We are all such massive fans. Talk soon, Wyatt!" And just like that, Wyatt heard the call end. *Massive fans?* Wyatt thought. *Porter & Herth are massive fans?*

Wyatt screamed with joy in his kitchen before remembering he had another call to make. He frantically found Caroline's text, clicked her contact information, and hit "dial."

His hands were still shaking with each ring until he heard another voice pick up.

"Hello, this is Caroline Haynes speaking," she said.

"Hi, Caroline, this — uh, this is Wyatt Brone returning your call," a new found confidence in his tone.

"Wyatt, hi, yes! Thank you so much for giving me a call back so quickly, I really appreciate that," she said.

"Of course. When *The New York Times* calls, you gotta call back, right?" Wyatt laughed, then immediately regretted an attempt at humor.

"Yes." Her quick and dry reply was exactly what he imagined it would be. Humor had never quite been Wyatt's forte. "Listen, I am working on a series about artists living in today's world, and I would absolutely love for you to be the first artist I highlight."

"Wow," Wyatt responded, shocked again, "that sounds amazing."

"Yes! It will be. We are essentially guaranteed a front-page expose. I do want to highlight anything you are willing to share with me. Your process, your life, your story, but most importantly, we want to highlight your paintings. I think they are an important next step in the evolution of contemporary art." *What in the hell…* Wyatt's mind raced with disbelief.

"Caroline, that is incredibly kind. Thank you so much," Wyatt smiled larger than he ever thought was possible, and still tried to maintain his composure.

"I'll take that as a 'yes,' then?" Caroline asked, kind but calculated.

"Absolutely, yes!" Wyatt responded, and laughed a little to himself.

"Amazing, I'll shoot you an email shortly, feel free to pass it on to your reps, and we can get all of the details coordinated and scheduled for when I'm in Los Angeles here in the next couple of weeks. I'm really excited, Wyatt. This is going to be incredible."

Wyatt stood silently in his kitchen. He looked down at his cell phone in his hand, and still felt his hands shaking and his heart racing. *What the hell was happening?* He thought. Controlling his trembling fingers as best he could, he called Melody back.

"Mel, I don't understand how this is all happening!" He said to his sister.

"Wyatt, I know it feels like it's happening overnight, but you have to keep in mind that Jackson just died." Melody hesitated before bringing it up.

"What do you mean?" Wyatt asked, curious.

"You're the painting nephew of the most renowned painter to ever live. He just died. Newspapers need headlines." Wyatt did not say anything initially in return, he just listened to his sister. He could hear the concern in her voice. "Ultimately, it doesn't matter, Wyatt. You have worked so hard for so long, and it's happening. It's finally happening."

For the first time in years, they shared a common joy brought on from Wyatt's art. For the first time, maybe ever, Wyatt felt pride in his passion.

He and Melody discussed his conversations with both Sylvia and Caroline, and Melody made notes to handle the follow-up conversations with both opportunities, getting things coordinated and booked officially.

"This is unbelievable," Wyatt managed to say, still in shock.

"Well, you better start believing it, Wyatt! This is happening. I am so proud of you. So incredibly proud, Wyatt," Melody's response almost brought tears to his eyes.

"Thank you, Mel." Wyatt replied, smiling wide.

Wyatt heard a "call waiting" tone bleep on his phone call with Melody, and he realized he was getting another call. He told his sister that he would call her back soon, and answered the call he was receiving. He said hello, and learned that it was the curator from the gallery that hosted his failed opening a few nights prior.

"Wyatt, I honestly can't believe I'm saying this, but as of this afternoon, we have officially sold every piece you gave us to showcase."

Impossible, Wyatt thought.

"I'm sorry, what?" Wyatt said back. He heard the curator laugh at his response.

"I know, trust me. I know. But yes. We have sold every one of your paintings."

What the hell, Wyatt thought.

"That's… that is amazing news," Wyatt said.

"I'm sorry if I was dismissive on our opening night, or rude, or whatever. This has just never happened like this before," the curator said.

"No, please, don't even worry about it, really. I'm happy to hear it turned out well." Wyatt said back.

"Listen, I have your commission payout check here at the gallery. But I would love it if you had more pieces we could display? I think we can capitalize on this momentum, and get more of your work into people's collections. What do you think?"

"I think that sounds like a plan. Thank you so much." Wyatt responded.

After working out a few minor details, and promising to get her in contact with his sister to work out the major logistics, Wyatt hung up the phone.

Wyatt could not believe what was happening. Not forty-five minutes before, he stood in front of his most recent work, contemplating throwing his brushes in the trash, and here he was, with a sold out gallery, multiple new openings, and on the verge of being on the front page of *The New York Times*. For the first time in his life, Wyatt understood the phrase, "What a difference a day makes."

Again, the beams of sunlight that shone through his windows caught Wyatt's eyes. He followed the solid beam of light as it cut through his space and into the secondary room.

The sunlight perfectly hit the back of his uncle's painting.

Wyatt remembered the letter.

"Never show, never tell; never stop, never sell; follow these to wildest dreams… for it will be yours." Wyatt said aloud. *Surely not,* he thought to himself. Then again… the proof was in the pudding.

He walked back into the room, and stared at the painting again.

"This can't be real," Wyatt spoke, standing alone in the room.

Unsure of what it all meant, he decided to lean in. He picked up his brush, and added another stroke. *Better safe than sorry.*

Wyatt heard his front door buzz, and quickly made his way over to it. He did not look through the peephole, but instead pulled it open.

Samantha stood in the doorway, tears filled her eyes.

"Woah… Sam, are you okay?" Wyatt asked, worried. Samantha immediately threw her arms around Wyatt, and cried onto his shoulder. "Oh, babe… come in, please. What's wrong?"

Wyatt kept his arm around Samantha, as he led her into his living space. She sat on his bed, and he immediately sat down next to her. "What's going on? Hey, are you okay?" Wyatt asked as he gently rubbed her back.

"Oh, Wyatt." Samantha said through muffled tears. "I'm so sorry."

"What are you sorry about?"

"I made a huge mistake. I love you, Wyatt. I don't want to do any of this without you. I don't care about what —" Wyatt interrupted her with a kiss. He kissed her hard.

"Samantha, it's okay. I love you too." He forced the words through a few tears of his own.

"I just want to be with you," she said.

"And we can figure out the rest along the way," he said, finishing her thought. They both smiled.

"Yes. Please." Samantha replied, resting her head back down on his shoulder.

The two sat on his bed in silence, holding each other.

After a few genuine, lovely moments, Wyatt pulled away from Samantha slightly. He looked at her, and debated whether to tell her about the painting and letter.

"What is it, Wyatt?" She asked, seeing the slight concern in his eyes.

"I just…" Wyatt was not sure how much to reveal. "I just have a feeling that things are about to get a little wild."

"Whatever happens, I'm just happy to be able to be by your side." Samantha smiled and touched his arm. Wyatt smiled back, and pulled her back into him, closer than before. And they sat, maybe closer than ever before.

Again the letter came into Wyatt's mind.

"To nev'r showeth and nev'r bid, f'r 'twill beest yours,
To nev'r stand ho and nev'r selleth, f'r 'twill beest yours,
Followeth these to wildest dreams, f'r 'twill beest yours."

CHAPTER 7

It started with a ring.

Wyatt heard his landline as it rang out through his open workspace loft, and bounced off the walls into his bathroom where he was brushing his teeth. Wyatt knew that Caroline Haynes would be exactly on time for their interview today, and he would be anything but. Frantic, he tried to keep his body calm to avoid the inevitable nervous sweats he knew he would feel at any moment.

Samantha, who had stayed at his loft the night before, called out from the kitchen so that he could hear her.

"It's your business line, I'll grab it!" Wyatt could hear a pleasant tone in her voice. A welcomed, pleasant tone. Wyatt quickly splashed some water on his face, and checked his watch. It was just a few minutes past ten in the morning, and his interview with Caroline was confirmed for around half past. He knew she would be on time, and also knew he would either not be ready, or be embarrassingly perspired… or both. He looked at himself in the mirror. *How is this happening?* He thought.

Samantha called out to him again, but this time he heard a slight hesitation in her voice. A tremble that he could not ignore. "Wyatt… can you come here for a second?"

"Yeah, babe, one sec," Wyatt called back to her. His mind raced with all of the things that could be waiting for him on the other end.

A mistake in the first report of gallery sales, and Wyatt actually made nothing; a miscommunication with Porter & Herth, and they contacted the wrong Wyatt Brone; or news that *The New York Times* had changed their minds, and decided to not waste their time on a Nobody, Try-Hard. Any of these outcomes could be within the realm of possibility, and Wyatt hated that his brain was broken in this way.

Wyatt quickly dried the beaded water off of his face, and tossed the towel back onto the counter. He walked out of his bathroom, and made his way back into his kitchen. He saw Samantha standing next to the counter, holding the phone receiver in her hand, and with a slight panic on her face. Not an urgent panic, but there was definitely a sense of confusion and concern. He could see it in her eyes.

"What is it?" Wyatt intentionally hushed himself to an exaggerated whisper. He hoped whoever was on the other end, with whatever news they had, would not hear him.

"I don't know. They said they are with the Los Angeles Police Department Homicide Division?" Wyatt heard Samantha hesitate as she said the word "homicide." Rightfully so, he understood that it was probably a jarring thing to hear, especially if the word was not a part of your world just a few moments before.

The first feeling that washed over Wyatt was a slight panic, like a school-aged child who had their name called into the principal's office. Then he remembered his failed commitment to go into the station and submit a formal statement around his uncle's suicide, and the panic was replaced with embarrassment. Regardless of why, the sweat he was hoping to avoid immediately came.

"Oh, shit," Wyatt said as he walked towards Samantha, "they are calling about Jackson. I told them I'd go answer some questions for them this week, I completely forgot."

"You forgot?" Samantha asked, a crinkle in her forehead, and the concern still present.

"Yeah, it's not a big deal. They are just confirming some details about his suicide, it just slipped my mind with everything going on." Wyatt reached out for the receiver. "Here, I can chat with them." Samantha handed the phone to Wyatt, and took a step away, still facing him.

"Hi, this is Wyatt."

Samantha kept her eyes on Wyatt as she moved her way around him in the kitchen. She proceeded to take over his morning coffee duties. She prepared the beans, added the dash of cinnamon, and filled the kettle with water before placing it on the stove. She turned the heat on, and then moved back towards Wyatt. She placed her hand on the back of his shoulder, and rested her head down on his chest.

"Wyatt. This is Detective Thomas Johns, we spoke at your apartment last week?" Det. Johns said on the other end of the line.

"Yes, hi Det. Johns, yes." Wyatt smiled at Samantha, a subconscious nod to tell her that it was, in fact, fine.

"Det. Foss and I wanted to give you a call since we never heard back from you about coming down to give us a statement." Wyatt could not read Det. Johns' voice at all. A skill Wyatt normally prided himself on.

"Yes, I'm so sorry, this week really got away from me." Wyatt responded, in the most calm tone he could muster.

"Listen, we have some availability today, if you're free."

"I'm so sorry, I can't today, but maybe this week." Wyatt again smiled at Samantha who cracked a small smile back. He could not tell if she believed him that everything was fine, but he did his best to make sure she did. He gently grazed the back of her head with his hand.

"Yeah, this week should be all right. Did you have a day in —" Before Det. Johns could even finish his thought, Wyatt jumped in and interrupted.

"Detective Johns, I'm so sorry, I am actually preparing for a thing I have. I promise I'll let you know about this week, and I'll make time to swing by. I just really have to get going," Wyatt felt bad for cutting the Detective off so quickly, but he also knew he was facing quite possibly one of, if not, the biggest opportunities of his career, and he could not be distracted with what he felt was total nonsense.

"If I didn't know any better, I'd probably start to think you were avoiding us, Wyatt." Det. Johns responded dryly.

For a moment, Wyatt's world slowed to a halt. Wyatt had never considered his reluctance to connect with the Detectives as anything but Wyatt simply avoiding an inconvenience that he felt was unnecessary. He definitely had not considered that it would be received as intentional avoidance.

"Oh, I — uh — ha, no. No, no, no. Just busy, is all." Wyatt shook his head, and knew that his nervous response probably did not help his cause in the slightest.

"Wyatt, I'm yanking your chain." Wyatt still could not detect anything in Det. Johns' tone to suggest the yanking of anyone's chain. Samantha began pouring the boiling water over the ground coffee beans.

"Oh, ha — got it. All right. Well, I really do have to go." Wyatt again responded awkwardly.

"This week, then?" Det. Johns said back.

"This week, I'll make it work."

Wyatt hung up the receiver, and took a breath.

At the station, Detective Johns also hung up the phone. He exhaled, frustrated, and turned to look at Detective Foss.

"He's dodging us," Det. Foss blurted out, impatiently.

"I don't know if he's dodging us, but something isn't adding up for me." Det. Johns added.

"We should just keep stopping by until he makes time to talk. I don't trust him."

"Ease up, Gerry. We just got to give him a little more time, but I'm definitely thinking we should look a little closer at what we know." Det. Johns said back.

Back at his loft, Wyatt looked to Samantha, who handed him a freshly brewed cup of coffee. The timing was perfect.

"This is probably a dumb question, but why does the L.A.P.D. want to talk to you about your uncle's suicide?" Samantha asked as she poured herself a cup from the same Chemex carafe.

"Not dumb at all, I had no idea before they came by last week." Wyatt took a sip.

"They came here?" Samantha replied, now more confused than concerned.

"Yeah, they just showed up. Apparently, even with suicides, they have to 'confirm' no foul play, or whatever. So they came by to get a statement since Mel and I are really the only two other people they can talk to." Wyatt looked towards the window of his loft. A breeze came through, and rustled his curtains.

"I'm sorry, Wyatt. I can imagine how frustrating that would feel." Samantha tried her best to console something she was not sure needed consoling.

"It's okay, it's just kind of annoying. Like… Jackson and I hadn't talked in months. I hadn't heard from him in even longer, so I don't know how anything I have to say would be helpful." Samantha put her hand back on Wyatt's arm, and gently rubbed it.

"Do they think anything suspicious happened? Seems —" Wyatt would not even let Samantha finish the question before he interrupted her.

"Don't be silly, of course not. They just keep saying they are doing their 'due diligence.' Apparently they have to do this every time someone…" Wyatt stopped himself, realizing his phrasing is probably a little too insensitive. "Well, you know what I mean."

"Yeah, I get it," Samantha responded.

"They just think I'm avoiding them now, which is annoying too. It'll be fine, I just need to find some time to make it into the station and give them whatever it is that they are looking for." Wyatt kissed the top of her head, and walked back into his bathroom.

As he made it back into the bathroom, and finished getting dressed, Wyatt wondered if there would be any implications underneath the hopefully benign joke Detective Johns had made on the phone. *What if I were avoiding them?* Wyatt thought. *I have not broken any laws, I have not done anything wrong. Maybe I have just been unusually busy.*

Wyatt tried convincing himself that he was starting to let his mind spiral into an anxious storm. It was a storm he was unfortunately all too familiar with already, and he definitely did not need two detectives stirring up anymore rough waters.

Was it a crime to avoid providing a statement to the detectives investigating your uncle's suicide? Was it a crime to shuffle them off of the phone as quickly as possible so you could prepare for an extremely important interview that could potentially catapult your career? Wyatt did not have the slightest idea. A small pit formed in his stomach, and made him think he would likely find out sooner rather than later. He could tell he was nervous about the answer to those hypothetical questions, however, because he found himself brushing his teeth again without thinking.

At least his breath would be fresh.

"Where is the piece Jackson left you?" Samantha called out from the other room, and Wyatt's face dropped. His heart raced, and his mind was immediately flooded with the panic of letting Samantha see the piece.

Even though he was not yet convinced of the validity of the letter's rules, he was certainly convinced that he was not ready to face any proverbial consequences, and therefore chose caution in not risking the rules to be true.

Wyatt ran out of the bathroom, and just barely caught the glimpse of Samantha walking into the secondary room.

"Samantha!" Wyatt shouted at the top of his lungs, as he rushed around the corner into the room to find a terrified Samantha. The sound of Wyatt's scream startled her, and she immediately jumped out of his way as he rushed past her, and threw the cloth over the piece.

"What the fuck, Wyatt!" Samantha yelled back, angry at his outburst and for scaring her.

"I'm sorry, I just — I can't..." Wyatt immediately realized that he could not explain why he reacted the way he did without sounding completely insane. "I just... I'm not... I'm not ready to show this to anyone yet," Wyatt pieced together the only cohesive sentence he thought was possible.

"Then just say that, Wyatt, Jesus Christ. You scared me to death," Samantha said as she walked out of the room, back into the kitchen.

Wyatt could feel his pulse in his neck. He took a deep breath and remembered the letter.

"To nev'r showeth and nev'r bid, f'r 'twill beest yours."

Wyatt quietly walked back into his bathroom, and splashed his face with water. *Get a grip, Wyatt,* he thought.

Caroline Haynes had become the preeminent art critic at *The New York Times*, and maintained that reputation for going on nearly three decades. With a keen eye on the current scene, a brilliant mind of where the scene had come from, and a distinct vision on where she felt the scene was heading, Caroline easily made a name for herself.

Over her tenure at the newspaper she had also developed a very particular way of curating art for the audience at *The Times.* They had learned to crave her specific and unique word, phrasing, and artist choices.

If Caroline Haynes said a piece or an artist were worth paying attention to, her audience listened. It was through this relationship that she had effortlessly created, and built up throughout her years that led her to her role as Chief Art Critic. She was a rare voice that had the ability to truly make or break someone's entire career.

The main reason Wyatt was now nervously brushing his teeth for a third time.

Caroline Haynes was exactly on time, as Wyatt had imagined she would be. She did not, however, look anything like what Wyatt would have imagined. There were two fairly distinct images that came to Wyatt's mind when he thought of what an "art critic" would look like. Obviously, he had encountered a few critics in the past, and the interactions definitely checked the boxes he was expecting. This only further validated his idea of what to expect when expecting an art critic.

First, the "Edna Mode."

Yes, that Edna Mode.

The Edna Mode from the 2004, computer animated, hit film produced by Pixar Animation Studios, and released by Walt Disney Studios. Edna Mode was a half-Japanese, half-German fashion designer and auteur whose main role in the film franchise was the designer of the costumes for the super heroes. Known for her short stature and calling everyone "dahling," Edna famously said, "no capes." Inspired by such personalities as Vogue's Anna Wintor, Edna wore thick, black framed glasses, had a fashionable "bob" haircut, and was also styled to a perfect sense of minimalism. This version of the art critic would stare at a piece for minutes at a time, in pure silence, before letting out a slight, "hm," before moving on.

The other art critic archetype Wyatt was used to encountering, and fully expecting was the "Ms. Frizzle."

Yes, that Ms. Frizzle.

Professor Valerie Frizzle, PhD, of the hit cartoon series *The Magic School Bus*, that ran from 1994 to 1997. Ms. Frizzle was eclectic, to say the least. Her wild red hair exploding in every direction, her purple, long-sleeved dress, covered in beakers and rocket ships, and her emphatic and loving motto, "Take chances, make mistakes, and get messy." The "Ms. Frizzle" art critic archetype was a simple one. The Ms. Frizzle is eclectic, eccentric, and cares deeply for every piece they feel moved by. This was easily the art critic that Wyatt preferred.

Caroline Haynes was neither of these character tropes. Caroline Haynes was simply Caroline Haynes.

She arrived exactly on time with her photographer, who Wyatt had not even considered would be joining her. Samantha greeted Caroline warmly, and Caroline immediately brought her in for a welcoming embrace. Pleasantries and hellos were exchanged in the entryway, before Wyatt heard Samantha say his name.

"Wyatt should be out in just a moment," Samantha said politely.

Wyatt finished calming himself down, and he walked into his living area. He could hear the photographer already snapping shots around his space, and he was so thankful he had cleaned things so intensely the day before.

Caroline stood just inside his entryway. They made eye contact as soon as Wyatt turned the corner.

Caroline Haynes smiled.

She had the kind of smile that immediately made Wyatt feel at ease. In that instant, she was not the feared, and brutal art critic, she was an old friend who was glad to see him. Wyatt smiled back.

"Wyatt Brone," Caroline said in a soft, and unexpectedly gentle voice.

Her thick, fashionable frames delicately rested on the bridge of her nose. Wyatt could tell her outfit was expensive, but it was not flashy or gaudy, by any means. It was modest, minimalist, and perfectly chosen for the occasion, but definitely designer from head to toe. Wyatt knew, because he continued catching Samantha staring, impressed with her style choices.

"Caroline, hi. It's lovely to meet you." Wyatt walked over to greet Caroline with a firm handshake, and she instinctively wrapped her arms around him and pulled him in for a friendly embrace. Wyatt did not resist at all, and instead hugged her like an old friend. There was such a pleasant warmth, and familiarity to Caroline. Wyatt and Samantha were both immediately entranced.

"Wyatt, this is my photographer Daniel, Daniel, this is Wyatt." Daniel let his camera rest around his neck, and walked over to shake Wyatt's hand. Wyatt shook it back.

"Beautiful space," Daniel responded, simple and plain.

"Thank you," Wyatt responded. Just like that, Daniel was back to taking quick shots of little details around Wyatt's loft. Paint splattered furniture, canvases peacefully resting against the wall. All of the details that *The New York Times* readers would no doubt notice.

"Wyatt," Caroline brought the conversation back to him. "It is just so wonderful to meet you, finally. My team has been really looking forward to this piece, and we are just so thrilled you were interested."

"Please, come in," Wyatt said as he ushered Caroline into his space, but she never took her eyes off of him. Her focus was intentional, she was a professional.

"And, that's so nice, of course I was interested. You're Caroline Haynes," Wyatt said, trying to flatter her. It must have worked, because she laughed graciously, and put her hand on his arm, a gesture of kindness and appreciation.

"Oh, stop." Caroline responded.

"I'm serious," Wyatt chuckled in return. "How could I pass up the opportunity to meet the newspaper that put my uncle on the map." Caroline stopped for a moment, and looked at Wyatt.

"I'm sorry?" She asked, confused.

"My uncle... Jackson Brone. *The Times* did a piece highlighting him in ... oh gosh, the early seventies? It made him a household name." Wyatt looked back at Caroline, and could see her putting the pieces together.

"Wyatt...Brone. Unbelievable." Caroline spoke almost to herself. "I'm so... I'm so sorry, Wyatt. I cannot believe I did not connect those dots." She smiled, not seeming phased by the revelation at all, and Wyatt could not tell if he felt embarrassed that she had not made the connection, or proud that she discovered Wyatt on the merits of his art, alone.

"Wait," Wyatt said. "You booked this without knowing that Jackson Brone was my uncle?" Wyatt asked, though even he was nervous for the answer.

"Wyatt, of course," she said through laughter, "We sought you out because we think your work is brilliant."

He could have burst into tears right then and there.

Wyatt realized he could not recall the last time someone unironically told him that they thought his work was anything positive, much less "brilliant." Adding on the fact that this compliment was coming from the most renowned art critic in the world was almost too overwhelming.

"Thank you, thank you so much." It was all Wyatt could think to respond with.

"That also answers my first question. It's Br-Own, and not Bro-Knee, so thank you for that." Caroline playfully smiled, and Wyatt laughed.

"Well, then for that reason alone, I'm glad it came up." He said back. Wyatt watched as Daniel expanded his range within Wyatt's space. Wyatt noticed that Daniel truly was taking shots of every detail. He felt a slight unease build inside of him, as he moved his gaze back to Caroline.

The three sat down in Wyatt's very recently cleaned and organized living space.

Caroline periodically interrupted her questioning to rave about how unique she felt his workspace loft was, and Wyatt periodically caught himself keeping a keen eye on where Daniel was roaming throughout the space.

"It just seems so creatively welcoming. Do you find it easy to create in such an open and welcoming space?" She asked with delicate, and particular phrasing.

"I have always felt… particularly lucky… to never run into much creative blocks. If I have a specific idea for a piece, I usually know every detail before I put paint to canvas. And I think that is a really lucky spot to start from as an artist." Even Wyatt felt impressed with his answer.

"Do you ever find it limiting? Living and creating in the same space?" Caroline asked, looking back at Wyatt.

"I think this space in particular has made it easy to compartmentalize the different aspects of my life. I have two separate rooms where I can create, and this room, where I can unwind. So I am sort of able to keep it all apart. Keeping the two truly separate makes all the difference. Work can be work, and life can be easy." Wyatt answered. Caroline smiled.

Wyatt caught, from the corner of his eye, the outline of Daniel walking into the secondary room. He felt his heart rate increase with each click of Daniel's shudder. After a few moments of tense stress, Wyatt abruptly called out to Caroline's photographer.

"Hi, Daniel!" Wyatt was immediately embarrassed at how loud and sudden his shout was. "I'm so sorry," he said to Caroline before he turned backwards Daniel, "could you please not take photographs in that room? I have some works I would prefer no one see quite yet…" Daniel emerged from the room, and Wyatt immediately felt embarrassed.

"I'm so sorry, Wyatt. I'm just taking space shots, I promise I haven't photographed any of your actual paintings." Daniel explained.

"Okay, no, it's okay. I'm sorry if I yelled." Wyatt backtracked.

"No need to apologize, Wyatt. I should have asked before I assumed."

"Thank you," Wyatt said. He then turned his gaze back to Caroline and Samantha who shared the same, puzzled look. Caroline, being the consummate professional she was, continued her line of questioning.

"You seem to have a relatively healthy creative, work, life balance for an artist. What do you attribute that to?" Caroline jotted down some notes on her notebook with a pen. At first, Wyatt was surprised that she was not using a tablet of some kind, but when he really thought about it, he was not surprised at all. Caroline Haynes was from a different generation.

"I do, I really do. I try to, anyway. I think it's just a matter of constantly reminding myself to be thankful for the opportunities I have been given so far. Along with the understanding that there really isn't anything else I would ever be qualified to do." Wyatt nervously smiled.

"If you weren't painting, what do you think you would be doing" Caroline asked, playfully poking a little deeper.

"Honestly? No idea. I can't imagine doing anything else." Wyatt answered honestly.

"How have you cultivated your audience so far?" Caroline asked, and Wyatt momentarily froze. He was not entirely sure if his answer would be good enough for *The New York Times.* He thought, *What audience?* Thankfully, Wyatt thought, Samantha jumped in to answer.

"Well, Wyatt has been consistently showing his work at galleries all across Los Angeles for years. L.A. might have the most well known art scene in the world, but when you're here, and in it, you know Wyatt Brone." Samantha said.

Wyatt felt proud of her interjection, but he could not tell if he believed her or not. The truth, to Wyatt's knowledge, was that you only knew the name Wyatt Brone in the Los Angeles scene because of the name Jackson Brone.

The three sat and talked for almost four hours. They discussed everything from Wyatt's upbringing in small town Texas, to how his passion for the creative world drove him into pursuing an impossible dream.

"Would teenage Wyatt daydream ahead about the beautiful work he would create as an adult?" She asked.

"Teenage Wyatt didn't know what day it was, much less that anyone would be interested in paint he put to canvas." Wyatt laughed.

"Well, I'm sure teenage Wyatt would be incredibly proud."

Caroline asked about Wyatt's approach, and process. She asked about his influences and his inspirations. Wyatt smiled with this question, and looked at Samantha.

"Samantha has always been here for me. In my highest of highs, and lowest of lows. She's my north star. Especially as an artist, it can be so easy to throw yourself down the emotional flight of stairs. No matter what, Samantha would always be there to help me back to my feet." Samantha smiled back at Wyatt, and he felt her squeeze his hand slightly.

"And you two have been together for how long now?" Caroline interjected, smiling.

"Almost…" Wyatt started before Samantha finished.

"Almost five years, I think." She said with a smile.

"Beautiful," Caroline said smiling. "Now, Samantha, does Wyatt ever put you to work? Managing anything, or helping with anything? Or do you just get to enjoy being this virtuosic artist's girlfriend?"

"Fiancé," Samantha hurriedly corrected Caroline. Wyatt shot a glance at her, confused. Samantha simply smiled back. An ear to ear grin beamed across Wyatt's face. He squeezed her hand hard.

This was everything he ever wanted.

The letter came to Wyatt's mind again, and he felt his heart rate tick up just slightly.

They all talked for a little longer, before Caroline checked her watch and seemed almost surprised at how long she had been there.

"I am so sorry, where is my head." Caroline jumped to her feet, and quickly started to gather her things. "I had no idea we'd been talking for so long!" She laughed, nervously, afraid she had overstayed her welcome. Wyatt and Samantha stood with her, and assured her that was not the case.

"Are you kidding?" Wyatt chuckled. "This was amazing, thank you so much."

"You've been so incredibly generous with your time," Samantha added.

"That's a word that isn't often used to describe me," Caroline said, and smiled at Samantha. "Generous. Huh." She smirked, and it made Wyatt and Samantha laugh.

"Really," Wyatt doubled down. "Thank you so much, Caroline. This was amazing."

Caroline Haynes hugged Samantha and they said goodbye, before Wyatt walked Caroline to his front door. He opened it, and Caroline took a step out of his loft, and into the hallway.

"Thank you again, Wyatt. It has been such a joy… an honor… and such a wonderful time meeting you and chatting." She said as she hugged Wyatt goodbye.

"No, Caroline, thank *you*. I owe you so much for this. This was really great," Wyatt said in response.

Caroline lingered for a second, and Wyatt thought she maybe had one more question to ask. Instead, he listened as Caroline made one final statement.

"Listen, Wyatt," she started, and he could tell she was being careful with the words she chose. "This article… I'm not going to hold back. I'm going to give my readers my God's honest truth of what I think about you." For the first time this afternoon with Caroline, Wyatt felt truly nervous. "Wyatt, I think you're brilliant. I think your paintings are a revelation. I think you have the potential to change everything. I'm going to tell my readers that." Wyatt felt his heart racing in his chest. "This article could very likely change everything for you. I just want you to … how do I put this delicately… I just want you to be ready for what comes next."

"What is that?" Wyatt asked, again nervous for her answer.

"Everything you've ever wanted." Caroline said.

Wyatt took a breath. Caroline noticed the exasperated sigh and laughed. "You'll be okay, I promise. But better prepared than caught off guard."

"Well, thank you. I'll try to not put the cart before the horse." Wyatt said, and smirked. His pulse was still pounding in his wrist.

"I'm just saying that the cart and horse are ready. Make sure you are, too." Wyatt smiled back, and struggled to contain his pure excitement. "This is just the beginning, Wyatt. Everything is about to change."

"Thank you, Caroline, so much." Wyatt hugged her again.

"The pleasure was mine, Wyatt. Truly," Caroline said as she hugged him back.

With that, Caroline Haynes walked away. Wyatt watched her board the elevator, and then disappear behind the closing door. He stood silent for a moment and tried to calm his heart rate. He took a deep inhale.

He turned, and walked back inside his space. He heard Samantha shut the door to his bathroom, and the shower sputtered to life. He took another breath and smiled to himself. Wyatt walked into the secondary room, and stood in front of the painting.

Almost immediately, he felt it calling him.

He picked up a brush, and dabbed some still moist paint from his palette onto its bristles.

Wyatt added a stroke of paint to the piece. He remembered the letter. He remembered the very specific last line of the letter.

"Followeth these to wildest dreams, f'r 'twill beest yours."

CHAPTER 8

Wyatt pulled her close.

He and Samantha laid quietly in his bed in the morning some days later. His arm intertwined with the curve of her body, they both laid on their sides. Wyatt had been awake for what he assumed was about forty-five minutes or so, but he assumed Samantha was still asleep and he did now want to wake her. Instead, he held her.

He subtly smelled her hair, and gently kissed the top of her head. Then he squeezed her again, just slightly. This was what he wanted.

Since Samantha had decided her leaving was a mistake, their relationship felt so effortless; so simple. It was as if all of their internal concerns, and ignored frustrations had just melted away. This was the second chance he had hoped for, but doubted he would ever experience. Wyatt intended to not let this fresh start melt away like everything else seemed to have.

"Good morning," Samantha said with a deep, cracking voice. Wyatt had been right, she was sleeping until that point.

"Good morning, love," Wyatt said back, quietly. He again kissed the top of her head.

Samantha slowly turned around on the bed, sort of stretching in the process, and faced Wyatt. The two locked eyes, and Wyatt smiled. "How did you sleep, baby?" Wyatt asked.

"Well. I was out like a log." Wyatt gently laughed under his breath.

"Hey, logs don't sleep." Wyatt laughed to himself, and he could almost feel Samantha's eyes roll out of her head.

"I… I hate you so much," Samantha said as she laughed and playfully pushed him away. Wyatt took this as a challenge, and immediately wrapped both of his arms around her, smothered her with kisses, and gently tickled her side. Samantha shouted at him through her laughter, and warded off his advances.

After a few moments or joyful play fighting, they kissed. It was a quick kiss, but a passionate kiss. Wyatt pulled Samantha close again, and the two laid still, arms around one another.

"What do you have to do today?" Samantha asked into Wyatt's chest.

"I have a lunch meeting with Mel, but other than that just resting. Caroline's write-up in *The New York Times* is printing today." Samantha immediately woke right up. She jolted upright, and slapped Wyatt hard in the chest. "Ouch!" Wyatt laughed.

"Wyatt! That's today?!" Samantha screamed, and smiled.

"It's probably already at your local Starbucks." Wyatt said through an ear-to-ear grin.

"Wyatt, that's amazing! Congratulations!" Samantha threw her arms around him, and hugged him tight.

"Thank you," was all he could say in return. Samantha erupted out of their bed, and ran to the bathroom. She called out as she ran away, "I have to go buy a copy!"

"Oh, stop it. They're sending me some, just take one of those." Wyatt called out after her. He saw her quickly pop her head out from around the bathroom door frame.

"I do not think so, Mister. I will be purchasing a copy at my local… newspaper… seller… place. Wherever you buy a newspaper. I will find a newspaper in Los Angeles, and I will purchase it, thank you very much!” Then her head disappeared right back into the bathroom.

“Suit yourself, Money-Bags McGee.” Wyatt could hear Samantha laugh out loud.

“Okay. A newspaper costs what, four dollars? I think I’ll be fine.”

“Just throwing money out the window every chance she gets,” Wyatt laughed, joking, and finally stood up out of bed himself. Wyatt laughed a little harder when he heard Samantha’s tone click up a full octave.

“Wyatt, stop! I want to be supportive,” she whined.

“Babe, I’m just teasing you. Go. Buy all of the copies you can find. I hear he’s super handsome.”

“Who?” Samantha asked, genuinely curious.

“The artist they interviewed… For the article… Me, I was talking about me.” Wyatt grimaced a wide, toothy smile. He had tried to land the ultimate dad joke, and realized it had fallen on Samantha’s absent ears. This time, Wyatt saw Samantha’s eyes roll out of her head, and she laughed.

“You’re so dumb,” she laughed.

“But you like me,” Wyatt smirked back.

“No, I love you. There’s a difference, look it up.” Samantha winked at him.

“I love you too,” he responded, and smiled. He was happy.

Wyatt walked into his kitchen, and began his daily morning routine. Coffee, a single piece of wheat toast with peanut butter, and either a banana or an apple. That morning, it would be an apple.

“What are you up to today?” Wyatt called out to Samantha.

“I’m meeting Amy for brunch, then I just need to swing by the office for a couple of hours, nothing crazy.” Wyatt heard the faucet turn on and off every three words, but he thought he understood the gist of what she said, and responded to the best of his ability.

"Sounds fun."

Wyatt took a sip of his coffee and Samantha finally emerged from the bathroom ready for her day. She tossed her arms around his neck, and Wyatt kissed her again.

"Have fun with your sister," Samantha spoke, face to face with Wyatt.

"Tell Amy I say hi," Wyatt responded.

"I will," Samantha said back.

Wyatt gently wiggled his nose across Samantha's, a traditional "kunik."

"I love you," Samantha raised the corner of her mouth into a smile as she looked into Wyatt's eyes.

"I love you too," Wyatt said back.

Wyatt took his time getting ready for his day. He also intentionally set his phone down far enough away from him where he would not feel tempted to check it every three minutes. He also made sure it was on silent mode, so he would not hear the buzzing or ringing of notifications, should they come in. That being said, he was a realist, and knew he relied on his phone to keep his life in order, so when he heard a set timer go off, he realized it was time to leave to meet Melody for lunch at their normal, favorite, rooftop spot.

Wyatt finished buttoning up his shirt, and walked towards his phone to leave when he heard his landline ring. *Shit,* he thought. He had wanted to unplug the receiver to ignore any incoming calls, but based on the ringing that echoed through his space, he had forgotten.

He decided to pick it up, knowing he was on his way out, and could not talk long to whoever was on the other end. He walked to the corded receiver, and picked it up, pressing it to his ear.

"This is Wyatt," he said into the phone.

"Wyatt, this is Sylvia. Sylvia Peregrine, Porter & Herth Gallery." Her voice was as quick and focused as ever.

"Sylvia, hi! Great to hear from you." Wyatt said back, and he checked his watch for the time. He was going to be late.

"Wyatt, you too, darling. Just saw your Time expose, truly incredibly, Wyatt. I hope you feel really proud, darling." Sylvia paused, and Wyatt smiled.

"Thanks, Sylvia, I'm just about to grab a copy to see how it turned out, myself." Wyatt responded.

"Oh, you'll love it. The photos are beautiful, the writing is incredible as always, it's a really masterful piece." Wyatt looks down, and suddenly found himself getting overwhelmed with the emotion of hearing this news.

"Thank you, Sylvia. It means a lot coming from you." He said in response.

"You've earned it, Wyatt. Wyatt, listen. I've been working with Melody on the details of our gallery with your work, but I have a favor to ask." Wyatt paused for a second before responding. He was not sure what was about to be asked of him, and he certainly did not know if it was a good thing or a bad thing that Sylvia fucking Peregrine was about to ask it.

"Uh huh?" He nervously responded, and took a breath.

"Listen, we normally do this very formally. We normally have all of the press and patrons, bullshit whatever. But we never usually have the artist at the opening. Don't ask why, it's just how we've always done it."

"Okay," Wyatt said, aware of the details of what she and Melody had agreed upon.

"Listen, Wyatt, we want you there. We want to have you at the opening. I know it's a little out of the norm for us, but we want you. We think it would be a really big change for the gallery, and we think you are the one to start with."

"Oh," Wyatt was not sure what to say. A part of him assumed this was a Melody decision. "I, uh—"

"Listen," Sylvia jumped in, and interrupted. "You don't need to answer right now, discuss it with Melody, and I'll do the same. But will you consider it?"

"Sylvia, of course. I'm actually on my way to meet her for lunch, so we can chat about it then." Wyatt said.

"Wonderful. I'll look forward to hearing from one of you. Have a lovely rest of your day, Wyatt!" Sylvia said before hanging up the line.

Wyatt smiled, and checked his watch again. He was definitely going to be late… again.

Wyatt sat in the backseat of his Lyft, headed toward the restaurant, and contemplated what the impact of this article could even have on his career. *Does anyone even read the newspaper anymore?* He wondered. All he had ever heard, for as long as he could remember, were Baby Boomers complaining about how it was a dying medium, killed off by the avocado toast obsessed millennial generation. *Sure, Sylvia mentioned how wonderful the write-up was*, Wyatt thought, fully acknowledging Sylvia is probably the only person in Los Angeles even remotely concerned with an artist's expose in *The New York Times*. Wyatt had no delusions of grandeur. He was not expecting this piece to be what would put him on the map, like it had his uncle decades earlier. It was simply a different world.

Wyatt lived in the world of Instagram, and TikTok. Where the only popular painting being done in the mainstream were Gen Z'ers applying elaborate makeup schemes while lip-synching John Mulaney stand-up bits.

Even so, now that Wyatt's phone was securely in his front right pocket, he felt a near constant buzz of notification alerts. Part of him worried they were all from Melody screaming obscenities via SMS messages, cursing Wyatt for once again being "just 5 minutes away." *Sorry Mel,* Wyatt thought.

He hopped out of the Lyft, rushed through the hotel's lobby, and barely caught the closing elevator door. Not that saving the two extra minutes was a deal breaker, but it made Wyatt feel less guilty.

The door slowly slid shut, and Wyatt exhaled slightly. He could feel a small bit of sweat pool on his lower back, and he tugged at it. The breeze from the sway of his shirt was cool against his skin. He glanced at the woman to his right, and they exchanged a soft smile. Wyatt's eyes moved down to her purse handle resting on her forearm, and the paper she held in her hand. *The New York Times.* Wyatt smiled, and looked ahead. The elevator came to a slow stop, the chime of their floor rang out, and Wyatt hopped out as quickly as he could.

He walked past the hostess stand without stopping, but was surprised to hear a quick, "Hi Wyatt! Welcome back," from one of the girls working it. He smiled politely, and kept walking.

Melody was sitting at her usual table, and her smile beamed the moment she and Wyatt caught eyes. She stood, and took a couple of steps towards her brother as he approached the table.

"I'm so sorry I'm late, I promise it wasn't actually my fault this time," Wyatt explained, but was muffled to silence by Melody's tight hug.

"I don't even care, hi, welcome," Melody said as her smile continued across her face.

"Sylvia called when I was on my way out," Wyatt again started to explain. "She said they want me at the gallery opening, did she tell you?" Wyatt noticed that Melody's expression had not changed, her smile had simply taken over her face and had not dissipated. "She said they never do it, but she felt like it would be a good opportunity to…" Wyatt trailed off, and gave his sister a strange look. Melody just stared back. "Alright, what's with you? You look like a creepy doll from a horror movie or something."

"Wyatt," Melody started to say, still smiling. "Your expose is blowing up." Wyatt just stared back with the cautious optimism of Charlie Brown gearing up to kick the football.

"Okay," is all Wyatt could muster.

"It's blowing the fuck up, Wyatt." Melody's smile had not wilted at all. It beamed as strong as it had started. "I've been fielding calls all morning asking to book you for more spots. *GQ, Vanity Fair, Esquire,* fucking *Vogue* wants you!" Melody exclaimed in a forced whisper. "Jesus, *Men's Health* asked if you'd take your shirt off." Melody started to laugh, and her smile got somehow even larger. Wyatt also laughed at the mention of his non-existent physique.

"Oh God, I hope you told them no," Wyatt said laughing. Melody's laughter was almost uncontrollable, and she nodded "yes" vehemently, and silently through her laughter. That only made Wyatt laugh a little harder too.

"Seriously though, Wyatt. This is insane!" Melody again tried to restrain her excitement and her volume.

"And all because —"

"Caroline Haynes. That's it. That is the approval everyone needed to finally appreciate you." Melody beamed with a sense of pride, not only in her client, but in her brother.

"Wow," Wyatt responded. Wyatt thought that maybe one article in *The New York Times* was actually all it took. "That's… that's amazing, Mel."

"That's not even the *half* of it, Wyatt." Melody smirked, and leaned back in her chair dramatically.

"I don't understand…" Wyatt was even more cautiously optimistic than before.

"Netflix wants to do a six-part *docuseries* on the 'plight of the modern artist,' and guess who they want as their focal point." Melody raised a single eyebrow.

"That isn't for real," Wyatt said in disbelief.

"It is. So is the H.B.O. offer for a similar series. Apparently they caught wind of Netflix's offer. This town is so dumb sometimes." Melody laughed again to herself. "To be fair, H.B.O. wants to do something a little more focused on the art world in Los Angeles, but still. You're the muse they want as the primary storyteller."

"Hold on, this is —" Wyatt felt his heart rate tick up, and his face felt flushed.

"Wyatt, that still isn't everything." Wyatt silent shook his head, and just laughed to himself. "MoMA wants to host an exhibit of your work. I started negotiations with them on what that would look like before I came here today."

"The Museum of Modern Art?"

"Yep." Melody again smirked, and Wyatt could tell she was eating this moment alive.

"Melody… this is… this is…"

"Wyatt, this is *happening*. It's all finally happening." Wyatt saw the tears begin welling in her eyes. She was proud. For a moment, Wyatt was too. He was proud of himself, and of them both.

"Mel, this is insane."

"I know! Isn't it exciting." Melody again laughed, and wiped some of the water from her eyes.

"All of this because of one fucking article?" Wyatt's utter disbelief dripped thick from his mouth.

"What have I told you from the beginning, Wyatt? It just takes one." Melody looked at her brother, and Wyatt almost said the words with her in unison. "You have been working towards this, Wyatt. This isn't by chance. This is you, and your work, finally getting the recognition it fucking deserved. The recognition it always has deserved."

She reached out, and took his hands in hers. They stared at each other, and smiled.

"This is unbelievable." Wyatt said graciously.

"Well, start believing it, kid. Because we've got some decisions to make." Melody said as she reached over to grabbed her bag from her feet. She pulled out some paperwork from her bag and tossed a small packet down onto the circular table. Wyatt picked the pages up, and their waitress came by.

"Have you two decided on anything I can get started for you?" The server asked. She smiled faintly at Wyatt, then looked to Melody.

"I'll take the quinoa and arugula salad, please, but could I get the lemon zest vinaigrette on the side?" Melody said without looking up from her menu. "And then, could we go ahead a get a bottle of the Mionetto?" Melody winked at Wyatt before she looked up to the server and smiled.

"The prosecco?" The server asked, and Melody nodded. "Do you have a preference between the Prosecco Brut, or the Prosecco Rose?" The server asked. Melody looked at Wyatt, and crinkled her nose to exaggerate giving the question genuine thought.

"Let's go Brut," Melody smiled again.

"Sound great," the server smiled, then looked at Wyatt, "And for you, sir?" Wyatt glanced back at his menu, and started to order his meal, when the server took a short, quick breath, almost startled. "Oh, my God, you're Wyatt Brone, aren't you?"

Melody's eyes went wide, and Wyatt stared at her.

"I am, yeah," Wyatt said back, with a hint of hesitation in his voice.

"I'm so sorry, I just saw you in *The Times* this morning. What a cool write up! Your work is so beautiful."

"Oh, wow," Wyatt chuckled somewhat awkwardly. "Thank you so much, that's really sweet."

"Okay, I'm so sorry. What can I get for you, Wyatt?"

There was something about the familiarity that the server now spoke with that appealed to Wyatt's ego. Something about the way she confidently used his name, even though they had never interacted before.

"I'll just do the habanero salmon, thanks."

"Of course, great choices, you two. Give me a moment, and I'll have that Prosecco brought out." She smiled at Melody, and then gave Wyatt a slightly bigger smile before she took their menus and walked away.

"What the hell was that?" Wyatt asked, and smirked at Melody. Her smile still beamed across her face, and Wyatt wondered how her cheeks had not given out yet.

"Wyatt, you better get used to that. This is just the beginning." Melody pushed her shoulders up so that they almost touched her ears, and Wyatt heard her squeal slightly, as if she was a child who just realized they had one last present under the Christmas tree. Wyatt just laughed, and shrugged her excitement off entirely. Melody handed him the papers again, and Wyatt took them in his hands. "Okay, back to business. These are the terms from both offers from Netflix and H.B.O. We should try and get a deal done while the excitement is there… so as soon as possible, really."

"Have you looked through them? What do you think?" Wyatt asked, and tossed the papers back onto the table.

"Honestly? You could take either. They are both great, the compensation is fair, and the exposure opportunity is nothing like we've ever had before. For you, I mean." A subtle jab at the lack of success and notoriety Wyatt has experienced up until this point. Wyatt rolled his eyes and laughed.

"Nice, thanks for that." He said.

"You know what I mean. Plus it's the goddamn truth, and you know it." Melody smirked back.

"My gut says H.B.O, but I have no justification." Wyatt sort of shrugged.

"Works for me." Melody said and picked the papers back up. "I'll reach out once I get back to the office, and see if we can't get this done."

Their server came back by with the bottle of Mionetto Prosecco Brut, and two pre-filled glasses. She set them down, and promptly walked away again. Wyatt and Melody took their flutes in their hands, and Wyatt's eyes caught the incessant bubbles in his glass. He looked past the glass to Melody just in time to connect eyes. She raised her glass, and Wyatt heard Melody say, "Congratu-fucking-lations, Wyatt. It's about time."

Wyatt's world slowed just slightly as he took a sip of the sparkling wine. All of the chaos of the last several weeks played through his mind like an old-time picture show. The grainy quality of the film of his memories, and the click of the reel rolled through moment after moment. Everything had felt like such a whirlwind of emotions from the failed gallery, the learning Jackson had passed, to now choosing a documentary series development deal with H.B.O. Again, Wyatt felt the tinge of confusion creep insidiously into the back of his mind. The painting, the letter, the promise of wildest dreams… so far he had followed the rules, and added a stroke of paint each day since receiving the work, and so far… it was working.

Internally, Wyatt shook his head, and thought, *grow up.* Rationally, Wyatt knew it was impossible that canvas, solvents, resins, colored pigments and additives were dictating a sudden burst of creative success.

Wyatt had worked his entire life for this exact moment. He had earned these opportunities, and he would be damned to let some sort of charmed, or cursed, painting be the reason. These successes were Wyatt's, and nothing else. He refused to believe it any other way. He held up his glass, and it met Melody's.

"Thank you, Mel. It is about goddamn time."

Clink.

They both took a sip, and set their glasses down, as their meals were dropped off at their table. Melody set her bag on the ground next to her feet, when they both heard a faint voice call out from a table nearby.

"Wyatt Brone?" The voice spoke, hesitant. Wyatt looked towards the voice, then back to Melody, before his eyes returned to searching for the phantom voice. A woman from a few tables over waved her hand, and stood up to approach them. Wyatt noticed the paper she held in her hands.

The New York fucking *Times.*

The woman quickly scurried over towards their table, and had a smile that matched Melody's.

"You're Wyatt Brone, aren't you?" The woman exclaimed, as she immediately crossed referenced the newspaper in her hands. "Yeah, this is totally you! You're the painter. From the paper." Wyatt was not sure how to respond, and simply awkwardly laughed and fidgeted in his chair.

"Hi, uh — yes, that's —" He started to respond before the woman yelled out to her friend back at their table.

"Susan, I told you, it's him! It's the guy from the paper!"

There is a certain phenomenon that occurs periodically in Los Angeles. Anytime someone sees anyone recognizable in public, their normal inhibitions immediately fall away. They lose their ability to rationally function as a normal, sane person in public. They create "a moment," mainly for themselves, but that moment always seems to garner the attention of everyone nearby. The crowd will start to take notice, not because the subject of the attention is *actually* well known or recognizable, but simply because it is Los Angeles, and they *might* be.

This was exactly what happened the moment Susan also got up from their table, and approached Wyatt and Melody.

People at nearby tables began hushed murmurs, and pointed and stared at Wyatt and Melody. At first, Wyatt uncomfortably obliged the two women for a photograph together, and he added a quick, scribble signature to their copy of *The New York Times.* It was after they both wanted individual photographs together that a few other cafe patrons stood up, and made their way over to Wyatt and Melody's table. One group begot another group, who begot another group, before there was a large crowd gathered around the small, rooftop, cafe table.

Wyatt could feel Melody getting slightly uncomfortable, and she started to disappear in the midst of the growing crowd. They had learned who it was they were now hounding, and the patrons began shouting his name. They asked for photographs, and autographs, and had started to become a little relentless.

Wyatt, standing next to the table, turned to his sister, and helped her gather her things. Melody tossed down a couple of twenty-dollar bills onto the table, and she and Wyatt started making their way through the crowd for a quick exit.

The cafe's staff stepped in just in time to help usher Melody and Wyatt through the crowd and into the elevator, where the door shut almost instantly behind them. They were alone, and immediately burst into laughter.

"Are you okay?" Wyatt asked, checking in on his older sister.

"Ha! Am I okay? Are you okay?!" Melody laughed back.

"I'm fine… good lord," Wyatt said laughing.

"You're it now," Melody laughed back. "You might need to start investing in some security."

"Don't worry, I still have the little handgun you yelled at me for getting. I'll be just fine." Wyatt laughed, held up his hand into a gun shape, and winked at his overprotective sister.

"I don't want to talk about that, you know how I feel about guns." She said.

"I know, I know. It's locked up, I promise. I have that stand up safe in my closet." He said. "What the hell was that up there?" Wyatt shook his head in joyous disbelief.

"I told you! It's happening."

"I guess people just really love art," Wyatt said, and they both laughed with each other as they felt the elevator start its descent to the lobby floor. "So fast, though! This is unbelievable…" Wyatt said again, and they both finally caught their breath.

"Wyatt, these are all of your wildest dreams. They're happening."

Wyatt looked at his sister, and they locked eyes. For a moment, his brain was transfixed on the words she chose to use. "Your wildest dreams."

Wyatt realized that he was blankly staring at her, so he smiled and exaggerated shaking his head, and laughed awkwardly.

"Yeah, I guess so." He said back.

"Buckle up, bro." Melody smirked. "This is just the beginning." The elevator doors chimed open, and a small crowd had already gathered in the lobby. Wyatt and Melody looked at each other and burst into laughter. They somehow made their way through the crowd, and out to the valet, where Melody already had a car waiting for them both.

Wyatt took a moment, breathed deeply, and then repeated the sentiment to himself. He forced a quick smile and looked down to his feet. His mind raced, and he took an even deeper breath.

"Just the beginning."

CHAPTER 9

Wyatt's ride home felt long.

It felt objectively longer than Wyatt knew it rationally was. Maybe it was the unending red lights along the boulevard, or perhaps it was the overpopulated city he continued to live in, though its population only increased. Whatever the reason for the delay, the typical, and anticipated fifteen to twenty minute ride from the rooftop cafe back to Wyatt's workspace loft seemed to last an hour, if not longer. Wyatt checked his watch… it was longer. Wyatt remained silent and still in the backseat of his Lyft, and tried to notice every detail of the buildings that he passed by. If this was the opening act, the prologue, of what his career would become, and it seemed to be shaping into the initial phases of just that, he wanted to make sure he stayed cognizant and present for every single, waking moment. To miss anything about what was surely to come would certainly be a disappointing loss. Wyatt knew this was the beginning of a moment in his brief life that he would likely never again experience: the moment before. He refused to let that loss become his reality, or his outcome.

Wyatt took a slow, deep, and drawn out breath, and noticed every passing detail. The cracked brick facade of the apartment buildings that lined Sixth Street and Spring Street in his downtown Los Angeles neighborhood. The various coffee shops and trendy eateries filled with millennials drowning out the frustration of not being able to afford a home with overpriced, oat milk lattes. The street vendors grilling bacon wrapped hot dogs with an assortment of grilled onions and peppers. A delicious, and shockingly filling snack available pretty much any time of day. Wyatt could almost smell the steam rising up from the grilled food as his car drove past.

Wyatt passed the same newspaper stand from the opening night of his gallery, and his heart skipped a beat. He realized the magazine his uncle had been on the cover of just a short week before had been replaced with a stack of the newest issue of *The New York Times* with *his* face on the front page. The image of the newspaper cover lining the side of the stand remained in Wyatt's mind. He thought about how his face had literally replaced his uncle's, and it was because of his art. *Unbelievable,* Wyatt thought.

Wyatt immediately felt the tears that had begun to well in his eyes, and a deep warmth of pride grew in his gut, and flushed his cheeks. It was something he was feeling within himself for the first time in as many years as he could remember. He was in the midst of realizing his dreams. Again, he made sure to truly, and viscerally, sit in every moment.

He arrived back at his loft building, and said a quick, "thank you," to his driver. Instead of the expected, "You're welcome," Wyatt simply heard the response of, "Five Stars, please."

"Sure thing," Wyatt responded, and let the car door cut off his response.

Wyatt stood on the cracked, urine stained sidewalk for just a moment. He took a breath and tilted his head up to look to the sky. The height of the buildings on his block never ceased to amaze him. They stood as a true feat of man's capacity to dream, the living proof that any height can be conquered, and any goal, no matter how outlandish or unrealistic, can, in fact, be achieved. He smiled, and felt the breeze gently roll across his face. In the midst of such unkept, metropolitan disarray, Wyatt found a moment of beautiful peace.

Overwhelmed with the morning, Wyatt shouted out with excitement. Luckily for him, a stranger shouting on the street in this particular area was not something novel, and no one around him seemed to care; or notice, for that matter. He did not feel embarrassed by the overwhelming emotions that boiled inside of himself. It felt nice to release some of the building anticipation in his nervous system.

For as long as Wyatt could remember, success in his art was his unachievable skyscraper. His paintings were the only thing he could imagine himself doing with, or giving his life to. Somehow, success in his art had also become the only thing that seemed the most unrealistic and out of reach for his future. After years and years of constant "no's," Wyatt had yearned deeply for just a single "yes."

The idea that all of these efforts and failures were beginning to potentially resolve in a perfect fourth was overwhelming, but an *overwhelmed* feeling that Wyatt both welcomed, and warmly, eagerly embraced. He had stayed ready, as they say, so he had no need to get ready.

He walked into his building, and the doorman immediately greeted him with a warm tone.

"Hiya, Wyatt! Great to see you. Morning going good?" He said with a smile and cheerful inflection. He dressed casually, even though he was at work. His jeans were expensive, his loose fitting button-up shirt was recently pressed, and his long hair was hidden underneath a designer beanie. He always had a kind demeanor, and sat behind the small desk just inside the building with his legs kicked up.

"Honestly, about as good as a morning can get," Wyatt said back, and smiled.

"My man! That's what I'm talking about." The doorman pointed at Wyatt, then pumped his fist in the air.

Wyatt saw his doorman press the button to call the elevator down to the lobby floor from wherever it was, and he gave the doorman a quick "thank you" nod. As Wyatt continued to walk away, and into the elevator hallway, Wyatt heard the doorman call out to him.

"Hey — uh, Wyatt! I saw the paper this morning. *The Times.* Very, very cool! Keep it up, my guy, very cool," he said.

Wyatt stopped, and smiled. He turned back towards the doorman, and nodded almost to himself. "Thank you, really. That means a lot," Wyatt said, before he turned and continued on his way to the elevator. Again, the doorman pointed at Wyatt, and pumped his fist in the air. Wyatt laughed as he heard the doorman repeat himself.

"My man. That's what's up."

The lift chimed, the elevator door slid open, and Wyatt stepped in.

Once inside, he leaned against the back wall of the metal box, and rested his body weight against the handrail. Again, Wyatt felt the tears pool in his eyes. He felt truly shocked, and could not believe this was happening.

His keys jingled in the lock on his door, before he heard the click of his dead bolt, and gently pushed his door open. He took a couple of steps in, shut the door behind him, and tossed his keys down into a small bowl on a table in his entryway. He gently stretched his head towards his shoulder to the right, and felt the soft crack of his neck. Wyatt repeated the moment to the left, and exhaled a slight sense of release from popping his neck in both directions.

The sun again burst through the small opening in his window shades. Wyatt's brain immediately caught a glimpse of the tiny dust particles as they danced in the beam of sunlight. He wondered how they choreographed each move in perfect unison with each other. Small, insignificant specks of nothing, creating an elaborate dance on an invisible stage. Wyatt found himself thankful, and felt lucky to be the audience of one.

Wyatt started walking towards the window to pull the shades open, and let the natural sunlight fill his room, when the hairs on the back of Wyatt's neck stood straight up. Like a faint whisper from over his shoulder, he felt a subtle pull towards the painting in his secondary space. For a moment, he thought he heard a whisper, before deciding it was in his head.

Wyatt slowly turned around to his left, and looked at the solitary, white door frame. Without hesitating, he slowly put one foot in front of the other, and stepped towards the room. At the doorway, he put his hand on the frame, and stood for just a moment.

There it was, facing the opposite end of the room.

The pulling intensified, and Wyatt quickly took several more steps in its direction.

Before another moment passed, Wyatt stood in front of the painting. He paused, and felt the sudden weight of silence as his eyes first caught glimpse of the painted canvas. The small, visible strokes of different colored paints layered on top of one another. The texture of individual bristles within each stroke.

Jackson came to Wyatt's mind. The work, and the time, that Jackson had no doubt dedicated to this piece, only to have Wyatt continue that journey for some yet unknown reason. What was Jackson's endgame with willing this piece to Wyatt? And more than that, what on earth was the reasoning for the note with no context? Wyatt always knew Jackson to be the eccentric type, but this seemed over the top, even for him.

Wyatt, feeling compelled by the urge to contribute to the painting's chaos, picked up his palette and a single brush. He took a slight step towards the piece.

Wyatt studied the piece. He took his closest examination of the canvas he had to this point. He noticed each individual stroke, each color. He recognized in the piece itself several, competing styles and techniques of painting. This confused Wyatt, and he leaned in, literally and figuratively.

Impressionism was an art movement in the late nineteenth century characterized by small, thin, yet very visible brush strokes.

Its use of open compositions and emphasis on the accurate representation of light and how light interacts with the world quickly became a hallmark trait of the movement's most relevant pieces. Impressionism's early stages in Paris in the late eighteen hundreds gave way to such great artists like Claude Monet, Edgar Degas, who, ironically, actually despised the term "impressionist," and maybe most famously, the post-impressionist Vincent Van Gogh; three of the more universally known impressionist painters. Then, of course, there was Jackson Brone.

Jackson Brone was known as an "abstract impressionist," combining the two recognizable styles. He used the techniques and styles of classical impressionism, but used this styles to build out abstract stories and imagery. Whereas Van Gogh would utilize these techniques to paint strikingly accurate self-portraits, and the vibrant sidewalk eatery in *Cafe Terrace at Night,* Jackson Brone used them to create visceral emotions on woven cloth. His use of short, thick strokes captured the essence of what he was feeling, as opposed to the movement of light, and passage of time in the physical world.

This was a subtle distinction, but proved paramount to the immense, global success Jackson had found during his career.

As a young and amateur artist, Wyatt wanted nothing more than to emulate, and be compared to his uncle. He was aware of the notoriety Jackson had gained, and he paid clear attention to how other creatives and non-creatives alike discussed his uncle's professional achievements. It was a universal respect that Jackson commanded, and it was all because of his art. His art and his mind.

It was all Wyatt wanted.

He wanted that attention. He wanted that adoration and admiration. If Wyatt was being very honest with himself, a part of him wanted that fame as well. That, however, had become something Wyatt let go of rather quickly. More so out of necessity, rather than desire.

Jackson never strayed from this technique. From his earliest works, to his final known completed piece, Jackson heavily utilized and fully relied on his impressionist style.

In examining this piece, however, Wyatt could easily see the influences of several other styles of painting. It perplexed Wyatt, and gave way to an even deeper intrigue about this piece. He wondered what played through his uncle's mind as the painting was being planned and created. It did not make sense.

Wyatt noted portions of the canvas that clearly displayed beautiful simply realist attributes. He thought he could make out the gentle features of a woman's face underneath a chaotic splatter of green. Wyatt noticed another example of what he assumed was an animal of some kind, very clearly in a Fauvist style. Bright, unrealistic colors outlining a creature he could not quite place in his mind. Wyatt also noticed several portions of the massive canvas that seemed to highlight aspects of the Madhubari style.

Wyatt, disoriented from the painting's lack of solidarity, took a step back and squeezed his chin in his hand. He could not make sense of it.

He had followed his uncle's career for his entire adult life, at times closer than he seemed to follow his own. Wyatt had never known Jackson to stray from his preferred style... abstract impressionism. *This just does not any make sense,* Wyatt thought. He was staring at it, however. He felt his mind start to wander, explaining away the unbelievable.

Perhaps Jackson has felt pigeonholed into the abstract impressionist box he had built himself into, and found solace in the experimentation of different techniques in a canvas never meant for anyone else's eyes? Again, the letter came to the forefront of Wyatt's mind.

"To nev'r showeth and nev'r bid, f'r 'twill beest yours..." ...to *never show and never tell, for it will be yours.*

For some reason, this made sense to Wyatt at this particular moment, and would explain away the first "rule" written down on the letter his uncle also left him. A safe space to express other styles and creative techniques that Jackson knew he could never let anyone see.

Wyatt's mind immediately called to question the following two statements from the letter.

"To nev'r stand ho and nev'r selleth, f'r 'twill beest yours…" …*to never stop and never sell, for it will be yours.*

If Wyatt was to believe that this canvas had become his uncle's creative safe room, then surely he could stand to believe that Jackson had imposed a commitment to himself to never cease working on it. To never stop trying new things, exploring new outlets, and mastering new styles and techniques. Again, the "rules" of this letter seemed to be falling into realistic sense for Wyatt's pragmatic mind.

Then there was the final "rule."

"Followeth these to wildest dreams, f'r 'twill beest yours…" …*follow these, to wildest dreams, for it will be yours.*

Again, Wyatt found himself begging for rationalization of this final command. Conceptually, Wyatt long understood the idea of the "hustle." American society as he knew it celebrated those that sacrificed everything for their craft, whatever that craft may be. Jackson, being recognizably the most favorite artist of his generation, would not have been free of that burden. Wyatt thought that it made sense for Jackson to have, again, committed to himself that if he continued developing his craft, and continued working on his art, and continued bettering himself as an artist writ large, that he would eventually see success in said art.

A commitment Wyatt had made to himself as a child, and success that Wyatt was seemingly on the precipice of experiencing.

There it was. Wyatt had cracked the code of this mysterious inheritance. He had unlocked the hidden message in the paint and oil of this work, and he felt a wave of calm wash over his entire body.

For a moment, he felt the presence of his uncle. He felt a warm sense of solidarity amidst the usual anxiety and apprehensive distress his relationship with Jackson had normally caused. He felt at peace, and he almost felt a sense that Jackson was proud of him too. A feeling he was undoubtedly putting within himself.

Wyatt exhaled, almost relieved at this sudden realization. There was no curse, and in the same instant, Wyatt felt a little foolish that he had even entertained the idea of a mysterious, magical enchantment of the stretch cloth on the thin wooden frame. Wyatt did still feel the urge to add paint to its surface, however.

Instead, Wyatt set his brush and palette down.

He took a small step back, and stared at the painting a little longer.

Admittedly, Wyatt still thought the letter he was given was a weird detail, and an object he could not quite explain. Now, however, having cracked the symbolism behind the words, Wyatt felt more at ease. He picked up the letter from a small table near the painting, folded it into a smaller square of paper, and slid it into a shoulder bag he had sitting in the corner of the room.

Wyatt walked out of the secondary room, and back into his kitchen.

He still felt a sense of calm about him, and he looked at a small, circular wall clock to see the time. It was just past 2:35 P.M. Wyatt laughed, and thought to himself, *it's five o'clock somewhere,* before he popped the cork of a bottle of whiskey, and poured himself two fingers of neat rye. He quickly tossed the liquor back, and poured himself another.

He walked his drink over towards his towering windows, and he felt the faint buzz of his cell phone in his pocket. He thought Melody must have an update about the H.B.O. contract that they had started discussing at their lunch, so he decided to answer the call quickly. Wyatt kept his eyes on the man on the street corner, yelling at tourists as they nervously walked past, Wyatt pulled the phone out of his pocket, and slid the virtual "answer" button across the bottom of the screen. He held the phone to his ear.

"This is Wyatt," he said. The very slight hint of a slur in his voice was a sudden reminder that Wyatt had not actually had the chance to eat any of his scheduled lunch with Melody earlier in the day.

"Wyatt, this is Det. Johns, L.A.P.D. Homicide division." Wyatt felt his heart skip a beat for a moment, and the dread of someone who accidentally answered a call they meant to screen. "Did I catch you at an okay time?"

Shit, Wyatt thought.

Within his group of friends, Wyatt had become known for screening his called. He had actually become quite good at avoiding nearly all unwanted interactions over the phone. Wyatt hesitated for a moment, frustrated with himself for answering the call without checking to see who it was from. Before Wyatt responded to the detective on the other line, he realized he was holding his personal cell phone.

Had he given the detectives his personal cell phone? He racked his brain, trying to remember each of his previous interactions with the detectives. He could not remember giving them anything, much less his protected, private, and personal cell phone number.

"Wyatt, are you there?" Det. Johns asked after a moment waiting.

Before Wyatt let too much silence pass by, he finally responded into the microphone of his cell phone, "Det. Johns, hi. I actually am sort of in the middle of so—" Det. Johns interrupted him. Something Det. Johns, to this point, had been careful not to do.

"Wyatt, listen, unfortunately our investigation has become a little more serious than before. I know we have mentioned wanting you to come down to the station, but at this point, I think we are actually going to *need* you to." There was a slight moment of silence.

"I don't understand," Wyatt said back slowly, trying to conceal his lack of food, and abundance of alcohol. "I thought you said this was a formality."

"We have had some recent updates that have taken this from a formality, to a little more serious." Det. Johns was short, and Wyatt could tell there was a slight edge to his voice.

"I think I need you to be a little more clear?" Wyatt hesitated, still trying to speak slowly.

"Well, Mr. Brone, we just think it would be best for you to come down to the station as soon as you are able to. We can discuss things with you there, and we can get that statement we need from you." Again, Det. Johns spoke quickly, with a cold, unwelcoming tone.

"I think —" Again, Wyatt was interrupted.

"We can have an escort pick you up as soon as you say you are free, and bring you down. If you think that would make it a little easier."

"With all due respect, Det. Johns, I —"

"With all due respect, Mr. Brone, we think it's time you made this a priority."

Wyatt stood for a moment in silence. He could feel his heart beat increasing with a sense of frustration, and slight anger. "Again, we can have a squad car at your door within ten minutes of you letting us know you are ready, but unfortunately, this is no longer a… casual request. We will compel you, if we need to, however we would prefer it not need to come to that." Again, Wyatt stayed silent for a moment. His thoughts raced and were as chaotic as paint normally is in his works.

"That won't be necessary, Detective." Wyatt gritted his teeth in his mouth, and took a slow deep breath through his nose.

"So you will make time for us?" Det. Johns asked, but still showed no warmth in his voice.

"Of course," Wyatt responded with a fake smile he hoped the detective could hear through the phone.

"Wonderful. When should we expect you?" Det. Johns asked.

"How is right now?" Wyatt asked, and pressed his fingers into his forehead. He could tell he was starting to get a headache, and knew he would need to shove something to eat into his stomach before meeting the two detectives.

"Now is great for us. Should we send an officer?" Det. Johns asked, still dry and unwelcoming.

"No, that's fine. I can be there within the next half hour or so?" Wyatt asked, again looking at the clock on his wall.

"Wonderful. We will see you then." Before Wyatt could respond, he heard Det. Johns hang up the other end of the line. Wyatt pulled the phone away from his ear, and looked at his cell phone's screen.

The glass display showed the words "Call Ended" and that the caller was from a blocked number. Again, Wyatt wondered how they even had gotten his personal number to begin with.

Wyatt stood next to his bed, chewing an entire banana in his mouth as he pulled a shirt over his chest. He walked into his bathroom, applied deodorant, and finished chewing his banana before he brushed his teeth.

Wyatt splashed some water onto his face, and rinsed his mouth out with mouthwash.

The last thing he wanted was for the two L.A.P.D. homicide detectives to smell alcohol on his breath when he reiterated to them that he did not, in fact, murder his uncle.

Surely, they are not stupid enough to think I actually killed Jackson, Wyatt thought to himself. Even the idea of that being a possibility seemed outlandish, and remarkably annoying to him. What would even be the point of killing his uncle? And what possible reason would *they* have to think as such? Wyatt had not even spoken to his uncle in longer than he could actually remember. The idea that these two strangers would honestly believe that he had something to do with his uncle's death made him angry, and beyond vexed.

Even so, there he stood. He fixed his hair, and tried to make himself look as presentable as possible.

He stared at himself in his dirty, smudgy bathroom mirror, splattered with water and toothpaste, and shook his head. *This is so fucking stupid,* he thought to himself.

He walked back into his kitchen and grabbed a piece of gluten-free, whole wheat bread before he turned to walk towards his front door. He shoved the whole slice of wheat bread into his mouth, and chewed it feverishly.

As Wyatt made his way towards his front door, he stopped in the doorway of his secondary room. He did not even look inside, but he felt that strange pull from before again. This time, however, it felt as though it was physically pulling his body towards the painting. It was as if this painting had its own gravitational field, and Wyatt was a satellite caught in its wake.

He slowly turned his head towards the painting, and he felt the rush of blood pounding in his fingertips. Chills gently shook his entire body, and he felt a ping of sensation as every single hair stood up on the back of his neck. *What is happening…* Wyatt thought.

He started to take a step towards the painting, before he grunted, and snapped himself out of it. Wyatt looked at the painting again. He tilted his head to the side, and almost felt like he could hear those same strange whispers, as he had before. Though he could not explain how, or why for that matter, Wyatt knew in his heart that the painting was calling to him. Again, he felt the undeniable urge to add paint to the canvas.

"What are you doing?" Wyatt asked himself, out loud. "This is insane. You're literally going crazy." Wyatt almost laughed at himself, and how absurd he felt in that moment. He shook his head, and again, resisted the unrealistic urge to work on the piece.

He continued his walk towards his front door, grabbed his keys from the table in the entryway, and opened his door to leave.

In the doorway, he paused for a moment, and looked back towards the room with the painting.

What was this feeling? What was this insane urge, and pull he felt from this object? It was simply canvas stretched onto a wooden frame. He had never experienced the urge to work on something so intensely before, not even one of his own pieces. It felt primal… uncontrollable. Wyatt knew he could not rationally explain what it was that he was experiencing, but he also knew he could not deny that he was, in fact, experiencing it. A strange phenomena that he had never felt before.

Confusion transformed into annoyance; frustration transformed into feeling slightly flustered. Unable to process it all, Wyatt simply left his loft. He closed the door and locked it behind him. Wyatt paused for just a moment. He inhaled his grief, and exhaled his joy. *What was that?* He thought. Wyatt then made his way to the elevator.

He pulled his phone out of his pocket, opened up his ride sharing app, and requested a car to the police station just down the street where he would finally meet with Det. Johns and Det. Foss. Wyatt felt nervous as the elevator rumbled, and made its way to the lobby floor. He reminded himself to breathe. He took another deep, slow breath and tried to calm his heart beat, and shook his head.

"Here goes nothing," Wyatt said to himself before sarcastically saying aloud. "Thanks, Jack."

CHAPTER 10

The station was freezing cold.

Located in the heart of downtown, the Los Angeles Police Department headquarters had a massive, beautiful building at the corner of West 1st Street and South Main St. Its massive stature loomed large in the neighborhood it stood in. From the outside, you would not be sure if you were looking at a contemporary opera theater, or a space station from the year 2744. Its triangle shaped roof only further drove home the futuristic, unnecessary size. It was completed in 2009 and is estimated to have cost $245 million. Compared directly to the former headquarters you would not even know they were built on the same planet, much less in the same city.

It's beautiful though, Wyatt thought. *It had better be.* Wyatt chuckled to himself, and smiled again as he looked up and around the massive, intimidating lobby.

His shoes clipped and clopped against the floor, and Wyatt felt a hint of embarrassment at the sound as he walked from the entrance doors to the main lobby desk to check in. The young man behind the desk smiled, and made note of Wyatt's arrival. He gestured over to a small set of chairs to the left, and let Wyatt know that someone would come get him shortly.

Wyatt sat in an uncomfortable, wooden chair in the lobby entrance way of the headquarters for the Los Angeles Police Department. Some sun broke through the towering wall of windows, and illuminated the lobby near a check in desk, but the heat stayed outside. In any other circumstance, the freezing room would have been a blessing of air conditioning that Wyatt would welcome with open arms, to the sun-like heat of his body's core. In that moment, however, Wyatt would have preferred a little warmth.

Wyatt nervously wrung his hands together, and noticed his fingers were losing their color. He was frantically bouncing his foot up and down on the ground to try to generate some level of heat. He quickly rubbed his hands against his dark, denim jeans and felt the sting of friction on his palms. He stopped bouncing his leg and focused on the feeling of the flats of both feet firmly against the ground. He did not know why he felt as nervous as he did. He laughed a little to himself thinking that he felt like a school aged boy that was just called into the principal's office for some unknown reason. Or like a driver on the road that notices a California Highway Patrol squad car trailing behind him. He knew he had done nothing wrong, but his blood pressure would suggest otherwise. He checked the time on his watch, and adjusted the band on his wrist. His appointment with Detective Thomas Johns and Detective Gerry Foss had been confirmed just fifteen minutes earlier than it was now. Wyatt rolled his eyes, and noticed that his leg had started chaotically bobbing up and down again.

He supposed that he did not feel nervous, per se, but rather uncomfortable. The overly chilled temperature of the room, the stale and flickering fluorescent lighting, and the loud, echoing clicks of heels and fine dress shoe soles against the marbled flooring was the perfect storm of some of Wyatt's least favorite things.

He tilted his head to the left until he cracked his neck and looked out the large, front building windows. Cars passed, people walked by, all oblivious to Wyatt's frustration about feeling like he was about to waste an entire afternoon with two people he had no interest in talking to. He did not understand why they had even become so desperate to get Wyatt in person for questioning. *Jackson died,* he thought. *No, Jackson killed himself. That is it. What the hell am I supposed to add?* He felt himself grow more and more agitated at his inevitable circumstance.

The faint, echoed clicks of heels on the floor got slightly louder, and Wyatt looked up to see a woman approaching directly towards him. She wore a simple blouse and neat skirt, and her glasses completed the very put together appearance of someone who was dressed for the job they wanted, not the job they had.

"Mr. Brone?" She asked with a soft voice. Wyatt cracked a small smile, and lifted his hand.

"That would be me," he said.

"Great to meet you, I'm Julie." She extended her hand, and he shook it.

"Nice to meet you as well," Wyatt responded. He gathered his things, stood up, and extended his hand to the woman. She smiled back, and shook his hand.

"Thank you so much for your patience as well, Det. Johns and Det. Foss are ready for you now," she said. "Please, just follow me, right this way," she turned and walked back in the same direction she had just come from.

Wyatt looked behind him at the chair he was sitting at to make sure he had not left anything behind, then he followed her to an entrance into the cold belly of the building.

The woman ushered Wyatt over to a line of security and metal detectors. Julie flashed her badge and passed through with no problems, while Wyatt set his belongings down on a table, and walked through the metal detector. He walked through, and heard a faint beep sound before one of the guards held up her hand, signaling Wyatt to stop for a moment. He watched her face as she scanned a screen behind him, and stared at it. After a few seconds, the woman motioned to Wyatt to continue on without saying a word to him.

"Thanks," Wyatt said, as he picked his things up, and made eye contact with Julie. She smiled at him, and he returned the gesture. Wyatt walked over to her, and Julie immediately started walking down the narrow hallway. Still cold, and still lit with unwelcoming, flickering fluorescent lights.

"It's just right down here," Julie said, and walked away. Wyatt kept pace.

He followed her in silence farther down the narrow hallway, before they arrived at an opened door to their left.

"Just in here, Det. Johns and Det. Foss will be in shortly. Make yourself comfortable." Wyatt peered inside the small room, and saw the makings of a stereotypical interrogation room. He slightly shook his head, annoyed, and if Julie had not been looking at him, he felt his eyes would have rolled out of his head.

"Thank you so much," he said instead.

"Can I get you anything? Water, coffee?" Julie asked.

"A coffee would be amazing, thank you."

"Cream and sugar?" She asked.

"Cream, no sugar. Thank you so much," Wyatt said.

Wyatt took a few steps inside the small, freezing room. He set his things down on the steel table, and expected to hear a response from Julie in the doorway. Instead, he heard the loud slam of the door against its frame. The concrete walls and flooring made the slam sound even louder. He jumped a little, and shot his glance to the now closed door.

"Well then," Wyatt laughed to himself. "Guess I'll make myself cozy."

Wyatt sat in the small, metal chair, and looked around the room. The two-way mirror on the far wall overlooking the entire space; the small divots on the metal table where they attach a suspect's handcuffs to; the small, almost cliche metal table with chairs on either side.

Wyatt felt chills sprint across his body, and realized why the police were notoriously so good at extracting false confessions.

"Is it always this cold in here?" Wyatt asked the two-way mirror, fully making a mockery of the situation.

Wyatt could see it already: Det. Johns sitting down, playing Dr. Good Cop, while Det. Foss paced around the room with the scowl of Mr. Bad Cop. He laughed to himself, before shaking his head.

What a waste of my fucking time, Wyatt thought.

Wyatt unsuccessfully tried to get comfortable in the impossible metal chair, and sat for an amount of time that started to make him frustrated. He looked at the watch on his wrist, and saw that this meeting was now almost forty-five minutes late.

He exhaled, and shook his head again. He debated how it would look if he left. He would feel it was justified, but then he thought better of it.

Finally, he heard the click of the door handle, and watched it creak open. Detectives Thomas Johns, and Gerry Foss, entered the small, dingy interrogation room. Det. Johns held two coffees, one in either hand, and Det. Foss tossed his coat down over the back of one of the chairs opposite Wyatt. They both greeted him with smiles and apologies.

"Wyatt, my God, I'm so sorry we are so late. You wouldn't believe the morning we've had," Det. Johns said.

"No worries at all, happy we could make this work." Wyatt responded, lying.

"Coffee, right? Julie handed it off to me," Det. Johns extended the second coffee in his hand to Wyatt while he took a sip from the other.

"Yes, thank you so much," Wyatt took the hot, paper cup from the Detective.

"Of course. It's not Blue Bottle, but it's hot and free."

"It'll do," Wyatt said and smiled at the men.

"Yes, it will." Det. Johns smiled back and pulled one of the chairs out from under the table. The legs squealed loudly against the floor.

Predictably, he sat down, and placed his coffee on the table, while Det. Foss remained standing, already staring at Wyatt.

Wyatt smiled, and quietly laughed to himself. *Here we go,* he thought.

"Wyatt, thank you so much for taking the time to come down and chat with us today, it means a lot. And it's extremely helpful for us." Det. Johns started in. "I know this has been sort of a hassle to get confirmed, but we appreciate it." He set his briefcase on the table, and lifted it open.

"Happy to help," Wyatt responded, keeping himself short.

"Some of this will likely feel weird, maybe uncomfortable, and unnecessarily formal, so just bare with us, if you don't mind. Our apologies in advance." Det. Johns continued as he pulled a small recording device from his opened briefcase, and set it down on the table.

"No problem," Wyatt responded, and then looked to Det. Foss who had yet to look away. "All part of the process, I'd imagine."

"That's right. All just part of the gig," Det. Johns clicked a button on the recording device. He looked up at Wyatt. "You don't mind do you?" Wyatt shook his head "no."

"By all means," Wyatt said.

"All part of the —" Det. Johns started to repeat himself, when Wyatt finished his thought for him.

"—part of the gig. I understand." Wyatt smiled. Det. Johns laughed, and pulled out a couple of file folders from his briefcase. He opened them, and settled for a moment.

"This is Detective Thomas Johns, and Detective Gerry Foss, with the Los Angeles Police Department Homicide Division. The date is June 17th, 2024. The time is 1524 hours. We are in Interview Room number 11. Wyatt, if you don't mind giving us your full name, and date of birth." He did not look up at Wyatt. Foss kept looking directly at Wyatt.

"My name is Wyatt Brone, my birthday is September 20th, 1991." Wyatt said and took a sip of coffee.

"Now Wyatt, you are here on your own free will, is that correct?" Det. Johns still did not look up from his papers.

"That is correct," Wyatt said.

"Thank you," Det. Johns finally broke his stare with the words on his papers, and smiled at Wyatt. "Thank you for coming in, Wyatt. Now as you are aware, Det. Foss and I are investigating the recent, and tragic death of your uncle, Jackson Brone. We are connecting with anyone we can that knew your uncle, or were particularly close with your uncle. As we have discussed, this investigation is primarily looking to confirm the currently stated cause of death, as suicide. Is this all accurate to your understanding?" Det. Johns looked back to his papers. Wyatt fidgeted a little in his seat, and he felt Det. Foss' eyes unrelenting, still singularly glued onto him.

"To my knowledge that is correct, yes." Wyatt said.

"And have you been in contact with anyone that has disclosed that they have interviewed with us?"

"I have not," Wyatt said, and there was a hint of confusion in the question. Wyatt realized he had not even asked Melody if she had connected with them, nor was he aware if they had interviewed her yet either.

"Great. Now, Wyatt, would you mind giving us a brief background of your relationship with your uncle, Jackson Brone?" Det. Johns again looked up from his papers for just long enough to shoot a small smile to Wyatt. Wyatt assumed this was his attempt to try to make Wyatt feel somewhat comfortable.

"Uh — my uncle and I had a — tenuous relationship, I would say?" Wyatt responded delicately.

"Tenuous? How do you mean?" Det. Johns followed up.

"We weren't very close. Maybe more so when I was younger, after my parents passed, but not really as an adult. My sister was always closer to Uncle Jack." Wyatt noticed how, as he predicted, Det. Foss had begun to pace slowly around the small room.

"Did you find yourself envious of your sister's relationship with your uncle?" Det. Johns asked, and Wyatt noticed he began to jot down certain anecdotes on his notepad.

"Absolutely not," Wyatt said. "We weren't close, but I didn't hate him. We didn't have a bad relationship, we just weren't close, is all."

"Understood," Det. Johns said, and smiled politely again. He jotted down something else, and then flipped one of his papers over. "Wyatt, I have some uncomfortable questions that I have to ask, so my apologies in advance, I am not intending any offense." Wyatt pushed his eyebrows together, and took his time responding.

"Okay," is all Wyatt had to say. Wyatt watched as Det. Johns looked at a paper in his hands, and Wyatt presumed they were notes for the upcoming questions.

"Do you know how long your uncle had been a patient of Dr. Erich Scholden?" Det. Johns asked, and both detectives looked at Wyatt for his answer.

"I — I don't know who that is." Wyatt furrowed his brow, confused. Det. Johns also looked confused.

"Dr. Scholden? Your uncle's psychiatrist." He said back.

Wyatt shook his head, and repeated his previous answer. "Like I said, I don't know who that is. I didn't know my uncle was seeing a psychiatrist."

"Wyatt, how aware were you of your uncle's mental state as of late?"

"How do you mean?" Wyatt asked, confused.

"Were you aware of his recent inpatient visit to the Reddick Neuropsychiatric Center?" Wyatt stared at Det. Johns face for a moment.

"I was not," he said back, still confused.

"So you were completely unaware that your uncle had a… sort of… breakdown a few weeks before he took his life?" Det. Johns wrote something down, then looked at Wyatt's face.

"I am finding out right now, actually," Wyatt said, and leaned back in his chair.

"Interesting." Det. Johns said. "Were you aware of your uncle's arrest on Thursday, May 11th?"

"I'm sorry?" Wyatt leaned back in.

"I'll take that as a 'no,' then." Det. Johns smiled, wrote more notes, then put his attention back on Wyatt. "Were you aware of his recent abuse of his prescription medications? He had multiple prescriptions for medications like Amisulpride, and Isordil?

"I didn't know my uncle was taking any particular medications." Wyatt said.

"So I can assume you are also unaware of his recent psychotic episodes? Which is why he had just gotten a recent prescription for Amisulpride?"

"I was not aware my uncle was taking any antipsychotic medication."

Wyatt watched as Det. Foss stopped pacing only to resume his stare. He also watched as Det. Johns jotted down more notes with every answer he gave.

"Wyatt, when was the last time you heard from your uncle?" Both detectives looked at Wyatt with almost a synchronized motion.

"Uh — it's been — it *had* been — I don't know, maybe... two months? Maybe three?"

"Can you try to remember?" Det. Foss finally spoke. Wyatt tried, but truly could not remember the last conversation he had had with his uncle.

"My sister, Melody, spoke with him a couple of weeks before my recent gallery opening, but I didn't. I would say probably two or three months, I'm sorry, I really don't remember when, exactly."

Det. Foss finally walked over to the table, and took a seat next to Det. Johns. He kept his eyes on Wyatt the entire time. Det. Johns finally continued on.

"Wyatt… it seems… odd — to me. It seems odd that your uncle would be so involved in your life, and yet you were completely unaware of anything we have just mentioned to you?" Both men again looked directly at Wyatt, intentional as to not break their stare. The room was still just as cold as it was before, but Wyatt felt a small bit of sweat form on his lower back.

"What do you mean? Jackson wasn't involved with anything about my life." Wyatt said back. "At least not since I was a boy."

The two detectives looked at each other. Det. Johns shuffled through a few of his papers, before he pulled a small stack of pages clipped together from the pile. He removed the paper clip that bound them together, and slid pages across the metal table to Wyatt.

"Are you sure about that, Wyatt?" Wyatt felt Det. Foss lean in a little, as he heard his voice for only the second time. Wyatt looked down at the pages that Det. Johns had slid over, and he felt his heart race a little.

Before him laid several sprawled out photographs, but printed and photocopied of the crime scene. Investigation photos the Detectives' team had taken when they arrived at Jackson's home after receiving the call from his neighbor.

Jackson's home was as lavish as one would expect it to be. Mid-century modern furniture filled the large living room space. Towering windows lined one entire wall of the room. Wyatt had only been to Jackson's home a few times, but Melody had visited many times over the years. Samantha had too, but Melody always described one particular element she found strange.

"There's no art," Melody told Wyatt one afternoon during their regularly scheduled lunch.

"What do you mean?" Wyatt asked, as he shoved a fork-full of salmon into his mouth.

"On the walls… Jackson. At his house. He has no art on the walls."

"Nothing?" Wyatt slowly cocked his head just slightly to the left and took another bite. "I'd have thought he would have some of his own." Wyatt chuckled to himself and rolled his eyes.

"I'm serious. Isn't that strange?" Melody asked again, and stared off into the distance.

"It's Jackson. It would be weird if it weren't weird." Wyatt said back before taking yet another bite.

Wyatt sat in silence for a moment looking at the photos set before him.

He noticed the bare walls.

He noticed the half finished paintings haphazardly leaned against the walls, much like how Wyatt himself handled his unfinished works.

Then, Wyatt noticed his face.

He took a slightly closer look at the photographs Det. Johns had laid out on the table. While there was no art on the walls of Jackson Brone's living room, Wyatt did notice that there were photographs of him strewn about the space.

Not all the same, but multiple photographs of Wyatt throughout his life were taped to the walls, sat on the table, were spread across the couch. Wyatt was everyone.

For some, this may have been a wholesome moment of appreciation from the absent father-like figure in the life of the lost boy. For Wyatt, he immediately felt a pit grow in the bilge of his stomach. Det. Foss' scratchy voice echoed out in Wyatt's mind again.

"Are you sure about that, Wyatt?" He asked a second time. Wyatt felt the detective lean in just slightly closer towards him.

"Is this a joke?" Wyatt asked, still staring at the images.

"We're afraid not." Det. Johns spoke up again.

Wyatt again studied the images and saw written, in what Wyatt hoped was deep red paint across one of the walls, he saw the words, "for it will be yours." Wyatt's heart raced, and he could feel his stomach turn. He was consumed with the phrase.

"We want to ask you again… when was the last time you spoke with your uncle, Wyatt?" Wyatt looked up at the men, and saw that their pleasant expressions had grown cold.

"My answer is the same," Wyatt responded. "I don't know exactly, but maybe a month or two. Three, maybe, I don't know."

"And you were entirely unaware of your uncle's mental decline?" Det. Johns asked, trying to remain gentle with his choice of words.

"I knew my uncle had… demons. I knew my uncle had social issues. But no, I didn't know he entered into any facility."

"Wyatt, help me out here," Det. Johns said, as he leaned back in his chair, and exhaled. "We're just trying to make sense of this. You say you don't know when you talked to your uncle last, and you say you didn't have any sort of relationship with him, and yet, in the room next to where his dead body is laying, your face is plastered all over everything."

"Trust me, it's weirder for me, I assure you." Wyatt's sarcasm was intentional and undeniable.

"Because from the looks of these photographs, it looks like either your uncle was stalking you, or…" Det. Johns started to trail off. Wyatt shot his glare to Det. Johns, and held it, waiting for the end of the sentence.

"Or what?" Wyatt finally asked, still staring at the detective. At this, Det. Foss jumped back into the conversation.

"Would you have any reason to hurt your uncle?" He asked.

Wyatt shot his glance to Det. Foss who still simply kept his stare fixed onto Wyatt.

"Excuse me?" Wyatt said.

"Would you have any reason to —"

"I heard what you said." Wyatt responded harsh and quick. "What the hell do you mean? Of course I didn't have any reason to hurt my uncle. Is that a joke?" Wyatt was the first to break eye contact with Det. Foss. He felt his face getting hot.

"Wyatt, we want to believe you…" Det. Johns took back over with his softer tone, but Wyatt was already annoyed by the implication.

"Should my lawyer be present?" Wyatt asked, and a hush fell over the small room.

"To be honest, we don't think it's entirely necessary, but if you feel more comfortable, you are welcome to." Det. Johns said.

"And my being here is voluntary, yes?" Wyatt asked again, less kind and more agitated. Det. Johns nodded.

"Yes," he said.

As soon as Wyatt saw Det. Johns' nod, Wyatt aggressively grabbed his things and stood up. "In that case, I'm done here. If you need anything else, please go through my attorney directly. Thank you for wasting my afternoon, gentlemen."

Det. Johns reached over slowly, and clicked the recording off.

Wyatt left the room in a hurry. He did not turn to look behind him, but he knew that Det. Johns and Det. Foss stayed exactly where they were in the interview room.

He left the building as quickly as he could. He did not bother calling a car, and opted to cool off by walking down the downtown street. Wyatt tried to take deep breaths to calm himself down, but it was not successful. He kept a brisk pace, and realized he had walked almost four city blocks before he stopped. His chest dramatically rose and fell with heavy breath, and his eyebrows still furrowed.

What the fuck was that? He thought. He could not tell if he was more disturbed by the images of his face in his uncle's home, or by the veiled insinuation that Wyatt could have possibly had something to do with his uncle's death. *This is unbelievable,* he thought.

Wyatt stopped for a moment, and stood at the corner of 4th and Spring St. He wondered why his uncle had so many printed images of him, and why they were chaotically plastered across the walls of his home. Try as he may, he could not for the life of him come up with any logical, believable reason. *And also,* Wyatt wondered, *what is with the…*

Wyatt remembered the letter.

"For it will be yours."

Wyatt remembered that morning when Maurice had explained that no one had read the letter except his uncle. *Jackson…* Wyatt thought, frustrated.

Then, Wyatt remembered the rules. *The rules!*

Never show, never tell; never stop, never sell; *follow these* to wildest dreams… for it will be yours.

Wyatt realized he did not add paint before he met the detectives.

Surely this was just a coincidence. Wyatt knew in his bones that there was zero chance of some sort of curse on this piece of painted cloth.

Up to this point, however, everything had been happening exactly how Wyatt would have hoped. Wyatt had been following the rules exactly how he interpreted them. Now, on the one day he does not obey the commands listed in the letter from his uncle, two homicide detectives think he may have murdered his uncle.

Great, Wyatt thought. *Thanks, Jack.*

Wyatt took a breath before he continued his walk back to his loft, realizing it was only a couple more blocks away. Wyatt also decided to add some paint when he got back.

Better safe than sorry.

As Wyatt passed 5th Street, less than a block from his building, he felt his cell phone vibrate in his pocket. He slipped the phone out of his pocket, into his hand, and saw "Samantha" on the display. He smiled for the first time since that morning, and tapped the "answer" button.

"Hey babe, I'm almost home, what's up?" He asked, and continued his walk.

"Wyatt…" Samantha said in a soft voice. "It's so beautiful."

Wyatt stopped, and instantly the busy sounds of Downtown Los Angeles faded away to a whisper of white noise. *Never show, never tell.*

"What is?" Wyatt hesitated asking a question he did not want the answer to.

"Your painting, Wyatt… it's…" Samantha's voice started to cut out, and Wyatt's heart sank deep into his diaphragm.

"Samantha, get out of there!" Wyatt shouted, as passing strangers shot glares at him. "Samantha? Can you hear me?"

"Wy— captivate— can't belie— hide this— love it." Wyatt was only getting every few words.

"Fuck, Samantha! Can you hear me?" When he did not get a response, he instantly hung up the call, and sprinted the remainder of the block back to his workspace loft. Sweat dripped from his hair, and he could feel his heart in his stomach.

He prayed the entire way that it was all an awful dream.

CHAPTER 11

Wyatt burst into the building.

The doorman was immediately surprised by the fear in Wyatt's eyes, and the speed at which he ran through the lobby.

"Woah! Excuse me, sir — oh, Wyatt, my bad!" The doorman called out to Wyatt as he rushed through the building's foyer.

"So sorry! I'm just in sort of a hurry." Wyatt called back.

"No worries! Everything okay?" The doorman asked as he stood slowly from his chair.

"Yep," is all Wyatt could respond with. "Sorry, could you just call the elevator?" Wyatt panted, completely out of breath.

"No worries, sure thing!" The doorman pressed the small button, calling the elevator, then sat back down, and picked up his phone again. Wyatt stood, staring at the intricately decorated steel doors, but the elevator did not come.

The doorman had pressed the button for Wyatt a million times before, and Wyatt always simply walked onto an open elevator car waiting for him. This time, for some reason, the elevator just did not come. Wyatt looked back to the doorman, who gave him his signature fist pump, and "my guy," this time adding a "hope you're good." Wyatt smiled back, lying through his undeniable panic.

Wyatt shifted his body weight back and forth from left side to right, as he stood in this building's lobby, and silently panicked. His breath heavy for a few more moments with no *ding* of an arriving elevator. Finally, he decided he could not wait any longer, and rushed towards the staircase entryway. He bullied his way through the heavy, metal door, and began his insane ascent up the fourteen-some-odd flights of stairs to his loft.

Panting, and sweating, Wyatt's adrenaline allowed him to continue his pace, floor after floor.

After climbing roughly one hundred and sixty-eight steps, Wyatt finally made it to his floor. He quickly burst through the stairway door and almost fell into his hallway. Not letting up, Wyatt sprinted towards the last door on the left; the front door to his loft.

He quickly pulled his keys from his pocket, and frantically searched through several to find his apartment key. Getting the key into the actual lock was an equally frustrating struggle. He finally heard the click of his deadbolt unlocking his door, and Wyatt slowly pushed the door inward. It creaked loudly as it swung open.

It was cold in his entryway. The contrast of the temperature stark against his flushed and sweaty skin.

Wyatt could not help but notice the dead quiet in his loft. The only noise he could even hear was the sound of his nervous, panicked breath, and the crackling of a wooden wicked candle flickering in his living room. His breath caught wind of the candle's scent as it put together the sound of the crackling wick. He thought it smelled like Christmas.

"Sam?" Wyatt hesitated before calling out again, "Babe?" His voice echoed off of the concrete floors loudly through the open floor plan of his workspace loft.

He took another step forward, and he heard the sole of his shoe press into the ground, but he did not get any response. His hand trembled slightly until he squeezed it into a fist, and held it closed. He held his fist so tightly that his knuckles slowly turned white. "Samantha?" He called out again as he walked cautiously into his kitchen's entryway. Once there, he stood silently for a moment, and placed his hand against the cold kitchen countertop.

To his left, Wyatt saw the clean, white paneling of the door frame to his secondary work space. The room he ran to through downtown. The room he was terrified to look into. The room where his uncle's painting rested. The room with the painting that called to him.

The room he dreaded Samantha would be in.

Tears had begun to pool under his eyes, and exhausted, he started slowly making his way towards the doorway, and towards the room. Through his shaky voice, Wyatt called out for his love again.

"Samantha, baby, please. Can you hear me?" Step after step, Wyatt took his time. More and more, with each step, Wyatt could see further into the cluttered, secondary room. "Sam…" Wyatt somehow managed to get out through his now flowing tears. The shaking in his voice matched the shaking on his hand.

He took another step, and saw the edge of the canvas.

Despite the war of anguish waging in his mind, Wyatt could almost instantly feel the pull of the painting calling out to him. The urge to add paint to its canvas replaced the shaking of his nervous hand. He clinched his eyes shut, and continued towards the entrance of the room.

Please, Samantha, he thought, desperately.

Finally, Wyatt turned the corner and peered directly into the room, and he gasped for air.

The room was empty. Samantha was not there. He frantically checked the entire room, but she definitely was not there.

"Wyatt?" He heard her soft tone call out from behind him, just outside of the room.

An immediate rush of desperate relief waved over him, and for a moment he felt weak in the knees. He locked his knees and stood firm, and before he turned to her, he looked again at the empty room around him, taking stock of the very real fear he had just experienced. He looked at his uncle's solitary canvas, and took a gigantic breath. He turned and saw the horror in Samantha's eyes as she evaluated the rush of emotions in his face. "What's wrong? Oh, my god… Wyatt… Are you okay?"

Samantha stood before him, just outside of the room, a cup of tea in her hand. She had a genuine concern in her eyes for the state Wyatt found himself in. She set down her cup of tea on the kitchen counter. Wyatt instantly rushed to her, and threw his arms around her.

"Hi," is all he could manage to say. Samantha hugged him back hard, and gave him a second to get his breath back. She gently rubbed her hand on his back, and held on for as long as he did. Based on the strength of his grip, she could tell he needed this more than she did.

"Wyatt, what in the hell is going on?" She almost laughed, unsure of how to interpret his obvious distress. Wyatt quickly pulled away from her, and looked her in the face.

"Samantha, on the phone… you said you were looking at a painting." He asked her, delicately. Samantha looked at him blankly, confused, like she was expecting more to that sentence.

"Yeah… I was…" She responded.

"Sam, I need you to tell me… which one?" His voice was shaking again, and she could tell he was nervous to ask. She crinkled her brow again, and tilted her head slightly towards his.

"The one in your room. The big new one that you started a couple of weeks ago?" Samantha gestured towards the room where his newest original painting was. He slowly followed her pointed finger with his eye line towards his primary work room. He wiped the tears from his cheek, and looked back at her.

"My new one," he said, and he started to laugh.

"Yeah, the big green one, in there." She said gesturing again. "I'm sorry, I know you said you wanted me to wait until it was finished. I was just excited to see how it was turning out. You know I like to see your progress. Get the full 'before and after' effect. I'm sorry, Wyatt, please don't be upset with me—" Samantha was completely ready to continue on, but Wyatt interrupted her before she could finish her thought.

"No, Sam," Wyatt smiled again. "It's okay. It's absolutely okay. It doesn't matter. I'm sorry I worried you." Samantha crinkled her forehead and again, she leaned in a little. "You're here, and you're okay. Nothing else matters."

"Are you okay?" She asked.

"Yeah, I am. I promise. I just— I thought you were looking at," Samantha returned the interrupting favor, and her face dropped to disappointment. She raised a single eyebrow.

"Your uncle's painting?" Wyatt could pick up the slight annoyance in her tone. He simply nodded in response as the shame started creeping in. Samantha kept her foot on the gas pedal. "You mean the only painting you've ever owned that you've asked me *not* to look at? For some unknown reason? That one?" Samantha smirked.

"Yep. That would be the one." Wyatt looked to the floor, and avoided her eyes.

"No, I didn't. I listen to you when you ask me for something. However weird I think it is." Samantha said.

"I'm sorry." Wyatt said back. "I'm embarrassed."

"Wyatt, it's okay. But why are you so upset? You're literally in tears, and you're sweating like you just ran a marathon… what's going on?" Samantha asked, and she put her hand on his arm. She wiped a tear from his cheek, and waited for a coherent response. Wyatt just forced a smile in return, and put his hand on hers, kissing it.

"Nothing, I promise, it's nothing."

"It's obviously not nothing, Wyatt. Your face is flushed, and you're panicked." Samantha did not let Wyatt off the hook.

"I promise, it's nothing," Wyatt insisted.

"Why are you so upset that you thought I looked at your uncle's painting?" She asked again, stern.

"I—" Wyatt did not have the words. He knew he could not give her the honest answer, because he knew how insane it would sound. "I — just — I'm not ready yet." Samantha looked at him, and took a second before she responded.

"Okay." She said plainly.

"Okay?" Wyatt asked for confirmation.

"Yeah. Okay," she said, "I understand."

"Stay here tonight?" He smiled, and hoped she smile would back. Samantha looked at him for a moment, and then smiled tenderly.

"Yeah. Of course." She wiped another tear from his cheek, and he kissed her forehead softly.

Later that night, Wyatt and Samantha laid in bed next to each other. Samantha had fallen asleep just moments before, but Wyatt laid restlessly awake, and stared blankly at the television as it flickered gently. The sound from the long cancelled sitcom barely audible over the hum of a bedside noise machine. Wyatt looked at Samantha peacefully sleeping. He watched a few repetitions of the gentle rise and fall of her chest, a rhythm he so loved. She was fast asleep; peaceful and content. Wyatt had no such luck. He watched as his sheer, wall length curtains danced in a subtle breeze coming through the crack in his window.

He laid, wide awake, for an hour or so before he gave into the relentless consciousness of his restless night. Wyatt carefully reached over to a small table to his right. His laptop sat atop, and he grabbed it. Maneuvering his body just slightly, Wyatt sat up slightly in his bed, and lifted the computer open. The light hit his face, and illuminated his room with a benign blue glow. Normally Wyatt would promptly be hit with a wave of concern that the light would wake Samantha, as she was only a foot away from it, but she had recently adopted sleeping with a solid black, silk sleep mask. She had not the faintest idea of the work Wyatt would begin pursuing, and so he continued on without care.

Wyatt opened up an internet browser on his laptop, and clicked into the search bar. The cursor ticked with anticipation for a moment or two, before he began to type: "Painting curse."

The first results were various YouTube videos entitled such things like "10 Cursed Paintings You Should NEVER Look At," etc. Wyatt quickly scrolled past to find the actual web search results of his search, and hopefully, some sort of cyber-peace-of-mind to the curious circumstance he found himself in. The first result hit he saw was a Wikipedia page about a painting entitled *The Crying Boy*, by Italian painter Giovanni Bragolin. He opened the article in a new tab on his web browser, and briefly scrolled through some of the text.

Skimming through the first few paragraphs, Wyatt learned that in 1985, a British tabloid reported that an Essex firefighter kept reporting that undamaged prints of this particular painting kept being found amidst the ruins of burned homes. With his interest piqued, Wyatt kept reading until he saw that the reason behind this phenomenon was a flame retardant varnish commonly used on the prints of this particular image. Wyatt clicked out of this Wikipedia page, and then tried to rub the sleep away from his eyes.

Page after page, Wyatt continued to skim through stories about, "The Curse of *The Crying Boy*." It seemingly had become a very popular urban legend in the small overlap between art fanatics and true crime enthusiasts. Wyatt then found a few articles about different well-documented potential curses around specific paintings, and the stories they've inspired. Works such as *The Picture of Dorian Gray* by Oscar Wilde, to the more contemporary novel *Rose Madder* by Stephen King.

Ultimately, Wyatt could not find anything related to his particular circumstance. Nothing about an inherited piece, nothing about a mysterious letter, and nothing about your wildest dreams coming true by following seemingly very mundane tasks.

Wyatt opened a new web browser search tab, and again, began to type:

"For it will be yours."

He clicked the "enter" button on his keyboard. The page took a moment to load, but then the search engine was filled with several results.

Unfortunately, however, it also proved to be a dead end. Result after result quoted various bible scriptures.

"Therefore I tell you, whatever you ask for in prayer, believe that you have received it, and it will be yours." A quote made popular by the Christian Jesus from the Book of Mark, Chapter 11, verse 24, from the New International Version. Or Luke, Chapter 4, Verse 7's gem, "Worship me, and all will be yours."

Ha, Wyatt laughed to himself, and rolled his eyes. He shook his head, disappointed, and shut his laptop. Wyatt sat for a moment. He again watched the faint flicker of the 90's comedy, and listened to a new silence that filled his room; the combination of the noise machine and the incessant, internal chatter of his sleepless mind. He lifted his laptop off of his lap, and carefully, quietly set it back down on top of the small, side table. Silently, he slid his legs off of the Tempur-Pedic mattress, and slipped out of his bed. Wyatt took his time, and made sure to not disturb Samantha. As quiet as a mouse, and as cautiously as he could manage, he stood to his feet and stretched his arms into the air. He yawned long, and exhaled without making a sound. Blood rushed to his head, and he smiled at the idea of falling over and waking Samantha, after being so careful not to disrupt her slumber.

Wyatt walked over to the edge of his loft, and stood at his window for a moment. Wyatt felt the wind kindly flow through the crack. It was cold. Wyatt thought it felt nice, and calming, but then remembered he had been running his air-conditioning all night.

He slowly closed the window, and when he heard the latch click shut, he looked back at Samantha. She was still peacefully sleeping, altogether undisturbed, and completely unaware of his restlessness.

After a moment, he felt his pulse pound the ends of his fingers. Wyatt looked towards the secondary room, and towards his uncle's painting. Again, and directly, it called to him. He needed to add paint to it. He walked towards the feeling, the urge, and subsequently towards the painting.

Once in the room, Wyatt noticed that the sound of the noise machine and air conditioner had almost completely dissipated. Wyatt looked at the small, wooden table next to the painting, and saw the letter. He lifted the letter, and again read its meticulous, and odd instructions, along with the more contemporary translations scribbled to the side.

"To nev'r showeth and nev'r bid, f'r 'twill beest yours… to never show and never tell, for it will be yours.

To nev'r stand ho and nev'r selleth, f'r 'twill beest yours… to never stop and never sell, for it will be yours.

Followeth these to wildest dreams, f'r 'twill beest yours… follow these, to wildest dreams, for it will be yours."

Wyatt looked at the blatant differences in handwriting differences between the old-style script and the adjacent scribbling translations. Wyatt could not understand why his uncle, Jackson, had written it in these ways in the first place. The blatant differences in script was still something Wyatt simply could not wrap his head around.

Wyatt's eyes scanned over the entirety of the letter, and once again, he noticed the other notes haphazardly jotted down in every space of the single page letter. Once more, his heart felt heavy for the mental decay his uncle must have experienced in his final days to produce such a deranged note.

Wyatt tried his best to read the cacography in the margins of the letter.

"Add new paint every day," Wyatt again read aloud to himself. "Any amount will do." Wyatt's eyes wandered a little farther down the page to another set of scribbled instructions. "Don't let anyone else look at it. No one."

Still farther down the page, "Do not remove or destroy the paint, just add in new layers." Again, on the far right, "Do not let anyone see, ever." Then finally, on the top of the page, "Everything will come true, everything."

Wyatt examined the letter closer than he ever had to this point. He could not help but notice that each individual addition of words and text were all in completely different script. It was all in different handwriting. Something in Wyatt's gut felt off.

It did not seem likely that Jackson had made this letter on his own, and he wondered how else it could have come to exist. Closely examining every inch of the paper, Wyatt noticed a faint grouping of numbers on the cat-eared corner that he had not seen previously.

The closest comparison Wyatt could make in his mind was the feeling he had the first time he had seen the United States Constitution in Washington D.C. The ink had faded so much on the paper that it was scarcely visible.

He walked to another small table in the corner of the room, and picked up a small pair of glasses that sat on it. He put them on, and held the page up again. He flattened the corner of the page out more, and took an even closer look.

Faintly, just faintly, he barely made out what the numbers looked like. He quietly said them out loud to himself.

"1881."

Puzzled, he squinted his eyes, and looked at the page again. There, just extremely faded ink, Wyatt swore he could make out the numbers *1881.*

What on earth? Wyatt thought. Was this a date? Was this another coded message? Wyatt still found himself stuck on the handwriting of the scribbled entries. His focus shifted back to the faded ink, and Wyatt saw yet another small grouping of numbers underneath the apparently "1881."

"1914."

Wyatt's stomach began to turn. He looked closer still. Underneath, another set of numbers.

"1972."

Wyatt stopped at the sight of this particular grouping of numbers.

1972.

To his own dismay, Wyatt recognized this set of numbers.

1972 was the year that Jackson Brone had suddenly become a household name.

1972 was the year that Jackson Brone's wildest dreams came true.

Wyatt felt slightly lightheaded at the sudden realization, or coincidence. He could not decide which it was. Logic still told him that this entire circumstance was simply due to his uncle's declining mental state, and ultimately were the manifestations of a rambling, crazy artist in his final days. Wyatt's better judgement told him that his most feared thought was actually real.

This painting was cursed.

This is insane, Wyatt scolded himself internally.

Wyatt felt frustrated at this constant, and self-diagnosed insane war waging in his mind. Between the scribbled and faded numbers, and the different styled handwritings, Wyatt started to feel slightly overwhelmed. He knew he needed answers he simply would not get tonight.

Is this painting cursed? Wyatt pondered. He felt foolish for entertaining the notion, but at this moment, as Wyatt stood, sleep-deprived in the room with his uncle's painting, it started to seem plausible. After all, almost as soon as Wyatt began adding paint to the canvas of this piece, things started to fall into place for him, *professionally* and personally.

Stop it, Wyatt, you sound insane.

Wyatt shook his head, in disappointment. Nothing about this made any sense to him, and he was starting to feel defeated by his lack of understanding.

He set the letter back down on the small, wooden side table, and shifted his focus back to the painting itself. The chaotic color, the thick layers, the varying styles and techniques. That same familiar pulsing sensation came back to his fingertips. Like the pin pricks of a sleeping limb.

Wyatt was overwhelmed with the urge to paint.

"What the hell are you?" He quietly spoke aloud to the painting standing solemnly before him.

He felt the consistent tingle in the ends of his fingers, and picked up a brush and his palette. There was a slight bit of paint still wet resting on the porcelain palette, and Wyatt swiped the brush against it. His heart raced, and he reached the brush towards the canvas.

Wyatt slid a small, yellow streak of paint across the blue, cloud shape. The end of the streak clumped together and Wyatt kept it as is. He stared at the single, yellow stroke blankly, and for a moment imagined it was a flower petal. He smiled slightly, and exhaled. The tingling in his fingertips instantaneously dispelled. Wyatt looked at his hand, and clinched his list tightly. His knuckles turned white again, and he released it. The blood rushed back in instantly.

"Any amount will do," he said to himself. "Guess so."

Wyatt set the brush and palette back down on the small table next to the painting, and just stared at it. He felt an insidious yawn build up in his stomach before making its way through his mouth. His eyes watered slightly as he exhaled. He tried to crack his neck, it did not work. He took another deep breath, before his attention was stolen by the gentle sounds of a light tap on the wooden door frame of the room he stood in.

Wyatt looked up, and saw Samantha standing there, leaning against the door frame, with a sheet wrapped around her body.

"Hey, kid," Wyatt said quietly, and smiled.

"What are you doing up?" Samantha asked, slowly, and still full of the restful sleep she had just woken up from.

"I couldn't sleep, so I thought I'd try and get some work done. I'm sorry, I didn't mean to wake you up." Wyatt quietly spoke, and he slowly made his way over to her. He kissed her forehead, and wrapped his arms around her. He flicked the room's light off, and gently ushered Samantha away from his uncle's painting.

"You didn't, I just woke up and you weren't there." She responded.

"Oh, I'm sorry. I'm feeling sleepy now though, let's get back to bed," Wyatt said.

As they walked back towards the bed, Wyatt peered over his shoulder back to the painting.

Almost as soon as he left the room, that familiar tingle in his fingertips was back. They pounded with the urge to keep painting. Samantha held his hand as they approached the bed, and she spread the sheet back out over it.

They both climbed in, and Samantha burrowed into the space between Wyatt's arm and his chest. A space she had coined "the nook."

"I love you," Samantha said lovingly. Wyatt could tell she was already falling back asleep. He smiled, and kept himself from laughing.

"I love you too," he said quietly back, and kissed the top of her head.

Wyatt put his hand on her ribs, and matched her gentle breath. He matched the gentle rise and fall of her chest, until they both drifted into a deep sleep.

CHAPTER 12

The smell of coffee woke Wyatt up.

The strong scent hit his brain before he even saw the light of the morning. As his eyes finally decided to open, he saw the sun peeking through his curtains, as they danced slightly. The window was opened, and the signature Los Angeles breeze made its way into the loft. Wyatt rubbed his face, took a deep breath, and gently slid his fingers across his cheeks and under his eyes. He yawned long, and put his hands through his hair as he sat up.

"Good morning, sleepy head," he heard Samantha's voice call out from behind him. He smiled as he stretched his back, and turned to face her. Samantha stood in the kitchen, holding a black, plastic spatula, and with her hair wrapped in a towel. "Did I wake you up? I was worried my shower would be too loud," she said as she turned back towards the eggs that sizzled in the skillet behind her.

"Not at all, I slept so hard. I must have really needed that," Wyatt said, as he forced himself to stand. He reached his arms into the air, and stretched his back again.

"Well, good then. You got it." He saw Samantha look over her shoulder and smile. "Coffee's still hot, come get some. I just finished making some breakfast too." Wyatt watched her plate some eggs next to a couple of slices of Turkey Bacon, and a piece of whole wheat toast covered with a smashed avocado and "Everything But The Bagel" Seasoning.

"You absolutely did not need to do all of this," Wyatt said with a smile as he slowly walked over towards the kitchen. He walked up behind Samantha, and gently wrapped his arms around her waist.

"I know, I wanted to. Here, eat up," she said. She gently closed her eyes as Wyatt kissed her neck. She enjoyed it for a moment before she laughed, and squirmed out of his grasp. "Ew, morning breath, gross!" Wyatt joined her laugh, and turned to walk towards the bathroom.

"Okay, okay, okay, fine," he said as he walked away. He walked into the bathroom, and called back to Samantha. "Where's your plate?" Wyatt grabbed his toothbrush, and spread a small amount of toothpaste on it as he heard Samantha call back.

"Ugh, I can't stay. I wish I could. I have to go into the office for a bit, so I grabbed an apple. I'll eat it on my way, and I think Cheryl is getting lunch for the team, anyway," she said. Wyatt heard the jingle of her keys as she picked them up from the counter.

Wyatt finished brushing his teeth, and looked at himself in the mirror. He just barely felt the tingle of desire to paint as it began to build in his fingers. He wrung his hands together, clinching them and releasing them, before he walked back into the kitchen.

Samantha had set his plate, full of incredible looking food, and a steaming cup of black coffee on the kitchen counter, in front of a sleek stool. She stood next to the arrangement, leaning against the counter, and smiled at him while she sipped her own cup of joe.

"Wow, thank you, this looks amazing," Wyatt said. He walked towards the feast, and sat down. He comically leaned in towards her. He spoke through puckered lips, "I'm all brushed now, I promise." Samantha smiled at him, giggled, and rolled her eyes. Their lips gently pressed together. Wyatt smiled, Samantha flipped her keys in her hand, and tossed a small purse over her shoulder.

"What do you have going on today?" She asked, as she finished off her coffee and rinsed out her porcelain mug in the kitchen sink.

"Mmm," Wyatt thought for a moment. "I think Melody is supposed to give me a call to chat about some gallery updates? I'm not sure what time though, to be honest."

"Oh, that's right!" Samantha's eyes lit up. "Porter & Herth, right?" She was beaming with pride.

"Yeah, the Los Angeles gallery has been open for a couple of weeks now." Wyatt desperately tried his hardest to play it cool, and coy. Samantha was not having any of his manufactured calm demeanor.

"And?!" She exclaimed. Wyatt laughed, and shrugged. "How has it been going?"

"I have no idea. They typically don't have the artists go to the openings. So no news is good news, I guess." Wyatt smirked, and Samantha knew she would not get anymore information. "Plus I'm only really used to getting bad updates, so the fact that it's been a few weeks could actually be a good sign," he said again and laughed.

"Oh, stop. I'm sure Melody is coming to give you an update of nothing but great news today." Samantha said as she smiled and playfully rolled her eyes.

"Here's to hoping, I guess," Wyatt said back, and he took a big bite of his avocado covered toast. Through the full mouth of the delicious breakfast, Wyatt managed to say, "This is amazing, by the way, thank you."

"Gross," she said and laughed. "But thank you, I'm glad you like it." Samantha checked her watch, and her internal pace promptly ticked up a notch. "Oh, shoot, I've got to run. Good luck today! Love you." Samantha turned and made her way towards Wyatt's front door.

"I love you, too," Wyatt said as he lifted the cup of hot coffee up to his lips. He slurped loudly, as he heard the door to his loft shut behind Samantha.

He exhaled loudly, and took another sip in silence, and finished his cup.

Wyatt sat for a moment, and appreciated the quiet that surrounded him. He closed his eyes, and took a deep breath. He slowly exhaled, and could feel his soul come alive in his chest. He repeated the breath exercise, and Wyatt felt his body settle in. He felt awake, he felt present, and ultimately, he felt grateful. In this exact moment, Wyatt had realized how lucky he felt for how dramatically, and quickly his life and career were progressing. Wyatt truly felt like all of his dreams were coming … true.

Wyatt again felt his fingers tingle, with that familiar urge to add paint to the canvas.

His knuckles had gone white from how tightly he clenched his fist together. He let go of the fist, and shook his hand out, hoping the tingles would subside. To further take the painting's calling off his mind, he walked into his kitchen and went through his normal morning coffee routine.

Wyatt boiled water, added fresh grounds and a pinch of cinnamon in the funneled neck of his glass carafe, and waited for his fresh pot to come together.

The tingles in his fingers did not dissipate. If anything, the urging had only become more intense. The longer Wyatt waited for the water to steep through the light roast grounds, the deeper the urging felt. Once he was finally able to pour and enjoy the first few sips of his morning coffee, Wyatt could no longer resist the urge that he was being drawn to.

He looked towards the secondary room, towards the painting, and slowly stood up from his kitchen stool. His eyes filled with a frustrated determination. He finished his toast and coffee, then slowly walked towards the canvas in the secondary room. With every step he took, the tingle in his fingertips pounded harder and harder, like his nerve-endings were imploding into themselves. Again, the canvas called to him. It drew him in, and he followed its summons until he stood face to face with the painting.

He stared at it for a moment, before he picked up his brush and palette and added a stroke. This time it was another simple stripe of egg shell toned paint directly on top of the yellow from the night before. Wyatt thought of the letter. *Just add new layers,* he thought. He took a deep breath, and exhaled slowly.

Finally, the tingling in his fingers disappeared.

Wyatt watched the thick line of paint flatten as it dried when he heard his door bell buzz. Curiosity billowed over his face, and he set his tools down. His brow faintly crinkled, Wyatt slowly made his way over to his front door's intercom. He pressed the button and cautiously spoke into the speaker.

"Hello?" Wyatt called out.

"Hey, it's Mel. Let me up?" Melody said back to him through the static of the old speaker.

"Yeah, of course," Wyatt said back, slightly taken by surprise, as he pressed a button on his speaker box and another buzz rang out.

The door squeaked predictably as Wyatt slowly pulled it open. Curiosity still rested on his brow, and he walked back into his kitchen. He picked his cup of light roast back up, took another sip, and waited.

Melody was not a loud person, so the only reason Wyatt knew she had made it to his loft was that same creaking of his door as she entered through it.

"Hello?" Melody comically called out, as she only took a few steps into his home. "Wyatt? Ya decent?"

Wyatt laughed from the kitchen and responded, "Nope, fully nude expecting my sister to walk in any minute, you big idiot. Yes, of course I'm decent." His smile genuine, he took another sip of his coffee. "I'm in here, come on in."

Melody walked around the corner into his loft, and set her purse down on his kitchen counter before tossing her arms around her brother and embracing him. Wyatt, still curious about why she was here in person, and not on the call they had planned, hugged his sister back.

"Morning, bro. What's up?" Melody spoke as she quickly made herself at home, and poured herself a cup of coffee.

"You tell me," Wyatt replied, and laughed again. "I thought we just had a call scheduled."

"We did." Melody smirked. "Sugar?" Wyatt pointed towards a cabinet next to the microwave hanging above the stove top, and Melody turned towards it. Wyatt stared at her blankly, and watched her make her coffee, before that same awkward smile creeped back onto his face.

"...and..." He goaded her to continue.

"...and," she said, and took the bait, "now it's an in person." Wyatt laughed, and shook his head.

"Jesus, Mel, do I have to beg? We are now having an in person because..." he again tried to get his sister to actually explain why she was standing in his kitchen.

"And we are now having an in person because sometimes you need to discuss things in person." Melody winked at her brother, and she knew she had won this round of the little game they were playing.

"Cut the shit, Mel," Wyatt blurted out through his jovial, and light-hearted, sibling annoyance. "Why are you here? You said you'd have gallery updates for me? Please, just say they're good. I don't think I can handle another failed gallery opening."

"Well... I have been engaged in a very interesting series of conversations with Sylvia Peregrine from Porter & Herth." At the mention of Sylvia's name, Wyatt's childlike expression turned to concern. To this point, his professional and artistic life had been completely dictated by the anticipation of professional breakthrough only for that anticipation to fall apart at the eleventh hour from circumstances that he often felt were entirely out of his control. Every ounce of Wyatt's emotional stability begged Melody to continue with good news.

"And?" Wyatt sheepishly replied, more gentle than before. Wyatt was nervous. Melody picked up on his concern, and immediately worked to quell his fear.

"No, no," she assured him. "This is good. It's great, Wyatt. It's so great." Melody watched as Wyatt's nerves dissolved, and his expression resumed its jovial curiosity.

"Okay," Wyatt continued, "…so?" Melody smiled wide.

"Sylvia let me know that their Los Angeles gallery of your work has been such a smash success that they want to expand it to more of their galleries."

Wyatt felt the world slow down for a moment.

"More of their galleries? Galleries? With an 's?' Plural? Wh— what does that mean?" He asked, while his nerves creeped back in with an undertone of excitement.

"New York." Melody said. Wyatt's eyes opened as wide as they could.

"They want to feature me in their New York gallery? You're kidding," he asked, in disbelief. Melody shook her head from side to side confirming that she was not, in fact, kidding. "New York?" Wyatt asked again. Melody nodded again.

"West 22nd Street in Chelsea." Melody let out a small "eek," like a high school girl who's crush just asked her to the homecoming dance. "But that's not it," she continued. Wyatt stared at her.

"What's not it?" Wyatt asked, cautiously.

"London. Soho," Melody said, and her devilish grin stretched from ear to ear. Wyatt almost exploded.

"London?!" He could not believe what Melody was saying.

"But that's not it," Melody said again, and she excitedly shook her fists in the air.

"No," Wyatt said, verbally pinching himself. "Fuck you," he said and laughed.

"Zurich. Switzerland." Melody said. Wyatt stared back at her with an empty expression. "They're taking you global, Wyatt."

Wyatt shouted with joy, and he embraced his sister. They hugged hard in his kitchen, jumped up and down, and shouted over each other at the raw excitement they both felt.

"Wyatt, there's one more bit." Melody spoke again, and Wyatt took a deep breath.

"Oh my God, how can there possibly be more?" Wyatt asked, adrenaline coursing through his veins.

"Sylvia said that they feel so confident that they will sell your works at all of their galleries, that they want to buy them from you outright in advance." Melody's eyes filled with sincere pride. She took a breath, and took her time with what she planned to say next. "Wyatt… I've negotiated 15 pieces for each gallery, and they are issuing us an advanced payment of $15,000,000."

Wyatt's entire world fell silent. The only sound Wyatt was confident he could hear was the beating of his own heart as it rumbled within his chest.

"I'm sorry — what?" Those were the only words Wyatt could muster because he simply refused to believe her.

"Fifteen million dollars, Wyatt. Up front. In advance. No matter what."

"Fifteen —" Wyatt could not finish the sentence.

"Fifteen million dollars, Wyatt." Melody opened her mouth, mocking a full scream without actually making any sound.

"Fifteen million dollars…" Wyatt lightly repeated the words, still in complete disbelief.

"You just became my highest grossing, and most successful, and most financially viable client of all time. I'm so proud of you." Melody laughed out loud. "Just saying that sounds so insane, doesn't it?" Wyatt laughed and playfully pushed her shoulder.

"Which part?" Wyatt responded, still in absolute shock.

"All of it! Are you kidding? Absolutely all of it!" They both laughed, and hugged again.

"This is insanity," Wyatt said. "And it's a done deal?" Melody nodded, and dug through her purse for a moment before she pulled out a small stack of papers clipped inside a blank manila folder.

"That's why I wanted to come in person, I have the agreement right here." She slapped the contract down on Wyatt's kitchen counter, and held a pen up towards him. She took a moment, and then clicked the pen open. "It's all here," she said, and Wyatt took the pen. He quickly skimmed through the pages.

"And you looked through it already?" Wyatt asked her.

"Already had legal look through it. All fairly standard gallery stuff. Payment will come in installments coordinated which each gallery opening. And it gets better… They actually want you at each opening, which I know is a little unusual, but she said they are expecting these openings to be huge. She thinks it would be a great press opportunity to have you attend each one, which I totally agree."

" Wyatt hesitated at this, but Melody continued on. "Like your own red carpet events, how amazing is that!"

Wyatt felt his hand shake, the pen hovering just a few inches above a $15,000,000 guaranteed payday. He clicked the pen shut. Melody saw his pause, and her sentence trailed off.

"Wyatt, what is it?" She asked, confused at his abrupt hesitation.

As he stared at the agreement, he thought of the rules of the letter that came with the painting. Specifically, the second rule. *To never stop, and never sell.*

To never stop.

Wyatt had been adding at least a single stroke of paint to the piece every day since he got it. Whether or not he believed it to actually be cursed, he knew for certain that he was not quite ready to put that to the test. He was not ready to risk the curse being real, and lose all he had gained. He remembered how he felt the moment he first saw the painting in his building's hallway. The shear size of the canvas was overwhelming. He knew that if the curse he had created in his mind was in fact real, the massive size of the canvas would prevent him from traveling with the painting in tow. Certainly trekking it across the country, and the world, would be a mere impossibility.

"I — I can't go. To the openings. I can't do that." He said to Melody, and struggled to get the words out of his mind. Melody now matched his previous confusion.

"What the fuck do you mean you can't go? They're paying you $15 million dollars, Wyatt. Of course you can go. You have to go to these openings."

"I can't, I'm sorry." He set the pen down on the counter.

"Why not?" As Melody responded, all of her joy slowly became confused frustration. Wyatt imagined telling her all of his scattered thoughts that were racing through his mind. He imagined the liberation he would certainly feel to explain that the painting he inherited from their uncle might possibly be cursed, and the actual source of all of his most recent success. He imagined how it would feel to explain the oddity of the letter that was included from their uncle, and how the painting came with a set of unexplainable, cryptic rules that Wyatt had essentially been blindly following since it came into his possession. And that, while he could not currently explain why, he kept feeling drawn to the painting. He could not imagine leaving the painting for days, or more likely weeks, on end, because if the curse was real... What would that mean? What consequences would come for breaking the mysterious rules of the painting? Wyatt was not certain he believed it, but he was certain he was afraid of it.

"I —" Wyatt struggled with how to explain this to his sister. "I just can't. I'm sorry. We need to renegotiate and have that request taken out of the contract."

"Wyatt, what the fuck is going on? I'm not asking them to take that out, that was a very specific request because of the size of this deal. I can't just —" Wyatt could feel her anger boiling.

"Mel, I'm sorry, I — I just can't go. I'll take less, it's fine. Please, just trust me."

Wyatt looked to his sister, and through her burgeoning rage, his eyes pleaded with hers. Wyatt knew she could see the genuine concern in his labored expression. Melody looked down and saw his hand trembling, and though she did not understand what scared him so about the once-in-a-lifetime proposition of these all-expenses paid trips around the world, her sibling compassion kicked into gear, and she metaphorically took a step back.

"Look, I don't need to get this agreement back to them for another week or so, so just, like, take a couple of days, and think about it. Is that okay? It would be insane to leave money on the table with a deal this size because you're scared to… fly, or whatever the fuck it is. Okay?" Melody looked at her brother, and reached her hand over to put it on top of his. She saw tears welling in his eyes, and felt concerned for her brother. "Hey, are you okay?" She asked him, and pulled him in to a hug. Wyatt snapped out of it for a moment, and wiped his eyes. "Hey, Wyatt, what's wrong?"

"Woah, ha," he uncomfortably tried to laugh off his sudden and intense emotional response. "Yeah, sorry, uh — yeah, that sounds great. I'll give it some thought." He took her hands in his, and squeezed them firmly.

"It'll be fine," Melody said, trying to comfort him. "We'll figure it out. You should feel really proud of this, Wyatt."

"Yeah. It'll be fine. Thank you, for everything," he said, and Melody grabbed her purse. "This is all really exciting, I'm just — overwhelmed, or something, I guess." He tried to make himself laugh to put Melody's immediate concern at ease.

"Yeah… Of course, no worries. Keep me posted, all right?" She said.

"Will do," Wyatt replied, and forced a smile.

They hugged, and Melody walked away. Wyatt heard the squeaking of his door, before it loudly closed.

With the piercing thud of his door shutting, Wyatt almost collapsed on the ground. The joy that turned to fear quickly became anger within him. He was angry that this painting had caused such a visceral reaction to what should have been a moment of pure celebration.

Almost instantly, he felt the tingle in his fingers come back. He rushed into the secondary room and stood face to face with the painting. He looked at the stroke of paint he had added that morning, and then at the various strokes of paint he had been adding over the past few weeks since coming into possession of the painting and letter.

The letter, Wyatt thought.

Wyatt looked for the letter in the room for a moment, before he found it resting on the small table near the painting itself.

Wyatt read through the rules aloud again, for what felt like a millionth time.

"*To nev'r showeth and nev'r bid, f'r 'twill beest yours…* to never show and never tell, for it will be yours.

To nev'r stand ho and nev'r selleth, f'r 'twill beest yours… to never stop and never sell, for it will be yours.

Followeth these to wildest dreams, f'r 'twill beest yours… follow these, to wildest dreams, for it will be yours."

Wyatt again examined the random scribbles throughout the page.

He had told himself over and over again that this letter was simply the manifestation of his uncle's declining mental health, and that there was nothing about this painting or this piece of paper that had been dictating the recent professional successes in his life.

Then, in a moment where his professional success confronted the potential curse of this piece, Wyatt succumbed. He bent to the will of the painting. And it filled him with anger.

He again intensely examined the scribbled ramblings of what his uncle had become. He thought about the distinct difference in handwriting between the different notations.

As he studied the tiny details of the writings on the page, Wyatt knew he desperately needed to talk to someone about this letter. He needed validation that this page was what he thought it was… what he hoped it was…

The last physical piece of his uncle's depression as he declined into madness.

He needed confirmation that he was not cursed.

Wyatt wanted confirmation that all of his recent success was something he had earned on his own.

He paced around his loft, racking his brain, trying to think of anyone he could confide in with this piece of his inheritance. He knew Melody was off of the table. He also knew Samantha would not understand what he would be trying to convey. It frustrated Wyatt that his inner circle had collapsed to such a small group over the recent years. He thought of professionals in his art world that he could reach out to, but no one came to mind. If he wanted the painting appraised, sure. He had several people he could call at this point for that, but that was not a service he was in need of. Wyatt knew he needed to discuss this with someone that would have intimate knowledge of his uncle's final days.

He thought of Maurice. He thought of how intimately close his uncle had been with Maurice, and how Maurice was the one who initially told Wyatt of the painting and the letter.

Then Wyatt remembered that Maurice was explicit about how he had not read the letter, and that no one had, except his uncle. Wyatt doubted that Maurice would be able to speak to the physical interpretation of his uncle's madness, beyond speculation anyway. Wyatt knew that if speculation was what he was after, he need not look beyond himself in the mirror.

He needed someone who could speak with authority to what it could potentially look like to witness the collapse of a man's mind. Perhaps a therapist, or a psychiatrist…

A psychiatrist, Wyatt thought. *That's it!*

Wyatt recalled his uncomfortable interrogation with Detective Johns, when they asked him about his uncle's final days. Wyatt remembered Detective Johns mentioning that his uncle had been seeing a psychiatrist.

"What was his name…" Wyatt asked himself, outlaid, as he paced his living room area. "Dr. —" Wyatt grunted with frustration. He had become so annoyed with his lack of ability to remember conversations in detail. An oversight that brought much frustration to those around him. "Dr. — An… Anderson? No, that's not it. Dr. — Erin? Aaron? Anders… ugh!"

Wyatt paced and paced, and grew more and more frustrated that he could not remember his uncle's psychiatrist's name. He pulled out his cell phone, and scrolled through his contacts until he found the number he was looking for.

Wyatt called Maurice.

It rang a few times before a voice on the other end picked up.

"Wyatt, hello. How are you?" Mauricie sounded tired on the other end of the call.

"Hi, Maurice. Sorry to call, I just had a quick question, I was hoping you could help me out?" Wyatt asked, and still nervously paced.

"No need to apologize, Wyatt. Of course, what can I help you out with?" Maurice responded with his typical soft, and kind demeanor.

"I'm trying to remember the name of my uncle's psychiatrist. Any chance you know?" Wyatt stopped pacing for a moment, and held his breath. He knew if Maurice could not remember, he would be entirely out of luck.

"Oh, yes, of course. Scholden — Erich Scholden. Teaches over at U.C.L.A., I believe. Runs a private practice in Westwood."

A wave of relief rushed over Wyatt, and he remembered Detective Johns saying the name.

"Erich Scholden, yes, that's it. Thank you so much, Maurice! I really appreciate it." Wyatt smiled, and Dr. Scholden ended the call.

Wyatt again looked at the letter he held in his hands.

The rules, the scribbles, and hopefully the answers he was seeking. Out loud,Wyatt mumbled to himself.

Finally, Wyatt knew who he needed to speak with.

"Dr. Erich Scholden."

CHAPTER 13

Wyatt stood on the sidewalk.

Dr. Erich Schoden's office building was plain, and unassuming. He shared an industrial space with a dentist, and a custom decal company "specializing in whatever you need." Wyatt looked at the main window of the decal business, and saw multiple merchandise options. T-shirts, stickers, hats, bandanas… all brandished with what appeared to be their slogan. "If you can think it, we can print it."

Wyatt approached the building, and looked for the suite numbers on the wall. He knew which suite he was looking for, but did not know where in this building it was. Based on the number outside the decal business, he knew he would be close.

He passed by a few other businesses before he arrived at Suite 109. Dr. Erich Scholden.

There was not much branding on Dr. Scholden's suite door. It simply had the suite number, one-zero-nine, and Dr. Scholden's LLC title.

Dr. Erich Scholden, M.D, PsyD.

Wyatt knocked on the door gently, but then after not receiving a response, he decided he had maybe been too gentle. He knocked again, this time slightly harder, and heard a faint voice from inside call out to him.

"Come on in!"

The office was cold.

While Dr. Erich Scholden was a simple man, he was a brilliant professional. His long, illustrious, and decorated career had included names even people in the most remote places on Earth had heard of, and yet, you would never know it from discussing his work with him. He never wore his accomplishments, though they indeed brought him great pride. Pride his ego simply kept to himself.

Dr. Erich Scholden was one of the few people on the planet whose career followed the thing they are actually passionate about. He had been obsessed with the intricacies and complexities of the human mind from quite a young age. By his early teenage years, he knew he was bound to go into the profession of psychiatry.

His office's walls were covered floor to ceiling in various accolades and achievements. His multiple degrees from multiple universities, recognitions from different private entities across the world, and even an achievement award from the American Psychiatric Association. What Wyatt assumed was the shrink's equivalent to an Academy Honorary Award from the Academy of Motion Picture Arts and Sciences. Wyatt thought of how intimidating it would potentially feel to walk into Dr. Erich Scholden's office only to see this monument to his successes staring you right in the face.

Wyatt took a deep breath, and remained in the, albeit, brief moment of solace that he was not here to receive treatment.

Dr. Erich Scholden leaned back in his leather, Vitra Grand Executive Highback desk chair. Wyatt noticed it did not squeak. Everything about this man, to Wyatt, felt expensive. Finally, after he settled in, Dr. Erich Scholden smiled at Wyatt.

"I believe this is the first opportunity for us to have met." Dr. Scholden said behind his thin, wire-rimmed glasses.

"I think so, yeah," Wyatt stuttered back. He could not understand why he felt so instantly anxious. "We may have met at a party once or twice," Wyatt corrected himself. "But you would have had no reason to remember me."

"I'm sorry, I don't recall. And my apologies for the circumstances now, of course." Dr. Scholden's voice was warm, and Wyatt believed the sincerity in his few words.

"Thanks, that means a lot." Wyatt smiled back. "And I also really appreciate you making time to see me today, especially on such short notice. It… it was important, and I appreciate you making it a priority." Dr. Scholden jumped onto the end of Wyatt's sentence almost in an attempt to prevent him from adding on any additional praise.

"But I must be transparent," Dr. Scholden continued. He took his time, and chose each word with precision and confidence. "I am… fairly unsure of what you are here to, or hoping to discover."

"Of course, I think I thought it would just be easier to discuss this in person, as opposed to trying to describe it over the phone." Wyatt slowly slid his fingertip against his beard, then started to reach for his bag. Before he could open it, Dr. Scholden stopped him.

"You understand that, even given the circumstances around your uncle's … passing … that I am bound by certain legal restraints on what I can and cannot be compelled to share. Contrary to popular belief, Patient and Provider Confidentially does, in fact, survive the patient." Dr. Scholden crinkled his brow, and spoke with his delicate tone. Wyatt stared back, confused at first.

"Oh, I — uh, sorry," Wyatt was not as succinct with his word selection, "I'm not here to chat about how crazy my uncle was, or anything like that." Wyatt tried to laugh at a poor attempt at his joke in bad taste. Dr. Scholden, predictably, was not amused.

"I try not to use that word here," he said and cordially smiled back at Wyatt.

"Oh, sorry, I didn't mean —" Wyatt could feel his toes tickle his uvula.

"It's okay. It's a common error. I also try to not judge anyone who sits in my office, regardless of their purpose for sitting there." Wyatt thought of how kind Dr. Erich Scholden seemed. "So. What is it that I can help you with, Wyatt?" He continued.

Wyatt again reached for his bag, and carefully slung open a flap revealing the bag's contents. His laptop, some magazines, and a couple of notebooks were visible for the moment that the bag was open.

Wyatt dug around, and stalled slightly with a few verbal cues. "Uh, um, eh —" Finally, he found what he was looking for, and pulled from his bag the letter he had received from his uncle as part of his inheritance.

"I don't suppose you and Uncle Jack ever discussed his will?" Wyatt asked. Dr. Scholden looked confused for a moment.

"We did not. That is not usually a topic I discuss with my patients." Wyatt nodded, and looked at the letter in his hands.

"I didn't think so, to be honest. Well, I inherited a piece of my uncle's work. A painting. There wasn't really any context around the piece, and to be frank, I didn't really want it at all. My uncle's lawyer informed me of it, and arranged for it to be delivered, so on and so forth." Wyatt wondered if the Doctor could notice the non-verbal cues Wyatt could feel himself developing. The anxious fidgeting of his fingers, the fact that he had pulled at his shirt and adjusted his position in the less expensive chair he sat in. *Surely,* Wyatt thought. "Anyway, to make a long story… not as long… I got the piece, and all that came with it was this letter."

Wyatt extended his hand across the desk, and handed the folded letter to Dr. Erich Scholden. Dr. Scholden took the letter from Wyatt and carefully unfolded it.

"I am fully confident that you are aware of the … relational struggles between my uncle and I." In any other environment Wyatt would laugh at himself for trying to sound so much more distinguished than he knew he was. "But this letter… it just seems odd."

Dr. Erich Scholden examined the letter in his hands. The texture and discoloration of the paper itself, the various scribbles, the different styles of text, and most obviously, the entirely different handwritings.

"I know you can't share a ton about how cra— how... mentally... disturbed... my uncle was before his death, but I am very much hoping you could give me some insight on this letter."

Dr. Scholden continued to examine the letter closely, without saying anything. He took his time, turned the page around, tilted his head. From Wyatt's point of view, Dr. Scholden seemed to be just as confused by it as Wyatt had felt from the beginning.

"This is... certainly peculiar." Dr. Scholden finally said.

"There are a ton of oddities about it, but the most obvious to me is that these scribblings seem to be in completely different handwriting. I mean, is that something my uncle could have done?" Wyatt asked carefully, hoping to get as much information from Dr. Scholden as possible.

"In my experience, certain psychoses can lend themselves to abnormal mental function." Dr. Scholden did not take his eyes off of the letter.

"So... yes?"

"In short, yes." Dr. Scholden responded quickly, and with certainty. "I obviously cannot disclose the details of your uncle's mental decline, but there are certain aspects of it that have been well-documented outside of these four walls."

"Yes," Wyatt agreed, perhaps too quickly. "Sorry," he awkwardly smiled at the Doctor.

"It is, in my professional opinion, entirely plausible that a rapid decline in mental stability could lend itself to the alteration of every day, normal motor functions; Handwriting being a prime example."

Wyatt nodded, and listened the Dr. Scholden intently.

"Now, I am not a graphologist, but even simply looking at this, I can see similarities in the different blurbs. Again, I am not necessarily the mind to make a decision like that, however —"

"Have you seen that before? A patient declining mentally so rapidly that they start writing… different?" Wyatt interrupted, and it gave Dr. Scholden pause.

"I — I have, yes."

"Have you seen it happen four or five times?"

"… I have not." Dr. Scholden responded.

"So while it is possible… in your opinion, is it likely?" Wyatt again asked carefully.

"I do not know if I would feel comfortable answering that."

"Look, Dr. Scholden, I know you can't tell me protected information because of confidentiality, or HIPAA, or whatever, but you can't look at this letter and suggest that everything about it is… normal…" Wyatt looked at Dr. Scholden, and took a breath. Dr. Scholden looked back at Wyatt, and then leaned back in his chair. He carefully removed his glasses and rubbed his eyes. "I'll take anything. I just need *something*." Dr. Scholden could feel the desperation in Wyatt's request.

"It is not a secret that your uncle's mental capacity declined remarkably quickly in his final weeks. He became detached; disinterested. He began being late to our appointments, which was wildly uncharacteristic to your uncle's extreme punctuality. His cognitive skills began to … deteriorate before my eyes, session to session." Wyatt listened intently, and leaned forward in his chair. "To be frank, I entirely assumed he was developing Early-Onset Alzheimer's Disease. I had begun working with his lawyer—"

"Maurice…" Wyatt was quick to interrupt.

"Yes, Maurice Pallen, to arrange for any necessary logistics if that diagnosis came. Your uncle simply never made it to his appointment." Dr. Scholden took a deep breath, and shook his head. Wyatt assumed he was disappointed for sharing as much as he just had.

"Look, I really appreciate all of this, it's really helpful," Wyatt tried to comfort the doctor.

"I really should not be sharing any of this with you," Dr. Scholden hesitated, but Wyatt encouraged him to go deeper.

"I understand, I'm just really trying to understand… you said he became obsessed?" Wyatt asked. After another moment, Dr. Scholden continued.

"Yes. He became singularly focused in his final weeks. An intense obsession, really." Dr. Scholden's voice trailed off slightly, and it gave Wyatt a sense of concern. He knew there was still more to be said.

"Obsessed with what?" Wyatt asked, admittedly afraid of the response.

"You," Dr. Scholden said plainly. "He had become obsessed with you."

Wyatt was shocked. He was not sure how to respond. He leaned back in his chair, and took a deep breath. He thought if he let the silence thicken to a certain point, the doctor would have to be compelled to continue. Wyatt was right.

"He became consumed with you, and your career achievements, and … he simply became obsessed with you, Wyatt."

"Anything else?" Wyatt again goaded the doctor into continuing.

"He also became consumed with what he kept referring to as his 'final' piece."

Wyatt froze in his chair. He recalled that exact phrase from his conversation with Mo, and how he had inherited his uncle's final piece.

"His final piece," Wyatt repeated after a long silence.

"He was consumed by it. It had become the only thing of any value to him. He was intent on ensuring that you would receive his final piece."

"So he was planning this all along in front of you, and what, you weren't compelled to stop him?" Wyatt had started to feel his heart rate increase, and his face warmed and his cheeks went flush.

"It's not that simple, Wyatt. His speech was speculative. It was metaphorical. It was forward thinking. He used... futurism. *He* was speaking as a futurist." The doctor tried to defend himself.

"He said, 'When I die, I'll make sure Wyatt — whom I've suddenly become obsessed with — gets my final piece — which I've also become obsessed with,' and you didn't think to talk to him about that more?" Wyatt felt his anger rising.

"As I said, it is not that simple, Wyatt. My responsibility was to listen, and to ensure my client's safety while in my presence. I have little to no control over my client's decision-making outside of these four walls; unfortunately. Your uncle used no such language to alert me to any threat level, whatsoever. Any more so than usual, I mean."

"I don't understand." Wyatt said.

"Yes, you do. You're an artist, just as your uncle was. You absolutely understand what I am saying." Dr. Scholden rubbed his face again. Wyatt understood. Not willing to become one of Dr. Erich Scholden's patients, Wyatt pressed the conversation forward.

"So coming back to the letter, then..." Wyatt spoke as he pointed at the paper as it rested on the desk where the doctor had left it. Dr. Scholden picked the letter up, and looked it over once more. "Do you actually believe... do you really genuinely believe that my uncle wrote all of the script on this letter?"

"What I think, what I believe, and what I can assume to be true based on my professional experience, unfortunately, can be very different things." Dr. Scholden responded.

"Humor me?" Wyatt asked.

"Scientifically? Yes. In my professional experience, and given the extremely rapid decline of your uncle's mental, cognitive function, I find it completely plausible that Jackson could have produced all of the varying script on this letter." Wyatt raised one eyebrow.

"But?"

"But —" Dr. Scholden hesitated before he continued. Wyatt understood that the doctor was carefully and meticulously searching for the right words to say. "I don't know. It seems... it just seems unlikely for a person in such dire mental condition to create to such varying, differing 'characters,' and to employ their individual penmanship all onto one letter. I don't know what would be the point, to put it in simple terms."

Wyatt thought for a long moment. All of the information he had been taking in read past his mind like a favorite novel. He knew what he wanted to ask as his one, final follow up question, but he was not sure he was ready to ask it. The concern, in Wyatt's mind, was how the doctor would respond to this final question.

Finally, Wyatt decided to give in, and leave all of his cards on the table.

"Dr. Scholden," Wyatt's voice trembled. The reaction caught the doctor's attention. "Do you believe in curses?"

Dr. Scholden looked up to meet Wyatt's eyes, and tilted his head to the side. He again noticed the distress in Wyatt's expression. There was a deep disquietude in Wyatts's eyes that was not lost on him.

"As in..." Dr. Scholden prompted Wyatt for more clarification.

"Curses. I don't know how to say that differently. Voodoo, hex, malediction... Curses. Like... a curse."

"Scientifically speaking?" Dr. Scholden responded.

Wyatt simply shook his head, "no." The doctor exhaled slightly, and rested back in his five-thousand-dollar desk chair.

"I think that there are things about our world of which we have no understanding of. And I am unsure if we will ever understand certain things. I am unsure if we are ever supposed to understand certain things. So, that being said, I do not know if I believe in the validity of curses. And while I understand that my opinion on the matter of curses is truly neither here, nor there, I do, however, believe in the validity of the hold that the idea of their existence can take on us. The grip on our reality which they can squeeze with tremendous force. And I do believe in the mental, physical, and psychological toll that grip can take on us, as people." Wyatt nodded slightly, and looked to his feet. He was not sure if that answer helped or not, but he was still glad he asked the question.

"Got it," Wyatt was not sure how to respond, and he could not find any other decent words.

"Wyatt," Dr. Scholden opened a drawer of his desk, and rummaged around slightly. "I want you to know that my professional relationship with your uncle is no deterrent to my ability to provide help to those in need."

Dr. Scholden reached out towards Wyatt, extending his business card. Wyatt just stared at it at first, before he finally took the card from Dr. Scholden's hands. He looked at it, and saw Dr. Scholden's office contact information.

"In my experience, some of the world's most brilliant artists are often the world's most tortured souls." Dr. Scholden gently smiled, and tried to make Wyatt feel comfortable. "No one is above getting the help they need, and are entitled to."

Wyatt set the business card back on Dr. Scholden's desk, and smiled back.

"Thanks, doc, but I think I'm all set for now." Dr. Scholden nodded, and smiled again.

"My door is always open to you," Dr. Scholden responded.

"Thank you for your time today," Wyatt was somehow both genuine, and ignored the passing moment. "I really appreciate your insight." Just as quickly as Wyatt had arrived, he left.

Wyatt arrived back at his loft quickly, after very little traffic home from the Santa Monica area where Dr. Scholden's office was. He walked through the door, and tossed his keys down onto the entryway table. The clank of his keys against the table loudly echoed throughout his loft, and he was taken aback by how quiet it was inside. He took a deep breath, and walked into the kitchen.

Almost instantly, after he crossed the loft's threshold, he felt that familiar tingle return to his fingertips. His heart beat pulsed in his wrists, and he again felt drawn to the painting. He wished he had elaborated to the doctor this exact feeling. This undeniable experience he had been having, and knew he would likely continue to have. If he had just articulated this feeling, he felt that Dr. Scholden would have been more willing to connect further.

He ignored the feeling, and walked over to his windows. He cranked them open slightly, and his loft was quickly filled with the cool, night breeze and the loud sounds of his downtown neighborhood. He felt the wind against his face, and took another deep breath.

He walked over to his bed, and sat on its edge. He took his watch off, and set it on the table. He stretched his hands into the air, and tilted his neck to each side until it cracked in both directions.

Again, the tingling bubbled up in his fingers. Again, he felt that same, familiar draw towards the painting in the room to his left.

He clenched his fist together, and again, ignored the pulling. He instead walked to his kitchen, and opened his refrigerator. He took out his water carafe, and grabbed a glass from his counter. He poured a glass of water, and drank it quickly. He had not realized how anxious he had felt before meeting with the doctor, and only now realized how dehydrated he felt. He poured another glass, and the tingling returned.

Frustrated, Wyatt walked into the secondary room and stared at the painting.

The pulsing intensified, the tingling like bursting blood vessels in his fingers.

Wyatt stood in front of the work, and again ran through all of the competing ideas in his mind. *Was this painting cursed?* Had his uncle knowingly put in his possession an actual cursed object? He knew that he and Jackson's relationship was strained at best, but would his uncle burden him with the responsibility of such a curse?

How realistic is the thought that this painting is actually magic? So far, the simple promise of the lyrical prose of the letter had held true.

"Wildest dreams," Wyatt said to himself.

It was true. All of the very specific ideas and definitions of success Wyatt had applied to himself had seemingly, suddenly, fallen into place. Again, the war waged in Wyatt's mind that these achievements were not due to a random curse, but to Wyatt's persistent hard work and determination.

Then again, that tiny voice in Wyatt's mind spoke up, and ruined everything. *Come on, Wyatt,* it would say, *do not be so naive. You are not even that talented in the first place.*

Wyatt was well acquainted with this voice. He had lived with it his entire life.

The only reason anyone gives a shit about you is because of this painting's curse.

Annoyed, frustrated, and starting to get angry, Wyatt walked out of the room.

He poured himself another glass of water, and quickly drank it down. He then found himself pacing in his living room talking out loud, working through all of his thoughts.

He laughed for a moment, and thought that he felt like he was going insane.

If this painting was magic, and was the reason behind his recent success and acclaim, then how would he not continue? And if the curse was not responsible, yet he continued obeying its commands, what would be the difference? Would that invalidate the acclaim the world assigned to him? If not one ever found out about the painting and its beautiful curse, who would care?

People only want to give the standing ovation because it makes them feel like they helped the production somehow. If someone chose to believe that Wyatt's art was the reason, then what would it matter if it was simply a curse?

Then again, if the curse is real, how quickly would Wyatt suffer his uncle's same fate? Assuming the validity of the curse, and that it led to his uncle's eventual demise, would Wyatt, by virtue of continuing to obey the rules, eventually run his course and lose his mind, just as Jackson had? Just how long were these curse's rules sustainable?

But then again, what if Wyatt was already suffering his uncle's fate, and letting the idea of this asinine curse devolve his own mind into its own tortured chaos?

Wyatt somehow found himself again standing in front of the painting, brush in hand. His fingertips numb with burning nerves.

"Am I going crazy," he said to himself out loud. "Probably says something that I'm talking to a painting." He smiled to himself.

He once again stared at the painting itself. The colors, the layers, the absolute chaos… it still made little to no sense to him. He again paid particular attention to the varying styles he had noticed previously. The images, the shadows, the different accidental impressionism from layers, upon layers of paint being so constantly added. *This is a curse? This is barely a painting,* he thought to himself.

He wondered where his uncle's final stroke of paint was. He wondered how much of what he could see was added by his uncle. He wondered how long this painting had been in his uncle's possession.

Was it possible that his uncle only saw success in his art because of this cursed piece? Would his uncle have been just another run of the mill, no named, struggling artist had it not been for someone else laying this burden upon him?

The thought simultaneously made him smile, and broke his heart. He felt regret for what he now understood were terrible things he had said and felt about his uncle. Perhaps he was beginning to understand that maybe his uncle was not neglecting him at all. Maybe his uncle was protecting him.

And then he remembered his uncle gave him this painting, and he felt defeated again. Even in death, Jackson made it difficult for Wyatt to feel anything but disappointment.

He was frustrated with how consumed he had instantly become with such an insane idea. He took a deep breath, and made a definitive commitment.

He had worked his entire career to be ready for this moment. He had earned these achievements. He had earned these accolades. He, and he alone, deserved this new life.

His success was not due to a piece of art.

There was no curse.

He refused to believe in it.

He could not believe in it.

Wyatt set the brush down without adding a stroke of paint, and almost instantly the tingling sensation dissipated. Validated that he made the correct, definitive decision, he walked out of the secondary room, clicking the light switch off on his way back towards his kitchen.

His mind only briefly flooded with the anxiety of a potential curse. The "what if's" fluttered through his id, only to fade away almost as quickly as they had appeared.

For the first time in a long time, Wyatt felt at peace.

CHAPTER 14

He awoke the next morning, and went about his normal routine. He took his time actually getting out of bed, then promptly made it; he walked to his kitchen in his t-shirt and underwear, and put on a kettle of water; he brushed his teeth, and decided between fixing his hair or wearing a hat for the day. Hat won, which it usually did.

Throughout his normal morning cadence, he was keenly aware that his fingertips had not tingled. His soul had not been called to, and his mind had not felt coerced into the secondary room to add benign paint to the cryptic piece on the easel. He smiled as he sipped his pour over coffee, and thought himself master of his domain.

He also had begun to think of how silly it was to be so worked up, and caught up, on some fantasy. *What curse,* he thought.

It was a beautiful day, he could actually hear birds singing over the chaotic sounds of the cars speeding through downtown intersections.

Also for the first time in weeks, Wyatt walked not into the secondary room with his uncle's painting, but to his primary workspace. His most current original painting stood on its own easel in the middle of the room. He realized he had not even thought of his own work since his uncle's painting had come into his loft. A regenerated excitement filled his spirit. He smiled from ear to ear, and felt eager to get to work.

He took a sip of his coffee, and stood silent, staring at his original work.

He felt pride.

It was almost as if he were looking at his own work with new eyes.

His style seemed somehow more clear. His intention seemed apparent. His delicate stroke felt feminine and important. He felt pride. Genuine, and real pride.

He studied all of his previous decisions as they sat on the canvas. The color choices, and how he chose to blend them; the layered moments, and the texture of them. He took a small step back to see the piece in its entirety, and he smiled wide. He realized he was in the midst of creating his favorite original piece. He had not felt this way about this particular painting since he had started on it several months prior. Again, he felt a sense of excitement, seeing it in this new light.

Wyatt picked up his paint palette, and added fresh blots of wet paint to the ceramic slab. He picked up his brush, and got to work.

The ideas and creative flow poured out of his mind and onto this canvas. He felt his brain perfectly syncopated with his hands. He moved quickly, but intentionally and precisely. He was painting exactly what he wanted, and what he knew was right.

Blues, and reds, and greens, and yellows; all good. *Good,* he thought to himself. *This is good.*

He felt so consumed by his unexpected burst of inspiration that he had completely lost track of time. He was snapped back into reality when his loft landline phone rang, and loudly echoed through his space. It caught him off guard, but he promptly set his brush and palette down, wiped his hands clean, and walked towards the receiver.

"This is Wyatt," he said.

"Hey babe!" Samantha's cheerful tone brought another smile to his face. "I'm running a few minutes late, but I am on my way! I'm so sorry," she said with an apologetic tone.

For a moment, Wyatt could not remember what she would be referring to. Late? Did they have plans? He knew he had a meeting scheduled with his sister later that afternoon, but Samantha was not coming to that. At least he did not remember inviting her. To be honest, Wyatt could not even remember what his meeting with Melody was about either. That meeting was also much, much later in the day. *Surely not,* he thought. He thought better than to ask again, so he responded plainly.

"Oh, no worries, love. Take your time, I'll be here."

"Great, thank you. I love you! See you in a bit," she said.

"See you soon," he replied.

He hung up the phone, and thought again about what he was forgetting. Regardless, he knew he could likely not go with paint on his hands.

He walked to his bathroom, and freshened up. He washed his face and hands, brushed his teeth, and opted to fix his hair after all.

"Maybe tomorrow, hat friend," he jokingly said to himself.

Wyatt put on an outfit that was casual enough without feeling casual, but not dressed up too much. An appropriately neutral outfit so he would essentially be prepared for whatever plans he had already committed to.

Almost as soon as he finished lacing his brown, worn, leather boots, his building door buzzed. He walked over, and pressed the button granting entrance. A few minutes later, there was a knock at his door.

For a very brief moment, Wyatt realized that he did not talk to whoever he had just buzzed in. He assumed it was Samantha, and just let the person into his building.

Immediately, he thought of the painting, the curse.

His heart raced, just slightly, he felt his face flush red. What had he done? What if this was the moment the curse proved itself true?

He had let a stranger into his building, and this would be his demise. He took slow step after slow step to the door, and all the while his imagination loomed with impending doom. Murder, kidnapping, stalking; whatever was on the other side of his door… he knew it would be terror.

His heart raced, he felt his pulse pounding in his chest. He finally made it to his front door, and gently turned the handle. The door slowly creaked open, and just as he was certain he would be face to face with his tragic end…

Samantha smiled through the crack. She stood in the hallway wearing a crewneck sweater, black yoga pants, and her brand new, cream colored, Nike Dunks. She smiled at Wyatt, and looked him up and down before she wrapped her arms around him, and kissed his cheek.

"You look nice," she said with a casual tone. Wyatt sort of laughed.

"Don't be mad?" He spoke sheepishly.

"Oh, god," Samantha said, sarcastically expected the worst. "What? What happened? What'd you do? What'd you forget?" She had a smile, so Wyatt knew she was not actually upset.

"All right, well, I spent some time this morning working on my newest piece," he started. Samantha cocked one eyebrow up, and listened.

"Okay…" Her words drawn out with skepticism.

"And it felt great, thanks for asking," he replied, and she laughed, "but I got so into that I completely lost track of time, and then when you called I could not, still can't, for the life of me, remember what we are doing today," his voice trailed off and drifted up into a higher octave. He squinted, embarrassed. Samantha laughed, and kissed his cheek again.

"You weirdo." She smiled, and Wyatt exhaled, relieved. "We," she said, her arms still wrapped around him, "are going to look at a house together. Over in Larchmont. Remember? It's that cute little two bedroom I found."

Everything came flooding back to Wyatt, and he did remember.

"Oh, my god, that's right!" He laughed to himself, and took a deep breath. "I do remember! And I'm so excited to do that," he said, and they both laughed. "I can't believe that is what slipped my mind."

"It's okay!" She made sure he knew she was not at all put off. "If I had a dollar for every time I forgot I had plans, or what those plans were, I'd probably buy a house for us by myself," she said, and again they laughed.

"Whew," Wyatt exaggerated a relieved motion with his hand on his forehand. "Okay, great. Let's go look at a fucking house."

"Let's do it." She smiled back at him.

It was only about a five mile drive from Wyatt's downtown loft at 6th and Spring St. to the Los Angeles neighborhood known as Larchmont Village, but as they sat into Wyatt's car, their GPS app said traffic would make this typical fifteen minute drive almost forty-five minutes. An expected amount of time for a weekday afternoon.

Samantha had a Spotify playlist playing through the speakers, and Wyatt felt the sun warming the left side of his body. Samantha rested her hand on his thigh, as a new James Blake song started softly in the background. Wyatt smiled to himself, and found himself thankful for how perfect this moment felt.

Moments like this erased the inevitable frustration that Los Angeles traffic caused.

Wyatt felt Samantha turn her head towards him, and she stared at him. He smiled slightly, and turned to meet her eyes with his. She smiled back.

"What?" He asked, playfully.

"Nothing." She said. "I love you."

"I love you too," he said back, eyes back on the car in front of them.

In hindsight, Wyatt would have to admit that this was maybe his most favorite forty-five-minute span he had experienced in a long time.

They pulled up outside the gorgeous home in Larchmont Village.

"Pretty good amount of street parking," Wyatt looked around at the area they found themselves in.

"It's got a great school district, it was recently renovated, this house is perfect." Samantha said, already beaming. Wyatt laughed, and they got out of the car.

The home was beautiful. Dated, in appearance, but quite lovely.

It had a yellowish, beige coat of paint on the exterior which made its bright red door pop. White trim outlined the outside of the home, and looked clean around the multiple, street facing window. Its second floor stretched the whole length of the home, and Wyatt could tell there would be plenty of space for the two of them. A tall chimney stood on the far left side of the home, and Wyatt had to admit, "This looks pretty cozy."

"Wait until you see inside," Samantha said, still bursting with excitement.

"Wait until *I* see inside?" Wyatt asked. "Have you already come?" Samantha smirked mischievously, and made a playful grimace, as if to apologize.

"Don't be mad?" She smirked again, and Wyatt laughed it off.

"You brat," he said through his chuckle.

"Hey, at least I didn't forget these plans." She playfully mocked his lapse in memory.

"Fair enough," Wyatt said back, and pulled her in for a hug. "Ready?" He asked.

"Ready," she squeezed his hand hard, and smiled back.

They walked up to the home, and knocked on the bright red door.

The real estate agent greeted them, and brought them inside. She showed the two around the entire home, highlighting all of its key features and built in amenities. The most exciting of which, to Wyatt, was an internal espresso machine literally built into the wall of the kitchen.

"Oh, my God, it's got wall coffee," Wyatt stage whispered to Samantha.

"Why do you think I am showing you *this house,*" she smirked again. Samantha knew exactly what she was doing.

After the guided tour around the entire home, the three of them reconvened in the main living room.

"Well," the real estate agent said, almost prompting the obvious excitement that Samantha was not well hiding. "What do we think?"

Wyatt felt Samantha look at him, letting him make the first move.

"It's really nice," he finally relented.

"The seller did just drop the price by $50,000, as well. So it is a fantastic time to make an offer." The real estate agent smiled at Samantha again, who was practically shaking in her Dunks.

"That's great. What does that bring the total to?" Wyatt asked, terrified of the answer.

Larchmont Village was a very clean and safe part of Los Angeles. And that was for a specific reason. It was also very expensive.

"The new total, after the price reduction, is now right at two-million, four forty-nine."

Wyatt felt his stomach in his throat.

Two and a half million dollars? He thought, and his wallet started boiling in his back pocket.

"So it's right in line with the budget we talked about," Samantha quickly jumped in, feeling the steam coming from Wyatt's ears. In truth, $2,449,000 was not an altogether terrible price for this house in this location. Having grown up incredibly poor, though, the number still made Wyatt's spine shiver. "And it's a forever home," Wyatt heard Samantha pleading through her rational word choice.

Wyatt had been budgeting to be able to make this type of decision as soon as he could. His recent burst of success had simply expedited his effort. *Strike while the iron is hot,* he told himself. The truth was, he could afford this investment right now. *It's now or never.*

"I'll definitely want to think it over," Wyatt said, "but this place is really wonderful. Thank you for everything today," he said to the agent. Samantha smiled wide again, and he felt her squeeze his hand hard. Part of him wanted to throw caution to the wind and say, "let's do it," but he thought better of it.

Samantha talked the entire way home, and Wyatt felt even more of an urge to call the real estate agent and make an offer. Instead, he listened to Samantha's vision for their future in their potential home.

He loved this woman.

He loved hearing her discuss their future.

He loved this moment.

"It has the perfect amount of rooms, so you can have multiple places to paint. I could set up my office in the den downstairs and work from home. We wouldn't get in each other's way, but we could still be at home together. Can't you see it?" She asked him, and stared out the passenger window.

"Honestly, I really can." He responded. And he was telling the truth. Continuous thoughts played through his mind, and he felt at peace.

"And I know it's expensive, but we both are able to right now. I'm in line for a massive promotion, and you've become a household fucking name. It's a perfect time for an investment like this."

He had to admit, she was making quite the compelling argument.

"You're not wrong." He said.

"I just love thinking about all of this, and knowing that it's with you." She smiled again, and put her hand back on his thigh.

He smiled back, and moved his left arm to touch the back of her head. He squeezed her hair gently, and felt her rest her head into his hand.

"Fuck it," Wyatt said. He felt Samantha look at him suddenly. "Let's do it."

"What do you mean?" She asked, quickly.

"When we get back to my loft, I'll call the agent and make an offer."

Wyatt could feel Samantha explode with excitement and joy.

"Are you sure? I know we talked about taking our time, and finding the right one —" She tried to rationalize their decision-making process, but Wyatt interrupted her.

"This is the right one, don't you think?" He briefly looked at her, and smiled. He could see that Samantha was almost in tears, and she nodded silently. "Right?"

"It is, I really think it is." Samantha could not hold in her smile. She leaned over the middle console to kiss his cheek again.

Later that afternoon, Wyatt finally arrived at his sister's office building. He was only about ten minutes late for his scheduled meeting with Melody, which was admittedly more punctual than he normally was for meetings. It was his first time at the space she had inherited from their uncle, so he assumed he could blame it on that. He knew her day must have gotten out of hand, because she had not even had the chance to text him her patented, "I hate you," like she always does when he runs late for their meetings; which was usually always.

He was greeted at the reception desk by a long-time employee of Melody's. Jessica sat cheerful behind the long desk in the main lobby of the building.

"Wyatt!" She exclaimed, and she hopped out of her chair to rush around the desk and give him a hug.

"Hey, Jess!" Wyatt replied.

"It's so great to see you. Isn't this space ridiculous?" Jessica was older than most would expect, but she was incredibly organized, and really loved Melody. She was a perfect fit for this particular role in Melody's growing enterprise.

"It's huge, yeah. I'm excited to see what Mel did with the space."

"You're going to love it. I'll ping her and let her know that you're here, but you're family," Jessica pointed to the far side of the lobby, "take the elevator to the fourth floor. That's Melody's floor."

Melody's floor? Wyatt thought.

"Thanks so much, Jess." Wyatt smiled, and started to walk towards the elevator.

As soon as Wyatt approached the elevator, the door opened, and Wyatt stepped in. He pressed four, and almost instantly the door opened again. Wyatt was shocked at how quick and smooth that elevator was. It was already an upgrade from the building he remembered from when it was his uncle's.

Wyatt soon realized that the fourth floor was not just more offices. The fourth floor was essentially a live-in loft. Full kitchen, multiple bedrooms, a huge living area with any and every amenity you could think of.

He moseyed his way through the beautiful space, peeking his head into any open doorway he could find. He was really impressed with how much Melody had already done to make this building so much more inviting. She had only had it for a few months, but it truly already felt brand new.

In one main living space, he noticed several beautiful pieces of pottery in square cubbies built into the wall. Each one had a small placard on the wall next to it explaining the piece, the artist, and the history of it.

Wyatt approached one, and read the card. Though the card explicitly said "please do not touch the art," his inner child brain immediately had the thought, *you should pick it up.* Almost as soon as the thought entered his mind, he heard Melody's maternal voice call out from an unknown office, "Don't touch it, Wyatt." He quickly retracted his hands, and looked around. He laughed at himself, and called out to her.

"How the fuck did you even know?" He heard Melody laugh back at him.

She walked into the room, and waved her hand, calling him towards her. She disappeared into a hallway, and Wyatt followed after her

"I always know," she said from the hallway. Wyatt just laughed and shook his head.

They walked into the main office of the floor, and Wyatt sat down on an incredibly comfortable chair.

"Melody, this… this place is amazing," he said.

"You like what I've done?"

"Love it. Do you stay here?" Wyatt gesticulated around the condo-style fourth floor.

"Sometimes, yeah, if it's a long day and I don't want to drive. But it's mainly for higher end clients, so they don't have to book an expensive room somewhere. They can just take their meetings here, and crash for a few nights." Melody poured herself a glass of water.

"That's really smart." Wyatt looked around.

Her office was gigantic. He felt proud of his sister. She had been building this empire for years, and with or without him, she was doing it.

"Especially for when my clients go under the knife, ya know?" Wyatt realized how clever his sister was. "So they don't have to worry about being seen by anyone they don't want to be seen by while they recover."

"Don't most facilities have housing?"

"Yeah, for $3,200 per night. Here they can stay for free." She grabbed a glass and asked, "Want a bourbon?" He enthusiastically nodded.

"Please, that would be awesome." Wyatt replied. "Why don't you just charge them like, half that rate," Wyatt said laughing.

"Because my average client relationship lifespan is eleven years. The industry average is five."

Wyatt laughed, and shrugged in agreement. *Touche,* he thought.

"I'm really proud of you, sis. This is amazing." Wyatt replied, and took the bourbon from her.

Melody finally sat down behind her desk and Wyatt watched as she exhaled long. She looked exhausted. She smiled back at him, and held up her own glass of bourbon.

"Cheers," she smiled as she sunk deeper into her comfortable desk chair. Wyatt laughed, and held up his glass to her.

"Cheers, sis."

They both took a sip, and Wyatt closed his eyes.

"Wow, that's incredible."

"It's good, right?"

"Amazing," Wyatt said.

"It was a gift from a new client," Melody said with a devious grin. Wyatt cocked an eyebrow up, and stared back at his sister.

"Is that right..." Wyatt raise one eyebrow and exaggerated tilting his head to the side.

Melody simply nodded back.

Wyatt knew his sister was not one to gossip in any way shape or form, so he understood that if he came right out and asked who, she likely would not tell him. Instead, he held up ten fingers, and started asking questions. Melody laughed, but played along.

"Film actor?" Wyatt asked, Melody nodded. Wyatt put his first finger down.

"Am I a fan?"

"Yes. Big time."

"Oh, interesting," Wyatt exaggerated an expression full of intrigue, and put down another finger.

"Has he had a film come out in the last year," Wyatt asked.

"Three." Melody answered, and Wyatt put down another finger.

"Oscar winner?" Wyatt asked, and Melody held back her laughter.

"One," she responded.

"He's won only one Oscar?" Melody nodded.

"Yes, and put another finger down, that question counts." Wyatt laughed, and reluctantly put another finger down.

"Fuck," Wyatt laughed even more. "Male or female?"

"Oh, great call. Male." Melody said.

Wyatt put one more finger down, and counted his remaining fingers. He had five fingers left. He thought for a moment, and his random Academy Award knowledge kicked in. There were only five contemporary male actors that have only won a single Academy Award.

"Pacino," Wyatt said.

"Nope," Melody responded, Wyatt put a finger down. Four left.

"McConaughey," Wyatt said.

"Nope," Melody laughed, and Wyatt put another finger down. Three left.

"Joaquin?"

Melody shook her head, Wyatt put a finger down. Two left. Wyatt grimaced, and his eyes went wide.

"Russell Crowe?"

Melody grimaced right back, but simply said, "Nope." Wyatt put a finger down. He was down to final finger, but he knew the answer.

"Shut the fuck up," Wyatt exclaimed.

Melody screamed out loud, and they celebrated.

"How the — how did that happen?" Wyatt asked, enthusiastically.

"I have no idea. I'm friends with some people on his agency's team, and they heard he was thinking about moving on from his management. They just made the introduction. We met a couple of days ago, and that's that." Melody was beaming with excitement and pride, and Wyatt could hardly contain himself.

"Here? You met him here?"

"Wyatt, he was sitting in that chair," Melody responded, and burst into laughter when Wyatt jumped out of the seat and walked around.

"He sat right here?" Melody laughed out loud at her brother and nodded.

"Right there," she said.

Wyatt rushed over to his sister, who stood and hugged him.

"What the fuck, Melody! That's amazing! Congratulations! Holy shit." They both sat back down, and while Melody still looked exhausted, there was now a chaotic energy in the room.

"It's honestly sort of insane. Things just keep happening, Wyatt, for both of us. All of the things we have wanted for so long. They're here, they're happening."

"This is… almost too much," Wyatt said through laughter.

"I'm going to be really honest with you, I do not remember why we were meeting today." Melody smiled and rolled her eyes. Wyatt raised his glass again to *cheers* his sister.

"Who cares. Let's just enjoy this whiskey from my favorite actor of all-time. What a world." Wyatt said. Melody raised her glass to him.

"Is everything good on your end?" She asked him. "Might as well try and get something done since you came all the way here."

"Are you kidding?" Wyatt asked, "That just made my week." Melody smiled, and stood up from behind her desk.

"Want some more?" She asked.

"Yes, please." Wyatt watched her walk over to a beautifully simple bar cart against her wall, and poured two more glasses of bourbon. She handed Wyatt his glass, and then picked up the bottle to show him.

Wyatt took the bottle from his sister, and held it in his hands.

"Wow," Wyatt said, "he touched this." Melody burst into laughter again, and sat back down.

"With his own hands," she said.

"With his own, one-time Oscar winning hands," Wyatt replied, and it made Melody laugh even harder.

Wyatt looked at the bottle.

It was not a particularly luxurious bottle of whiskey. It was a Blanton's Straight From the Barrel Bourbon Whiskey, valued at anywhere between three-hundred and four-hundred dollars per bottle. Not particularly, or outlandishly, expensive, but still more than a normal person would likely spend on bourbon whiskey. The bottles iconic horse and jockey bottle stoppers had become the brand's recognized trademark feature. So much so, that the company had begun selling the stoppers in collectable sets that came in a velvet bag to give as gifts, or to own yourself.

It also just happened to be one of Wyatt's favorite brands.

"We like the same whiskey," he said. Melody looked at her brother and saw a funny pride in his eyes. As if this were validating his taste in liquor.

"You have so much in common already," she humored him.

"And now I'm officially only one-degree of separation, how insane is that," Wyatt said laughing.

"What a time to be alive." She said.

"What a time to be alive." Wyatt smiled, and echoed his sister. "I'm proud of you, kid," he said to his sister, playfully.

"I'm proud of us," she said in return.

That night, once Wyatt returned home from his busy day, he stood silently in his kitchen for a moment. He noticed just how quiet his loft felt. There was no street noise, no dancing curtains, and finally, no urge to paint his uncle's piece. There was no tingling in his fingers, and no pull towards his secondary room. If there was a curse, he had broken it. He took a deep breath, and genuinely felt at peace.

"It was all in my head," he said to himself, smiling.

After a moment, he decided to test the limits on his new-found freedom from the canvas.

Wyatt walked into the secondary room, and stood directly in front of the painting.

Nothing.

It was like a space heater that had been unplugged from the wall. It did nothing. No tingles, no urges, it was just a lonely painting standing by itself in a neglected room.

Wyatt again smiled.

"It really was all in my head," he said again.

He walked out of the room, confident and feeling accomplished. He had broken the feeling this painting had over him for several weeks now. He did not add any more to it. He was not sure he would ever need to add anything to it ever again.

Thanks again, Jack, he thought.

Wyatt finally laid down in his bed, and almost immediately drifted into a heavy, burden-free sleep.

CHAPTER 15

The morning felt normal.

Wyatt felt a damp discomfort on his legs from the warmth underneath his duvet cover. He swung it up and over and exposed his legs to the cool air that circulated in his loft. Over the noise of a static sound machine, and ceiling fan on high, Wyatt heard the pitter patter of something against his window. *What is that?* He thought as he still laid in his bed.

Before Wyatt even opened his eyes, he could feel that something was not right. The cool air turned stale; unsettled and almost disgruntled. He felt like a middle school student realizing he was late for class before even fully waking up. He opened his eyes, and almost instantly, his heart picked up its pace. He quickly looked around, and although everything seemed to be in order, the dread mounted in his chest. His curtains danced, just barely, in the wind, but where there had been sunlight that glinted through the crack in the same window, there was a bland sense of grey. Wyatt realized the pitter patter were drops of rain that gently showered down over the city. All of the things his morning had become accustomed to in the recent months were already turning on their heads.

He could not explain how he knew, but in his soul, he knew something was wrong.

Despite the rain, Wyatt tried to keep his mind off of the nagging sense that his world would soon crumble, and went about his typical morning routine. A quick shower, and the brushing of teeth. Coffee, and toast with a schmear of inevitable dread.

He had decided that rain in Los Angeles was an omen, and convinced himself that something catastrophic had happened, so through his first waking hour, he actively avoided looking at his phone. Surely, if something terrible had come to pass, not looking at it could potentially delay his destruction.

When he walked past the secondary room, he paused slightly for just a moment.

Again, he felt no drawing, no unexplainable calling to him. He felt no tingles in his fingers, and no sensation prickled down his spine. For a fleeting moment, in what he knew would become a terrible morning, he smiled. Again, he felt validated in his decision to hold a proverbial middle finger to his uncle's "cursed" painting. Wyatt's moment of comfort was short-lived.

His cell phone rang loudly, and it caught Wyatt off guard. He was always very intentional about not only keeping his phone silenced, but he also kept a regular schedule of the feature, "Do Not Disturb." Again, he panicked slightly, and understood that if his phone was ringing out loud, it meant that someone had already tried to call him several times. His phone was telling him that he could not avoid the day any longer.

Reluctantly, he answered his phone.

"This is Wyatt," he said, keeping his voice from shaking.

"Wyatt, hello, this is Courtney Manning calling from Porter & Herth." Her voice was cold, and calculated. The tone of someone with not enough time, and too many tasks to complete.

"Courtney, hi. I don't believe we have spoken before." Wyatt paused, and waited for the other shoe to drop.

"We have not, and I wish we were today under better circumstances." There it was. "Wyatt, I'm calling with some rather unfortunate news." Wyatt felt his world slow. "Sylvia Peregrine passed away yesterday evening." The sounds of the falling rain and his busy, city street faded into a pure silence, and he listened. "I'm not sure if you were aware, but she had been in a fairly ferocious battle with breast cancer, and, well, yesterday she lost that fight."

"Oh, my God," is all Wyatt could think to say. "That's… that's so terrible, I'm so sorry to hear that. Were you close with Sylvia?" He asked. He noticed that her tone did not change much.

"Yes, we were. Everyone here at Porter & Herth is remarkably close, so this was a fairly significant blow to our team." She responded with a stoic calm.

"I can imagine," Wyatt responded. "I'm so sorry, Courtney, how terrible."

"Yes, it really is." There was a moment of silence, before she got right back to business. "Wyatt, I'm calling because with Sylvia's passing, the gallery is making a few changes to our upcoming global season."

Wyatt did not know quite how to respond. Instead, he opted to remain silent, and hoped that it would prompt Courtney to continue speaking on her own. His tactic worked.

"Sylvia's replacement here at Porter & Herth has decided to terminate our agreement to carry your works at our international galleries. We would still love to host your work here at our Los Angeles headquarters, but we will not be carrying your paintings in our London gallery, or our Zurich gallery." Wyatt had a decision to make. He could either continue his method of silence, or he could finally speak up.

"Sylvia's replacement? Who is replacing her?" Wyatt asked, and tried to remain calm.

"I am," she responded.

"I… uh— Understood." He responded, solemnly.

"I know this is likely coming to you as a complete shock, but I wanted to reach out personally and let you know that it is nothing personal. This was simply a business decision that came after Sylvia's passing." She showed no emotion in her words, or even how she chose to put those words together. If you were an outsider looking in, you would assume she hardly knew Sylvia.

"No, I — uh, I understand. I'm disappointed, obviously. But I understand." Wyatt was performing his best diplomatic facade. He was proud with how composed he sounded given how intensely his hands were shaking, and how nauseated he felt. "And what about New York?"

"We will not be carrying your work in our New York gallery either. Just here in Los Angeles. That is, if you would still like us to."

"Got it." Wyatt responded. The only feeling he could articulate to himself was "gutted." "Heartbroken" felt too cliched. "Well," Wyatt continued, "thank you for letting me know. I'm sure this was as difficult for you to say as it is for me to hear."

"You are not wrong, Wyatt. I really am sorry." For the first time, Wyatt heard a hint of sadness in her voice. "There is one last piece, and it's something we can work out with our respective teams."

The pit in Wyatt's stomach made itself known again.

"We are issuing an advance reversal on any funds we had in escrow or paid as an advance for these particular galleries. We will revalue the Los Angeles gallery, and clawback the balance of what we have paid. Our legal team has submitted the necessary paperwork to the State, as well as your representative… Melody Brone." He felt his face flush with heat.

"Anything else?" Wyatt tried his best to match her cold tone.

"No," she said plainly, "I believe that is all of the updates I have for you at this time. Our team will be in touch with Ms. Brone, and we will work out the logistics. Thank you again for the time this morning, and again, I really am sorry."

"I'm sorry for your loss, Courtney. I hope you and the team have the help you need through what I'm sure is a difficult," *click.* The mocking dial tone rang out loudly in Wyatt's ear as Courtney ended the phone call. Wyatt was promptly filled with anger.

Did she just fucking hang up on me? He thought. It took every ounce of resolve for Wyatt to not instantly call her back and give her an ear full. He was incensed, and shocked. He could not believe that had just happened.

He fumed, and paced around his kitchen. The automated tea kettle sang out with a piercing screech, but Wyatt could barely hear it. His own internal thermometer was simultaneously boiling.

"Who the fuck does she think she is?" Wyatt exclaimed to himself. "I'm Wyatt fucking Brone, show me some goddamn respect." Tears filled in Wyatt's eyes, and for the first time in a long time, he leaned into the anger. He breath thinned, and his anger peaked. He clenched his fists, and exhaled as much as he could… which was not much.

"Un-fucking-believable," he said again, aloud, and continued his pacing. He felt a new tingle in his fingers, and it was not an urge to paint, but an urge to *destroy.* Immediately, he rushed into the secondary room. He found himself, again, face-to-face with the painting. The apex of his recent rage. His brain did not try and sniff out the meaning, or hidden mystery. Instead, his mind was flooded with the thoughts and visualizations of ripping this piece from its easel, and slamming it into his original hardwoods.

There was a faint voice within Wyatt that begged him to calm down, but he was determined to ignore it entirely. He reached with both of his hands, and grabbed the painting by its edges. Just before he lifted the piece off of its wooden stand, he heard his phone again ring loudly. He let go of the piece, and walked directly to where he set his phone down on his kitchen counter, steadfast in his desire to tell Courtney exactly how he felt about the update she just gave only moments ago.

Wyatt picked up his cell phone, and without looking to confirm it was her, he tapped "answer," and his hateful words began to flow out of his mouth like a burst pipe carrying petrol from Alberta to Illinois.

"Listen, you two-bit, hack curator wannabe. I'm Wyatt fucking Brone. Do you hear me? I wouldn't want my *art* to be shown at any of your… fucking… sloppy excuses for art galleries. Your team wouldn't know actual art if it poured out of your fucking ass and plopped onto a canvas in front of you. Your entire team is a disgrace, and, and I hope you all rot in fucking hell." He felt a cathartic release before the wave of inevitable guilt rushed over him. He exhaled deeply for the first time that morning. He shook his head, and put his free hand through his hair.

Just before he started to apologize for his outburst, he heard the unphased voice of a man on the other end.

"Mr. Brone," the voice said. Wyatt felt a jolt of shame shock his core. "This is Detective Thomas Johns, from the L.A.P.D. Homicide Division. Have I caught you at a bad time?"

A bad time? Wyatt thought. *Nope, only the worst possible time.*

"Oh, ha, Det. Johns, hi, I'm so sorry," Wyatt knew there was no possible way to recover.

"All good. Rough morning?" Wyatt could almost hear the spiteful smirk through the phone.

"I've definitely had better. What can I do for you?" Wyatt took a deep breath, and shook his head more.

"Wyatt, we need you to come back down to the station for a couple more questions Detective Foss and I have." There was a bit of silence just after he spoke. Wyatt employed the same tactic as he had with Courtney just moments before, but to different ends. Det. Johns said nothing. There were several awkward moments of genuine silence before Wyatt finally blinked.

"Can I ask what about?" Wyatt said.

"Well, we are still in the same investigation." Det. Johns was short, and Wyatt was already annoyed.

"Look, Thomas…" Wyatt felt his frustration boiling into his words.

"Detective Johns," was the response. Wyatt clinched his eyes together, before he continued.

"I have… quite a bit to do today, so can this wait until —" Again, Wyatt was interrupted.

"Unfortunately, it cannot." The detective said. "Mr. Brone, it cannot wait." Wyatt took a deep breath, and waited again to see if there was more. "Det. Foss and I just spoke with your uncle's psychiatrist. You may know him... Mr. — my apologies, Dr. Scholden? Are you familiar with him? Of course you are. Anyway, Dr. Scholden spoke with us, and he had some remarkably interesting new information to share with us."

Wyatt could feel his stomach turn, and he replayed every word he spoke to the psychiatrist. Any inkling of insinuation he may have uttered, any disparaging comment he may have made about his uncle.

"So at this point, we are no longer *asking* you to come in. We will compel you, if we must. We'd prefer not to, though. As you can imagine. Just makes things easier if you say, 'okay,' and we get it taken care of. Make sense?" Wyatt's eyes went in and out of focus. He tried to remember a time he felt such uncontrollable rage.

"I understand." Wyatt responded through gritted teeth.

"Great. So we will see you... Tuesday? Say, around noon?" Wyatt could almost hear Det. Johns wry smile through the phone.

"I'll see you then," Wyatt said softly. After another silent moment, he heard the detective hang up on the other end, and the line went dead. Wyatt closed his eyes, and took a deep breath.

He gently set his phone back down on the granite countertop. He felt overwhelmed, and for a moment of respite, he just leaned against his counter. How could all of this have happened in the short twenty-five minutes since he had decided to open his eyes?

He finally took his kettle off the stove top burner, and set it down on a vacant one. The steam slowly subsided, and the whistle faded into a quaint boil, unlike the rage and frustration Wyatt felt. If anything, the kettle and his internal flames paralleled each other.

He was not sure quite what to do next. He had lost literally millions of dollars in yet to be received revenue, and simultaneously was slowly becoming the primary suspect in a murder he had absolutely nothing to do with. Wyatt felt like his brain could not process the information he had just taken in quickly enough, and he felt his head spin slightly. He was not sure where to turn, or who to talk to, or even what to ask if he did. The only person who continued to pop into his head was the person whose name just appeared on the display of his cell phone.

Melody Brone calling…

Wyatt answered his phone, and simply held it to his ear without saying anything. Before she spoke, Wyatt could hear the exhaustion Melody exuded. The two sat in a silent stalemate, but Wyatt could feel the genuine concern within it.

"I don't know what happened." He finally spoke.

"I don't either, but I'm finding out." Melody responded.

"Can they…" Wyatt desperately searched for something meaningful to say.

"Well, honestly, no. We have a contract, and the ink has dried. But then again, Meta."

The end of Melody's response confused Wyatt more than it consoled him.

"Huh?" Wyatt asked, confusion stopped him in his place.

"Meta," Melody repeated herself.

"Say it one more time, Mel, maybe I'll get it then," Wyatt responded, frustrated.

"Meta," Melody said, sarcastically.

"I don't know what that means, Melody. Meta? What do you mean?" Wyatt asked.

"Meta. Facebook. Meta, you know?" She said.

"Explain it to me like I'm five," Wyatt said. He popped his bluetooth headphones into both ears, and walked to his wardrobe. As Melody responded, Wyatt finally started to get some normal clothes on.

"Facebook changed its company name to Meta," she started.

"Okay…"

"Well, there was already a company named Meta. So Facebook asked for permission at first, but Meta said 'no.' Then Facebook changed their name to Meta, anyway."

"I don't understand how that applies," Wyatt said, and slid a crewneck sweater on.

"So, we have a fucking deal with Porter & Herth, and they are tearing it up anyway."

"Okay, so this is why I have you, right? As my representation?"

"Yes, and my lawyers are already drafting documentation. I just don't know how much we can do. Hope for the best, prepare for the worst, I guess." Melody sounded defeated.

"That… doesn't sound great." Wyatt matched her.

"We will do what we can do, and take the rest from there." Wyatt nodded to himself.

"Okay." He said.

"I'm getting a call, mind swinging by the office? We can chat more about what our game plan should be."

"Yeah, that sounds great, I'll head over soon." He said. He took his headphones out of his ears, and slid them back into their white, plastic case.

Wyatt took a deep breath, and walked over to the window.

The sound of the rain increased, and Wyatt stole a peak towards the sky. He could not remember the last time the sky over Los Angeles had such a consistent layer of grey.

He had a feeling it was an omen. He had just hoped that he was wrong.

So far, he was not wrong. And he was devastated about it.

He shut his window, and the sound of the rain became muffled, and dull. He closed the thin blinds, and walked away from the window.

There was a nervous energy coursing through his body that he had not felt since school. It was equivalent to the first day of an important job for which he felt actively unprepared.

Presented with the two options to either nervously pace his apartment for a few hours, or to just head to Melody's office, he chose the latter.

He made it downstairs just as his Lyft arrived.

"Carlos?" Wyatt asked through the open driver's side window. The man nodded.

"For Wyatt?" Wyatt nodded back and climbed into the backseat.

The driver pulled away from Wyatt's building, and Wyatt stared out the window. He watched the buildings pass quickly, and he closed his eyes for a moment. He hoped that leaving his apartment would help him feel less overcome with frustration, but those feelings had yet to subside.

"Crazy weather today, huh?" Wyatt was snapped out of his agitated spiral by the sound of his Lyft driver making small talk.

"Sure is," Wyatt reluctantly responded.

"I don't remember the last time it rained like this. Not here, at least. You from here?" The driver continued.

Instinctively, Wyatt pulled his phone out of his pocket, and held it to his ear.

"This is Wyatt," he said into phone call with no one, as he looked to the driver, and motioned a "I'm so sorry, I have to take this," gesture. "Yeah, I am heading there now," he continued talking to his phone call of nothingness.

He kept this charade going the forty-five-minute ride to his sister's office. Most of the fake conversation was simply "uh huh's" and "yeah, I get it," but he still preferred it to making small talk; Wyatt's least favorite aspect of human life.

He arrived at Melody's, and immediately jumped out of the car. The driver took the hint, and focused solely on getting Wyatt out of his car. He got there quickly, but primarily at the cost of Wyatt's equilibrium. He felt slightly nauseous, but he was there. He pushed through, and walked into the building.

He passed the lobby staff without even saying hello. He approached the elevator, and it opened without him even needing to press anything. He looked back at the receptionist, and smiled at her. He held up a hand, saying "thank you," and she just smiled back. Wyatt stepped into the elevator, and Melody's office floor was already illuminated.

The doors chimed and opened, and Melody was standing just outside the doors. His arms crossed, and a scowl on her face.

"Nice to see you too," Wyatt said. Melody did not respond, she just turned and walked away. Anxious, Wyatt followed close behind her.

"Melody... I don't like that face..." he spoke with a thick layer desperation in his voice. "Talk to me, what happened?" He was on her heels, and she walked straight into her office.

Melody walked around her desk, and hit a button on her answering machine. She stared at Wyatt as the machine beeped.

"Melody, you still use an answering machine?" His attempt at humor was interrupted by a familiar voice.

"Melody, hi, this is Caroline Haynes with *The Times*. I wanted to get a hold of you. We've come into some... well, some disturbing information about your brother Wyatt's work," the voice said.

"I don't understand," Wyatt said over the recording.

"Keep listening," Melody spoke calmly, her expression remained stoic. Caroline's recording continued.

"We have come into ... well a couple of tips that are suggesting that Wyatt's work isn't actually his, and that they are... primarily works he inherited from your uncle, Jackson Brone."

Wyatt shot his glance directly at Melody. She stared back.

"What the fuck? Melody, you know that isn't true..."

"As you know," Caroline's recording continued, "if these allegations are even remotely true, this is the end of your brother's career."

"Melody, this... this is insane," Wyatt's voice cracked with anger and desperation.

"I'm calling because I wanted to give you a chance to respond before I move forward with this story, but I'm finalizing a first draft right now. Give me a call," the recording beeped, and Caroline's message was over.

Wyatt's heart rate exploded. For a moment, he had thought his rage capacity for the day had been met, but he learned he had a little left in the tank.

"Melody," Wyatt pleaded.

"Wyatt, I know it's not true. But who the fuck would even insinuate that?" Melody said.

"Call her back!" Wyatt did not mean to raise his voice, but he could not help himself.

"I will, I just wanted to play it for you first." Melody clicked a few buttons on her desk phone, put it on speaker, and they both heard the ring.

"There's no possible way it's true, correct?" Melody asked Wyatt, then shrugged. She had to, and he knew it.

"There's zero chance this is remotely true, and you of all fucking people would know it."

After a few loud rings, they heard Caroline's soft voice on the other end.

"Caroline Haynes," she said.

"Caroline, what the fuck is that?" Melody got straight to the point. Wyatt was taken aback slightly, he had never heard Melody use such direct language to a professional peer before.

"Melody, hi," Caroline was not phased at all.

"What are you even talking about?" Melody pushed harder.

"I'm just following up on a story that I'm sending to print tomorrow. It's customary to try and get a statement first. It's only right," Caroline spoke with such a casual ease, Wyatt felt his anger bubble up from his gut again.

"Well, it isn't even remotely true." Melody said, doing her job.

"Which is what we all assumed you would say," Caroline responded.

"Caroline, listen. Wyatt and my uncle were hardly even on speaking terms. Wyatt was barely even in the will, for crissake," Melody snapped. Wyatt smirked at her, and again, she shrugged.

"I understand, and to be honest, I didn't even think much of it at first, but the more we dug, the more—"

"The more *what*, Caroline? Who the fuck would even say something like this? Let alone corroborate this bullshit?" Melody said.

"Melody, you know I will not reveal my sources."

Wyatt fumed, and paced around Melody's office. There was a beat of silence on the phone.

"Well, first, my official statement is that these allegations are categorically false. That's on the record." Melody's tone again straightened, and became as sharp as a razor. "My second, off-the-record statement, is that you better fucking hope this slanderous allegation from this ridiculous 'source' is airtight. Because if you move forward with this, we will come down on you so hard you will have to turn to the fucking *Post* for work, do you understand?" Wyatt felt a sting of pride electrocute his spine. He knew his sister was tough, but he did not realize she was a full on badass.

"Melody—" Caroline's tone shifted slightly, but Melody refused to take her foot off her throat.

"I said, do you understand?"

There was a beat of silence on the line. Wyatt and Melody locked eyes. After another moment, they heard Caroline take a breath before she spoke.

"I understand."

Click.

Dial tone.

Melody pressed a button, and the line went dead.

The two again stood in momentary silence.

"It's not true, right?" Melody asked, then smirked. Wyatt rolled his eyes. "I'm sorry, too soon?" She laughed, and tried to break the tension.

"Yes, too soon." Wyatt responded.

"Wyatt, come on. We both know that story is absolute garbage. There's zero reality in which it's even remotely true."

"Who the fuck would make that up?" Wyatt put both hands on his head, and took a deep breath.

"It doesn't matter, she won't run it."

"How do you know?" Wyatt asked Melody, who sat down behind her desk.

"I just do." She responded.

"So what do we do now?" Wyatt was afraid to ask.

"We wait, I guess. I make some calls, and find out who the fuck tried to betray us."

"Well, today is officially canceled." Wyatt said, and sat down across from her.

"Yeah, what is going on? Did you change a routine or something, and rip the space-time continuum? Good lord," Melody lit a cigarette, and took a deep drag.

Wyatt thought of the painting. Wyatt thought of the rules of the curse.

A panic shot down his spine.

He had not painted yesterday. He had directly broken the agreement of the curse, and in a matter of hours, his life had begun falling apart.

"I'll get to the bottom of it, don't stress." Melody said calmly. "Why don't you head home and try and get some rest? We'll figure out the gallery shit tomorrow."

Wyatt silently nodded, his mind now consumed with the reality that the curse was real. This, to him, was the proof he needed.

"Yeah, I need to go home," Wyatt's panic quickly became apparent. Melody looked at him, concerned.

"Wyatt," she spoke with a tone specifically curated to get his attention. They locked eyes. "Whatever happens, it's going to be fine, I promise." Wyatt forced a smile, and nodded again.

"I know, thanks."

Wyatt left her office, and rushed home.

His car arrived back at his building, and Wyatt felt like running through the lobby.

He passed the doorman, keeping his greeting normal, and frantically rushed to his door.

The moment he entered into his loft, he walked directly to the painting.

There it was. Wyatt stood, and faced it. For the first time in a couple of days, Wyatt felt his fingers tingle with the sensation to add paint to the canvas. Tears filled his eyes, and he felt like the painting had begun taunting him. The painting knew the day he had, and it was mocking him for ignoring it.

Wyatt wept. Alone, in this room of his rejected art, he wept. He wept because he knew the painting was right. He had ignored the warning, and today, he had begun paying the consequences of that decision.

Still reluctantly, Wyatt picked up his brush and palette, and added paint.

Wyatt added a dramatic amount of paint.

Part of him hoped that the amount would make up for the lost day, part of him hoped it would favor some level of forgiveness for neglecting the curse, but mainly, he just painted.

Before he had realized how much he had done, he snapped out of it, and saw essentially a brand new piece of art before him. He had covered almost the entire canvas with a new, fresh coat of paint.

New movements, new styles; a new story being told. For the first time since he inherited this work, it felt like his. It felt like a piece he normally would be proud of.

In this moment, he felt nothing but disgust. He felt disgust with himself, with his circumstance. He felt weak, and his fingers continued to tingle. Again, he felt taunted. Scolded, like a child.

Finally, after two full hours had come and gone, Wyatt set down his brush and palette. His fingers ached, and his back matched the pain. He was exhausted, and felt dehydrated from all the tears shed.

Demoralized, Wyatt took a deep breath, and walked out of the room. He clicked the light off, and hung his head low. He was defeated.

CHAPTER 16

Wyatt did not sleep.

His mind raced with the day he had experienced, and the weight of his anxiety felt like a gravity blanket. The spinner rings he normally removed before bed were active in his thumb and index finger from sunset to sunrise. He almost felt as if the beams of light from the morning sun would be his salvation. If he could just wait it out until he saw that light, he would be fine.

He sat for hours, and stared into his ceiling. He tried to focus on the monotonous sound of his fan and white noise machine, but he failed. All he could think about was the day he had. The conversations, the missteps, then impending doom he was certain to wake up to.

Then the canvas. The rules. The curse. The idealistic future he had just gotten a taste of, and hoped was not being permanently stripped away.

The rules were so simple, how stupid are you? He struggled to guard himself from his own scorn. *You had everything, you idiot.*

When the alarm he set rang out around eight in the morning, he exhaled and rubbed his eyes. He felt hopeful when he initially set the alarm, but the sleepless night just made him anxious that he had to start a new day.

The floor was cold against his bare feet. He paid no mind to the window, still closed, and the lack of breeze with dancing curtains. He simply walked to his bathroom in silence, and brushed his teeth. He readied for his day, and forced himself to see his morning routine through. Breakfast, coffee, all in almost complete silence. He did not check his phone, listen to music, or podcasts, or turn on his television. He resigned himself to a quiet morning before discovering what fallout was certainly coming from Caroline's new piece in *The New York Times*.

His doorman was kind when Wyatt walked through the lobby towards his building's exit. He gave his normal, signature fist pump, and smiled when Wyatt passed by. Wyatt smiled back, and said a simple, "Morning, bud."

Wyatt walked down the sidewalk of his busy, downtown street, wireless headphones in each ear. He still did not listen to anything, but rather, had them in as a tactic to avoid interacting with anyone else. After a couple of blocks, he approached a small cafe. This particular place had become his normal spot for the mornings when he did not feel like making coffee. Even though he had made some this particular morning, he found some comfort in getting another one. This cafe also typically carried the most recent issue of *The New York Times*, conveniently.

He ordered a hot oat milk latte, and perused the magazine wall while he waited. The newest issue of *The New York Times* always took the last vacant shelf spot on the far left side of the cafe. Wyatt forced himself slowly towards it. He read each headline along the way, another tactic to force him to move slowly.

Headlines like "Spotlight Story: Did We Blow Our Best Chance to Tackle Climate Change?" Or, "This Celebrity Reacts to This Celebrity's Recent Split: He's an Attention Whore!" Or finally, "Keanu Reeves Donated More Than Half of His 'Matrix' Salary to Cancer Research." Wyatt debated picking that one up. Instead, he smirked to himself, and thought how he always knew Keanu was the coolest. *What a guy,* he thought to himself.

He had wanted to move slower than he did, and before he knew it, he stood face to face with the most recent addition of *The New York Times.* Certain he was moments away from seeing his name slandered across the front page, he closed his eyes, and took a deep breath. He braced for the worst, and felt the hairs on the back of his neck stand at attention.

When he opened his eyes, he saw it. There it was, again. His name. Sprawled across the front page of the historic newspaper. His heart sank. Everything he had worked for, and every dream he had finally seen being realized were mere words away from falling apart.

Despite everything inside of his urging him not to, Wyatt picked up the paper, and held it in his hands.

Finally, he read the headline in full.

"Mysterious Phenom Artist, Wyatt Brone, Has More Secrets, by art critic Caroline Haynes."

He furrowed his brow, and found the headline curious. He reluctantly started to read Caroline's words.

"It is not often *The Times* makes space for a contemporary artist on its historic front page. Space often reserved for military decisions and U.S. Presidential elections is rarely given to such topics. This artist, however, is anything but ordinary. Overnight sensation, and once in a generation art talent, Wyatt Brone, seems to still have some gas in the creative tank. The Los Angeles-based artist who recently became a remarkable household name, with sold out galleries all over the country, is holding onto something special. A single, unfinished canvas."

Wyatt felt confused more than anything else. This article seemed anything but the veiled threat he overheard during Melody's phone call with Caroline just the day before. The article went on.

"According to our sources, despite the recent gallery sell outs across the country, the artist is holding onto one final piece of art. Something being called, 'the unfinished piece.' There is little known about this specific work, other than the fact that it is quickly becoming one of the most anticipated pieces of contemporary art in modern history. The speculation is that it is a piece started by his renowned uncle, Jackson Brone, given to Wyatt to complete. A work like this has never existed."

Wyatt had prepared for anger and heartbreak, he had not prepared for this.

He felt his phone vibrate in his pocket, and knew in his heart it was Melody. He answered the call, and held it up to his ear.

"You seeing this?" He said before anything else.

"What is happening?" Melody said on the other end. Wyatt thought she sounded just as confused as he felt. "You are finishing one of Jackson's pieces?"

"No, no fucking way. You know Jack would have never given me anything like that. Your guess is as good as mine," Wyatt responded. He read the next sentence aloud to his sister through the phone. "Listen to this… 'Though this latest piece has been shrouded in secrecy from its beginning, it likely will not remain hidden for long. If Wyatt Brone has proven anything over the last six months, it is the simple fact that contemporary art is not dead. And now, with the prospect of a combined artistic effort, he will even keep his uncle's legacy alive.' Like… what the fuck?"

"I guess my tough voice works," Melody smirked, and Wyatt laughed.

"I knew you were tough, but good lord, Mel," Wyatt said.

"What piece is she talking about? Is it the piece Jack left you in his will?" Melody asked, with genuine curiosity.

"No, no way, I have literally no idea," Wyatt responded. "And who is *this* source?"

"No idea either. I'll give her office a call, and see what I can dig up." Melody said.

"Sounds good, thanks, Mel." His conversation ended just as the barista called out his name.

"Wyatt?" The barista shouted from behind the espresso bar.

He slipped his phone into his pocket, and took the paper up to the cashier. He grabbed his coffee, and took out his wallet.

The worker looked at him, and scrunched her eyes together a little.

"Wyatt, as in, Wyatt Brone?" The barista said, curious. Wyatt was taken by surprise a little, but a small smile creeped out from his lips.

"Yes…" he said.

"You're in *The Times* today!" The barista referenced the paper in his hands. Wyatt laughed, and straightaway, he felt embarrassed.

"Yes," he said through a chuckle, "and yes, I'm embarrassingly purchasing a copy of it." Wyatt held out a ten-dollar bill.

"The hell you are," the barista said, then typed in a couple of buttons on her screen. "I'm an art major at U.C.L.A. and we just had an entire discussion about you. Your coffee is on me today. The paper too. It's dope to meet you." She smiled.

"Oh, you're probably thinking of my uncle. He's a regular topic in university lectures around here," Wyatt said, deflecting.

"No dude. Jackson is old news. You're Wyatt Brone. You're changing the course of art, man. But finishing one of his pieces? Pretty fucking rad, if you ask me." The barista said plainly what Wyatt struggled so hard to believe. A smile streaked across his face. Somehow, the day he had just a day before had been completely erased from his mind, and his sleepless night no longer mattered.

"Well, thanks. Tell your professor to keep it up," Wyatt responded, and the barista laughed.

"I never do this, but can I grab a selfie?" She asked, timid.

"Sure," Wyatt smiled, and posed for a photo with her. "Thanks again," he said, before he walked out of the cafe.

When he got back to the street, the city felt lighter somehow. For the first time that morning, Wyatt noticed the rain had cleared. The sky was clear and blue. The breeze was cool, and the traffic was insane. The city felt normal again. A random encounter, an unexpected article, and a free oat milk latte, and all was right again.

Even his steps felt easier.

Wyatt pulled his phone back out of his pocket, and dialed a number as he started his short walk home.

"Wyatt," Caroline said as she answered.

"Caroline," he responded, smiling."

"I'm assuming you saw the piece."

"I did. And it read strikingly different from how my sister had made it sound like it would," he took a sip of his coffee.

"News changes quick. I had a story ready for print, but another story surfaced, and I decided it took precedent. So I wrote the more… *vibrant* story that is turning out to be true." Caroline kept her words short, and intentionally vague.

"Can I ask how? You keep mentioning sources but you don't seem to make any other references?" Wyatt was certain Caroline could hear him raise a suspicious eyebrow when he asked her this question.

"Wyatt, like I told your sister, we don't reveal our sources." Caroline said no more.

"I understand, it's just… It's odd. I don't recall talking to anyone about any of my paintings recently, like, at all. Especially not any collaborative pieces with my dead uncle. So you can imagine that my curiosity is piqued." Wyatt spoke as he approached his building's front door.

"It doesn't necessarily matter anymore, though, does it?" Caroline said, and she was correct.

"Well, thanks. I guess. I always appreciate the kind words." He harshly replied, and hung up. He again slipped his phone back into his pocket, and smiled. Then he walked back into his building.

For the next couple of hours, Wyatt worked on one of his newer works, but he kept feeling distracted by his uncle's piece. It became a distraction, and he felt like he could not focus on the work at hand, so at one moment, he walked into the secondary room, and added a stroke of paint.

Like an addict, as soon as he did, the urging left him. Like an itch that needed to be scratched, and then got exactly what it wanted. He finally felt able to focus on his actual piece of art, and eventually lost track of his day.

Once he felt like his creative tank was emptied, he showered, and started preparing dinner for he and Samantha. He checked the time, and panicked slightly. He realized she should be arriving any minute.

With dinner preparation in full swing, he heard his door buzz. He walked over to the intercom, and held down the button to respond.

"Hey Sam, that you?" Wyatt asked, expecting Samantha over for dinner.

"It's me!" Samantha responds. Wyatt smiled, and then buzzed her into his building.

A few minutes later, he heard a set of keys jingle in his locked front door, and the squeak of the hinges swinging open. Samantha walked in. He was standing over the stove, chicken sizzling in a cast iron on the stove. She walked up behind him, and wrapped her arms around his waist. He smiled, and she kissed his neck.

"Smells amazing," she said, and over-exaggerated a large inhale. Wyatt laughed, and flipped the chicken over. Once he did, he set his utensils down, and snaked around to face her. She smiled back, and they kissed, gently.

"You smell amazing," Wyatt said back, and it made Samantha laugh.

"Whatcha making?" She asked, and hugged him hard.

Wyatt squeezed back, and held her for a moment. "Dinner," he said, and she laughed again, loudly.

"You brat," she said, and playfully smacked him on the arm. Wyatt laughed, and turned his attention back to the food.

"Want a glass of wine?" She asked as she grabbed some glasses from a cabinet. She picked a bottle of wine out from the small cluster on the countertop, popped it open.

"I saw *The Times* this morning." She said as she took a small sip of her cabernet sauvignon and leaned against a simple, black and metal bar stool. Without looking at her, Wyatt smiled.

"Oh yeah?" He replied.

"Yep," she said.

"What'd you think?" He asked, and finally turned around.

"Pretty… interesting stuff there, ya know?" She replied, wryly.

"Ha, yeah? You think?" Samantha nodded, smirking. "Which part, exactly? Ya know, just, for the record…"

"Um…" She pretended to think hard. "Oh! The super-secret new expensive and mind-blowing piece of art you are collaborating on with Jackson? Maybe?" She smirked again, and raised one eyebrow.

"Oh, that part." Wyatt chuckled. "I honestly don't know what they're talking about."

"Wyatt, come on!" Samantha exclaimed, and walked over to him. She set her glass of wine down on the counter, and swung her arms around him again.

"I'm serious, actually," Wyatt said and smiled. "I don't have any secret new pieces. And I definitely haven't been working on anything that my uncle started, that's insane. Also, I haven't talked to anyone about my new work except you." Wyatt paused, and made his eyes go comically large. "Et tu, Brute?! Are you their secret source?" Wyatt playfully accused her.

"Uh—" Samantha played along with his silly bit. "You caught me. It was me. I broke the clock tower." They laughed together. "No, of course not. I don't even know what I would say."

"So yeah, I have no idea what they are talking about. You know the new pieces I'm working on, they aren't secret, and they aren't Jack's. But hopefully they are expensive." Wyatt laughed again.

"And you're sure it isn't the piece in this room over here that you, uh…" Samantha sort of trailed off, but Wyatt knew what she was referring to.

"No," he responded flatly. "No one even knows about that piece except you and Melody, and I don't plan on showing it to anyone."

"Oh, come on, Wyatt. Why is it so secretive? That has to be the one they are talking about." Samantha responded. She slowly started taking steps towards the secondary room, and smirked at Wyatt with each step.

"Sam, stop. I'm serious. It's not funny. You promised me." Wyatt was not joking, and Samantha straightaway picked up on the urgency in his voice.

"Okay, okay… I'm just teasing. I won't look at it." She said.

"Thank you," Wyatt looked at her, and wondered if he hurt her feelings.

"I just don't understand why it's so private. Your uncle showed me everything he was working on," Samantha said with a hint of sarcasm.

"Well, my uncle was also a piece of shit, so," he responded quickly, and almost just as quickly regretted it.

"Okay, well," Samantha threw her words away, and Wyatt tried to backtrack.

"I'm sorry, Sam, I didn't mean that, it's just… this week has just been really intense, and I don't want to talk about that painting. Just not right now." He tried to smile at her, but he knew he ruined the evening's mood.

When Wyatt woke up the next morning, Samantha had already left. He assumed she had left early for work, but something in his gut told him it was the night before.

Still in bed, he got a call from Melody on his phone. He looked at his phone, then the time. It was only seven in the morning. He did not have any pertinent meetings scheduled for the day, so he ignored her call. He rolled over in bed, and closed his eyes. The way a child would when already late for school. *Five more minutes,* he thought.

His phone rang again, and he rolled back over to look. It was Melody. Again.

He answered the call, and held it up to his ear.

"It just better be 7 A.M. worth it, Mel," he replied, his voice still deep with a night well slept, and a fresh morning lacking words.

"Ms. Brone, we would like to feature your client Wyatt Brone's art at our Los Angeles and San Francisco galleries, but we also want the collab piece from Wyatt and Jackson… Ms. Brone, I'd like to offer five million dollars, cash, for the Wyatt and Jackson piece from *The Times*… Melody, call me, I need the piece from *The Times*, name your price… Wyatt, I'm getting blown up with people wanting this fucking piece of art."

"Tell them no," he responded plainly.

"What the fuck, I'm not passing up on all of these possibilities. You have a new piece, and you're doing it with our dead uncle? First of all, what the fuck? Thanks for letting me know. Regardless, people *want* it. So let's decide who to sell it to." Melody said.

"Melody, I said no. It's not up for debate." Wyatt's frustration spewed out. He was now fully awake.

"Wake the fuck up, Wyatt. You're an artist. This is what you do." Melody's tone and quick delivery made her point known. "And if you're finishing a piece that our uncle started, don't be an idiot about this. That's going to be desired. And it's going to come at a massive payday."

"I'm not working on anything from Jack. Full stop. I have new works that will probably be finished soon. But the piece everyone thinks they want, isn't up for sale. Or viewing. Or anything. So again, my representative-Melody-Brone, respectfully, tell them to fuck off." Wyatt replied and sat up in bed. "How does anyone even know about it? I inherited a piece from Jack, yes, but it's not a collaboration."

"Well, the court of public opinion would say otherwise." Melody said.

"Okay, well, I don't know what you want me to say, Melody." Wyatt replied. "Swing by my loft later, and we can chat about this more, but right now, I have nothing else to add. I have to go, I need to go work on *my* pieces." Wyatt hung up before he gave Melody a chance to respond.

Wyatt tried to go about his morning, but he could not figure out how anyone found out about the piece he had inherited from his uncle. Much less, why anyone would think it was something he was working on *with* his uncle, postmortem. He made breakfast and coffee, took a shower, dressed, and talked Samatha into meeting him for an early afternoon coffee. He told her he wanted to apologize for the night before, and hoped that she would be able to meet him on her lunch break. She agreed, and when it was time, he headed to her office.

When he readied to leave to meet Samantha, he walked past the secondary room. He looked at the painting, and felt nothing but frustration. For a moment, he wished he had never inherited it. He felt the tingling in his fingers, and the urge to add that day's stroke of paint, but instead he huffed his breath, and rolled his eyes. He held out his middle finger to the canvas in defiance, and left his apartment. He slammed the door behind him.

He got to Samantha's office a few minutes early, and waited in the main lobby. He saw her as soon as she started down the steps from the second floor, where her office was. He smiled at her, and she smiled back. He could tell she was still upset. She made it down the stairs, and walked up to him. He hugged her and smiled gently again.

"I'm sorry, babe," he said. "I was an ass, and I think I've just been sort of stressed out, and I took it out on—"

"It's okay, Wyatt. I don't care about the painting, I just don't want there to be secrets between us." Samantha said, and interrupted him.

"I know, I know. I'm sorry. I promise I will explain everything as soon as I can, I just can't yet. Please, trust me." He pleaded. For a moment, he worried that she would not let this explanation suffice. The truth was, he wondered how much of what he just said he actually believed. Would he explain everything? Would he discuss the inheritance, the curse, the rules? Would he tell her everything? If he was being honest with himself, he was not sure. But right now, it is what he felt, so it is what he said.

"Okay," Samantha said, and smiled. They embraced. For the moment, he felt at ease.

They walked through the neighborhood near her office, and talked about everything. Everything except the painting he inherited from his uncle. They stopped at a small coffee stand at the corner next to her building, and Wyatt got them a couple of lattes. While there, someone waiting for their coffee recognized Wyatt from the newest issue of *The New York Times*, and asked him for a photograph. He smiled at Samantha, and he thought she looked proud. She was proud of him. She knew he was finally experiencing the success he deserved. At least, that is what he told himself.

"Ah, I have to get back to a meeting, we should start walking back," Samantha said.

"Oh, I'm sorry, I completely lost track of time." Wyatt said.

He pulled his phone out of his pocket to see exactly what time it was and he saw a few texts and missed calls from Melody. For some inexplicable reason, he felt a weight in his gut. He and Melody had text messaged each other and spoke to each other over the phone all day, every day for years, but for some reason, Wyatt felt sick. He stopped walking, and froze. He stared at his phone, unable to bring himself to open the messages.

"Wyatt? Everything okay?" Samantha asked, but Wyatt did not look up.

Reluctantly, he swiped his phone open, and stared at the notification over his text message app. It said there were three unread messages. He knew they were all from Melody, and he knew it was not good. He could not explain how, he just knew, in his soul.

"Wyatt, you're scaring me…" Samantha said.

Reluctantly, he tapped the text message icon on his phone, and the app opened. He tapped into his conversation with Melody, and all of his fears came to fruition.

Message one, *"Why would you want to keep this hidden? It's stunning."*

Message two, *"Is this the piece you're working on with Uncle Jack?"*

Message three, *"Wyatt, this is beautiful."*

Wyatt's heart sank. He instantly began sweating, and hyperventilating.

Melody looked at the canvas.

Wyatt broke the second rule.

"Wyatt, what's going on?" Samantha asked, again to no response. He tried to catch his breath, but his attempts to breathe only made him even more light-headed. He immediately dialed Melody on his cell phone. He turned to Samantha, and she saw the panic in his eyes.

"I have to go," he responded, and she instantly knew she needed to help.

"I'll call a car right now," Samantha replied, and began working on her phone.

"Come on, Mel, please pick up." Wyatt begged.

"Hi, this is the voicemail of Melody Brone, if this is important, call me again, if this isn't important, leave a message!" *Fuck.* Wyatt immediately hung up the call, and dialed again.

After a minute, a car pulled up, and Wyatt got into it. He made sure the driver had his address, and they were off. He did not realize he had not said anything to Samantha.

"Hi, this is the voicemail of Melody Brone, if this is important, call me again, if this isn't important, leave a message!"

"Fuck!" Wyatt shouted, and the driver immediately looked back at him. "Sorry, I'm just... having an emergency." Wyatt said. His mind was consumed with all of the worst case scenarios it could come up with. The problem was that he did not have a single idea what they were.

Another call, another voicemail. Wyatt sat in the backseat, fully in tears, and was not sure what to do. In a last resort, he made another phone call.

"9-1-1, what's your emergency?" A female dispatch officer answered.

"My name is Wyatt Brone, and I think something terrible has happened."

He gave the dispatch his address, and answered as many questions as he could, explaining that he could not answer them all. He begged for her to believe him, and she did. She agreed to send an officer to the residence.

The driver slowly crept up to Wyatt's building, and before he came to a complete stop, Wyatt burst out of the backseat. He ran through the lobby, and rushed to his floor as quickly as he could. He made it to his hallway, and saw his front door ajar.

He froze, and he felt his heartbeat in his throat. He felt like throwing up, but continued towards his door.

He gently pushed the door open farther, and took a quiet step inside.

"Melody?" Wyatt called out, still in tears. "Can you hear me? Are you here? Melody?"

He walked a few more steps in his loft, and he saw the door frame of the secondary room. His heart pounded in his chest, and he was convinced it would burst out onto the floor. His breath was thin, and tears streamed from his face.

"Melody? Come on, Mel, please…" he begged.

Wyatt took another step, and he saw something on the floor in the doorway of his secondary work room. It looked wet, like spilled paint. In a manic moment of absolute dread, Wyatt realized what he was looking at.

It was blood.

He gasped for air, and worried he would pass out. He somehow persuaded his legs to move, and rushed into the room. There, he saw exactly what he did not even realize that he feared the most.

Wyatt saw Melody's body, lifeless, laying on the floor in front of the painting.

"No!" He screamed, and rushed to his sister's aid.

The thin handle of a single paint brush from Wyatt's work station was lodged deep into her throat, and protruded through the other side. Warm blood still spilled out of the grotesque wound.

Wyatt froze in panic and fear. Though blood still poured from her neck, he knew she was dead. Wyatt's sister was dead.

He wrapped his arms around her, and cupped her face in his face. He wept, and screamed for help. He did not know what else he could do at that moment. Her blood felt warm on his hands, but her body felt cold and heavy. There was no life in her eyes. Wyatt felt for a pulse, but quickly realized he did not know what he was doing. He wept harder, and held his dead sister.

For just a moment, Wyatt looked up and saw the painting before both of them. It stared back at him, mocking his lack of obedience. In a burst of anger, he stood up, and threw the painting off of its easel. It smashed into a large stack of discarded canvas' that were leaned up against the wall, but its wooden frame and cloth were not harmed. It silently sat, the painted side facing the wall. Wyatt knelt back down with his dead sister.

A few moments later, he heard shuffling at his front door. He heard the door creaked as it carefully swung open in its frame. He cried out for whoever it was.

"Please, help! In here, please!" He screamed.

"Mr. Brone?" He heard a man say.

"Yes, please help, in here, please!" Wyatt screamed desperately. He moaned, he felt sick, and he was still hyperventilating.

Two L.A.P.D. officers entered the room, and were taken aback.

"Please help," Wyatt begged through his tears.

Just behind the two officers, Wyatt saw two more men enter his home; Detective Thomas Johns, and Detective Gerry Foss. He made eye contact with Detective Johns, and wept.

CHAPTER 17

The room was colder than before.

Wyatt recalled the distinct chill he felt as he waited in the lobby of the Los Angeles Police Department headquarters, but he had now found himself in the holding cell of the Los Angeles Police Department Metropolitan Detention Center.

He was alone, sitting on a wooden bench attached to the stagnant white, concrete wall. The cement and other mixture of aggregates was cold to his touch. The single, recessed fluorescent light flickered from the ceiling above him. He stared into the epoxied concrete flooring.

He sat in silence, his hands still stained purple with his sister's blood. His clothes dried, but now rigid, and stiff where the blood had dried. Admittedly, Wyatt did not have a clue on how the criminal system worked in the City of Los Angeles, but from the true crime documentaries Samantha had been obsessed with, he assumed they could hold him for a few days before releasing him. He remembered that it was a Thursday, so if they held him the entire allotted amount of time, he could potentially be there until Monday, or maybe even Tuesday.

Normally, this thought would have likely caused an immediate sting of stress and anxiety, but Wyatt simply felt numb. The image of Melody's lifeless body burned into his eyes, like an old television left on the same channel for too long.

The blank, emptiness in her eyes when he tilted her face towards his. The way her hair gently fell, undisturbed when he lifted her head in his hand. The dull thud her hand made when it hit against the floor as he picked her lifeless body up into his. All of these images and sensations just played on a relentless loop of torture. He was not sure of the time, or even how long he had been sitting in this room. Only that he had been brought there that day. His brain tried to piece the day together, but even then, it was struggling to place the timeline.

He had not slept, he walked to get coffee, he saw the piece from Caroline Haynes in *The New York Times*. Then Melody called him.

The barista recognized him, he took a selfie with her — *wait, no.* He thought. *Was that the day before? Today, Wyatt. What happened today?*

He did not sleep much. Samantha was gone when he woke up because they had fought before they went to sleep. He remembered that he went to sleep angry. He should not have done that. To not go to bed angry is an incredibly simple task told to him his entire life by people far wiser. Yet, last night he did. He could not help but look at where he was now, and tears welled in his eyes. *Focus, Wyatt. What happened next?*

Melody woke him up. She called him early, and he was still partly asleep. He remembered his cell phone lighting up and ringing out, and the fog still in his eyes from a restless night. He remembered feeling annoyed before he even looked to see who was calling him so early. He remembered feeling even more annoyed when he saw his sister's name on his display screen. Tears again welled to the brink of falling when he thought how ruinous such annoyance seemed.

Wyatt felt his foot tremble, bouncing anxiously up and down, when the reality of his predicament began to set into his mind. He remembered locking eyes with Detective Thomas Johns. The fear, and panic, he certainly communicated to the detective just through his expression.

Wyatt pulled his legs up from the ground, laid down on the wooden bench. Balling himself into the fetal position, Wyatt wept. His large frame barely fit, and he knew the point was not physical comfort; rather, emotional. He wrapped his arms around himself, and mourned his sister.

Wyatt was snapped back into reality with the loud *clank* of the holding cell's lock sliding open. A correctional officer pulled the steel door open, and it creaked as loudly as one would expect. Wyatt slowly sat back up, and the officer held up a set of handcuffs without saying anything.

Though Wyatt had never found himself in this situation before, he instinctively knew he was going with this officer to a new location. He slowly stood, and wiped his tears. He took a couple of steps towards the officer, and held his wrists out towards the officer.

The office silently locked Wyatt's wrists tightly into the handcuffs, grabbed his shoulder hard, and pulled him out of the cell. He slightly shoved Wyatt forward, and Wyatt took a couple of steps forward. Wyatt thought how strange it felt being in his normal clothes, still maroon with his sister's blood, in handcuffs, being led down a hallway by an officer.

"Third door on the left, let's go." The officer's voice was deep, and gravelly. Wyatt shifted his focus from the floor to the open door down the hallway. He counted the doors on the way; third on the left. The two men walked in silence down the hallway, until Wyatt was just a step or two inside the empty room, third door on the left. He turned towards the officer, who unlocked his hand cuffs, and shut the door behind him.

Wyatt stood alone in a new room.

A blank table. A chair on one side, two on the other. Wyatt knew where he was. He was in another interrogation room.

Wyatt rubbed his wrists with his hands. He looked down, and saw indents in his skin where the handcuffs were, though they were only bound briefly. He walked over to the side of the table with a lone chair, and he took a seat. He repeated many of his actions from the previous room, just in a new room. He looked around, and realized many of the features were actually the exact same.

The recessed, fluorescent light in the ceiling. The bland, off-white walls and sealed concrete flooring. He took a deep breath, and started to exhale it slowly. In a moment of pure emotion, Wyatt was overcome with tears. He again buried his head in his hands, and wept.

He stopped himself, and wiped his tears. He sat in silence for another few minutes, until the door clicked open. He looked towards the frame, and saw Detective Johns and Detective Foss both walk into the interrogation room.

Detective Foss set down a couple of folders onto the table, and took a seat, but Detective Johns stood at the table for a moment, his arms crossed across his abdomen.

The three men simply existed in the same room for a moment. No one spoke. Wyatt looked down at the table, and the men kept their eyes on him. Wyatt wondered if they were waiting for him to speak first. A poor idea, as Wyatt knew he had nothing to say.

To Wyatt, the silence somehow simultaneously felt like an eternity, but also passed in the blink of an eye. Time had stopped making sense to him. Detective Gerry Foss was the first of the men to speak, and broke the silence in a very administrative way. He opened the folder in front of him, took out a paper, and clicked the pen in his hand before he took a breath, and looked up at Wyatt.

"Mr. Brone, this is the Los Angeles Police Department. I'm Detective Gerry Foss, this is Detective Thomas Johns, you have spoken with both of us on previous occasions." Wyatt did not respond or react. He kept his eyes on the table. "We want to start today by just getting some information. We want to make sure this is for the record. These questions are standard, and very routine. Would you please provide us your first name?" He finished his question, and again, the three men sat in the thick silence. Wyatt, without looking up, quietly responded.

"Wyatt," he said in a tired voice.

"Is that your legal first name?" Det. Foss replied. Wyatt nodded.

"Yes," he said.

"Middle name?" Foss then asked.

"I don't have one," Wyatt replied. Det. Foss again jotted down some notes on the paper in front of him.

"Last name?" Foss asked.

"Brone," Wyatt said.

"Mind spelling that?" Foss asked, an edge of sarcasm in his voice.

"B - R - O - N - E." Wyatt said, and still stared down directly at the table.

"And what is your date of birth?" Det. Foss spoke, but did not look up from his notes.

"September 20th, 1991." Wyatt said quietly.

The detective continued on asking more basic questions, formally, such as Wyatt's current address, and social security number. Wyatt meekly answered them all, and never looked up from the table. He had begun rubbing his hands together gently. Not out of pain, or anxiety, just as an act of comfort to himself.

"Okay," Det. Foss continued, "I'm going to read you something, and I want to make sure you understand it, okay?" Wyatt nodded without saying anything. "You have the right to remain silent. Anything you say can and will be used against you in a court of law. You have the right to talk to a lawyer, and have them present with you while you're being questioned. If you cannot afford a lawyer, one will be appointed to represent you before any questioning, if you wish. You can decide at any time to exercise these rights, not answer any questions, or make any statements. Okay." Det. Foss finished reading the statement, and reached into the folder to grab another paper. He slid this page in front of Wyatt, and handed him a pen. "Would you mind signing this paper showing that I read you these rights?"

Wyatt picked up the pen, and signed the page on a line at the bottom, next to a "X" Det. Foss had added just a moment prior. Once Wyatt was finished, Det. Foss took the page back, and slid it back into the folder.

Det. Foss leaned back in his seat, and crossed his arms. Thomas Johns finally shifted his weight, and took a seat. He rubbed his face with his hands, and took a breath before he started.

"Do you want to talk to us about today? Det. Johns said. Wyatt did not reply. The detectives could see the remnants of tears, still pooled in the bottom of Wyatt's bloodshot eyes. "I have to know if you want to talk to us about today, Wyatt."

"I can talk to you," Wyatt's words came soft, and he tried to hold back the tears.

"Good. All right. Why don't we start with you walking us through your day?" Det. Johns leaned against the table, with both his elbows resting on the surface, and his hands clasped together just under his chin.

"I woke up around seven this morning, because she called me, her call woke me up—" Wyatt started, but was almost instantly interrupted.

"She? Who? Melody?" Det. Foss asked.

"Melody, yes," Wyatt responded. "She called me early, and woke me up."

"What did she call you so early for?" Det. Johns asked.

"About an article that had just been published. It mentioned a piece of art, and she had been getting a lot of … inquiries about it." Wyatt said. He took his time with each word, finding them with caution and certainty. Simultaneously, he wanted to be careful about how he said every response, and he also wanted to hold back his emotions as much as possible. He had already begun to gather that these men were not entirely on his side. "We … fought a little over the phone, before I told her I had to go."

"You fought? Over the phone?"Det. Foss again jumped in.

"We didn't *fight,* we disagreed." Wyatt clarified.

"You just said *fought.* So did you fight? Or did you disagree?" Det. Foss pointed in.

"We disagreed. About what to do about the painting." Wyatt replied, and still looked down. "We got off the phone, and I met Samantha for lunch."

"Samantha Garcia, correct?" Det. Johns asked. Wyatt nodded. "And Samantha is your partner, correct?"

"My fiancé, yes." Wyatt said. "Samantha and I had lunch, and walked around the city, and then I got a couple of text messages from Mel," as Wyatt mentioned her name again, he started to lose control on his tears. It was only for a moment, but the dam had started to crack.

"And what did the text messages say?" Det. Foss asked.

"Uh — they, uh —" Wyatt stumbled over his words for a moment. "She sent me a text to, uh — tell me how beautiful she thought a painting was. In my loft." Wyatt broke down as he finished his sentence. He thought of the moment he looked at his phone. That moment of dread he felt just before he opened his text message app. How he somehow knew something terrible had happened, and that there was nothing he could do.

The genuine and searing fear he felt as he read the messages she had sent.

Why would you want to keep this hidden? It's stunning — Is this the piece you're working on with Uncle Jack? — Wyatt, this is beautiful.

The tears streamed down Wyatt's face. The image of the text messages burned into his brain.

"What time would you say you were with Samantha?" Det. Johns asked.

"I… I don't remember exactly. I called 9-1-1 in a Lyft on the way back to my loft." Wyatt said.

"So, you get these texts, you tell Samantha you have to leave, then you take a Lyft home?" Det. Johns asked. Wyatt nodded. "So you were with Samantha the entire time before you went home and found Melody?" Again, Wyatt nodded.

"Well, there are some inconsistencies we are curious about," Det. Foss started, "I believe everything you just said, except for the part where you aren't at home when your sister is murdered." Det. Johns took a breath, and let Det. Foss dig in. "Wyatt, the fact of the matter, is that no one has a key to your apartment except you, Samantha and Melody. Samantha has an alibi, she was at work. We already checked with her, and she confirmed this. That only leaves you."

"I was with Samantha, you can verify that too." Wyatt said.

"And if you learned that Samantha told us otherwise?" Det. Foss spoke cold, pointed, and short. For the first time, Wyatt looked up from the table, and made eye contact with the detective.

"She never said that, because it isn't the truth. Samantha called the Lyft for me from her phone. These are … verifiable facts." Wyatt said, harshly. "If you want to say something, Detective, say it. Otherwise, I think you should let me go."

"Listen, Wyatt," Det. Johns said, and took back over the conversation. "We just want to get the details of your day, so we can put together an accurate timeline."

"I just gave you every detail on what has become the worst day of my entire life. You can confirm them on your own." Wyatt said, and he started to lose his temperature. "Now am I being arrested, or can I leave?"

"We can hold you for forty-eight hours, so calm down." Det. Foss snapped back.

"Well, then take me back to the fucking cell—" Wyatt raised his voice for the first time a long time.

"That's enough," Det. Johns raised his voice just so, and interrupted both men. "Gerry, take a walk." Without breaking his eye contact with Wyatt, Det. Foss abruptly stood up from his seat and walked out of the room.

Once Det. Foss closed the door behind him, Det. Johns stood from his chair, and turned to face the door. He took a few labored breaths, and rubbed his face with his hands.

"You understand how this looks for us, yeah? Please at least say that." Det. Johns said reluctantly. "A highly known figure that's closely related to another well-known public figure who mysteriously kills himself, is found with the body of another family member? Come on, Wyatt." Det. Johns turned to face Wyatt, but Wyatt still stared down at the table. "And now we are here with you, again, face to face, and you're being evasive, and … it's just all very suspect."

"I'm being evasive?" Wyatt said through gritted teeth. "I just came home to find my sister dead—"

"In your apartment, yes. With your fingerprints all over the piece of wood lodged in her esophagus." Det. Johns interrupted Wyatt, and Wyatt sensed the anger in his voice.

"It was a paint brush. In my studio. I'm an artist. Of course, it had my fingerprints on it." Wyatt shook his head, and again had begun losing the battle to hold back his tears.

"This just doesn't square. I've been in this business for 25 years, Wyatt. I know when something doesn't seem all there. This… this whole fucking mess doesn't add up." Det. Johns spoke sincerely, but there was a definite threatening tone added in.

"Are you keeping me here, or am I free to leave?" Wyatt replied plainly.

"You're free to leave. But I'm telling you right now," Det. Johns quieted his voice, and leaned over the table, getting his face close to Wyatt's. "I'm just missing the connecting piece. I will find it. And I will take you down."

The two men stared at each other in silence for a few moments. Wyatt finally exhaled, looked back down at the table, and smirked. He was intentionally feigning an air of sarcasm to the detective, but also, full aware of his own innocence, felt sad for the detective too.

Wyatt slowly stood up, and without saying another word, Wyatt left the room.

As he walked down the hallway, he passed Det. Foss, who was leaning up against the wall, one foot on the ground, one foot on the dirty baseboard. Det. Foss stared Wyatt down as he walked pass. Wyatt did not look up. He kept walking until he was out of the building.

Samantha was waiting for him outside, and she smiled, with tears in her eyes, as he approached her car. She hugged him hard, and he cried in her arms. They stood, stoic and quiet, for a few moments, and just embraced each other. Finally, they both got into Samantha's car, and she drove away.

It took them about forty-five minutes to get to Samantha's apartment in West Hollywood from downtown at that hour. The traffic had been predictably terrible, but Wyatt did not mind. If he was being honest, he hardly noticed the traffic at all. Samantha, wanting to be sensitive to the traumatic day he had experienced, opted to not resume her customized "summer beat bops" playlist she had built on Spotify. She did not play anything at all. They just sat on the freeway, in bumper-to-bumper traffic, in complete, and welcomed silence.

They parked in her building's garage, and took the service elevator on the back of the building up to the seventh floor. Wyatt did not have any of his belongings with him, but remembered that he had a pair of sweatpants and a couple of plain t-shirts at Samantha's.

Samantha fumbled her keys in her hands for a moment, before she opened the door, and they walked inside. She set her keys down on a small table in her entryway, and took her shoes off. She turned to Wyatt, and kissed his cheek.

"Can I get you anything? Some water? A glass of wine? Anything" She winced, and gently rubbed his face with her hand. Wyatt forced the tiniest of smiles, and shook his head "no." Samantha nodded, and walked into her apartment. She grabbed a glass from a kitchen cabinet, and poured a glass of water for him, anyway. Wyatt followed her in, slowly, and watched her.

"Here, drink it. Please." She said tenderly.

Wyatt did not say anything, but his brain was racing a mile a minute. Everything he knew he needed to say had been boiling up from the moment he sat into her car.

"Samantha, I need to tell you something." He finally found a way to put words together. Samantha stopped what she was doing, and turned to face him. "And … it's going to sound insane. It really is, but there isn't any way around it, I have to tell you." Wyatt's eyes welled with tears yet again, and Samantha knew he was getting to his breaking point.

"Wyatt, you're scaring me," she said, and remained as calm and as gentle as she knew how to be.

"I inherited a painting from my uncle," Wyatt started.

"Yeah, I know," she responded in the habit of trying to be comforting. She walked around her kitchen counter, and touched his arms with her hands.

"The painting had a… letter attached to it? On the back of it. And the letter was… odd. Strange. It felt old. And it had a set of rules written on it, and then there were lots of other scribbles, and thoughts, and notations, all over this single piece of paper." Wyatt realized that explaining this would be more difficult than he anticipated, and he hated the fact that even to him, he already sounded crazy.

"Rules?" Samantha asked.

"Yeah, like… guidelines? But they were written in… like… old English. Some sort of… aged dialect." He replied. "I don't remember exactly how they are phrased like that, but one of the notations in the margins, had sort of, rewritten then, in a way to understand." He searched for the three lines of text that accompanied the painting.

"Okay…" Samantha replied, and gently rubbed his shoulder.

"To never show, and never tell, for it will be yours. To never stop, and never sell, for it will be yours. Follow these to wildest dreams, for it will be yours." Wyatt felt almost out of breath when he finished speaking. He felt that saying these commands out loud was expelling some internal demon that had been weighing him down. He looked up at Samantha, who simply stared back at him, blank faced and confused.

"…I don't… understand." She finally said.

"I didn't either, at first. But the more time I spent with it, I realized they were instructions. I realized that this painting has some sort of… curse on it, and as long as I followed these instructions, everything I wanted would happen." Wyatt hesitated as he ended his thought, but he had already committed to finishing it. Samantha lifted a single eyebrow, but did not say anything in return. "I know it sounds crazy, but it worked. It happened. All I had to do was add a stroke of paint to the canvas every day, and literally everything started changing…" he continued, a hint of desperation had begun to creep into his seeking cadence. "And it worked. It happened to my uncle. He went from being a *nothing*, to being everything at the drop of a dime. It was literally happening with him. I bombed at a gallery opening, what, seven weeks ago? Then Jackson leaves me this painting, and I've been on the front page of *The New York Times*, twice. That doesn't just happen to people, Sam."

"First of all, your uncle came up in a different time, and that shit happened to people like Jackson. Wyatt, you have *worked your ass off* to get to where you are. You didn't just appear on the cover of *The Times*. They sought you out, because of how hard you work every single fucking day at your art. So don't cut yourself short with some … fantasy."

"You aren't listening, Samantha. I followed the rules, and they happened." He said again.

"Wyatt…" Samantha said, and tried to slow him down.

"I added paint, and… and suddenly, *The New York Times* wants to do an article on me, and… and *you* decide you want to be together and get married, and… and Porter & Herth decides they want to showcase my work worldwide." Wyatt sped up as he talked, and the tears had begun to fall again. "When I added paint… everything, *everything* fell into place."

"Wyatt, hang on…" Samantha tried again to slow him, to no avail.

"Then I stopped adding paint, and everything came crashing down. Caroline Haynes at *The Times* said she was going to run a piece that would have ended my career, and Porter & Herth drops me from all of their galleries except one." Wyatt shook her hands off of his arms, and paced around her living room.

"Wyatt, you're scaring me…" Samantha pleaded.

"Don't you understand? Melody looked at the painting. She wasn't supposed to see it— no one was supposed to see it. I broke the rules. And—"

"Are you saying the painting killed your sister?" Samantha stared at him with genuine fear in her eyes. "Wyatt…"

"Why do you think I didn't want you to look at it? Why I couldn't show you the piece? Samantha, I didn't know what would happen—" Wyatt seemed to be falling apart at the seams.

"Wyatt, stop," Samantha spoke with slightly more force in her voice.

"Samantha, are you listening? This is all my fault, I broke the rules, and the curse killed Melody." Wyatt wept. He stood alone in her living room, his arms wrapped around his torso. He squeezed himself tightly, and he wept.

Slowly, Samantha walked over to him, and again, gently touched his arm. "Wyatt, baby…" She spoke slowly and carefully. "Wyatt, love, there are no such things as curses. Magic isn't real, you didn't kill your sister."

"I need to go to my apartment, I haven't added any paint today," Wyatt started to plead.

"Wyatt, no, you can't," Samantha interjected.

"I have to, Samantha, I have to. I don't know what will happen if I miss today," Wyatt cried hard, and forced the words out through his tears.

"Wyatt, you can't. Stop, slow down. Just for a minute. Listen to yourself. You can't go anyway, your apartment is still an active… there are still police officers there." Samantha caught herself from saying the words *crime scene.* "Wyatt, you didn't kill your sister."

"I did, I… I didn't obey the rules—" Wyatt continued.

"You didn't obey the rules? Of what? A painting? A painting is oil and canvas, Wyatt, its materials… nothing else… that's it." She tried her best to console him, but she did not know if she would see any success in her attempts. "I know that this has been a terrible, awful day. And I know that you have so many questions, and no answers, but Wyatt… Melody took her own life. Melody killed herself. It had nothing to do with you, and there is nothing you could have done to stop it or prevent it. And I know how difficult that is to hear, and how impossible that may seem to understand, but you have to believe me." Samantha teared up as she spoke too. "This is not your fault. Magic isn't real. There is no cursed painting. This is just a shitty, terrible day."

Wyatt took a few deep breaths, and again stood in silence. Samantha finally hugged him again, and just held onto him in her living room. They said nothing, they just stood there together.

Samantha exaggerated her deep breaths, and tried to get Wyatt to mimic them, subconsciously.

"I promise," Samantha continued, "everything will be fine. Let's just have tonight, okay?" He listened to her, but did not immediately respond. After a moment, he put his arms around her, and held her tight too.

She closed her eyes, and buried her head in his chest.

He stared blankly at the wall, his heart raced.

Wyatt stayed at Samantha's apartment that night. He did not add a stroke of paint to the canvas that day. As he laid awake in her bed, Wyatt realized something that made his gut ache. Not only did he not add paint that day, he told Samantha about the letter.

Again, Wyatt had broken the rules.

CHAPTER 18

He woke up alone.

Not due to an argument, or residual anger from the night before; Samantha had an early meeting. He stretched his arms out wide, and took a deep breath before he opened his eyes. In a moment of dull pain, he realized this was essentially the first morning of his life waking up into a world without his sister.

The weight was palpable, heavy, and numbing.

He opened his eyes, and stared at Samantha's popcorn ceiling. He laid for a few moments in excruciating silence, before he forced his limbs into action, and eventually stood up. Every movement, and every breath felt labored.

Wyatt made his way into Samantha's kitchen and tried to replicate his morning routine, but quickly realized that he had no clue where anything was kept. After searching for a few moments, in hopes to find some coffee grinds, he accepted defeat and walked back into her bedroom. He did not have an appetite anyway.

He got dressed in a plain, dark blue t-shirt he had left at Samantha's house what felt like ages ago, and a new pair of jeans Samantha had delivered to her house the previous evening. He heard his cell phone chime, and his heart ached. His first thought was, "What does Melody need?"

The dull, sucking feeling in his chest subsided only for a moment. He looked at his phone, and saw a voicemail notification on the display screen. He swiped it open, hit play, and enabled the speakerphone. He heard a voice speak on the other end.

"Hello Wyatt, this is Sonya Walter with the Los Angeles Police Department. I'm calling to let you know that the majority of our team has vacated your apartment, and you are free to return at your convenience." Wyatt breathed a slight sigh of relief, though he admittedly had no desire to set foot back in his apartment. "That being said, some members of our team will need to be in and out for a few days, and we will have some portions of your apartment sectioned off for our forensics team to continue gathering data. If it's more convenient for you to stay elsewhere, you can make the decision that is best for you. We will be in contact if our team needs anything from you, take care."

Wyatt stared at his phone screen for a few moments, before pressing the power button on the side once, and the display clicked off. He took a deep breath, and looked around him. It was in that exact moment that he realized he had no plans that day. Melody had been the primary component of his professional calendar, and he did not have that anymore.

He remembered his laptop did have his calendar synced with Melody's office, and anything he needed to do would be linked there. His laptop was at his loft. He took another, smaller breath, and stood up. He knew, as much as he wished he could avoid it, he needed to go home.

Wyatt walked through Samantha's apartment, grabbed his keys, and headed out the door.

The drive from Samantha's West Hollywood two bedroom to Wyatt's downtown loft felt especially long today. Wyatt's anxiety and dread slowly built momentum with every passing streetlight. He would have preferred anything rather than having to take a step back into his apartment.

He walked into the lobby of his building, and already felt anxious about having to interact with anyone. His Door Man greeted him, and acknowledged the somber mood and tragedy. Wyatt expressed his gratitude, and forced a smile, before he walked over to the elevator and pressed his floor. The elevator chimed and the doors closed.

Wyatt caught a glimpse of his reflection in the brushed steel elevator door.

For the first time in the last day or two, Wyatt almost laughed. He looked like a disaster. His hair was greasy, and disheveled. His shirt was just slightly too small, and his jeans just slightly too tight. The brushed steel reflection he was looking at was warped and distorted, but he knew it was not all that far off from reality.

The chimes rang out again, and the doors slowly slid open. Two police officers stood just outside the door in the hallway of Wyatt's floor. They smiled and nodded at him, and parted so he could step out of the elevator. Wyatt knew they did not realize it was him, or that they were just in his loft. They took a step into the elevator, and pressed a button before the door closed again. Wyatt looked to his door, and saw it open. One more officer stood outside his door, and two more walked out. Wyatt knew there would be more inside.

He finally started walking to his door, and the police officer just outside stopped him.

"I'm sorry, this is a closed location," the officer said. Wyatt was caught off-guard for a moment, and stumbled over his words.

"I, uh— sorry, this— fuck, uh…" *Great start,* Wyatt thought. "I live here." He finally stuttered out.

"Oh, my apologies. Do you have an ID?" The officer asked.

Instinctively, Wyatt checked his pockets, but realized that his wallet was inside his loft.

"Sorry. I do, it's just… in there." Wyatt said, and pointed inside his loft. "Small table on the right-hand side of the bed. I'll wait here." He said. The officer looked inside, and called out to another officer.

"Hey, Matthews, you got eyes on a wallet… top right-hand side of the bed?" The officer looked at Wyatt and asked, "In the drawer or sitting on top?

"Should be on top," Wyatt responded quietly.

"Should be sitting on top," the officer again called out.

After a few quiet moments, a disembodied voice called out from inside Wyatt's living room. "Got it," the voice called out.

"Mind bringing it over?" the officer asked. Wyatt smiled at the officer.

Another officer walked into view, and handed the man the wallet. The officer took the wallet, and flipped it open. He pulled out the California driver's license, and held it up to compare Wyatt's face. It was obviously Wyatt.

"Date of birth?" The officer said. It took all of Wyatt's might to resist rolling his eyes. Instead, he simply opted to cooperate. He recited the month, day and year or his birth.

The officer nodded, and handed Wyatt his driver's license back. "Welcome home, Wyatt. We have a few areas roped off, at this time you are not permitted into those areas. If you haven't gotten one yet, someone from our office should be in touch with more details."

"Yeah, someone called me earlier, I don't remember her name," Wyatt responded. The officer took a small step out of the way, and Wyatt walked inside.

He barely recognized his space. Everything was moved, or covered in tagged, or caution tape. Several people with clipboards stood discussing various things. Down the thin hallway, Wyatt saw a photographer taking shots of various things in his bedroom. Wyatt felt out of place, and definitely in the way. He used his restroom, and excused himself past the photographer in his bedroom to pack some clothes in a black, Herschel Supply Co. weekender bag.

Wyatt took a long, hot shower, and brushed his teeth. He thought about how it felt slightly violating that he was expected to co-exist with so many intrusive strangers in his home. He could hear people talking in his living room, and the photographer as he continued capturing moments in his space.

He teared up, and looked in the mirror. *What the fuck happened?*

He got ready to leave again, and walked past the entrance of the secondary room. The painting still leaned against the wall, where Wyatt had thrown it to the side.

His fingertips tingled with the urge to add paint to it.

The room was sectioned off with bright yellow caution tape. Wyatt knew he could not add paint to the canvas even if he wanted to. At this point, he just wanted to destroy it. Another act that he knew the rules prohibited him from performing. His eyes moved slowly from the painting against the wall to the floor in front of where the painting stood. The wood darkened from the large pool of Melody's blood. Again, Wyatt felt overcome with emotions. Not just the deep, and unbearable sadness from losing his sister, but the overwhelming sense of guilt from getting her wrapped up in the mess he found himself in.

Every decision that he had ever made that led him to this moment contributed to his sister's demise. He was fully, and unequivocally to blame. And it was too late — there was nothing he could do to change it.

Melody was gone, and that was that.

A single tear fell from his eye, and splashed against the floor at his feet. His knees felt weak, and he was afraid that they would buckle.

His guilt and shame was interrupted, when he felt his cell phone buzz with an incoming phone call. He wiped his tears, and pulled his phone out of his pocket.

Unknown Caller...

He tapped the green "Answer" button anyway.

"This is Wyatt," he said through a soft, graveled voice.

"Wyatt, hi, this is Caroline Haynes, from *The New York Times*." Her voice sounded gentle, and caring.

"Hey…" Wyatt said. He looked around his place. Everyone still seemed undeterred at his presence, so he walked back towards his door and took a few steps outside. "…Caroline, how's it going?"

"Wyatt, I am so, so profoundly sorry for your loss. Melody… well, she was a bulldog. And your biggest champion with our team." Caroline smiled lightly as she spoke. She was sincere, and Wyatt believed her.

"Thanks, Caroline. Really. That means a lot." He smiled gently, and looked at the ground.

"Listen, I'm calling with some unfortunate news, and I know now is not a great time, but again… we run what's relevant." Wyatt heard the sincerity and concern in Caroline's voice almost instantly click off, and her business, serious tone clicked on.

"Listen, Caroline…" Wyatt tried to interrupt her to voice his indifference to whatever she had to say, but business Caroline carried on.

"We have sources that suggest you are under investigation for the potential murder of your uncle."

Wyatt stood silently in the hallway of his building, the police officer stood just outside his door. It took everything to keep Wyatt from responding with the rage he felt, but he wisely opted to keep his mouth shut.

"We verified. We have two Los Angeles Police Department Homicide Investigators on record, and willing to be named in the piece. And now… with the news of your sister, our team feels even more justified to run this story." Caroline spoke quick, and calculated. Wyatt thought meticulously about how quickly Caroline's phone calls transition from friend to foe.

There was silence on the line for a moment. Wyatt's mind raced with all the things he wanted to say, and then again with all the things he actually should say. Instead, he said nothing.

"Wyatt, are you there?" Caroline asked, her voice still cold to the touch. He still said nothing. His pragmatic brain screamed to just remain silent. Instead, his anger took over.

"Caroline, if you run this story, I will file a slander lawsuit against you and the Los Angeles Police Department. This is categorically false, and I will bring you down."

If Wyatt was honest with himself, a small part of his ego felt relieved. Relieved that he stood up for himself, and spoke the truth. Another part of Wyatt screamed with fear that he was at the point of no return.

"Good luck, Wyatt," Caroline paused for just a moment, and then she ended the call. He slid his phone back in his pocket, and tried to focus on his breathing.

"We're all set for today," a voice said from behind him. Wyatt snapped out of his thoughts, and turned to see the officer from outside his loft standing in front of him.

"Thanks," Wyatt said with a thin voice.

"Please don't cross the caution tape, we'll likely have another team in tomorrow to wrap up a few things." The officer said, and Wyatt nodded. A few more people left Wyatt's loft as he made his way back inside. He locked the door behind him, and leaned against the door. He cried, and fell down to sit on the ground.

He could not believe this was all happening.

After a few moments of self-pity, Wyatt forced himself back onto his feet, and walked up to the caution tape blocking the entrance of his secondary room.

Wyatt crossed the tape.

He walked over to the painting, and picked it up off of the ground. Even with the genuine anger he felt for this piece of canvas and wood, he was gentle with it, and carefully placed it back onto its easel.

Wyatt took a step back and looked at the painting.

He no longer saw its complex textures and color palette. He only saw a sloppy disregard for the things that brought him joy in art. His hands pounded with the urge to add paint to the canvas, but his mind was consumed with the thoughts of ruining it. The thoughts of the many ways he could destroy the painting right now in this moment. He wanted to.

He wanted to end this nightmare.

He knew the rules were clear about not destroying the painting, but he contemplated if he cared anymore. He had accidentally broken rules already, and he had cost his sister her life by doing so. *What else could go wrong?* He thought, sarcastically.

His mind raced with different ideas of how he could end the curse and obliterate the canvas itself. A control burn right there in his loft… slicing it into shreds with a poultry kitchen knife… or just covering it with simple rubbing alcohol, and taking a paint scraper to it… His heart raced, and matched the speed his mind was running with the fantasy of destroying the piece.

Then he thought of Samantha. The idea of something awful happening because he destroyed this painting, and it being involved with Samantha gave him a pause. Up to Melody's death, he assumed that his life would be the only one potentially affected by this curse. Now, everyone in his life was on the table.

Wyatt could not bear the idea of something bad happening to Samantha.

Tonight he would not destroy the painting. Instead, he simply picked up the moving cover, and draped it back over the painting. Though his hands pounded with the urge to add to it, he instead turned, and walked out of the room.

He grabbed his keys, and with a new determination, he rushed out of his loft. Before too long, Wyatt found himself outside of the office of Dr. Erich Scholden.

Wyatt stood, outside of the building, and stared at the building. A part of him could not remember how he even arrived, and a part of him screamed to leave. He saw someone exit the building, and as they passed him, they stared at him. Their eyes showed concern, and Wyatt realized he must look insane.

His feet kicked into gear, and the next thing he knew, he was inside, standing before an equally concerned receptionist.

"Can I help you, sir?" The young woman asked, gently. Wyatt could tell that she had experience working with distraught, and desperate patients. He stared back blankly for a moment, and tried to remember how to speak. He thought that even if he could remember how to use words, what words would he even use? Finally, he found some that sufficed.

"Dr. Erich Scholden." Wyatt said. The young woman did not break her eye contact, and instead continued.

"Is the Doctor expecting you?" She asked, while she reached for a desk phone.

"No, but it's important." Wyatt responded.

"Okay…" the young woman cautioned, and dialed a few numbers on the phone. "You can wait over there, I'll reach out to his office. What is your name?"

"Wyatt Brone," he said. The young woman's eyes widened. She nodded, and Wyatt did not move. After a few moments of awkward silence, the young woman spoke into the phone.

"Wyatt Brone is here to see Dr. Scholden… uh huh… no, he is not… Okay, thank you." The young woman hung up the receiver, and lightly smiled at Wyatt before she spoke. "Unfortunately, Dr. Scholden is not available at this time."

"Feel free to call him back, and let him know that I won't leave until he sees me. I'll stay all day if I have to." Wyatt said, and the young woman could almost hear the desperation in his voice.

"I'm really sorry, sir, Dr. Scholden's schedule is just—"

"Listen." Wyatt said, and there was a new tone of anger in his words. "I am not going anywhere. Erich can make some fucking time." The young woman looked scared, and she slowly reached back for the phone receiver.

She dialed a couple of numbers again, and Wyatt relented back towards the waiting area. She spoke so quietly that Wyatt could not make out the words. After a few moments, she stood, and forced a smile at him.

"He'll see you now. Last office on the right, just down this hallway." She said to Wyatt, and Wyatt smiled as he walked past her desk.

"Sorry, I didn't mean to raise my voice," Wyatt said as he walked past. He did not wait for her to accept his apology, or even respond. He did not care. He beelined straight towards Dr. Scholden's office door, and as he reached for the handle, Erich opened the door.

"What the fuck is your problem?" Erich said, disappointment behind his eyes.

"Is that how you talk to all of your patients?" Wyatt sarcastically responded.

"You, Wyatt, are not my patient. And at this point, you're essentially a criminal." Erich said, and walked back into his office. Wyatt followed him in, and shut the door behind him. "Did you have to scare Mandy? She just started a few days ago."

"Sorry, I didn't mean to… I wasn't trying to be rude to her." Wyatt said, and Dr. Scholden took a seat behind his desk.

"Well, maybe you should apologize to her on your way out." Erich said, and looked out his window. "What are you doing here, Wyatt? I have nothing else to say," he continued.

"Melody died." Wyatt said, and Dr. Scholden looked directly at him.

"Wyatt, I'm so sorry. I had no idea." He said, and Wyatt could tell he was sincere. "I didn't know her, but your uncle spoke of her incredibly highly." Wyatt nodded, and looked to the ground. "What happened?"

Wyatt took a deep breath, and without looking at the doctor, and said, "She killed herself." Dr. Erich Scholden almost gasped. His line of work put him in close contact with many suicides; Wyatt's uncle being one of the more recent examples. It still was never easy to hear, and it was always a shock. "She looked at the painting, and she shoved one of my wooden paint brush handles into her neck. I got home too late, and she was dead."

The two men stayed in the silence for a few moments.

"What do you mean she looked at the painting?" Dr. Erich Scholden finally broke the silence, and asked.

"The painting I told you about, the cursed—" Wyatt started to explain, but the doctor would not let him finish his thought.

"Wyatt, stop. There are no such things as curses," he said with confidence.

"No? Well, I believe I mentioned the painting's rules to you last time we spoke, and what would happen if I broke the rules? *Everything terrible.* I'm getting dropped from galleries, I'm under investigation for my uncle's death apparently, and now my sister— my sister kills herself. No such thing as curses? Then how do you explain any of this? Huh, doc?" Tears welled in Wyatt's eyes, and he was out of breath.

Dr. Scholden saw the hopelessness in Wyatt's eyes. He took a couple of breaths, and carefully took his glasses off of his face, and set them onto the top of his desk. He rubbed his eyes.

"Wyatt," he started, a distinct shift in his tone. "I can't explain any of it. No one can. But sometimes that is how things happen. They're unexplainable. But our brains — we need reason to grasp onto; especially in the face of unspeakable tragedy." Dr. Erich Scholden spoke with a careful gentleness.

Wyatt just shook his head, and looked down. Tears openly fell from his eyes now, and he rubbed his hands together.

"Wyatt, it's in your head. This… this *curse* is your brain's way of explaining what cannot be explained. It isn't real… there is no curse. It's in your head." The doctor continued, his eyes locked onto Wyatt.

"So what do I do now?" Wyatt asked, and despair filled every syllable. Dr. Scholden leaned back in his chair, and exhaled.

"I don't know." He said. He crossed his arms, and tensed his muscles. "You could destroy it." At this, Wyatt looked up. "It's obviously causing you incredible distress, unnecessarily in my opinion, so rip the weed out at its roots. Destroy the painting, so you have the ability to move on. Mourn your uncle. Mourn your sister. Move on with your life."

Silence again fell over the room, save for the sounds of Wyatt's muffled weeping.

"And what if you're wrong?" Wyatt asked, he still looked at the ground.

"I'm not, Wyatt. You know I'm not," the doctor responded, and brushed the notion aside. "If for no other reason than just... peace of mind. Get rid of the fucking thing."

Wyatt left Dr. Erich Scholden's office in no better headspace than he had been upon his arrival. He felt exhausted, and at the end of his emotional rope. He opened an app on his phone, and ordered a car to take him home.

Wyatt looked up at the Los Angeles skyline in front of him. A helicopter slowly curled the city, and Wyatt closed his eyes for a moment. The sounds of the city brought him a fleeting moment of respite, but his nagging shame slowly crept back in. He took a deep breath, and waited for his ride home basking in the sounds of the chaos; both in his city and in his mind.

He made sure to check the box in the app again so he could sit in silence on his ride home as well. It made the ride feel long, but everything he had done for the last 48 hours felt longer than it had been.

Samantha was already at his loft when he arrived back. She had some take out and a heavy pour of Cabernet Sauvignon waiting for him. She hugged him hard, and avoided asking him how his day was. They ate in silence, but sat next to each other at his kitchen counter. Samantha had some music playing, and tried her best to make Wyatt feel as comfortable as possible. She knew he would talk when he felt up to it. She did not push the subject.

Wyatt did not speak for a long time. They finished their dinner, and Samantha topped off both of their glasses. Samantha laid back down next to him, and rested her head on his shoulder. Finally, he spoke.

"Do you remember what I told you? About the painting?" He asked.

"About how you think it's haunted?" She replied.

"I'm thinking about destroying it," Wyatt said. He did not look at her.

"Isn't it one of your uncle's last paintings?" She responded, skeptically.

"Not exactly," Wyatt tried to reply, but Samantha cut him off.

"Wyatt, you can't do that. I know you and Jackson had your differences, but think about what you're saying." She said.

"You don't understand, Sam… it's… there's something wrong," Wyatt tried again.

"Because you think there's a ghost haunting cloth and wood?" She asked, more pointed. "You realize how insane you sound?"

"I just… I need to get rid of it. For me, and for you."

"What do you mean, for *me?*" Samantha asked, and he knew she was confused by his statement.

"It's … dangerous. I don't know what will happen, but I have to end this. The way I feel, the confusion, the fear, the anger. It's all stemming from this fucking painting. I have to get rid of it." Wyatt said, and Samantha saw that he was afraid.

"Okay," she responded. "Okay… hey…. It's okay. Everything is fine. Do what you need to do, I understand." Wyatt nodded, and forced a smile. "Plus, if it gets you focused back on your own work, then even better." Samantha stood up, and cleaned up their takeout containers. Wyatt smiled.

"I guess it has been a minute, huh?" He said.

"Too long," Samantha smiled. Samantha grabbed Wyatt by the sleeve of his shirt, and pulled him with her into his main work room. "Like this one," Samantha said as they both walked to stand in front of one of Wyatt's newer original pieces. He had not finished it yet, but it was one he was particularly proud of. "This is so gorgeous, and when is the last time you even looked at it?"

"It's… it's been awhile." Wyatt said.

"See? It needs your attention. Or even this one," Samantha said, and turned to face another one of Wyatt's unfinished originals. "These are amazing, Wyatt. They deserve to get finished."

"Maybe you're right," Wyatt said, and put his hand through her hair.

"I know this is an impossibly hard week. But you're an artist, Wyatt. You need to create again. And if getting rid of that painting will do that, then… you need to do it." Samantha said.

He kissed her. They smiled. Wyatt felt human again.

Samantha held up her glass of wine, and smirked at him.

"I'll get us some more," Wyatt said, and laughed. He walked out of the room, and headed back towards his kitchen. Samantha continued to look at some of Wyatt's unfinished works.

On his way back to the kitchen, Wyatt felt his cell phone vibrate in his pocket. He pulled the phone out of his pocket, and swiped to answer.

"Hello?" Wyatt said as he grabbed the bottle of wine, and filled his own glass.

"Wyatt, hello. It's Courtney. Porter & Herth" Her voice was soft, and precise.

"Courtney, hi. Wasn't expecting a call from you." Wyatt said, and popped the cork back into the bottle.

"Yes, my apologies for calling so late, too. Listen, Wyatt. We were sent an advanced copy of a piece Caroline Haynes is working on at *The New York Times*." Wyatt took a breath, and leaned forward, against his kitchen counter. "I know there will likely be multiple stories, and conflicting reports, but at this time, we at Porter & Herth cannot in good conscience continue to highlight your works at any of our galleries. We will fulfill our financial obligations as stated in our existing, modified contract, but we will be removing your works, effective immediately."

Wyatt was not sure how to respond. He just took another deep breath. Every ounce of him wanted to explode, but he thought of everything that had occurred over the last few days, and what

Samantha had just told him. Maybe this was a chance to go back to what brought him joy. *Painting.*

"Thanks for letting me know, I understand you need to do what you feel is best." Wyatt did not smile, but he felt a small glint of pride in his response.

"I'll make sure our team communicates financial fulfillments, and we wish you the best." Courtney was quick to end the call. Wyatt did not have a chance to respond, but he ultimately knew he did not need to. He simply slid his phone back into his pocket. He grabbed the bottle of wine, and his glass.

Wyatt walked back into his main work room.

"I think there's still enough left in this bottle—" he started to speak, but the room was empty. He looked around, but Samantha was not there. "Samantha?" Wyatt called out, and slowly walked out of the main work room.

Wyatt walked into a hallway, and he could feel his heart begin to race. "Sam? Where'd you go?" Samantha did not respond. "Samantha? This isn't funny," he called out, and walked a little quicker.

He instinctively felt himself walking towards his secondary work room.

"Samantha!" Wyatt yelled.

Finally, Samantha responded, and her words made Wyatt's world come to a screeching halt.

"Wyatt, it's stunning," Samantha said. Her voice echoed throughout his loft.

"Samantha!" Wyatt yelled.

Crash!

The sound of glass smashing against the floor rang out, and Wyatt knew it was coming from his secondary work room. He sprinted towards the doorway. "Samantha!" He yelled again.

Wyatt froze as he turned the corner and looked into his secondary room.

Samantha had removed the cover from his uncle's painting, and stood solemnly facing it. Tears in her eyes, and the long, thin stem from her broken wine glass in her left hand. Wyatt saw the remainder of her shattered glass on the floor at her feet.

"Samantha…" Wyatt said tenderly, but it was too late.

"Wyatt…" she whispered, completely entranced by the canvas. Tears began to fall from her eyes.

Samantha slowly raised the glass stem towards her head. She gently stabbed the stem of the broken wine glass into her neck, and dragged it across her throat. Blood poured from the wound, and spilled everywhere. Samantha, having slit her own throat, fell to the ground.

"Samantha, no!" Wyatt screamed, and ran towards her. He wept, and screamed. "No, no, no! Samantha, no!" He cradled her head, blood poured out of her neck, and onto the floor.

Wyatt held his hand against the wound, but it was too deep. Blood spilled out at a rate Wyatt had not known possible. Samantha began to choke on her own blood, and her body convulsed.

Wyatt watched her die.

In his arms, he watched the life disappear from her eyes. Her body became still.

Wyatt screamed loudly, and cried hard. He prayed he was in the midst of a terrible nightmare. He screamed for help. No one heard to answer him. He screamed anyway. Wyatt screamed until the back of his throat bled.

CHAPTER 19

Samantha was dead.

Her body was still warm to his touch.

Wyatt could not take his hands away from her face, and her head. It took Samantha almost a full sixty-seconds to die. Wyatt held her in his arms as she gasped for breath though her severed esophagus. Her eyes filled with panic and regret. Wyatt knew there was nothing he could do but watch. He frivolously held his hand to the wound in her neck, but it was too deep. There was nothing he could do to stop the inevitable death. It came. Samantha's body went limp in Wyatt's arms, and he screamed out again, devastated.

It takes around twelve hours for a deceased human body to become cold to the touch. Samantha had just barely ceased gurgling on her own blood. Though the air had left her lungs, her heart had stopped beating, and her brain function had ended, Samantha's eyes were still wide open. She lifelessly stared at Wyatt. All Wyatt felt he could do was silently weep, and stare back. Eventually he gently touched her face, and closed her eyes. Blood streaked down her forehead to cheeks from his fingers.

Since her heart had stopped, so had the massive amount of blood that poured from her neck. Wyatt let go, relented the pressure he held against her neck, and looked at the wound. The large slit was deep, and at first glance Wyatt almost vomited in his mouth. He could see the fiber of her neck muscles. The yellow layer of thin fat just underneath her skin made Wyatt's stomach turn. It was brutal, utter carnage. Wyatt grabbed a cloth from his small work table, and delicately wrapped it around her neck. He could not bear to see her like this. Dead. Lifeless.

Wyatt again found himself covered in the blood of someone he loved, virtually in the same spot on the hardwood floor of his secondary workspace. He looked at the lake of blood around him with the images of Melody's body still fresh in his mind. He moaned out of the sheer pain and weight of reality. He did not know what to do.

Samantha was gone. In two days' time, he had watched two of the most important people in his life leave this planet in his arms. What was he supposed to do?

He wept. He touched Samantha's hair, her face, her lips. He uttered hushed whispers under his breath, and apologized.

"I'm so sorry, I'm so sorry," he managed to say. "Please forgive me."

After several minutes, his focus shifted from his dead fiancé to the painting at his three o'clock. His sorrow and misery turned to fury. He felt his stomach turn with rage. He choked back a deep breath.

With nothing left to lose, Wyatt decided that he knew what he needed to do. It would only be a question of if he could bring himself to actually do it. The moment the thoughts began to enter his mind, his fingers tingled.

Wyatt gently laid Samantha's body flat, down onto the floor, and cried hard as he touched her face one more time. He then brought himself to his feet, and pulled his cell phone from his pocket. He raised his phone to eye level to unlock the divide and make a phone call.

At first, his locked phone screen did not recognize his face due to the amount of Samantha's blood on him. He did his best to wipe it away, keep it off of the camera lens on his phone, and eventually got past the security on his phone. He opened the phone app and dialed a number.

The call rang a few times without anyone picking up. A voicemail message started speaking, but Wyatt hung up before it finished. He quickly dialed the number again. IT rang several times again before someone finally answered. Then a man picked up.

"Hello?" The voice said on the other end.

"Detective Thomas Johns?" Wyatt said with a broken, monotonous voice.

"Yes. Who is this?" Detective Thomas Johns asked.

"It's Wyatt Brone." Wyatt replied, his voice still flat and stagnant.

"Wyatt… uh— hi… what's… uh— Wyatt, this is my cell phone… How did you get this number?" Det. Johns asked, a hint of concern in his voice.

"I need you to know that I did not have anything to do with my uncle's death. We were not close, we had our problems, but I did not kill my uncle." Wyatt started. His voice was weak, and shaky when he spoke.

"Wyatt, what's going on? Where are you right now?" Det. Johns' tone shifted from seeming caught off guard, to being at work.

"I need you to know that I did not have anything to do with my sister Melody's death. She was my business partner. She was my best friend. She was… my *sister*. I did not kill my sister. I need you to know that," Wyatt said. His tears had dried, and he had a new resolve.

"Wyatt, are— are you at home? Slow down, just tell me where you are." Det. Johns' voice became more forceful, and assertive.

"And I need you to know that I had nothing to do with Samantha's death either. We were planning our wedding, and buying a home. She was my fiancé, and the love of my life. I did not kill Samantha. Thomas, you have to believe me." Wyatt's face was blank, expressionless. He wondered if the detective would believe him. He assumed that the detective would not believe a word of what he was saying, but a part of him hoped the detective could hear the sincerity in his voice, and the intentional choice of words.

"Wyatt, did you hurt Samantha? Where are you? Are you at home? Is Samantha with you? Can you put Samantha on the phone, Wyatt?" Wyatt could hear scrambling on the detective's end of the line.

"I need you to send an ambulance to my loft on 6th Street. I'm going to call for an ambulance, I'm at home at my loft on 6th and Spring."

"Wyatt, listen to me —" *click.* Wyatt hung up the phone.

He took a breath, and then dialed 9-1-1. When the operator picked up, he explained that Samantha had slit her own throat, and that he needed an ambulance. The operator tried to ask several follow up questions, but Wyatt simply provided his address, and said "she's already gone," before he hung up.

They tried to call him back several times, but Wyatt did not answer. Instead, he turned his phone off, and set it down on the small table next to the painting's easel.

According to the Los Angeles Fire Department ambulatory statistics, the national ambulance response time average is around seven minutes. A national standard that the L.A.F.D. openly concedes to routinely failing. Given the circumstances of the last several weeks, Wyatt felt comfortable with the confidence that they would arrive quickly that evening. Wyatt checked his watch.

He stoically walked from the secondary work room, and down the thin hallway towards his bedroom. He walked into his bedroom, and to the left towards his closet.

He opened his walk-in closet door, and pushed some of his hanging clothes out of the way, revealing his safe. He calmly turned the knob on the safe's door, and put in the security code. He heard the click and pop of the lock opening, and Wyatt swung the heavy, steel door open. From the safe, Wyatt pulled out an all-black, six-round Ruger G.P. 100 revolver. He grabbed a small box of ammunition from a shelf lower in the safe, and then calmly loaded the revolver one bullet at a time. Once loaded, Wyatt closed the chamber, and slipped it into his belt behind his back.

Next, from the same shelf where the ammunition was, Wyatt grabbed a small, 1-quart tin of "Painter's Solvent." A liquid specifically designed to strip paint from anything. After several unintentional accidents of ruining original pieces he had spent countless weeks creating, Wyatt had begun keeping this small, blue tin of acetone in his safe. He set the tin down on top of his safe, then closed and locked the strongbox.

Wyatt grabbed the tin of acetone, took the revolver back out from his belt, and walked out of his bedroom. He moved back down the hallway towards the secondary work room, revolver in one hand, acetone in the other. He turned the corner, and paused momentarily when his eyes again found Samantha's body lying limp on the floor. Wyatt felt a deep sadness in his gut, the guilt and shame overwhelming, but he pressed on. He again checked his watch. Based on when he placed the call to 9-1-1, Wyatt assumed he had another two to three minutes before an ambulance arrived.

Wyatt set the revolver down on the small table next to the painting's easel, before he popped open the tin can of solvent.

His fingers pounded.

Not with the familiar urge to paint, but now with the new urge to *stop.* It was an intense feeling he had not yet experienced in his time with this cursed object. It was as if the painting was attempting to defend itself from its own destruction. Wyatt paused only for a moment, then he jerked the tin can towards the canvas, and the solvent sprayed across the piece.

The blues, and yellows, and greens, and reds… covered in methylene chloride. There was no dramatic bubbling, or expulsion of an evil spirit. There was just an odorless liquid seeping through layers upon layers of paint.

The solvent ate through the paint quicker than the Blitzkrieg through the open fields of Poland at the beginning of World War II.

Layers and layers of paint, who knows how old, had begun peeling away from the canvas. It curled in the weight of the chemical reaction, and fell to the floor. Wyatt had not anticipated what it would feel like, but he knew nothing would bring back the death of Melody or now Samantha.

As the canvas became more and more bare, Wyatt took a paint brush from atop his workstation near the painting, and began stabbing the canvas with its handle. Puncture hole after hole, Wyatt ravaged the cloth. He had become out of breath, and stopped for a moment. He looked at the many holes now in the canvas, and set the brush down.

He began to weep again.

This was it.

Wyatt stuck his fingers into the holes he had created, and pulled. The canvas ripped apart in his hands.

He finally took a step back, and looked at the wreckage before him.

Hardly any paint, large holes ripped into its cloth… Wyatt had destroyed the piece.

After a few more moments, he crumpled to the ground, exhausted. It was as if a yoke had evaporated from his shoulders.

He took a deep breath, and moved back towards Samantha's body. He again cradled her in his arms. He could not take his eyes off of her lifeless body. He gently touched her hair, and cupped her face in his hands.

"I'm so sorry, Samantha, I'm so sorry," he struggled to get the words out. "It's over now."

Wyatt took another breath, and checked his watch again.

One minute.

He took a quick look around the room. So many paintings unfinished, and leaned against all four walls. Paint splotches everywhere, and this one painting in the middle of the room, torn apart.

Wyatt's life's work. Hours, and hours of work no one would ever witness. Years of his adult life, created from nothing, poured onto canvas that would be thrown away in a matter of hours. This was what everything was for, and in this moment, Wyatt realized it was nothing.

An internal clock in his mind counted down from ten.

Wyatt pressed the tip of his revolver into his temple and pulled the trigger.

A loud *crack* ripped through his loft, and his body fell to the left. Blood poured from his head, and his eyes blinked one last time.

Wyatt and Samantha's bodies laid lifeless and together in this room for several more minutes before paramedics arrived. Several L.A.P.D. officers burst through Wyatt's front door, and entered his loft, guns drawn. Immediately behind them entered Detective Thomas Johns and Detective Gerry Foss. As the tactical officers discovered their bodies, a small group of them continued on, and cleared each room of the apartment. The detectives saw the bodies, and for some reason felt defeated. Detective Foss almost immediately took notes of the scene, and began ordering other officers to complete certain tasks. Detective Johns slowly walked into the secondary room, and looked at Wyatt and Samantha. His heart broke under the curiosities his mind conjured up about their final moments.

He wondered if, whatever happened, had been preventable. After a few moments, he too went into action, and assisted in the preliminary stages of the investigation to come.

The following afternoon, a large group of press had gathered outside the L.A.P.D. headquarters downtown. A small, makeshift stage and podium stood vacant. Reporters chattered, and photograph flashes came and went. After a few chaotic moments of anticipation, an old, gruff man in uniform walked up to the podium.

He adjusted the microphone, and instantly reporters began hurling questions. He predictably ignored them all, and cleared his throat. The questions died down, and he leaned in towards the microphone.

"My name is Joseph Anderson, I'm Police Chief for the City of Los Angeles. Joining me here momentarily will be L.A.P.D. Homicide Detectives Thomas Johns and Gerry Foss. We are here today to make an announcement regarding the investigation into the deaths of Jackson and Melody Brone." The police chief looked to his left, and motioned the detective to come to the podium. "Ladies and gentlemen, Detectives Thomas Johns and Gerry Foss."

The detectives arrived at the podium, and shook the police chief's hand. Detective Johns stepped up to the microphone, and adjusted it for himself. Detective Foss stood just off his right shoulder.

"Hello, everyone. My name is Detective Thomas Johns, L.A.P.D. Homicide Division. This is my partner, Detective Gerry Foss. We are the two detectives that have been investigating the death of artist Jackson Brone. Yesterday evening, at approximately eighteen hundred hours, we received a call from Jackson Brone's nephew, Wyatt Brone. He informed us that an ambulance was needed at his residence, the same residence where we discovered the body of his sister, Melody Brone just two days before. Upon arriving, we found Mr. Wyatt Brone dead in the same room as his fiancé, Samantha Garcia, also deceased. At this time, our team of investigators is hard at work to determine the exact events of the evening, but at this time we have enough evidence to suggest that this was, in fact, a murder suicide. We believe Wyatt Brone was the perpetrator in the murder of his uncle, Jackson Brone; his sister, Melody Brone; and now his fiancé, Samantha Garcia. At this time, we anticipate letting our team conclude their investigation, but we are confident that we will consider this case closed moving forward. Wyatt Brone has been, and will remain the primary suspect in all three homicide investigations. These were violent crimes, committed by a violent individual, and though we mourn the lack of justice we were able to impart, we are at peace knowing this criminal activity is at an end. At this time, we are not going to take any questions, and we will provide updates as we have them. Thank you all for being here."

The detectives left the podium to another flurry of reporters yelling questions. They ignored them. They shook the hand of the police chief again, and went inside.

At Wyatt's apartment, a forensic team conducted many of the same acts. Photographing evidence, and taping off areas of the loft. Wyatt and Samantha's bodies were wheeled out on stretchers, in standard, black body bags.

A few moments after their bodies were removed from the loft, two more investigators rolled a large object out of the loft. It was covered by a cloth tarp, and almost touched the ceiling.

It was the painting.

It was placed on a moving truck, and left the downtown loft building, headed for the Los Angeles Police Department Headquarters, just a few blocks away.

A short time later, Detective Johns sat at his desk when he heard a light rapping on the frame of his opened office door. He looked up and saw Detective Foss leaning into the doorway. When their eyes met, Detective Foss raised his brows, and smiled.

"It's here," he said, and smirked.

"You're kidding, already?" Det. Johns practically left up from his seat, and the two hurried down the hallway.

"I can't stay, but I'll walk with you."

The two men stepped into the opened elevator, and pressed the button for the fourth floor. A small, hand-written note taped next to the floor button crudely read, "EVIDENCE."

When they reached the fourth floor, Detective Johns was the first one off the elevator car. The men walked to a desk at the end of the hallway. They presented their badges, and Detective Foss said something to the clerk. She looked at their credentials, and bused the door open.

"Third row on the left, you can't miss it, it's fucking huge." She said in an uninterested tone.

Detective Foss spoke up as Detective Johns hurried into the Evidence Room.

"I gotta head back down, I'm meeting with Sarge on another case he wants us on. I'll catch you later." Det. Foss walked back down the hallway towards the elevator.

Detective Johns slowly walked through each row of evidence in the large depository. He paused for a moment, as he felt a slight tingle in his fingertips. He wrung his hands together, and continued. With each step, his fingers pulsed harder and harder. He could not quite understand what was happening. Finally, he reached the third row on the left, and he looked towards the end of the narrow walkway.

As his eyes met the large, covered object, his fingers burst with the pounding of desire.

It was a pulse, a tingle, and an urge he had never experienced before. All of his logic, and foresight left his mind, as he stared at the large canvas.

Slowly, he removed the cloth bindings, and let the cover gently slide off of the painting, and onto the floor.

Detective Johns stood, staring at the work.

Tears filled, his eyes, and his heart flooded with the urge to add paint to its face.

He thought… no, he knew… somehow… he needed to take this painting home.

THE END

ABOUT THE AUTHOR

Trey Everett is a Texas-born author, screenwriter and musician. While his family had no professional creative ties, he was always drawn to the arts. For college, he moved to Southern California and attended the American Academy of Dramatic Arts, studying film & television. After many years of flirting with success, he settled back into his original passion; storytelling. Now based in Los Angeles, he focuses on carefully and meticulously crafting stories he is most compelled to tell.

BENEATH THE SURFACE
TREY EVERETT

NOTE FROM TREY EVERETT

Word-of-mouth is crucial for any author to succeed. If you enjoyed *For It Will Be Yours*, please leave a review online—anywhere you are able. Even if it's just a sentence or two. It would make all the difference and would be very much appreciated.

Thanks!
Trey Everett

We hope you enjoyed reading this title from:

www.blackrosewriting.com

Subscribe to our mailing list – *The Rosevine* – and receive **FREE** books, daily deals, and stay current with news about upcoming releases and our hottest authors.
Scan the QR code below to sign up.

Already a subscriber? Please accept a sincere thank you for being a fan of Black Rose Writing authors.

View other Black Rose Writing titles at www.blackrosewriting.com/books and use promo code **PRINT** to receive a **20% discount** when purchasing.